PRAISE FOR
DAVID GEMMELL

"I am truly amazed at David Gemmell's ability to focus his writer's eye. His images are crisp and complete, a history lesson woven within the detailed tapestry of the highest adventure. Gemmell's characters are no less complete, real men and women with qualities good and bad, placed in trying times and rising to heroism or falling victim to their own weaknesses."
—R. A. SALVATORE

"In the best sense of the word, you could say that Gemmell's a brand; an assurance of passionate, cleanly written prose, imaginative plots, and, above all, terrific storytelling. For anyone who appreciates superior heroic fantasy, David Gemmell's offerings are mandatory."
—*Time Out London*

"Gemmell is very talented; his characters are vivid and very convincingly realistic."
—CHRISTOPHER STASHEFF,
author of the Wizard in Rhyme novels

"Gemmell is a fine writer who has paid his dues in a crowded field."
—*Contra Costa Times*

By David Gemmell
Published by Ballantine Books

LION OF MACEDON
DARK PRINCE

ECHOES OF THE GREAT SONG

KNIGHTS OF DARK RENOWN

MORNINGSTAR

DARK MOON

IRONHAND'S DAUGHTER

THE DRENAI SAGA
LEGEND
THE KING BEYOND THE GATE
QUEST FOR LOST HEROES
WAYLANDER
IN THE REALM OF THE WOLF
THE FIRST CHRONICLES OF DRUSS THE LEGEND
THE LEGEND OF DEATHWALKER
HERO IN THE SHADOWS
WHITE WOLF
THE SWORDS OF NIGHT AND DAY

THE STONES OF POWER CYCLE
GHOST KING
LAST SWORD OF POWER
WOLF IN SHADOW
THE LAST GUARDIAN
BLOODSTONE

THE RIGANTE
SWORD IN THE STORM
MIDNIGHT FALCON
RAVENHEART
STORMRIDER

IRONHAND'S DAUGHTER

A Novel of The Hawk Queen

DAVID GEMMELL

BALLANTINE BOOKS • NEW YORK

A Del Rey® Book
Published by The Random House Publishing Group
Copyright © 1995 by David A. Gemmell
Excerpt from *The Hawk Eternal* by David Gemmell copyright © 1995 by David A. Gemmell

All rights reserved under International and Pan-American Copyright Conventions. Published in the United States by Del Rey Books, an imprint of The Random House Publishing Group, a division of Random House, Inc., New York. Originally published in Great Britain by Legend Books, a division of Random House UK Limited (London), in 1995.

Del Rey is a registered trademark and the Del Rey colophon is a trademark of Random House, Inc.

www.delreybooks.com

ISBN 0-345-45838-9

Manufactured in the United States of America

First American Edition: December 2004

OPM 9 8 7 6 5 4 3 2 1

IRONHAND'S
DAUGHTER

Prologue

Sunlight glinted on steel as the knife blade spun through the air to thud home in the chalk-circled center of the board. The woman chuckled. "You lose again, Ballistar," she said.

"I let you win," the dwarf told her. "For I am a creature of legend, and my skills are second to none." He smiled as he spoke, but there was sadness in his dark eyes and she reached out to cup her hand to his bearded cheek. He leaned in to her touch, twisting his head to kiss her palm.

"You are the finest of men," she said softly, "and the gods— if gods there be—have not been kind to you."

Ballistar did not reply. Glancing up he drank in her beauty, the golden sheen of her skin, the haunting power of her pale blue-grey eyes. At nineteen Sigarni was the most beautiful woman Ballistar had ever seen, tall and slender, full-lipped and firm-breasted. Her only flaw was her close-cropped hair, which shone like silver in the sunlight. It had turned grey in her sixth year, after her parents were slain. The villagers called it the Night of the Slaughterers, and no one would speak of it. Pushing himself to his feet he walked to the fence post, climbing the rail to pull Sigarni's throwing knife from the board. She watched him stretching out his tiny arms, his stunted fingers unable to curl fully around the hilt of her blade. At last he wrenched it clear, then turned and jumped to the ground. He was no larger than a child of four, yet his head was huge and his face heavily bearded. Ballistar returned her blade and she slid it home into the sheath at her hip. Reaching to her right she lifted a pitcher of cool water and filled two clay goblets, passing one to the dwarf.

Ballistar gave a wide grin as he took it, then slowly passed his tiny hand across the surface of the water. She shook her head. "You should not make those gestures, my friend," she said seriously. "If you were seen by the wrong man, you would be flogged."

"I've been flogged before. Did I show you my scars?"

"Many times."

"Then I shall not concern myself with fears of the lash," he said, passing his hand once more over the drink. "To the long-dead King over the water," he said, lifting the goblet to his lips. A sleek black hound padded into sight. Heavy of shoulder, slim of flanks, she was a hare and rabbit hound, and her speed was legendary. Highland hunting hounds were bred for strength, stamina, and obedience. But most of all they had to be fast. None was swifter than Sigarni's hound. Ballistar laid down his empty goblet and called to her. "Here, Lady!" Her head came up and she loped to him, pushing her long muzzle into his beard, licking at his cheek. "Women find me irresistible," he said as he stroked the hound's ears.

"I can see why," Sigarni told him. "You have a gentle touch."

Ballistar stroked Lady's flanks and gazed down into her eyes. One eye was doe-brown, the other opal-grey. "She has healed well," he said, running his finger down the scar on the hound's cheek.

Sigarni nodded, and Ballistar saw the fresh flaring of anger in her eyes. "Bernt is a fool. I should never have allowed him to come. Stupid man."

"That *stupid* man loves you," chided Ballistar. "As do we all, princess."

"Idiot!" she snapped, but the anger faded from her eyes. "You know I have no right to such a title."

"Not so, Sigarni. You have the blood of Gandarin in your veins."

"Pah! Half the population have his blood. The man was a rutting ram. Gwalchmai told me about him; he said Gandarin could have raised an army of his bastard offspring. Even Bernt probably has a drop or two of Gandarin's blood."

"You should forgive him," advised Ballistar. "He didn't mean it." At that moment a red hawk swooped low over the clearing, coming to rest on a nearby bow perch. For a moment or two it pranced from foot to foot, then cocked its head and stared at the silver-haired woman. The hound gave a low growl, but slunk back close to Ballistar. Sigarni pulled on a long black gauntlet of polished leather and stood, arm outstretched. The hawk launched itself from the fence and flew to her.

"Ah, my beauty," said Sigarni, reaching up and ruffling the russet-colored feathers of the bird's breast. Taking a strip of rabbit meat from the pouch at her side, she fed it to the hawk. Swiftly and skillfully she attached two soft collars to the hawk's legs, then threaded short hunting jesses through brass-rimmed holes in the collars. Lastly she pulled a soft leather hood from the pouch at her side and smoothly stroked it into place over the bird's beak and eyes. The hawk sat motionless as the hood settled, and even turned its neck to allow Sigarni to lean forward and tighten the braces at the rear. The woman turned her gaze back to the dwarf and smiled. "I know that Bernt acted from stupidity. And I am more angry with myself than with him. I told him to loose Lady only if there was a second hare. It was a simple instruction. But he was incapable even of that. And I will not have fools around me."

Ballistar said nothing more. There were, he knew, only two creatures in all the world that Sigarni cared for—the hound, Lady, and the hawk, Abby. Sigarni had been training them both, determined that they would work together as a team. The training had gone well. Lady would seek out the hares and scatter them, while Abby swooped down from the trees in a kill that seemed swifter than an arrow. The danger

area came when only a single quarry was sighted. Hawk and
bird had raced each other to make the strike. Abby won both
times. On the second occasion when Lady darted in to try to
steal the kill, Abby had lashed out, her beak grazing the
hound's flank. Sigarni had grabbed Lady's collar, dragging
her back. In an effort to retrain Lady, Sigarni had allowed the
cattle herder, Bernt, to accompany her on the training hunts.
His duty was to keep Lady leashed, and only release her
when more than one hare was sighted. He had failed. Excited
by the hunt, Bernt had loosed the hound at first sight of a single hare. Abby had swooped upon it, and Lady had sped in
to share the prize. The hawk had turned, lashing out with her
cruel beak, piercing the hound's right eye.

"You are hunting today?" asked the dwarf.

"No. Abby is above her killing weight. I let her have the
last hare we took yesterday. Today we'll just walk awhile, up
to the High Druin. She likes to fly there."

"Watch out for the sorcerer!" warned Ballistar.

"There is no need to fear him," said Sigarni. "I think he is
a good man."

"He's an Outlander, and his skin has been burned by sorcery. He makes me shudder."

Sigarni's laughter pealed out. "Oh, Ballistar, you fool! In
his land all people have dark skins; they are not cursed."

"He's a wizard! At nights he becomes a giant bird that flies
across High Druin. Many have seen it: a great black raven,
twice normal size. And his castle is full of grimoires and
spells, and there are animals there—frozen. You know Mar-
ion—she was there! She told us all about a great black bear
that just stands in the hallway, a spell upon it. You keep clear
of him, Sigarni!"

She looked into his dark eyes and saw the reality of his
fear. "I shall be careful," she said. "You may rely on it. But I
will not walk in fear, Ballistar. Have I not the blood of Gandarin in my veins?" Sigarni could not quite mask the smile
as she spoke.

"You should not mock your friends!" he scolded. "Magickers are to be avoided—anyone with sense knows that. And what is he doing here, in our high, lonely places? Eh? Why did he leave his land of black people and come here? What is he seeking? Or is he perhaps hiding from justice?"

"I shall ask him when next I see him," she said. "Come, Lady!" The hound rose warily and paced alongside the tall woman. Sigarni knelt and patted her flanks. "You've learned to respect Abby now," she whispered, "though I fear she will never learn respect for you."

"Why is that?" asked Ballistar. Sigarni looked up.

"It is the way of the hawk, my friend. It loves no one, needs no one, fears no one."

"Does it not love you, Sigarni?"

"No. That is why she must never be called in vain. Each time she flies to the fist I feed her. The day I do not, she may decide never to return. Hawks know no loyalties. They stay because they choose to. No man—nor woman—can ever own one."

Without a word of farewell the huntress strode off into the forest.

Chapter One

Tovi closed the double doors of his oven, removed his apron, and wiped the flour from his face with a clean towel. The day's bread was laid out on wooden trays, stacked six high, and the smell of the baking filled his nostrils. Even after all these years he still loved that smell. Taking a sample loaf, he cut through the center. It was rich and light, with no pockets of air. Behind him his apprentice, Stalf, breathed a silent sigh of relief. Tovi turned to the boy. "Not bad," he said. Cutting two thick slices, he smeared them with fresh butter and passed one to the boy.

Moving to the rear door, Tovi stepped outside. Above the stone and timber buildings of the village the dawn sun was clearing the peaks and a fresh breeze was blowing from the north. The bakery stood at the center of the village, an old three-story building that once had been the council house. *In the days when we were allowed a council,* thought Tovi sourly. The buildings surrounding the bakery were sturdily built, and old. Farther down the hill were the simpler timber dwellings of the poorer folk. Tovi stepped out into the road and gazed down the hill to the river. The villagers were stirring and several women were already kneeling by the waterside, washing clothes and blankets, beating them against the white rocks at the water's edge. Tovi saw the black-clad Widow Maffrey making her way to the communal well. He waved and smiled and she nodded as she passed. The smith,

Grame, was lighting his forge. Seeing Tovi, he strolled across. Soot had smeared the smith's thick white beard.

"Good day to you, Baker," said Grame.

"And to you. It looks a fine one. Nary a cloud in sight. I see you have the Baron's greys in your stalls. Fine beasts."

"Finer than the man who owns them. One of them has a split hoof, and both carry spur scars. No way to treat good horses. I'll take a loaf, if you please. One with a crust as black as sin and a center as white as a nun's soul."

Tovi shook his head. "You'll take what I give you, man, and be glad of it, for you'll not taste a better piece of bread anywhere in the kingdom. Stalf! Fetch a loaf for the smith."

The boy brought it out, wrapped in muslin. Dipping his huge hand into the pocket of his leather apron, Grame produced two small copper coins that he dropped into Stalf's outstretched palm. The boy bowed and backed away. "It'll be a good summer," said Grame, tearing off a chunk of bread and pushing it into his mouth.

"Let us hope so," said Tovi.

The dwarf Ballistar approached them, laboring up the steep hill. He gave an elaborate bow. "Good morning to you," said Ballistar. "Am I late for breakfast?"

"Not if you have coin, little man," said Tovi, eyes narrowing. The dwarf made him feel uncomfortable, and he found himself growing irritable.

"No coin," the dwarf told him affably, "but I have three hares hanging."

"Caught by Sigarni, no doubt!" snapped the baker. "I don't know why she should be so generous with you."

"Perhaps she likes me," answered Ballistar, no trace of anger in his tone.

Tovi called for another loaf which he gave the dwarf. "Bring me the best hare tonight," he said.

"Why does he anger you so?" asked Grame as the dwarf wandered away.

Tovi shrugged. "He's cursed. He should have been laid

aside at birth. What good is he to man or beast? He cannot hunt, cannot work. If not for Sigarni maybe he would leave the village. He could join a circus! Such as he could earn an honest living there, capering and the like."

"You're turning into a sour old man, Tovi."

"And you are getting fat!"

"Aye, that's the truth. But I still remember the wearing of the Red. That's something I'll take to the grave, with pride. As will you."

The baker nodded, and his expression softened. "Bonny days, Grame. They'll not come again."

"We gave them a fight, though, eh?"

Tovi shook his head. "We showed them how brave men die—that's not the same, my friend. Outnumbered and out-classed we were—their knights riding through our ranks, cutting and killing, our sword blades clanging against their armor and causing no damage. Gods, man, it was slaughter that day! I wish to Heaven I had never seen it."

"We were badly led," whispered Grame. "Gandarin did not pass his strength to his sons."

The smith sighed. "Ah, well, enough dismal talk. This is a new day, fresh and untainted." Spinning on his heel, the burly blacksmith strode back to his forge.

The boy, Stalf, said nothing as Tovi reentered the bakery. He could see his master was deep in thought, and he had heard a little of the conversation. It was hard to believe that Fat Tovi had once worn the Red, and had taken part in the Battle of Colden Moor. Stalf had visited the battle site last autumn. A huge plain, dotted with barrows, thirty-four in all. And each barrow held the dead of an entire clan's fighting men.

The wind had howled across Colden Moor and Stalf had been frightened by the power and the haunted wailing of it. His uncle, Mart One-arm, had stood with him, his bony hand on the boy's shoulder. "This is the place where dreams end, boy. This is the resting place of hope."

"How many died, Uncle?"

"Scores of thousands."

"But not the King."

"No, not the King. He fled to a bright land beyond the water. But they found him there, and slew him. There are no Mountain Kings now."

Uncle Mart walked him onto the moor, coming at last to a high barrow. "This is where the Loda men stood, shoulder to shoulder, brothers in arms, brothers in death." Lifting the stump of his left arm, he gave a crooked smile. "Part of me is buried here too, boy. And more than just my arm. My heart lies here, with my brothers, and cousins, and friends."

Stalf dragged his mind back to the present. Tovi was standing by the window, his eyes showing the same faraway look he had seen that day on the face of Mart One-arm.

"Can I take some bread to me mam?" asked Stalf. Tovi nodded.

Stalf chose two loaves and wrapped them. He had reached the door when Tovi's voice stopped him. "What do you want to be, lad, when you're grown?"

"A baker, sir. Skilled like you." Tovi said no more, and the boy hurried from the bakery.

Sigarni loved the mountain lands, the lush valleys nestling between them, and the deep, dark forests that covered their flanks. But mostly she loved High Druin, the lonely peak that towered over the Highlands, its summit lost in cloud, its shoulders cloaked in snow. There was, in High Druin, an elemental magnificence that radiated from its sharp, defiant crags, a magic that sang in the whispering of wind-breath before the winter storms. High Druin spoke to the heart. He said: "I am Eternity in stone. I have always been here. I will always be here!"

The huntress let Abby soar into the air and watched her swoop over High Druin's lower flanks. Lady bounded out over the grass, her sleek black body alert, her one good eye scanning for sign of hare or rat. Sigarni sat by the Lake of Tears, watching the brightly colored ducks on the banks of the small island at the center of the lake. Abby circled high above them, also watching the birds. The hawk swooped down, coming to rest in a tree beside the lake. The ducks, suddenly aware of the hawk, took to the water.

Sigarni watched with interest. Roast duck would make a fine contrast to the hare meat she had eaten during the last fortnight. "Here, Lady!" she called. The hound padded alongside and Sigarni pointed to the ducks. "Go!" hissed Sigarni. Instantly the dog leaped into the water, paddling furiously toward the circling flock. Several of the birds took wing, putting flat distance between them and the hound, keeping low to the water. But one took off into the sky and instantly Abby launched herself in pursuit.

The duck was rising fast, and Abby hurtled down toward it with talons extended.

At the last possible moment the duck saw the bird of prey—and dived fast. For a heartbeat only Sigarni thought Abby had her prey, but then the duck hit the water, diving deep, confusing the hawk. Abby circled and returned to her branch.

The huntress gave a low whistle, summoning Lady back to the bank. The sound of a walking horse came to Sigarni then, and she rose and turned.

The horse was a tall chestnut, and upon it rode a black man, his cheeks, head, and shoulders covered in a flowing white burnoose. A cloak of blue-dyed wool hung from his broad shoulders and a curved sword was scabbarded at his waist. He smiled as he saw the mountain woman.

"When hunting duck, it is better for the hawk to take it from below," he said, swinging down from his saddle.

"We're still learning," replied Sigarni affably. "She is wedded to fur now, but it took time—as you said it would, Asmidir."

The tall man sat down at the water's edge. Lady approached him gingerly, and he stroked her head. "The eye is healing well. Has it affected her hunting?" Sigarni shook her head. "And the bird? Hawks prefer to feed on feather. What is her killing weight?"

"Two pounds two ounces. But she has taken hare at two-four."

"And what do you feed her?"

"No more than three ounces a day."

The black man nodded. "Once in a while you should catch her a rat. Nothing better for cleaning a bird's crop than a good rat."

"Why is that, Asmidir?" asked Sigarni, sitting down beside the man.

"I don't know," he admitted with a broad smile. "My father told me years ago. As you know the hawk swallows its prey—where it can—whole and the carcass is compressed, all the goodness squeezed out of it. It then vomits out the cast, the remnants. There is, I would imagine, something in the rat's pelt or skin that cleans the bird's crop as it exits." Leaning back on his elbows, he narrowed his eyes and watched the distant hawk.

"How many kills so far?"

"Sixty-eight hares, twenty pigeons, and a ferret."

"You hunt ferret?" asked Asmidir, raising a quizzical eyebrow.

"It was a mistake. The ferret bolted a hare and Abby took the ferret."

Asmidir chuckled. "You have done well, Sigarni. I am glad I gave you the hawk."

"Three times I thought I'd lost her. Always in the forest."

"You may lose sight of her, child, but she will never lose sight of you. Come back to the castle, and I will prepare you a meal. And you too," he said, scratching the hound's ears.

"I was told that you were a sorcerer, and that I must beware of you."

"You should always heed the warnings of dwarves," he said. "Or any creature of legend."

"How did you know it was Ballistar?"

"Because I am a sorcerer, my dear. We are expected to know things like that."

"You always pause at my bear," said Asmidir, gazing fondly at the silver-haired girl as Sigarni reached out and touched the fur of the beast's belly. It was a huge creature, its paws outstretched, talons bared, mouth open in a silent roar. "It is wonderful," she said. "How is it done?"

"You do not believe it is a spell then?" he asked, smiling.

"No."

"Well," he said slowly, rubbing his chin, "if it is not a spell, then it must be a stuffed bear. There are craftsmen in my land who work on carcasses, stripping away the inner meat, which can rot, and rebuilding the dead beasts with clay before wrapping them once more in their skins or fur. The results are remarkably lifelike."

"And this then is a stuffed bear?"

"I did not say that," he reminded her. "Come, let us eat."

Asmidir led her through the hallway and into the main hall. A log fire was burning merrily in the hearth and two servants were laying platters of meat and bread on the table. Both were tall, dark-skinned men who worked silently, never once looking at their master or his guest. With the table laid, they silently withdrew.

"Your servants are not friendly," commented Sigarni.

"They are efficient," said Asmidir, seating himself at the table and filling a goblet with wine.

"Do they fear you?"

"A little fear is good for a servant."

"Do they love you?"

"I am not a man easy to love. My servants are content. They are free to leave my service whenever it pleases them to do so; they are not slaves." He offered Sigarni some wine, but she refused and he poured water into a glazed goblet that he passed to her. They ate in silence, then Asmidir moved to the fireside, beckoning Sigarni to join him.

"Do you have no fear?" the black man asked as she sat cross-legged before him.

"Of what?" she countered.

"Of life. Of death. Of me."

"Why would I fear you?"

"Why would you not? When we met last year I was a stranger in your land. Black and fearsome," he said, widening his eyes and mimicking a snarl.

She laughed at him. "You were never fearsome," she said. "Dangerous, yes. But never fearsome."

"There is a difference?"

"Of course," she told him, cocking her head to one side. "I *like* dangerous men."

He shook his head. "You are incorrigible, Sigarni. The body of an angel and the mind of a whore. Usually that is considered a wonderful combination. That is, if you are contemplating the life of a courtesan, a prostitute, or a slut. Is that your ambition?"

Sigarni yawned theatrically. "I think it is time to go home," she said, rising smoothly.

"Ah, I have offended you," he said.

"Not at all," she told him. "But I expected better of you, Asmidir."

"You should expect better of yourself, Sigarni. There are dark days looming. A leader is coming—a leader of noble blood. You will probably be called upon in those days to aid him. For you also boast the blood of Gandarin. Men will follow an angel or a saint, they will follow a despot and a villain. But they will follow a whore only to the bedchamber."

Her face flushed with anger. "I'll take sermons from a priest—not from a man who was happy to cavort with me throughout the spring and summer, and now seeks to belittle me. I am not some milkmaid or tavern wench. I am Sigarni of the Mountains. What I do is my affair. I used you for pleasure, I admit it freely. You are a fine lover; you have strength and finesse. And you used me. That made it a balanced transaction, and neither of us was sullied by it. How dare you attempt to shame me?"

"Why would you see it as shame?" he countered. "I am talking of perceptions—the perceptions of men. You think I look down upon you? I do not. I adore you. For your body *and* your mind. Further, I am probably—as much as I am capable of it—a little in love with you. But this is not why I spoke in the way I did."

"I don't care," she told him. "Good-bye."

Sigarni strode from the room and out past the great bear. A servant pushed open the double doors and she walked down the steps into the courtyard. Lady came bounding toward her. Another servant, a slim dark-eyed young man, was waiting at the foot of the steps with Abby hooded upon his wrist. Sigarni pulled on her hawking glove.

"You were waiting for me?" she asked the young man. He nodded. "Why? I am usually here for hours."

"The master said today would be a short visit," he explained.

Sigarni untied the braces and slid the hood clear of Abby's eyes. The hawk looked around, them jumped to Sigarni's fist. When the huntress lifted her arm and called out "Hai!" the hawk took off, heading south.

Sigarni flicked her fingers and Lady moved close to her side, awaiting instructions. "What is your name?" she asked the servant, noting the sleekness of his skin and the taut muscles beneath his blue silk shirt. He shook his head and moved away from her.

Annoyed, the huntress walked from the old castle, crossing the rickety drawbridge and heading off into the woods. Her mood was dark and angry as she went. The mind of a whore, indeed. Her thoughts turned to Fell the Forester. Now there was a man who understood pleasure. She doubted if there was a single woman within a day's walk who hadn't succumbed to his advances. Did they call him a whore? No. It was "Good old Fell, what a character, what a man!" Idiotic!

Asmidir's words rankled. She had thought him different, more . . . intelligent? Yes. Instead he proved to be like most men, caught between a need for fornication and a love of sermonizing.

Abby soared above her, and Lady ran to the side of the trail, seeking out hares. Sigarni pushed thoughts of the black man from her mind and walked on in the dusk, coming at last to the final hillside and gazing down on her cabin. A light was showing at the window and this annoyed her, for she wished to be alone this evening. If it was that fool, Bernt, she would give him the sharp side of her tongue.

Walking into the yard, she whistled for Abby. The hawk came in low, then spread her wings and settled on Sigarni's glove. Feeding her a strip of meat she removed the hunting jesses; then carrying her to the bow perch, she attached the mews ties, and turned toward the cabin.

Lady moved to the side of the building, lying down beside the door with her head on her paws.

Sigarni pushed open the door.

Fell was sitting by the fire, eyes closed, his long legs stretched out before the blaze. It angered her that she could feel a sense of rising excitement at his presence. He looked just the same as on that last day, his long black hair sleek and glowing with health, swept back from his brow and held in place by a leather headband, his beard close-trimmed and as soft as fur. Sigarni took a deep breath, trying to calm herself.

"What do you want here, Goat-brain?" she snapped.

Then she saw the blood.

There were wolves all around him, fangs bared, ready to rip and tear. A powerful beast leaped at him. Fell caught it by the throat, then spun on his heel hurling the creature into

the pack. His limbs felt leaden, as if he were wading through
water. The wolves blurred, shifting like smoke, becoming
tall, fierce-eyed warriors holding knives of sharpened
bronze. They moved in on him, smoothly, slowly. Fell's arms
were paralyzed and he felt the first knife sink into his shoul-
der like a tongue of fire . . .

He opened his eyes. Sigarni was kneeling beside him with
a needle in her hand, and he felt the flap of flesh on his shoulder drawn tight by the thread. Fell swore softly. "Lie still,"
she said and Fell obeyed her. His stomach felt uneasy. Snapping the thread with her teeth, she sat back. "Looks like a
sword cut."

"Long knife," he told her, taking a deep shuddering breath.
He said no more for a while, resting his neck against the
thick, cushioned hide of the chair's headrest. Focusing his
gaze on the far timbered wall he ran his eyes over the weapons hanging there—the long-handled broadsword with its
leaf-shaped blade and hilt of leather, the bow of horn and the
quiver of black-shafted arrows, the daggers and dirks and
lastly the helm, with its crown and cheek guards of black iron
and the nasal guard and brows of polished brass. Not a speck
of rust or tarnish showed on them.

"You keep your father's weapons in good condition," he
said.

"That's what Gwal taught me," she told him. "Who gave
you the wound?"

"We didn't exchange names. There were two of them.
Robbed a pilgrim on the Low Trail. I tracked them to Mas
Gryff."

"Where are they now?"

"Oh, they're still there. I returned the money to the pilgrim
and made a report to the Watch." His face darkened. "Bastards! You could almost feel their disappointment." He
shook his head. "It won't be much longer, you know. They'll
look for any excuse."

"You've lost a lot of blood," she said. "I'll make some broth."

He watched her move away; his eyes lingered on the sway of her hips. "You're a beautiful woman, Sigarni. Never saw the like!"

"Look on and weep for all you've lost," she said, before disappearing into the back room.

"Amen to that," he whispered. Resting his head once more, he remembered the last parting two years before, Sigarni standing straight and tall and proud . . . always so proud. Fell had walked across the glens to Cilfallen and paid bride price for Gwendolyn. Sweet Gwen. In no way did she match the silver-haired woman he had left, save in one. Gwen could bear children, and a man needed sons. Ten months later Gwen was dead, the victim of a breech birth that killed both her and the infant.

Fell had buried them both in the Loda resting place on the western slope of High Druin.

Sigarni returned to his side. "Flex the muscles of your arm," she ordered.

He did so and winced. "It's damned sore."

"Good. I like to think of you in pain."

"I buried my son, woman. I know what pain is. And I'd not wish it on a friend."

"Neither would I," she said. "But you are no friend."

"Your mood is foul," he admonished her. "Had a falling-out with your black man, have you?"

"Have you been spying on me, Fell?" It irritated him that she did not deny the association.

"It is my work, Sigarni. I patrol the forest and I have seen you enter the castle, and I have seen you leave. How could you rut with such as he?"

She laughed then, and his anger rose. "Asmidir is a better man than you, Fell. In every way." He wanted to strike her, to slap the smile from her face. But the growing nausea finally swamped him and with a groan he pushed himself from the chair, staggered to the door, and just made it to open ground before falling to earth and vomiting. Cold sweat shone upon his face in the moonlight, and he felt weak as a day-old calf as he struggled to rise. Sigarni appeared along-side him, taking his arm and looping it over her shoulder. "Let's get you to bed," she said, not unkindly.

Fell leaned into her. The scent of her filled his nostrils. "I loved you," he said as she half carried him up the four steps to the doorway.

"You left me," she said.

When he woke it was daylight, the rising sun shining through the open window. The sky was clear and Fell saw the hawk silhouetted briefly against the blue. With a groan he sat up. His shoulder was burning, and his ribs were badly bruised from the fight with the two Outland robbers.

Rising from the bed he moved to the window. Sigarni was standing in the sunlight, the hawk on her glove, the black hound lying at her feet. Fell's mouth was dry, and all his long-suppressed emotions surged to the surface. Of all the women he had known—and there had been many—he had loved only one. And in that moment he knew, with a sicken-ing certainty, that it would always be thus. Oh, he would marry again, and he would have sons, but his heart would re-main with this enigmatic mountain woman until the daggers of time stopped its beat.

Though still weak from loss of blood, Fell knew he could stay no longer in sight of Sigarni. Gathering his cloak of black leather he pulled on his boots, took up his longbow and quiver, and walked from the rear of the cabin, heading back on the long trail to Cilfallen. There was a maid there, of marriageable age, whose father had set a bride price Fell could afford.

"I hate this place," said the Baron Ranulph Gottasson, leaning on the wide parapet and staring out over the distant mountains. Asmidir said nothing. It was cold up here on the

Citadel's high walls, the wind hissing down from the north, cutting through the warmest clothes. But the Baron seemed not to notice the inclemency of the weather. He was dressed in a simple shirt of black silk and a sleeveless jerkin of the finest black leather. He wore no adornments, no silver enhancements to his black leather leggings, no chains or ornate discs attached to his knee-length boots. As Asmidir stood shivering on the battlements, the Baron turned his pale, hooded eyes on the black man. "Not like Kushir, eh? Too cold, too bleak. Ever wish you were back home?"

"Sometimes," Asmidir admitted.

"So do I. What is there here for a man like me? Where is the glory?"

"The kingdom is at peace, my lord," said Asmidir softly. "Thanks mainly to your good self and the Earl of Jastey."

The Baron's lips thinned, the hooded eyes narrowing. "Don't speak his name in my presence! I never met a man so gifted with luck. All his victories were hollow. Tell me what he has ever done to match my conquest of Ligia? Twenty-five thousand warriors against my two legions. Yet we crushed them, and took their capital. What can he offer against that? The Siege of Catium. Pah!"

"Indeed, sir," said Asmidir smoothly, "your deeds will echo through the pages of history. Now I am sure you have more important matters to attend to, so how may I be of service to you?"

The Baron turned and beckoned Asmidir to follow him into a small study. The black man stared longingly at the cold and empty fireplace. Does the man not feel the cold? he wondered. The Baron seated himself at a desk of oak. "I want the red hawk," he said. "There is a tourney in two months and the red hawk could win it for me. Name a price."

"Would that I could, sir. But I sold the hawk last autumn."

The Baron swore. "Who to? I'll buy it back."

"I wouldn't know where to find the man, sir," Asmidir lied smoothly. "He came to my castle last year. He was a traveler,

I believe, perhaps a pilgrim. But if I see him again I shall direct him to you."

The Baron swore again, then lashed his fist against the desktop.

"All right, that will be all," he said at last.

Asmidir bowed and left the study. Descending the spiral staircase he moved down into the belly of the fortress, emerging into the long hall where the feast was in progress. Red-liveried servants were carrying platters of food and drink and more than two score of knights and their ladies were seated at the three main tables. Fires were blazing merrily at both ends of the hall and minstrels sat in the high gallery, their soft music drowned by the chatter of the guests.

Asmidir was not hungry. Swiftly he walked from the hall, and down the long stairs to the lower chambers and the double-doored exit. His thoughts were somber as he recalled the Baron's words. Asmidir remembered the conquest of Ligia, the battles and the massacres, the rapes and the mutilations, the torture and the destruction. A rich, independent nation brought to its knees, humiliated and beggared, its libraries burned, its holy places desecrated. Oh, yes, Ranulph, history will long remember your bloody name! Asmidir shivered.

Revenge, so the proverb claimed, is a dish best served cold. Is that true? he wondered. Will there be any satisfaction in bringing the man down?

Wrapping his cloak more tightly about his broad shoulders, Asmidir left the fortress building and moved across the courtyard. A young man hailed him and he turned and smiled at the newcomer—a tall young man, slender and brown-eyed, his long blond hair drawn back from his brow and tied in a tight ponytail. He was carrying an armful of rolled maps. "Good afternoon, Leofric. You are missing the feast."

"Yes, I know," said the other dolefully. "But the Baron

wants to study these maps. It doesn't pay to keep him waiting."

"They look old."

"They are. They were commissioned some two hundred years ago by the Highland King, Gandarin the First. Fine work, most of them. Beautifully crafted. The mapmakers also had some method of judging the height of mountains. Did you know that High Druin is nine thousand seven hundred and eighty-two feet high? Do you think it could be true, or did someone just invent the figure?"

Asmidir shrugged. "It sounds too precise to be an invention. Still, I am glad you are enjoying your work."

"I enjoy the detail," said Leofric, chuckling. "Not many do. It pleases me to know how many lances we have, and the state of our horses. I like working on projects like this. Did you know there are four hundred and twelve wagons employed around the Five Towns?" The young man laughed. "Yes, I know, it is a little boring for most people. But you try to go on a campaign without wagons and the war is over before it begins."

Asmidir chatted with the young man for several minutes, then bade him farewell and walked swiftly to the stable. The hostler bowed as he entered, then saddled the chestnut gelding. Asmidir gave the man a small silver coin.

"Thank you, sir," he said, pocketing the coin with a swiftness that dazzled the eye.

Asmidir rode from the stable, through the portcullis gate, and out into the wide streets of the town. He felt the eyes of the people upon him as he passed through the marketplace, and heard some children calling out names. A troop of soldiers marched past him and he pulled up his horse. The men were mercenaries; they looked weary, as if they had marched many miles. Leofric planning the logistics of war, more mercenaries arriving every day . . . The beast is not far off, thought Asmidir.

Passing through the north gate, Asmidir let the horse

break into a run as it reached open ground. He rode thus for a mile, then slowed the beast. The chestnut was powerful, a horse bred for stamina, and he was not even breathing hard when Asmidir reined him in. The black man patted the gelding's neck.

"The dreams of men are born in blood," he said softly.

Fell was sitting by the roadside, catching his breath, when the small two-wheeled cart moved into sight. Two huge grey wolfhounds were harnessed to it, and a silver-haired man sat at the front with a long stick in his hands. Seeing the forester, the old man tapped his stick lightly on the flanks of the hounds. "Hold up there, Shamol. Hold up, Cabris. Good day to you, woodsman!"

Fell smiled. "By Heaven, Gwalch, you look ridiculous sitting in that contraption."

"Whisht, boy, at my age I don't give a care to how I look," said the old man. "What matters is that I can travel as far as I like, without troubling my old bones." Leaning forward, he peered at the forester. "You look greyer than a winter sky, boy. Are you ailing?"

"Wounded. And I've shed some blood. I'll be fine. Just need a rest, is all."

"Heading for Cilfallen?"

"Aye."

"Then climb aboard, young man. My hounds can pull two as well as one. Good exercise for them. We'll stop off at my cabin for a dram. That's what you need, take my word for it: a little of the water of life. And I promise not to tell your fortune."

"You *always* tell my fortune—and it never makes good listening. But, just this once, I'll take you up on your offer. I'll ride that idiotic wagon. But I'll pray to all the gods I know that no one sees me on it. I'd never live it down."

The old man chuckled and moved to his right, making room for the forester. Fell laid his longbow and quiver in the back and stepped aboard. "Home now, hounds!" said Gwalch. The dogs lurched into the traces and the little cart jerked forward. Fell laughed aloud. "I thought nothing would amuse me today," he said.

"You shouldn't have gone to her, boy," said Gwalch.

"No fortunes, you said!" the forester snapped.

"Pah! That's not telling your fortune; that's a comment on moments past. And you can put the black man from your mind, as well. He'll not win her. She belongs to the land, Fell. In some ways she *is* the land. Sigarni the Hawk Queen, the hope of the Highlands." The old man shook his head, and then laughed, as if at some private jest. Fell clung to the side of the cart as it rattled and jolted, the wheels dropping into ruts in the trail, half tipping the vehicle.

"By Heaven, Gwalch, it is a most uncomfortable ride," complained the forester.

"You think this is uncomfortable?" retorted the old man. "Wait till we get to the top of my hill. The hounds always break into a run for home. By Shemak's balls, boy, it'll turn your hair grey!"

The hounds toiled up the hill, pausing only briefly at the summit to catch their breaths. Then they moved on, rounding a last bend in the trail. Below them Gwalch's timber cabin came into sight and both dogs barked and began to run.

The cart bounced and lurched as the dogs gathered speed, faster and faster down the steep slope. Fell could feel his heart pounding and his knuckles were white as he gripped the side rail. Ahead of them was a towering oak, the trunk directly in their path. "The tree!" shouted Fell.

"I know!" answered Gwalch. "Best to jump!"

"Jump?" echoed Fell, swinging to see the old man following his own advice. At the last moment the dogs swerved toward the cabin. The cart tipped suddenly and Fell was hurled headfirst from it, missing the oak by inches. He hit the ground hard, with the wind blasted from his lungs.

Fell forced himself to his knees just as Gwalch came ambling over. "Great fun, isn't it?" said the old man, stopping to take Fell by the arm and pull him to his feet.

Fell looked into Gwalch's twinkling brown eyes. "You are insane, Gwalch! You always were."

"Life is to be lived, boy. Without danger there is no life. Come and have a dram. We'll talk, you and I, of life and love, of dreams and glory. I'll tell you tales to fire your blood."

Fell found his longbow and quiver, gathered the fallen arrows, and followed the old man inside. It was a simple one-roomed dwelling with a bed in one corner, a stone-built hearth in the north wall, and a rough-hewn table and two bench seats in the center. Three rugs, two of ox skin, one of bear, covered the dirt floor, and the walls were decorated with various weapons—two longbows, horn-tipped, several swords, and a double-edged claymore. A mail shirt was hanging on a hook beside the fire, its rings still gleaming, not a speck of rust upon it. On a shelf sat a helm of black iron, embossed with brass and copper. A battle-axe was hanging over the fireplace, double-headed and gleaming.

"Ready for war, eh, old man?" asked Fell as he sat down at the table. Gwalch smiled, and filled a clay cup with amber liquid from a jug.

"Always ready—though no longer up to it," said the old man sadly. "And that is a crying shame, for there's a war coming."

"There's no war!" said Fell irritably. "There's no excuse for one. The Highlands are peaceful. We pay our taxes. We keep the roads safe."

Gwalch filled a second cup and drained it in a single swallow. "Those Outland bastards don't need an excuse, Fell. And I can smell blood in the air. But that's for another day, and it is a little way off, so I won't let it spoil our drinking. So tell me, how did she look?"

"I don't want to talk about her."

"Ah, but you do. She's filling your mind. Women are like

that, bless them! I knew a girl once—Maev, her name was. As bright and perfect a woman as ever walked the green hills. And hips! Oh, the sway of them! She moved in with a cattle breeder from Gilcross. Eleven babies—and all survived to manhood. Now *that* was a woman!"

"You should have married her yourself," said Fell.

"I did," said Gwalch. "Two years we were together. Great years. All but wore me out, she did. But then I had my skull caved in during the Battle at Iron Bridge, and after that the Talent was on me. Couldn't look at a man or woman without knowing what was going on in their minds. Oh, Fell, you've no idea how irksome it is." Gwalch sat down and filled his cup for a third time. "To be lying on top of a beautiful woman, feeling her warmth and the soft silkiness of her; to be aflame with passion and to know she's thinking of a sick cow with a dropping milk yield!" The old man laughed.

Fell shook his head, and smiled. "Is that true?"

"As true as I'm sitting here. I said to her one day, "Do you love me, woman?" She looked me in the eye and she said, "Of course I do." And do you know, she was thinking of the cattle breeder she'd met at the Summer Games. And into her mind came the memory of a roll in the hay with him."

"You must have thought of killing her," said Fell, embarrassed by the confession.

"Nah! Never was much of a lover. Roll on, roll off. She deserved a little happiness. I've seen her now and again. He's long dead, of course, but she goes on. Rich, now. A widow of property."

"Are all the weapons yours?" asked Fell, changing the subject.

"Aye, and all been used. I fought for the old King, when we almost won, and I fought alongside the young fool who walked us onto Colden Moor and extermination. Still don't know how I battled clear of that one. I was already nigh on fifty. I won't be so lucky in the next one—though we'll have a better leader."

"Who?"

The old man touched his nose. "Now's not the time, Fell. And if I told you, you wouldn't believe me. Anyway I'd sooner talk about women. So tell me about Sigarni. You know you want to. Or shall I tell you what you're thinking?"

"No!" said Fell sharply. "Fill another cup and I'll talk— though only the gods know why. It doesn't help." Accepting the drink he swallowed deeply, feeling the fiery liquid burn his throat. "Son of a whore, Gwalch! Is this made of rat's piss?"

"Only a touch," said the old man. "Just for color. Now go on."

"Why her? That's the question I ask myself. I've had more than my fair share of beautiful women. Why is it only she can fire my blood? *Why?*"

"Because she's special." Gwalch rose from the table and moved to the hearth. A fire had been expertly laid and he ignited his tinderbox, holding it below the cast-iron firedog until flames began to lick at the dry twigs at the base. Kneeling, he blew on the tongues of flame until the thicker pieces caught. Then he stood. "Women like her are rare, born for greatness. They're not made to be wives, old before their time, with dry breasts drooping like hanged men. She's starlight where other women are candle flames. You understand? You should feel privileged for having bedded her. She has the gift, Fell. The gift of eternity. You know what that means?"

"I don't know what *any* of this means," admitted the forester.

"It means she'll live forever. In a thousand years men will speak her name."

Fell lifted his cup and stared into the amber liquid. "Drinking this rots the brain, old man."

"Aye, maybe it does. But I know what I know, Fell. I know you'll live for her. And I know you'll die for her. *Hold the right, Fell. Do it for me!* And they'll fall on you with their

swords of fire, and their lances of pain, and their arrows of
farewell. Will you hold, Fell, when she asks you?" Gwalch
leaned forward and laid his head on his arms. "Will you
hold, Fell?"

"You're drunk, my friend. You're talking gibberish."

Gwalch looked up, his eyes bleary. "I wish I were young
again, Fell. I'd stand alongside you. By God, I'd even take
that arrow for you!"

Fell rose unsteadily, then helped Gwalch to his feet, carefully steered the old man to the bed, and laid him down. Returning to the fire, he stretched himself out on the bearskin
rug and slept.

It was the closest Sigarni could come to flight. She stood
naked on the high rock beside the falls and edged forward,
her toes curling over the weather-beaten edge. Sixty feet
below the waters of the pool churned as the falls thundered
into it. The sun was strong on her back, the sky as blue as
gemstone. Sigarni raised her arms and launched her body
forward. Straight as an arrow she dived, arms flung back for
balance, and watched the pool roar up to meet her. Bringing
her arms forward at the last moment she struck the water
cleanly, making barely a splash. Down, down she sank until
her hands touched the stone at the base of the pool. Spinning,
she used her feet to propel her body upward. Once more on
the surface she swam with lazy grace to the south of the
pool, where Lady anxiously waited. Hauling herself clear of
the water, she sat on a flat rock and shook the water from her
hair. The sound of the falls was muted here, and the sunlight
was streaming through the long leaves of a willow, dappling
the water with flecks of gold. It would be easy to believe the
legends on a day like today, she thought. *It seems perfectly
natural that a king should have chosen this place to leave the
world of men, and journey into the lands of Heaven.* She
could almost see him wading out, then turning, his great
sword in his bloodstained hand, the baying of the hounds

and the guttural cries of the killers ringing in his ears. Then, as the warriors moved in for the kill, the flash of light and the opening Gateway.

All nonsense. The greatest King of the Highlands had been slain here. Sorain Ironhand, known also as Fingersteel. Last spring, during one of her dives, Sigarni's hands had touched a bone at the bottom of the pool. Bringing it to the surface she found it to be a shoulder blade. For an hour or more she scoured the bottom of the pool. Then she found him, or rather what was left of his skeleton, held to the pool floor by heavy rocks. The right hand was missing, but there were rust-discolored screw holes in the bones of the wrist, and the last red remnants of his iron hand close by.

No Gateway to Heaven—well, not for his body anyway. Just a lonely death, slain by lesser men. Such is the fate of kings, she thought.

A light breeze touched her body and she shivered. "Are you still here, Ironhand?" she asked aloud. "Does your spirit haunt this place?"

"Only when the moon is full," came a voice. Sigarni sprang to her feet and turned to see a tall man standing by the willow. He was leaning on a staff of oak, and smiling. Lady had ignored him and was still lying by the poolside, head on her paws. Sigarni reached down to where her clothes lay and drew her dagger from its sheath. "Oh, you'll not need that, lady. I am no despoiler of women. I am merely a traveler who stopped for a drink of cool mountain water. My name is Loran." Leaning his staff against the tree he moved past her and knelt at the water's edge, pausing to stroke Lady's flanks before he drank.

"She doesn't . . . usually . . . like strangers," said Sigarni lamely.

"I have a way with animals." He glanced up at her and gave a boyish grin. "Perhaps you would feel more comfortable dressed." He was a handsome man, slender and beardless, his hair corn-yellow, his eyes dark blue.

Sigarni decided that she liked his smile. "Perhaps *you* would feel more comfortable undressed," she said, her composure returning.

"Are you Loda people always so forward?" he asked her amiably.

Returning the knife to its sheath, she sat down. Lady stood and padded to her side. "What clan are you?" she asked.

"Pallides," he told her.

"Are all Pallides men so bashful?"

He laughed, the sound rich and merry. "No. But we're a gentle folk who need to be treated with care and patience. How far is it to Cilfallen?" He stood and moved to a fallen tree, brushing away the loose dirt before seating himself.

Sigarni reached for her leggings and climbed into them. "Half a day," she told him, "due south." Her upper body was still damp and the white woolen shirt clung to her breasts. Belting on her dagger, she sat down once more. "Why would a Pallides man be this far south?" she inquired.

"I am seeking Tovi Long-arm. I have a message from the Hunt Lord. Do you have a name, woman?"

"Yes."

"Might I inquire what it is?"

"Sigarni."

"Are you angry with me, Sigarni?" The words were softly spoken. She looked into his eyes and saw no hint of humor there. Yes, I am angry, she thought. Asmidir called me a whore, Fell left without a word of thanks or good-bye, and now this stranger has spurned my body. Of course I'm bloody angry!

"No," she lied. He leaned back and stretched his arm along the tree trunk. Sigarni swept the dagger from the sheath, flipped the blade, then sent the weapon slashing through the air. It slammed into the trunk no more than two inches from his hand. Loran glanced down to see that the blade had cut cleanly through the head of a viper; the rest of its body was thrashing in its death throes. He drew back his hand.

"You are an impressive woman, Sigarni," he said, reaching out and pulling clear the weapon. With one stroke he decapitated the snake, then cleaned the blade on the grass before returning it hilt first to the silver-haired huntress.

"I'll walk with you a ways," she said. "I wouldn't want a Pallides man to get lost in the forest."

"Impressive *and* blessed with kindness."

Together they walked from the falls and up the main trail. The trees were thicker here, the leaves already beginning to turn to the burnished gold of autumn. "Do you usually talk to ghosts?" asked Loran as they walked.

"Ghosts?" she queried.

"Ironhand. You were talking to him when I arrived? Was that the magic pool where he crossed over?"

"Yes."

"Do you believe the legend?"

"Why should I not?" she countered. "No one ever found a body, did they?"

He shrugged. "He never came back either. But his life does make a wonderful story. The last great King before Gandarin. It is said he killed seven of the men sent to murder him. No mean feat for a wounded man." Loran laughed. "Maybe they were all stronger and tougher two hundred years ago. That's what my grandfather told me, anyway. Days when men were men, he used to say. And he assured me that Ironhand was seven feet tall and his battle-axe weighed sixty pounds. I used to sit in my grandfather's kitchen and listen to the tallest stories, of dragons and witches, and heroes who stood a head and shoulders above other men. Anyone under six feet tall in those days was dubbed a dwarf, he told me. I believed it all. Never was a child more gullible."

"Perhaps he was right," said Sigarni. "Maybe they were tougher."

Loran nodded. "It's possible, I suppose. But I was a Marshal at last year's games. The caber toss from Mereth Sharp-eye broke all records, and Mereth is only five inches above six feet tall. If they were all so strong and fast in those days, why do their records show them to be slower and less powerful than we are today?"

They crossed the last hill before Cilfallen and Sigarni paused. "That is my home," she said, pointing to the cabin by the stream. "You need to follow this road south."

He bowed and, taking her hand, kissed the palm. "My thanks to you, Sigarni. You are a pleasant companion."

She nodded. "I fear you spurned the best of me," she said, and was surprised to find herself able to smile at the memory.

Still holding to her hand he shook his head. "I think no man has ever seen the best of you, woman. Fare thee well!" Loran moved away, but Sigarni called out to him and he turned.

"In the old days," she said, "the Highland peoples were free, independent, and unbroken. Perhaps that is what makes them seem stronger, more golden, and defiant. Their power did not derive from a hurled caber, but a vanquished enemy. They may not have all been seven feet tall. Maybe they just *felt* as if they were."

He paused and considered her words. "I would like to call upon you again," he said at last. "Would I be welcome at your hearth?"

"Bring bread and salt, Pallides, and we shall see."

Chapter Two

If Loran was as disappointed in Fat Tovi the Baker he took pains not to show it, for which Tovi himself was more than grateful. The Pallides clansman had bowed upon entering the old stone house, and had observed all the customs and rituals, referring to Tovi as Hunt Lord and bestowing upon him a deference he did not enjoy even among his own people.

Tovi led the clansman to the back room, laid a fire, and asked his wife to bring them food and drink, and to keep the noise from the children to as low an ebb as was possible with seven youngsters ranging from the ages of twelve down to three.

"Your courtesy is most welcome," said Tovi uncomfortably as the tall young man stood in the center of the room, declining a chair. "But as you will already have noticed, the clan Loda no longer operates under the old rules. We are too close to the Lowlands, and our traditions have suffered the most from the conquest. The title of Hunt Lord is outlawed, and we are ruled by lawyers appointed by the Baron Ranulph. We have become a frightened people, Loran. There are fewer than three thousand of us now, spread all around the flanks of High Druin. Seventeen villages of which my own, Cilfallen, is the largest. There are no fighting men now, saving perhaps Fell and his foresters. And they report to the Baron's captain of the Watch. I fear, young man, that the old ways are as dead and buried as my comrades on Colden Moor." Tovi sniffed loudly, and found himself unable to meet the clansman's steady stare. "So, let us dispense with the formalities. Sit you down and tell me why you have come."

Loran removed his leaf-green cloak and laid it over the back of a padded chair. Then he sat and stared into the fire for a few moments, gathering his thoughts. "We of the Pallides," he said at last, "suffered great losses at Colden. But we are far back into the mountains and the old ways have survived better than here. Our young men are still trained to fight, and retain their pride. As you say, you are close to the Lowlands and the armies of the Outlands, and so I make this point without criticism. As to my visit, my Hunt Lord wishes me to tell you that the Gifted Ones of the Pallides have been experiencing dreams of blood. It is their belief that a new war is looming. They have seen blood-wolves upon the Highlands, and heard the cries of the dying. They have seen the Red Moon, and heard the wail of the Bai-sheen. My Hunt Lord wishes to know if your own Gifted Ones have dreamed these things."

"We have only one man with the Gift, Loran. Once a warrior—and a mighty one—he now travels the mountains in a cart drawn by hounds. He is a drunkard and his dreams are not to be relied upon."

The door opened and Tovi's wife entered, carrying a wooden tray on which sat two tankards of ale and a plate of bread and beef. Laying it down on the table she took one glance at her husband, smiled wearily, and left without a word. From beyond the open doorway the sound of children playing could be heard, but the noise was cut off once more as the door closed behind her.

"Drunkard or no," said Loran, "has he dreamed?"

Tovi nodded. "He says a great leader is coming, a warrior of the line of Ironhand. But it is nonsense, Loran. The Outlanders have five thousand men patrolling the Lowlands. Five thousand! If there was the merest hint of rebellion they could treble that number in a matter of weeks. All their wars are won. They have armies sitting idle."

"That is precisely what troubles my Hunt Lord," said Loran. "A warrior race with no wars to fight? What can they do? Either they will turn on themselves like mad dogs, or they will find an enemy. What your drunkard says about a great leader is echoed by our own Gifted Ones, and also by the Seer of the Farlain. No one knows this leader's name, nor his clan. There is a mist shrouding him. Yet we must find him, Lord Tovi. All indications are that the Outlanders will lead an invasion force here in the spring. We have less than seven months to prepare."

"To prepare?" stormed Tovi. "For what, pray? Fell and his foresters number around sixty men. I could raise perhaps another two hundred, and some of those would either be greybeards or children. Prepare? If they come, we die. It is that simple. The Loda were never the largest of the clans. The Pallides and the Farlain always outnumbered us. Still do. And you have the high passes that can be defended, and the hidden valleys to hide your cattle and goats. What do we have? I was a warrior, boy. I was a captain. I know how to use land in war. If I had ten thousand men I couldn't protect my own villages. You want to talk of preparation? Talk of pleading with the Baron, of sending an entreaty to the Outland King, of dropping to our bended knees and begging for life. The first I'll accede to, the second I'll put my name to, and the third I'll never do! But they are our only options."

Loran shook his head. "I don't believe that to be true. If we can find the leader to unite us, we can formulate a strategy. The people of Loda could leave their homes and draw back into the deeper Highlands. We have the autumn before us and could move food and supplies farther back into the mountains. If you agree, I can arrange for temporary homes to be erected in Pallides lands."

Tovi shook his head. "There must be another way, Loran. There must be! We cannot fight them with any hope of success. And what could they gain from invading the Highlands? There is no gold here, no plunder. Would you declare war to capture a few cattle herds?"

"No, I wouldn't," agreed Loran. "But armies are like swords. They must be kept sharp and in use. The Outlanders will, as I have said, need to find some enemy."

Tovi sighed and rose from his chair, pausing before the fire and staring into the flames. "I am not the Hunt Lord, man. I am the baker. I don't have power, and I don't have resources. I don't even have the will."

"Damn you, man!" stormed Loran, rising from his chair. "Have you lost so much? I met a whore on the road with more fire in her belly than you." Tovi's face went white and he lunged forward, his large hands grabbing the front of Loran's pale green tunic, dragging the younger man from his feet.

"How dare you?" hissed Tovi. "I stood on Colden Moor, my sword dripping Outland blood. I watched my brothers cut down, my land swallowed by the enemy. Where were you when I fought my battles? I'll tell you—you were sucking on your mother's tit! I have lost much, boy, but don't presume to insult me."

"My apologies, Hunt Lord," said Loran softly, holding to Tovi's angry gaze. There was no hint of weakness in the mild manner in which Loran spoke, and Tovi's eyes narrowed.

"You did that on purpose, Pallides. You think to fire my blood through anger." Tovi released the younger man, then nodded. "And you were right." Clumsily he tried to brush the creases from Loran's tunic. "Damn it all, you are right. Live under the yoke long enough and you start to feel like an ox." He laughed suddenly, the sound harsh. "I do not know how gifted are your Gifted Ones, Loran, but we will lose nothing by at least sending supplies back into the high country. And tonight I will call a meeting of the Elders to discuss the rest of your proposal. You are welcome to stay here the night and meet them."

"No," the younger man told him. "I want to see the drunkard you spoke of."

"It is a long walk and it will soon be dusk."

"Then I'd best finish this meal and be on my way." Loran tore a chunk from the bread and bit off the crust as Tovi returned to his seat.

"You mentioned a whore? We have only one whore in Cilfallen, and she rarely leaves her house."

"A young silver-haired woman. She offered herself to me without even asking a price."

Tovi suddenly chuckled. "You should consider yourself most fortunate that you did not call her a whore to her face."

"How do you know I did not?"

"The last man who called her such a name had his jaw broken in three places. It took two men to pull Sigarni away from him; she was about to cut his tongue out." The smile faded. "She is the last of the true bloodline of Gandarin. Any son of hers would be the undisputed heir to the crown. And it will never happen."

"She is barren?"

"Aye. She was due to wed Fell, the Forest Captain. Old Gwalch, our Gifted One, proclaimed her infertile. She is no whore, Loran. True she has enjoyed many lovers, but she picks only men she likes, and there is no price to pay. She is a woman of fire and iron, that one, and well liked here."

"You are saying I should feel flattered?"

"Did you not?" countered the baker, a twinkle in his eye.

"She is very beautiful. I watched her make a dive into Ironhand's pool and it took the breath away. I have always spurned those I thought to be whores. Now I am beginning to regret my decision."

"You may never get another chance, boy."

"We will see."

The sandy-haired young man sat with his head in his hands, his eyes bleary with drink. Before him was a half-empty tankard. Ballistar climbed to the bench seat and then perched his small body at the edge of the table. "Getting drunk won't solve anything, Bernt," he said.

"She doesn't want to see me," said Bernt. "She says she will never see me again." He looked across at the dwarf. "I didn't mean to do it, Balli. I got excited. I wouldn't have hurt Lady, not for all the world. I just wasn't thinking. I was watching Sigarni. She looked so beautiful in the morning sunlight. So beautiful." The young man drained the tankard and belched. Ballistar looked at him—the square face, the deep-set blue eyes, the powerful neck and broad shoulders— and knew envy. All that *height* wasted on a dullard like Bernt. Ballister felt guilty at the thought, for he liked the young man. True, Bernt was not bright, yet he had a warmth and a compassion lacking in other, more intelligent men. In truth he was a sensitive soul.

"I think," said the dwarf, "that you should just lie low for a while. Lady is almost healed and she is hunting well. Wait for a little while, then go out and see Sigarni again. I expect she'll relent. You were always good for her."

"*Was*. That's the word, isn't it? *Was*. I could never talk to her, you know. Didn't understand much of what she said. It all flew over my head. I didn't care, Balli. I was just happy to be with her. To . . . love her. I think all she needed from me was my body." He laughed nervously and looked around to see if anyone was listening, but the two other drinkers in the tavern were sitting by the fire, talking in low tones. "That's what she told me," he continued. " 'Bernt,' she said, 'this is your only skill.' She said I took away all her tension. She was wrong, though, Balli. It's not my only skill. I was *there* for her. She couldn't see that. I don't know what I'm going to do!"

"There are other women," said Ballistar softly. "You are a good young man, strong, honest. You have a great deal to offer."

"I don't want anyone else, Balli. I don't. All my waking moments are filled with thoughts of her. And when I sleep I dream of her. I never asked for anything, you know. I never . . . made demands. She didn't ever let me sleep in the bed, you know . . . afterward. I always had to go home. It didn't matter what the weather was like. Once I even went home in a blizzard. Got lost, almost died. Almost died . . ." His voice faded away, and he bit his lip. "She didn't care, not really. I always thought that I would, sort of, grow on her. That she would realize I was . . . important. But I'm not important, am I? I'm just a cattle herder."

The dwarf shifted uneasily. "As I said, Bernt, you should give her a little time. I know she likes you."

"Has she spoken of me?" asked the young man, his eyes eager, his ears hungry for words of encouragement.

Ballistar looked away. "I can tell, that's all. She's still angry, but underneath . . . just give it time."

"She didn't say anything, did she, Balli? Except maybe that I was a fool."

"She's still angry. Go home. Get something to eat."

The young man smiled suddenly. "Will you do something for me, Balli? Will you?"

"Of course," answered the dwarf.

"Will you go to her and ask her to meet me at the old oak grove tonight, an hour after dark?"

"She won't come—you know that! And she doesn't keep clock candles, she has no use for them."

"Well, soon after dusk then. But will you ask her? Tell her that it is so important to me. Even if she only comes to say good-bye. Will you tell her that? Will you? Tell her I have never asked for anything save this one time."

"I'll go to her, Bernt. But you are only building up more pain for yourself."

"Thank you, Balli. I'll take your advice now. I'll go home and eat."

The young man levered himself up, staggered, grinned inanely, and lurched from the tavern. Ballistar clambered down from the table and followed him.

It was a long walk on tiny legs to Sigarni's cabin, more than two hours. And it was such a waste, thought Ballistar.

The afternoon was warm, but a gentle breeze was blowing over High Druin as the dwarf ambled on. He walked for an hour, then sat for a while on a hillside resting his tired legs. In the distance he could see a walker heading off toward the higher hills. The man wore a leaf-green cloak and carried a long staff; Ballistar squinted, but could not recognize him. He was heading toward Gwalch's cabin. Ballistar chuckled. He wouldn't be walking that straight when he left!

Rising once more, he set off down the slope and along the deer trails to Sigarni's cabin. He found her sitting by the front door, cutting new flying jesses from strips of leather. Lady was nowhere to be seen, but Abby was sitting on her bow perch. She flapped her wings and pranced as she saw Ballistar. The dwarf gave a low bow to the bird. "It is good to see you as well, Abby."

"Just in time," said Sigarni. "You can make some herb tea. Somehow I never make it taste as good as yours."

"My pleasure, princess."

Ballistar climbed the steps and entered the cabin. An old iron kettle was hissing steam over the fire. Taking a cloth to protect his hands, he lifted it clear. In the back room he found the packs of dried herbs he and Sigarni had gathered in the spring. Mixing them by eye, he added hot water and cut a large portion of crystallized honey, which he dropped into the mixture. He stirred the tea with a long wooden spoon and sat quietly while it brewed. How to tackle Sigarni? How to convince the silver-haired huntress to meet the boy?

After several minutes he filled two large pottery cups with tea and carried them out into the afternoon sunlight. Sigarni took the first and sipped it. "How do you make it taste like this?" she asked.

"Talent," he assured her. "Now, are you going to ask me why I have walked all this way?"

"I assume it was because you felt in need of my company."

"Under normal circumstances that would be true, princess. But not today. I have a favor to ask."

"Ask it—and I'll consider it," she said.

"I was hoping for a little more than that," he admitted.

"Just ask," she said, a little coldly.

"I saw Bernt today . . ."

"The answer is no," she said flatly.

"You don't know the question yet."

"I can hazard a guess. He wants me to take him back."

"No! Well . . . yes. But that is not the favor. He asks if you will meet him after dusk at the old oak grove. Even if it is only to say good-bye. He said it was vital to him."

"I have already said good-bye." Returning her attention to the leather jesses, she said nothing more.

Ballistar sighed. "He also said that he had never asked you for anything—save this once."

She looked up and he braced himself for her anger. But her words were spoken coldly, and without emotion. "I owe him nothing. I owe you nothing. I owe no one. You understand? I did not ask him to love me, nor to follow me like a dog. He was an adequate lover, no more than that. And now he is part of my past. He has no place in the present. Is that clear?"

"Oh, it is clear, princess. Callous, unkind, unfeeling. But very *clear*. And of course it would be so time-consuming for you to walk to the oak grove. After all, it is more than a mile from here."

She leaned back and looked into his face. "Now we are both angry, little man. And for what? Bernt is a dolt. I have no need of fools around me. But since it is a favor to you, I shall grant it. I shall go to Bernt, and I shall tell him good-bye. Does that satisfy you?"

He grinned and nodded. "And as a reward I shall prepare you a meal. What provisions do you have?"

"Abby killed a duck this morning."

"I shall cook it with a berry sauce," he said.

* * *

They ate well, the duck being young and plump. Ballister cooked it to perfection; the skin was crisp and dark, the flesh moist, the red berry sauce complementing the flavor. Sigarni pushed aside her plate and licked her fingers. "If I had an ounce of common sense I'd marry you," she told the dwarf. "I never knew a man who could make food taste so fine."

Ballistar was sitting in the hide chair, his little legs jutting out. He nodded sagely. "Well," he said at last, "you could *ask* me. But I would only say no."

Sigarni smiled. "Not good enough for you, dwarf?"

"Too good, probably. Though that is not the reason. There is something about you, Sigarni. Like the Crown of Alwen— all men can see it, but none can touch it."

"Nonsense. Men can touch me. I like men to touch me."

"No, you don't," he argued. "I don't think you have ever allowed a man to touch your heart. No man has ever opened the window of your soul."

She laughed at him then. "The heart is a pump for moving blood around the body, and as to the soul . . . what is that exactly?" She held up her hand. "No, don't try to explain it. Let it lie. The meal was too fine to finish on an argument. And you had better go, or you'll be walking back in the dark."

The dwarf scrambled down from the chair, and gathered up the plates. "Leave them," said Sigarni. "Be off with you, Ballistar. I have a need to be alone."

"Don't be too hard on Bernt," said Ballistar from the doorway.

"I'll treat him like an injured puppy," she promised.

After the dwarf had gone Sigarni cleaned the plates and built up the fire. She did not relish seeing the young cattle herder, for she was determined never to renew their relationship. It was not that he was a poor lover, nor even that he was dull. In the early days, last autumn, she had enjoyed his quiet company. However, during the spring he had become like a weight around her neck, following her everywhere, declaring his love, sitting and staring at her, begging for love like a dog begs for scraps. She shuddered. Why could he not enjoy what they had? Why did he need more than she was prepared to give? Idiot!

Pouring herself a goblet of honey mead from a flagon that Gwalch had given her, she moved to the doorway and sat down beside Lady. The hound looked up, but did not move. Idly Sigarni stroked the soft fur behind the beast's ears. Lady lay still, enjoying the sensation for several minutes, then her head came up and she stared intently toward the tree line. "What is it, girl?" whispered Sigarni.

As horse and rider emerged from the trees, Sigarni swore softly. It was Asmidir. He was dressed now in clothes of black and riding a tall black gelding. His burnoose of black silk was held in place by a dark band of leather, with an opal set at the center. The horse advanced into the yard. Abby spread her wings and let out a screech on her bow perch. Lady merely stood, alert and waiting.

"Come to see your whore?" asked Sigarni as the black man rode up. He smiled amiably, then dismounted. Draping the reins over the gelding's head, he climbed the three steps to the porch.

"You are too prickly, Sigarni. I need to speak with you. Shall we go inside? Your northern weather plays havoc with my equatorial bones."

"I'm not sure you are welcome," she told him, rising to stand before him in the doorway.

"Ah, but I am, for friends are rare in life, and not to be idly tossed aside. Also I can see from your eyes that you are pleased to see me, and I sense in you a tension only sex will resolve. Am I at fault in any of these observations?"

"Not so far," she agreed, stepping aside and ushering him into the room. Once inside he stopped and sniffed.

"You have been having a feast," he said, nostrils flaring. "The aroma makes my mouth water. Duck, was it?"

"Yes. Ballistar cooked it for me. Now, he is a true sorcerer when it comes to food. You should employ him."

"I'll think on it," he said, removing his cloak and laying it over the back of the chair. Sitting down by the fire he sat for a moment in silence staring into the flames. Sigarni sat on his lap, leaning to kiss his cheek.

"I'm glad you came," she said. Reaching up, he ran his fingers through her silver hair and drew her close. Pushing one arm under her thighs, he stood and carried her through to the back bedroom.

For more than an hour they made love, but skilled as he was, Sigarni could feel a different tension within him. After her second orgasm she stopped him, pushing him gently to his back. "What is wrong, my friend?" she asked him, rising up on her elbow and stroking the sleek dark skin of his chest. He closed his eyes.

"Everything," he said. He reached for her, but she resisted him.

"Tell me," she commanded.

"I would have thought," he said, forcing a smile, "that you would have the good grace to let me achieve my own climax before entering into a dialogue."

She chuckled and bit his ear. "Then be quick," she told him, "for I have other matters to attend to!"

"Your wish shall be obeyed, mistress!" he said, rolling over and pinning her shoulders.

Sigarni felt loose-limbed and wonderfully relaxed as she sat by the fire and sipped her mead. Relaxed in the chair, Asmidir sat naked, save for his cloak, which he had wrapped about his shoulders against the draft from the warped wood of the door.

"Now tell me," she said.

"There is a war coming," he told her.

"Where?"

"Here, Sigarni. I was at the Citadel a few days ago. I saw the mercenaries arriving, and I know the Baron is studying maps of all the lands around High Druin. It is my belief that he intends to bring an army into the mountains."

"That cannot be," she said. "There is no one to fight him."

"That is largely immaterial. He hates his position here, and probably sees a Highland war as his best chance of being recalled south in triumph. It does not matter that he will face a rabble of poorly armed villagers. Who will know? He has his own historian. His army will be able to pillage and plunder the Highlands, and he will gather to himself a force to make him a power in the land. He may even be looking ahead and planning a civil war. It doesn't matter what his motives are."

"And how does this concern you, Asmidir? You are not of this land, and you are a friend to the Outland King."

"I served him, but he has no friends. The King is a hard, ruthless man, much like the Baron. No, for me it is . . . personal." He smiled thinly. "I came here because of a prophecy. It has not been fulfilled. Now I am lost."

"What prophecy?"

He shrugged. "It does not matter, does it? Even shaman can make mistakes, it seems. But I have grown to love this harsh, cold land with a fierceness that surprises me. It is as strong as my hatred for the Baron and all he represents." He sighed and turned his head toward the fire. "Why is it that wickedness always seems to triumph? Is it just that evil men freed from the constraints of basic morality are stronger than we?"

"It is probably just a question of timing," she said, and his head jerked around.

"Timing?"

"We have had two kings of legend here, Gandarin and Ironhand. Both were good men, but they were also strong and fearless. Their enemies were scattered, and they ruled wisely and well. But this is the time of the Outland Kings, and not a good time for the peoples of the Highlands. Our time will come again. There will be a leader."

"Now *is* the time," he said. "Where is the man? That was the prophecy that brought me here. A great leader will rise, wearing the Crown of Alwen. But I have traveled far, Sigarni, and heard no word of such a man."

"What will you do when you find him?"

He chuckled. "My skill is strategy. I am a student of war. I will teach him how to fight the Outlanders."

"Highland men do not need to be taught how to fight."

He shook his head. "There you are wrong, Sigarni. Your whole history has been built on manly courage: assembling a host to sweep down on an enemy host, man against man, claymore crashing against claymore. But war is about more than battles. It is about logistics, supplies, communication, discipline. An army has to feed, commanders need to gather reports and intelligence and pass these on to generals. Apart from this there are other considerations—morale, motivation, belief. The Outlanders, as you call them, understand these things."

"You are altogether too tense," she told him, leaning forward and running her hand softly down the inside of his thigh. "Come back to bed, and I will repay you for the pleasure you gave me."

"What of these other matters you had to attend to?" he asked.

For a moment only she thought of Bernt, then brushed him from her mind. "Nothing of importance," she assured him.

At noon the following day Ballistar found Bernt hanging from the branch of a spreading oak. The young cattle herder was dressed in his best tunic and leggings, though they were soiled now, for he had defecated in death. The boy's eyes were wide open and bulging, and his tongue was protruding from his mouth. When Ballistar arrived at the oak grove a crow was sitting on Bernt's shoulder, pecking at his right eye.

Below the corpse was a hawking glove, lovingly made and decorated with fine white beads. Urine from the corpse had dripped upon it, staining the hide.

Chapter Three

The oxen found pulling the wide wagon too difficult over the narrow deer trails to Gwalch's cabin, so Tovi was forced to take the long route, down into the valley and up over the rocky roads once used by the Lowland miners when there was still a plentiful supply of coal to be found on the open hillsides. The baker had set off just after dawn. He always enjoyed these quarterly trips into Citadel town. Gwalch was an amusing, if irritating, companion, but the money they shared from their partnership helped Tovi to maintain a pleasant and comfortable lifestyle. Gwalch made honey mead of the finest quality, and much of it was shipped to the south at vastly inflated prices.

One of the oxen slipped on the rocky shale. "Ho there, Flaxen! Concentrate now, girl!" shouted Tovi. The wagon lurched on, the empty barrels in the back clunking against one another. Tovi took a deep sniff of the mountain air, blowing cool over High Druin. At the top of the rise he halted the oxen, allowing them a breather before attempting the last climb into the forest. Tovi applied the brake, then swung to stare out over the landscape. Many years before he had marched with the Loda men down this long road. They were singing, he recalled; they had met the Pallides warriors down there by the fork in the stream. Seven thousand men— even before the Farlain warriors had joined them.

All dead now. Well . . . most of them anyway. Gwalch had been there. Fifty years old and straight as a long staff. The

King had been mounted on a fine southern horse, his bonnet adorned with a long eagle feather. Every inch a warrior he looked. But he had no real heart for it. Tovi hawked and spat, remembering the moment when the King fled the field leaving them to stand and die.

"Blood doesn't always run true," he said softly. "Heroes sire cowards, and cowards can sire kings."

The air was crisp, the wind beginning to bite as Tovi wrapped his cloak across his chest. Didn't feel the wind back then, he thought. I did a week later, though, as I fled from the hunters, crawling through the bracken, wading the streams, hiding in shallow caves, starving and cold. God's bones, I felt it then!

High above him two eagles were flying the thermals, safe from the thoughts and arrows of men. Tovi released the brake and flicked the reins over the backs of the oxen. "On now, my lads!" he called. "It's an easier trip down for a while."

Within the hour he arrived at Gwalch's cabin. The old man was sitting outside in the sunshine with a cup of mead in his hands. There were three horsemen close by, two grim-faced soldiers still sitting their saddles, and a cleric who was standing before the old man, arguing and gesticulating. The soldiers looked bored and cold, Tovi thought. The cleric was a man he recognized: Andolph the Census Taker, a small, fat individual with ginger hair and a face as white as Tovi's baking flour.

"It is not acceptable!" Tovi heard the cleric shout. "And you could be in serious trouble. I don't know why I try to deal fairly with you Highlanders. You are a constant nuisance."

Tovi halted the wagon and climbed down. "Might I be of service, Census Taker?" he inquired. Andolph stepped back from the grinning Gwalch. "I take it you know this man?"

"Indeed I do. He is an old friend. What is the problem?"

Andolph sighed theatrically. "As you know, the new law

states that all men must have surnames that give them indi-
viduality. It is no longer enough to be Dirk, son of Dirk.
Gods, man, there are hundreds of those. It is not difficult,
surely, therefore, to find a name that would suffice. But not
this old fool. Oh, no! I am trying to be reasonable, Baker,
and he will not have it. Look at this!" The little man stepped
forward and thrust a long sheet of paper toward Tovi. The
baker took it, read what was written there, and laughed
aloud.

"Well, it *is* a name," he offered.

"I can't put this forward to the Roll Makers. Can't you see
that? They will accuse the old man of making a mockery of
the law. And I will be summoned to answer for it. I came
here in good faith; I like a jest as well as the next man, and it
did make me laugh when first I saw it. But it cannot be allowed to stand. You see that, don't you?"

Tovi nodded. There was no malice in the little man, and as
far as was possible with an Outlander, Tovi quite liked him.
It was a thankless task trying to take a census in the Highlands, especially since the object was to find new taxpayers.
"I'll speak to him," he said, handing back the paper and
walking over to where Gwalch sat. The old man was staring
at one of the soldiers, and the man was growing uncomfortable.

"Come on, Gwalch," said Tovi soothingly, "it is time for
the fun to stop. What name will you choose?"

"What's wrong with Hare-turd?" countered Gwalch.

"I'll tell you what's wrong with it—it'll be carved on your
tombstone. And you'll not be surprised when future generations fail to appreciate what a fine man you were. Now stop
this nonsense."

Gwalch sniffed loudly, then drained his mead. "You
choose!" he told Tovi, staring at the soldier.

The Baker turned to the Census Taker. "When young he
was known as *Fear-not*. Will that do?" Andolph nodded.
From a leather bag he took a quill and a small bottle of ink.

Resting the paper against his saddle, he made the change and called Gwalch to sign it. The old man gave a low curse, but he strolled to the horse and signed with his new name.

Andolph waved the paper in the air to dry the ink. "My thanks to you, Tovi Baker, and good-bye to you . . . Gwalch-mai Fear-not. I hope we will not meet again."

"You and I won't," said Gwalch, with a grin. "And a word of advice, Andolph Census Taker: Trust not in dark-eyed women. Especially those who dance."

Andolph blinked nervously, then climbed ponderously into his saddle. The three horsemen rode away, but the soldier Gwalch had been staring at swung around to look back. Gwalch waved at him. "That is the man who will kill me," said Gwalch, his smile fading. "He and five others will come here. Do you think I could have changed the future if I had stabbed him today?"

Tovi shivered. "Are we ready to load?" he asked.

"Aye. It's a good batch, but I'll not be needing the new barrels. This is our last trip, Tovi. Make the best of it."

"What is the point of having the Gift if all it brings is gloom and doom?" stormed Tovi. "And another thing, I do not believe that life is mapped out so simply. Men shape the future, and nothing is written in stone. You understand?"

"I don't argue with that, Tovi. Not at all. Sometimes I have dreamed of moments to come, and they have failed to arrive. Not often, mind, but sometimes. Like the young cattle herder who loved Sigarni. Until yesterday I always saw him leaving the mountains to find employment in the Lowlands. Last night, though, I saw a different ending. And it has come to pass."

"What are you talking about?"

"Bernt, the broad-shouldered young man who works for Grame the Smith . . ."

"I know him . . . what about him?"

"Hanged himself from a tree. Late last night. Dreamed it sitting in my chair."

"Hell's teeth! And it has happened? You are sure?"

The old man nodded. "What I am trying to say is that futures can be changed sometimes. Not often. He shouldn't be dead, but something happened, one small thing, and suddenly life was over for Bernt."

"What happened?"

"A woman broke a promise," said Gwalch. "Now let's have a swift drink before loading. It'll help keep the cold at bay."

"No!" said Tovi. "I want to be at the market before mid-morning." Gwalch swore and moved away to the barrel store, and together the two men loaded twelve casks of honey mead alongside the empty barrels Tovi had brought with him. "Why don't you let me leave the empties here?" asked the baker. "You might change your mind—or the dream may change."

"This dream won't change, my friend. There'll be no market for our mead come springtime. You know that; you've spoken to the Pallides man."

"What did you tell him?" asked Tovi as the two men clambered to the driving seat of the wagon.

"Nothing he didn't already know," answered Gwalch. "The Pallides Gifted Ones are quite correct."

"And that was all?"

Gwalch shook his head. "There is a leader coming. But I wouldn't tell him who, or when. It is not the right time. He impressed me, though. Sharp as a stone of flint, and hard too. He could have been a force one day. But he won't survive. You will, though, Tovi. You're going to be a man again."

"I am already a man, Gwalchmai Hare-turd. And don't you forget it."

In the pale moonlight the friendly willow took on a new identity, its long, wispy branches trailing the steel-colored water like skeletal fingers. Even the sound of the Falls was muted and strange, like the whispers of angry demons. The undergrowth rustled as the creatures of the night moved abroad on furtive paws, and Sigarni sat motionless by the waterside, watching the fragmented moon ripple on the surface.

She felt both numb and angry by turn; numbed by the death of the simple herder, and angry at the way the dwarf had treated her. Sigarni had spent three days in the mountains trapping fox and beaver, and had returned tired, wet, and hungry to find Ballistar sitting by her door. Her spirits had lifted instantly; the little man was always good company, and his cooking was a treat to be enjoyed. Greeting him with a smile, Sigarni had dumped her furs on the wooden board and then returned Abby to her bow perch. Returning to the house, she saw that Ballistar had moved away from the door. He was standing stock-still, staring at her, his face set and serious, the expression in his eyes unfathomable. Sigarni saw that he was carrying a hawking glove of pale tan, beautifully decorated with white and blue beads.

"A present for me?" she asked. He nodded and tossed her the glove. It was well made of turned hide brushed to a sheen, the stiches small and tight, the beads forming a series of blue swirls over a white letter S. "It's beautiful," she said gaily. "Why so glum? Did you think I wouldn't like it?" Slipping it on, she found it fit perfectly.

"I never saw a crow peck out a man's eye before," he said. "It's curious how easily the orb comes away. Still, Bernt didn't mind. Even though he was in his best clothes. He didn't mind at all. Scarce noticed it."

"What are you talking about?"

"Nothing of importance, Sigarni. So, how was Bernt when you saw him?"

"I didn't see him," she snapped. "I had other things to do. Now what is wrong with you? Are you drunk?"

The dwarf shook his head. "No, I'm not drunk—but I will be in a while. I shall probably drink too much at the wake. I do that, you know. Funerals always upset me." He pointed at the glove she wore. "He made that for you. I suppose you could call it a love gift. He made it and he put on his best tunic. He wanted you to see him at his very best. But you didn't bother to go. So he waited until the dawn and then hanged himself from a tall tree in the oak grove. So, Sigarni, that's one fool you won't have to suffer again."

She stood very still, then slowly peeled off the glove. "It was on the ground below him," said Ballistar, "so you'll have to excuse the stains."

Sigarni hurled the glove to the ground. "Are you blaming me for his suicide?" she asked him.

"You, princess? No, not at all," he told her, his voice rich with sarcasm. "He just wanted to see you one last time. He asked me to tell you how important it was to him. And I did. But nothing is important to him anymore."

"Have you said all you want to say?" she asked, her voice soft but her eyes angry.

He did not reply, he merely turned and walked away.

Sigarni sat in the doorway for some time, trying to make some sense of the events. Ballistar obviously held her responsible for Bernt's death, but why? All she had done was rut with him for a while. Did that make her the guardian of his soul? *I didn't ask him to fall in love with me,* she thought. *I didn't even work at it.*

You could have gone to him as you promised, said the voice of her heart.

Sorrow touched her then and she stood and wandered away from the house, heading for the sanctuary of the waterfall pool. This was where she always came when events left her saddened or angry. It was here she had been found on that awful night when her parents were slain: She was just sitting by the willow, her eyes vacant, her blond hair turned white as snow. Sigarni remembered nothing of that night, save that the pool was the one safe place in a world of uncertainty.

Only tonight there was no sanctuary. A man was dead, a

good man, a kind man. That he was stupid counted for nothing now. She remembered his smile, the softness of his touch, and his desperation to make her happy.

"It could never be you, Bernt," she said aloud. "You were not the man for me. I've yet to meet him, but I'll know him when I do." Tears formed in her eyes, misting her vision. "I'm sorry that you are dead," she said. "Truly I am. And I'm sorry that I didn't come to you. I thought you wanted to beg me back, and I didn't want that."

Movement on the surface of the pool caught her eye. A mist was moving on the water, swirling and rising. It formed the figure of a man, blurred and indistinct. A slight breeze touched it, sending it moving toward her, and Sigarni scrambled to her feet and backed away.

"Do not run," whispered a man's voice inside her mind.

But she did, turning and sprinting up over the rocks and away onto the old deer trail.

Sigarni did not stop until she had reached her cabin, and even then she barred the door and built a roaring fire. Focusing her gaze on the timbered wall, she scanned the weapons hanging there: the leaf-bladed broadsword, the bow of horn and the quiver of black-shafted arrows, the daggers and dirks and the helm, with its crown and cheek guards of black iron and the nasal guard and brows of polished brass. Moving to them she lifted down a long dagger, and sat honing its blade with a whetstone.

It was an hour before she stopped trembling.

Gwalchmai's mouth was dry, and his tongue felt as if he had spent the night chewing badger fur. The morning sunlight hurt his eyes, and the bouncing of the dog cart caused his stomach to heave. He broke wind noisily, which eased the pressure on his belly. He always used to enjoy getting drunk in the morning, but during the last few years it had begun to seem like a chore. The great grey wolfhounds, Shamol and Cabris, paused in their pulling and the cart stopped. Shamol was looking to the left of the trail, his head still, dark eyes alert. Cabris squatted down, seemingly bored. "No hares today, boys!" said Gwalch, flicking the reins. Reluctantly Shamol launched himself into the traces. Caught unawares, Cabris did not rise in time and almost went under the little cart. Angry, the hound took a nip at Shamol's flank. The two dogs began to snarl, their fur bristling.

"Quiet!" bellowed Gwalch. "Hell's dungeons, I haven't had a headache like this since the axe broke my skull. So keep it down and behave yourselves." Both hounds looked at him, then felt the light touch of the reins on their backs. Obediently they started to pull. Reaching behind him, Gwalch lifted a jug of honey mead and took a swallow.

Sigarni's cabin was in sight now, and he could see the black bitch, Lady, sitting in the dust before it. So could Shamol and Cabris, and with a lunge they broke into a run. Gwalch was caught between the desire to save his bones and the need to protect his jug. He clung on grimly. The cart survived the race down the hill, and once on level ground Gwalch began to hope that the worst was over. But then Lady ran at the hounds, swerving at the last moment to race away into the meadow. Shamol and Cabris tried to follow her, the cart tipped, and Gwalch flew through the air, still clutching his jug to his scrawny chest. Twisting, he struck the ground on his back, honey mead slurping from the jug to drench his green woolen tunic. Slowly he sat up, then took a long drink. The hounds were now sitting quietly by the upturned cart, watching him gravely. Leaving the jug on the boardwalk, he stood and walked to where the cart lay. Righting it he moved to the dogs, untying the reins. Shamol nuzzled his hand, but Cabris took off immediately toward the woods in search of Lady. Shamol ambled after him.

Gwalch recovered his jug and went into the house. He found Sigarni sitting at the table, a dagger before her. Her hair was unwashed, her face drawn, her eyes tired. Gwalch gathered two clay cups and filled them both with mead, pushing one toward her. She shook her head. "Drink it, girl," he said, sitting opposite her. "It'll do you no harm."

"Read my mind," she commanded.

"No. You'll remember when you are ready."

"Damn you, Gwalch! You're quick to tell everyone's fortune but mine. What happened that night when my parents were butchered? Tell me!"

"You know what happened. Your . . . father and his wife were killed. You survived. What else is there to know?"

"Why did my hair turn white? Why were the bodies buried so swiftly? I didn't even see them."

"Tell me about last night."

"Why should I? You already know. Bernt's ghost came to me at the pool."

"No," he said, "that wasn't Bernt. Poor, sad Bernt is gone from the world. The spirit who spoke to you was from another time. Why did you run?"

"I was . . . frightened." Her pale eyes locked to his, daring him to criticize her.

Gwalch smiled. "Not easy to admit, is it? Not when you are Sigarni the Huntress, the woman who needs no one. Did you know this is my birthday? Seventy-eight years ago today I made my first cry. Killed my first man fourteen years later, a cattle raider. Tracked him for three days. He took my father's prize bull. It's been a long life, Sigarni. Long and irritatingly eventful." Pouring the last of the mead, he drained it in a single swallow, then gazed longingly at the empty jug.

"Who was the ghost?" she asked.

"Go and ask him, woman. Call for him." She shivered and looked away.

"I can't."

Gwalch chuckled. "There is nothing you cannot do, Sigarni. Nothing."

Reaching across the table she took his hand, stroking it tenderly. "Oh, come on, Gwalch, are we not friends? Why won't you help me?"

"I *am* helping you. I am giving you good advice. You don't remember the night of the Slaughter. You will, when the time is right. I helped take the memory from you when I found you by the pool. Madness had come upon you, girl. You were sitting in a puddle of your own urine. Your eyes were blank, and you were slack-jawed. I had a friend with me; his name was Taliesen. It was he—and another—who slew the Slaughterers. Taliesen told me we were going to lock away the memory and bring you back to the world of the living. We did exactly that. The door will open one day, when you are strong enough to turn the key. That's what he told me."

"So," she said, snatching back her hand, "your only advice is for me to return to the pool and face the ghost? Yes?"

"Yes," he agreed.

"Well, I won't do it."

"That is your choice, Sigarni. And perhaps it is the right one. Time will show. Are you angry with me?"

"Yes."

"Too angry to fetch me the flagon of honey mead you have in the kitchen?"

Sigarni smiled then, and fetched the flagon. "You are an old reprobate, and I don't know why you've lived so long. I think maybe you are just too stubborn to die." Leaning forward, she proffered the flagon, but as he reached for it she drew it back. "One question you must answer. The Slaughterers were not human, were they?" He licked his lips, but his eyes remained fixed on the flagon. "Were they?" she persisted.

"No," he admitted. "They were birthed in the Dark, Hollow-tooths sent to kill you."

"Why me?"

"You said one question," he reminded her, "but I'll answer it. They came for you because of who you are. And that is all I will say now. But I promise you we will speak again soon."

She handed him the flagon and sat down.

"I cannot go to the pool, Gwal. I cannot."

Gwalchmai did not answer her. The mead was beginning to work its magic, and his mind swam.

The Baron Ranulph Gottasson ran a bony finger down the line on the map. "And this represents what?" he asked the young blond man shivering before him. Leofric rubbed his cold hands together, thankful that he had had the common sense to wear a woolen undershirt below his tunic, and two pairs of thick socks. His fleece-lined gloves were in his pocket, and he wished he had the nerve to wear them. The Baron's study at the top of the Citadel was always cold, though a fire was permanently laid, as if to mock the Baron's servants. "Are you listening, boy?" snarled the Baron.

Leofric leaned over the table and felt the cold breeze from the open window flicker against his back. "That is the river Dranuin, sir. It starts on the northern flank of High Druin and meanders through the forest into the sea. That is in Pallides lands."

The Baron glanced up and smiled. The boy's face was blue-tinged. "Cold, Leofric?"

"Yes, sir."

"A soldier learns to put aside thoughts of discomfort. Now tell me about the Pallides."

I'm not a soldier, thought Leofric, I am a cleric. And there is a difference between the discomfort endured through necessity and the active enjoyment of it. But these thoughts he kept to himself. "The largest of the clans, the Pallides number some six thousand people. It used to be more, but the Great War devastated them. In the main they are cattle breeders, though there are some farms which grow oats and barley. In the far north there are two main fishing fleets. The Pallides are spread over some two hundred square miles and live in sixteen villages, the largest being Caswallir, named after a warrior of old who, legend claims, brought the Witch Queen to their aid in the Aenir Wars."

"I don't care about legends. Just facts. How many people in Caswallir?"

"Around eleven hundred, sir, but it does depend on the time of the year. They have their Games in the autumn and there could be as many as five thousand people attending every day for ten days. Of course, these are not all Pallides. Loda, Farlain, and even some Wingoras will attend—though the Wingoras are all but finished now. Our census shows only around one hundred and forty remain in the remote Highlands."

"How many fighting men?"

"Just the Pallides, sir?" asked Leofric, sitting down and opening a heavy leather-bound ledger. The Baron nodded. "It is difficult to estimate, sir. After all, what constitutes a fighting man in a people with no army? If we are talking men and older boys capable of bearing arms, then the figure would be . . ." He flicked through three pages, making swift mental calculations, then went on: ". . . say . . . eighteen hundred. But of these around a thousand would be below the age of seventeen. Hardly veterans."

"Who leads them?"

"Well, sir, as you know there is no longer an *official* Hunt Lord, but our spies tell us that the people still revere Fyon Sharp-axe, and treat him as if he still held the title."

Lifting a quill pen, the Baron dipped the sharpened nib into a pot of ink and scrawled the name on a single sheet of paper. "Go on."

"What else can I tell you, sir?" asked Leofric, nonplussed.

"Who else do they revere?"

"Er . . . I don't have information on that, sir. Merely statistics."

The Baron's hooded eyes focused on the younger man's face. "Find out, Leofric. All possible leaders. Names, directions to their homes or farms."

"Might I ask, sir, why we are gathering this information? All our agents assure us there is no hint of rebellion in the

Highlands. They do not have the men, the weapons, the training, or the leaders."

"Now tell me about the other clans," said the Baron, his quill at the ready.

Ballistar sat perched on the saddle of the small grey pony and stared around at the village of Cilfallen. Despite his fears, he gazed with a sense of wonder at this unfamiliar view. The pony was only ten hands high, barrel-bellied with short stubby legs—a dwarf horse for a dwarf. And yet, Ballistar estimated, he was now viewing the world from around six feet high, seeing it as Fell or Sigarni would see it.

Fat Tovi emerged from his bakery, and smiled at the dwarf. "What nonsense is this?" he asked, transferring his gaze to the man on the black gelding who was waiting patiently beyond Ballistar.

"The sorcerer Asmidir has asked me to cook for him," said Ballistar boldly, though even the words sent a flicker of fear through him. "And he has given me this pony. For my own."

"It suits you," said Tovi. "It looks more like a large dog."

Grame the Smith wandered over. "She's a fine beast," he said, stroking his thick white beard. "In years gone by the Lowland chariots were drawn by such as she. Tough breed."

"She's mine!" said Ballistar, grinning.

"We must leave," said the man on the black gelding, his voice deep. "The master is waiting."

Ballistar tugged on the reins and tried to heel the pony forward, but his legs were so short that his feet did not extend past the saddle and the pony stood still. Grame chuckled and walked back to his forge, returning with a slender riding crop.

"Give her just a touch with this," he said. "Not too hard, mind, and accompany it with a word—or sound—of command."

Ballistar took the leather crop. "Hiddy up!" he shouted, swiping the crop against the pony's rear. The little animal reared and sprinted and Ballistar tumbled backward in a somersault. Grame stepped forward and caught the dwarf, then both fell to the ground. Ballistar, his bearded face crimson, struggled to his feet as Asmidir's servant rode after the pony and led her back. Tovi was beside himself with mirth, the booming sound of his laughter echoing through the village.

"Thank you, Grame," said Ballistar, with as much dignity as he could muster. The smith pushed himself to his feet and dusted himself down.

"Think nothing of it," he said. "Come, try again!" Pushing his huge hands under Ballistar's armpits he hoisted the dwarf to the saddle. "You'll get the hang of it soon enough. Now be off with you!"

"Hiddy up!" said Ballistar, more softly. The pony moved forward and Ballistar lurched to the left, but clung onto the pommel and righted himself.

With the village behind them Ballistar's fear returned. He had been sitting quietly behind the tavern when the dark-skinned servant found him. Had he been asked beforehand whether he would be interested in a journey to the wizard's castle, Ballistar would have answered with a curt shake of his head. But two gold pieces and a pony had changed his mind. Two gold pieces! More money than Ballistar had ever held. Enough to buy the little shack, instead of paying rent. More than enough to have the cobbler make him a new pair of boots.

If he doesn't sacrifice you to the demons!

Ballistar shivered. Glancing up at the man on the tall horse, he gave a nervous smile, but the man did not respond. "Have you served your master long?" he inquired, trying to start a conversation.

"Yes."

And that was it. The man touched heels to the gelding and moved ahead, Ballistar meekly following. They rode for more than an hour, moving through the trees and over the high hills. Toward midmorning Ballistar saw Fell and two of his foresters, Gwyn Dark-eye and Bakris Tooth-gone; he waved and called out to them.

The three foresters converged on the dwarf, ignoring the dark-skinned rider. "Good day to you, Fell," said Ballistar. Fell grinned, and Ballistar experienced renewed pleasure in the fact that he could look the handsome forester straight in the eye.

"Good day to you, little friend. She is a fine pony."

"She's mine. A gift from the sorcerer."

"He is not a sorcerer!" snapped the servant. "And I wish you would stop saying it."

"The black man wants me to cook for him. Duck! Sigarni told him about me; he's paid me with this pony." Ballistar decided not to mention the gold pieces. Fell he liked above all men, and Gwyn Dark-eye had always been kind to him. But Bakris Tooth-gone was not a man Ballistar trusted.

"Are you sure he doesn't want to cook *you*?" asked Gwyn. A slightly smaller man than Fell, and round-shouldered, Gwyn was the finest archer among the Loda.

Ballistar looked down upon him and noticed the man had a bald spot beginning at his crown. "On a day like today the thought does not concern me," said Ballistar happily. "Today I have seen the world as a tall man."

"Enjoy it," sneered Bakris. "Because when you get off that midget horse you'll return to the useless lump you've always been." The words were harshly spoken, and they cut through Ballistar's good humor. Fell swung angrily on the forester but before he could speak Ballistar cut in.

"Don't worry about it, Fell. He's only angry because I've got a bigger prick than him. I don't know why it should concern him. Everyone else has too!"

Bakris lunged at the dwarf, but Fell caught him by the shoulder of his leather jerkin and dragged him back. "That's enough!" roared Fell. The sudden commotion caused the pony to move forward. Asmidir's servant nudged his gelding alongside and the two riders continued on their way. Ballistar swung in the saddle and looked back at the foresters. When he saw Bakris staring after him he lifted his fist and waggled his little finger.

Asmidir's servant chuckled. "You shouldn't be so swift to make enemies," he observed.

"I don't care," said Ballistar.

"And why is it that you Highlanders value so much the size of the male organ? Size is of no relevance, not to the act itself nor to the pleasure derived."

Ballistar glanced up at the man. Ah, he thought, so you've got a small one too! Aloud he said, "I wouldn't know. I have never had a woman."

It was midafternoon when they topped the last rise before the castle. Ballistar had never traveled this far before and he halted his pony to stare down at the magnificent building. It was not a castle in the true sense, for it was indefensible, having wide-open gateways with no gates, and no moat surrounding it. It had once been the house of the Hunt Lord of the Grigors, but that clan had been annihilated in the Lowland wars, the few survivors becoming part of the Loda. A three-storied building, with a single tower by the north wall that rose to five stories, it was built of grey granite, and the windows were of colored glass joined by lead strips.

"We are late," said the servant. "Come!"

Ballistar's heart was pounding and his hands trembled as he flapped the reins against the pony's neck.

Two gold pieces seemed a tiny amount just then.

Chapter Four

Autumn was not far off, but here in the Highlands even the last days of summer were touched by a bitter cold that warned of the terrible winters that lay ahead. Two fires blazed at either end of the long hall, and even the heavy velvet curtains shimmered against the cold fingers of the biting wind that sought out the cracks and gaps in the old window frames.

Asmidir pushed away his empty plate and leaned back in his chair. "You are a fine cook," he told the dwarf. Two servants entered, lighting lanterns that hung in iron brackets on the walls, and the hall was filled with a soft glow.

"Can I go now?" asked Ballistar. The little man was sitting at the table, on a chair set upon blocks of wood.

"My dear fellow, of course you can go. But it is already becoming dark and your pony is bedded down for the night in a comfortable stall. I have had a room prepared for you. There is a warm fire there, and a soft bed. Tomorrow one of my servants will cook you a breakfast and saddle your pony. How does that sound?"

"That is wondrous kind," said Ballistar uneasily, "but I would like to be on my way."

"You fear me?" asked Asmidir mildly.

"A little," admitted the dwarf.

"You think me a sorcerer. Yes, I know. Sigarni told me. But I am not, Ballistar. I am merely a man. Oh, I know a few spells. In Kushir all the children of the rich are taught to make fire from air, and some can even shape dancing figures from the flames. I am not one of those. I was a nobleman—a warrior. Now I am a Highlander, albeit somewhat more dusky than most. And I would be your friend. I do not harm my friends, nor do I lie. Do you believe me?"

"What does it matter whether I believe you or not?" countered the dwarf. "You will do as you wish."

"It matters to me," said Asmidir. "In Kushir it was considered unacceptable for noblemen to lie. It was one of the reasons the Outlanders—as you call them—defeated the armies of the Kushir King. The Outlanders kept lying: they signed treaties they had no intention of honoring, made peace, then invaded. They used spies and agents, filling Kushir soldiers with fear and trembling. An appalling enemy with no sense of honor."

"But you fought alongside them," said Ballistar.

"Yes. It is a source of endless regret. Come, sit by the fire and we shall talk." The black man rose and walked to the fireside, settling his long frame into a deep armchair of burnished leather. A servant appeared and drew back Ballistar's seat, allowing the little man to slide from his cushions to the floor. Asmidir watched as he climbed with difficulty into the opposite armchair, then, waving away the servant, he leaned forward. "You treat your affliction with great courage, Ballistar. I respect that. Now what shall we speak of?"

"You could tell me why you served the Outlanders," said the dwarf.

"Swift and to the point," observed Asmidir with an easy grin. "It all came down to politics. My family was accused of treason by the Kushir King. He was hunting us down at the time the Outlanders invaded. My sister and my wife were executed by him, my father blinded and thrown into a dungeon. We have a saying in Kushir—*the enemy of my enemy must therefore be my friend*. So I joined with the Outlanders."

"And now you regret it?"

"Of course. There is no genuine satisfaction in revenge, Ballistar. All a man unleashes is a beast which will destroy even those he loves. Cities were laid waste, the people slaughtered or sold into slavery. A rich, cultured nation was set back two hundred years. And even when they had won, the slaughter continued. The Outlanders are a barbaric people, with no understanding of the simplest economic realities. The Kushir was rich because of trade and commerce. The lines of trade were severed, and treaties with friendly nations broken. There was a Great Library at Coshantin, the capital; the Outlanders burned it down." Asmidir sighed and lifted an iron poker, idly stabbing at the burning logs.

"You grew to hate them?"

"Oh, yes! Hatred as strong and tall as High Druin. But two men more than any other, the Baron Ranulph and the Earl of Jastey. The King himself is merely a merciless savage, holding power through ruthlessness and manipulation. The Baron and the Earl hold the balance of his power."

"Why are you telling me this?" asked Ballistar. "It is not wise."

Asmidir smiled. "It is a question of judgment, my friend. Do you trust Sigarni?"

"In what way?"

"Her instincts, her values, her courage . . . whatever?"

"She is intelligent and does not suffer fools. What has this to do with anything?"

"She *trusts* you, Ballistar. Therefore so do I. And as for the risk . . . well, all life is a risk. And time is running too short for me to remain conservative in my plans. Sigarni tells me you are a great storyteller, and somewhat of a historian. Tell me of the clans. Where are they from, how did they come here? Who are their heroes and why? What are their noble lines?"

"You are moving too fast for me," said Ballistar. "A moment ago we were talking of trust. Before that, revenge. Now you want a story. Tell me first your purpose."

"A clear thinker . . . I like that. Very well. First I shall tell you a story." Asmidir clapped his hands and a servant came forward bearing a tray on which were two golden goblets filled with fine red wine. Ballistar accepted the first, holding it carefully in both hands. As the servant departed Asmidir sipped his drink, then set the goblet aside. Leaning back, he rested his head on the high back of the chair. "With Kushir in ruins I went home to my palace. An old man, dressed in a cloak of feathers, was waiting for me there. His face was seamed with wrinkles and lines, his hair and beard so thin they appeared to be fashioned from the memory of wood smoke. He was sitting on the steps before my door. A servant told me he had arrived an hour before, and refused to be moved; they tried to lay hands upon him, but could not approach him. Knowing him to be a wizard, they withdrew. I approached him and asked what he wanted. He stood and walked toward my home. The door opened for him, though there were no servants close, and he made his way to my study. Once there, he asked me what I felt about the destruction of my land and my part in it. I did not answer him, for my shame was too great. He said nothing for a moment, then he bade me sit and began to talk of history. It was fascinating, Ballistar. It was as if he had witnessed all the events himself. Perhaps he had. I don't know. He spoke of the growth of evil and how, like a plague, it spreads and destroys. It was vital, he said, that there should always be adequate counterbalances against the forces of wickedness.

"Yet he insisted, we had reached a period of history when there was no balance. The Outlanders and their allies were conquering all in their path. And those nations still resisting the advance of the Outlanders were doomed, for there were no great leaders among them. Then he told me of a conquered nation, and a commander yet to come. He said—and I believed him utterly—that here, in the north, I would find a prince of destiny, and from the ashes of Highland dreams would come a dynasty that would light our way forward into a better future. I came here with high hopes, Ballistar, and yet what do I find?

"There is no leader. There is no army. And in the spring the Outlanders will come here with fire and sword and exterminate hundreds, perhaps thousands, of peaceful farmers, cattlemen, and villagers." Asmidir threw a dry log to the dying blaze. "I do not believe that the ancient one lied to me . . . and I cannot accept that he might have been mistaken. Somewhere in these lands there is a man born to be king. I must find him before midwinter."

Ballistar drained his wine. It was rich and heavy and he felt his head swimming. "And you think my stories might help you?" he asked.

"They might provide me with a clue."

"I don't see how. Legend has it that our ancestors passed through a magic Gateway, but I suspect our history is no different from other migrating peoples. We probably came from a land across the water, originally as raiders. Some of our people then grew to love the mountains, and sent back ships for their families. For centuries the clans warred upon one another, but then another migrating group arrived. They were called the Aenir, ancestors of the Outlanders. There was a great war. After that the clans formed a loose-knit confederacy."

"But you had kings? From where did they come?"

"The first true King was Sorain, known as Ironhand. He was from the Wingoras, a mighty warrior. Hundreds of years ago he led the clans against the Three Armies and destroyed them. Even the Lowland clans respected him, for he risked everything to free their towns. He vanished one day, but legend has it he will return when needed."

Asmidir shook his head. "I doubt that. Every nation I know of has a hero of myth, pledged to return. None of them do. Did he have heirs?"

"No. He had a child, but the babe disappeared—probably murdered and buried in the woods."

"So what of the other kings?" inquired Asmidir.

"There was Gandarin, also known as the Crimson—another great warrior and statesman. He died too soon and his sons fought among themselves for the crown. Then the Outlanders invaded and the clans put on their red cloaks of war and were cut down on Colden Moor. That was years ago. The young King fled over the water, but he was murdered there. Anyone known to share the blood of Gandarin was also put to the sword. And the wearing of the Crimson was banned. No Highlander can have even a scarf of that color."

"And there is no one left of his line?"

"As far as I know there is only Sigarni, and she is barren."

Asmidir rubbed his tired eyes and tried to disguise the dejection he felt. "He must be somewhere," he whispered, "and he will need me. The ancient one made that clear to me."

"He could have been wrong," volunteered Ballistar. "Even Gwalch is wrong sometimes."

"Gwalch?"

"The Clan Gifted One. He used to be a warrior, but he was wounded in the head and after that he became a prophet of sorts. People tend to avoid him. His visions are all doom-filled and gloomy. Maybe that's why he drinks so much!"

Asmidir's spirits lifted. "Tell me where to find him," he said.

Sigarni was angry with herself. Four times that morning she had flown Abby, and four times the red hawk had missed the kill. Abby was a little overweight, for there had been three days of solid rain and she had not flown, but even so she was acting sluggishly and the tourney was only two weeks away. Sigarni was angry because she didn't know what to do, and was loath to ask Asmidir. Could Abby be ill? She didn't think so, for the bird was flying beautifully, folding her wings and diving, swooping, turning. Only at the point of the kill did she fail. The pattern with the red hawk was always the same—swoop over the hare, flick her talons, tumbling the prey, then fastening to it. Sigarni would run forward, covering the hare with her glove, then casting a piece of meat some distance from the hawk. The bird would glance at the tidbit, then leave the gloved hare to be killed and bagged by Sigarni. But not today.

Sigarni lifted her arm and whistled for Abby. The hawk dived obediently from the high branch and landed on the outstretched fist, her cruel beak fastening to the tiny amount of meat Sigarni held between her fingers.

"What's wrong with you, Abby?" whispered Sigarni, stroking the bird's breast with a long pigeon feather. "Are you sick?" The golden eyes, bright and impenetrable, looked into her own.

Returning to the cabin, Sigarni did not take Abby to her bow perch but carried her inside and set her on the high back of a wooden chair. The cabin was cold and Sigarni lit a fire, banking up the logs and adding two large lumps of coal from the sack given to her by Asmidir. From the cupboard she took her scales, hooking them to a broad beam across the center of the cabin. Fetching Abby, she weighed her. Two pounds seven ounces: five ounces above her perfect killing weight.

"What am I to do with you, beauty?" she asked softly, stroking the bird's head and neck. "To keep you obedient I must feed you, yet if you do not fly you get fat and lazy and are useless to me. If I starve you, all your training will disappear and I will be forced to start again as if it never was. Yet you are intelligent. I know this. Is your memory so short? Mmmm? Is that it, Abby?" Sigarni sighed. Taking the hawk's hood from the pouch at her belt, she stroked it into place. Abby sat quietly, blind now, but trusting. Sigarni sat by the fire, tired and listless.

Lady scratched at the door and Sigarni opened it, allowing the hound to pad inside and stretch her lean black frame in front of the fire. "I hope you've already eaten," she told the hound, "since we've caught nothing today." Lady's tail beat

against the floor and she tilted back her head, looking at
Sigarni through one huge, brown eye. "Yes," said the woman,
"I don't doubt you have. You're the best hare hound in the
Highlands. You know that, don't you? Faster than the
wind—though not as fast as Abby."

The darkness was growing outside and Sigarni lit a small
lamp that she hung over the fireplace. Stretching out her
legs, she removed her wet doeskin boots and her oiled
leather trews. The warm air from the fire touched the bare
skin of her legs and she shivered with pleasure. "If only I
wasn't hungry," she said aloud, stripping off her buckskin
shirt and tossing it to the floor. The fire crackled and grew,
casting dancing shadows on the walls of the cabin.

"I have the bells of Hell clanging in my head," said
Gwalch, walking from the bedroom, clutching his temples.

"Then you shouldn't drink so much, Gwal," she said with
a smile.

"All right for you but I . . ." He stopped as he saw her
nakedness. "Jarka's balls, woman! That's not decent!"

"You said you'd be gone, old fool. It would be decent
enough were I alone!"

"Ah, well," he said with a broad grin, "I think I might as
well make the best of it." Pulling up a chair, he gazed with
honest admiration at her firelit form. "Wonderful creatures,
women," he said. "If God ever made anything more beautiful He has never shown it to me."

"Since your eyes are standing now on reed stalks, I take it
that you are a breast man," she said with a laugh. "Now Fell
is a legs and hips man. His eyes are naturally drawn to a
woman's buttocks. Strange beasts, men. If God ever made
anything more ludicrous She's never shown it to me."

Gwalch leaned back and roared with laughter. "Blas-
phemy and indecency in the same breath. By Heavens,
Sigarni, there is no one like you. Now, for the sake of an old
man's feelings, will you cover yourself?"

"Feel the blood rising, old man?"

"No, and that is depressing. Dress for me, child. There's a good girl."

Sigarni did not argue, but slipped a buckskin shirt over her head. It was almost as long as a tunic and covered her to her thighs. "Is that better, Gwal? You weren't so worried when I lived with you, and you bathed me and washed my hair."

"You were a child and titless. And you were hurt, lass."

"How do you kill a demon, Gwal?" she asked softly.

He scratched at the white stubble on his chin. "Is there no food in this house? By God, a man could die of starvation visiting you."

"There's a little cold stew, and a spare flagon of your honey spirit. It's too fiery for my taste. You want that, or shall I heat up the stew?"

He gave a wicked grin and winked. "No, lass. Just fetch me a drop of the honeydew."

"First a bargain."

"No," he said, his voice firm. "I will tell you no more. Not yet. And if that means a dry night, then so be it."

"When will you tell me?"

"Soon. Trust me."

"Of all men I trust you most," she said, moving forward to kiss his brow. She fetched him the flagon and watched as he filled a clay cup. The liquid was thin and golden, and touched the throat like a flame. Gwalch drained the cup and leaned back with a sigh.

"Enough of this and a man would live forever," he said.

She shook her head. "You are incorrigible. Do you know the legend of Ironhand?"

"Of course. Went through a Gateway, to return when we need him."

"And will he return?"

"Yes. When the time is right." He drank a second cup.

"That's not true, Gwalch. I found his bones."

"Yes, I know. Under several boulders in the pool of the falls. Why did you tell no one?"

Sigarni was surprised, though instantly she knew she should not have been. "Why do you ask, when you already know the answer?" she countered.

"It is not polite to answer a question with a question, girl. You know that."

"People need legends," she told him. "Who am I to rob them of their power? He was a great man, and it is nice for people to think that he actually managed to kill all the assassins, instead of being done to death by the murdering scum."

"Oh, but he did kill them all! Seven of them, and him wounded unto death. Killed them, and their war hounds. Then he sat by the pool, his strength fading. He was found by one of his retainers, a trusted man, loyal and steadfast. Ironhand told him to hide his body where none could find it until the chosen time. You see, he had the Gift. It came on him as he was dying. So the word went out that Ironhand had crossed the Gateway and would one day return. And so it will be."

Gwalch filled a third cup and half drank it. Leaning forward, he placed the cup on the hearthstone, then sank back, his breathing deepening.

"When will he come back, Gwalch?" whispered Sigarni.

"He already has once," answered the old man, his voice slurring. "On the night of the Slaughter. It was he who killed the last demon." The old man began to snore gently.

Fell loved the mountains, the high, lonely passes, the stands of pine and the sloping valleys, the snow-crowned peaks and the vast sweep of this harsh country. He stood now above the snow line on High Druin staring out to the north, the lands of the Pallides and farther to the distant shimmering river that separated the Pallides clan from the quiet, grim men of the Farlain. This was a land that demanded much from a man. Farming was not easy here, for the winters were harsh beyond compare, the summers often wet and miserable, drowning the roots of most crops, bar oats that seemed to thrive in the Highlands. Cattle were bred in the valleys, hard, tough, long-haired beasts with horns sweeping out, sharp as needles. Those horns needed to be sharp when the wolves came, or the black bears. And despite the long hair and the sturdiness of their powerful bodies, the vicious winters claimed a large percentage of the beasts—trapped in snowdrifts, or killed in falls from the icy ridges and steep rises.

It was no land for the weak of spirit, or the soft of body.

The cool dusk breeze brushed the skin of his face and he rubbed his chin. Soon he would let his close-cropped beard grow long, protecting his face and neck from the bitter bite of the winter winds.

Fell climbed on, traversing a treacherous ridge and climbing down toward the supply cave. He reached it just before nightfall. The flap that covered the narrow opening was rotting and he made a mental note to bring a new spread of canvas on his next visit. It wasn't much of a barrier, but it kept stray animals from using the cave as shelter, and on a cold night it helped to hold in the heat from the fire. The cave was deep, but narrow, and a rough-built hearth had been set some ten feet from the back wall below a natural chimney that filtered smoke up through the mountain. As was usual the fire was laid, ready for a traveler, with two flint rocks laid beside it. By the far wall was enough wood to keep a blaze burning for several nights. There was also a store cupboard containing oats and honey, and a small pot of salted beef. Alongside this were a dozen wax candles.

It was one of Fell's favorite places. Here, sitting quietly without interruption, he could think, or dream. Mostly he thought about his role as captain of the foresters; how best to patrol the forests and valleys, to cull the deer herds, and hunt the wolves. Tonight he wanted to dream, to sit idly in the cave and settle his spirit. Swiftly he lit a fire, then removed his cloak and pack and stood his longbow and quiver against the wall. From the pack he pulled a small pot and a sack of oats. When the fire had taken he placed the pot over it and made several trips outside, returning with handfuls of snow that he dropped into the pot. At last when there was enough water he added oats and a pinch of salt, stirring the contents with a wooden spoon. Fell preferred his porridge with honey, but he had brought none with him and was loath to raid the store. A man could never tell when he would need the provisions in the small store cupboard, and Fell did not want to be stuck on High Druin in the depths of winter, only to remember that on a calm night in late summer he had eaten the honey on a whim.

Instead he cooked his porridge unsweetened, then put it aside to cool.

Sigarni's face came unbidden to his mind and Fell swore softly. "I must have sons," he said aloud, surprised how defensive the words sounded.

"A man needs love also," said a voice.

Fell's heart almost stopped beating. Leaping to his feet, he spun around. There was no one there. The forester drew his double-edged hunting knife.

"You'll have no need of that, boy," said the voice, this time coming from his left. Fell turned to see, sitting quietly by the fire, the oldest man he had ever seen, his face a maze of firelit wrinkles, his skin sagging grotesquely around the chin. He was wearing a tunic and leggings of green plaid, and a cloak that seemed to be fashioned from feathers of every kind, pigeon, hawk, sparrow, raven . . . Fell flicked a glance at the canvas flap over the doorway. It was still pegged in place.

"How did you get in here?" he asked.

"By another doorway, Fell. Come, sit with me." The old man stretched out a fleshless arm and gestured to the forester to join him.

"Are you a ghost?"

The old man thought about it. "An interesting question. I am due to die long before you were born. So, in one sense, I suppose I am already dead. But no, I am not a spirit. I am flesh and blood, though there is precious little flesh left. I am Taliesen the druid."

Fell moved to the fire and squatted down opposite the old man. He seemed harmless enough, and was carrying no weapon, but even so, Fell kept his dagger in his hand. "How is it that you know me?" he asked.

"Your father gave me bread and salt the last time I came here, nineteen years ago, by your reckoning. You were six. You looked at my face and asked me why it no longer fit me." The old man gave a dry chuckle. "I do so love the young. Their questions are so deliciously impertinent."

"I don't remember it."

"It was the night of the twin moons. I had another man with me; he was tall and recklessly handsome, and he wore a shirt of buckskin emblazoned with a red hawk motif."

"I do remember," said Fell, surprised. "His name was Caswallon and he sat with me and taught me how to whistle through my teeth."

The old man's face showed a look of exasperation. He shook his head and whispered something that sounded to Fell like a curse. Then he looked up. "It was a night when two moons appeared in the sky, and the Gateways of time shimmered open causing a minor earthquake and several avalanches. But you remember it because you learned to whistle. Ah well, such, I fear, is the way of things. Do you intend to share that porridge?"

"Such was not my intention," said Fell testily, "but since you remind me of my manners I am obliged to offer you some."

"It never does a man harm to be reminded of his manners," said Taliesen. Fell rose and fetched two wooden bowls from the cupboard. There was only one spoon, which he offered to the old man. Taliesen ate slowly, then put aside his bowl half finished. "I see you've lost the art of porridge in this time," he said. "Still, it will suffice to put a little energy into this old frame. Now . . . to the matter at hand. How is Sigarni?"

"She is well, old man. How do you know her?"

Taliesen smiled. "I don't. Well, not exactly. My friend with the hawk shirt brought her to the people who raised her. He risked much to do so, but then he was an incautious man, and one ruled by an iron morality. Such men are dangerous friends, but they make even more deadly enemies. Thankfully he was always more of a friend."

"What do you mean *brought* her? She lived with her father and mother until . . ."

"The night of the Slaughter . . . yes, yes, I know. But they were not her parents. Their child died in her cot. Sigarni was a . . . changeling. But that is all beside the point. I take it the invasion is not under way yet? No, of course it isn't. I may be getting old, but I still have a certain Talent when it comes to Gateways. It is now six days from the end of summer, yes?"

"Four days, but you make no sense, old man," said Fell, adding more wood to the fire. "What invasion?"

"Four days? Mmmmm. Ah well, close enough," said the old man, looking down at his gnarled hand and tapping his thumb to each of the fingers, as if working on some simple calculation. He stood and wandered to the doorway, pulling back the flap and looking up at the sky, scanning the bright stars. "Ah yes," he said, returning to the fire. "Four days. Quite right. Now, what was your question? The invasion. Mmmm. Where to begin? The descendants of the Aenir, the conquerors of the Lowlands. What do you call them . . . Outlanders? Yes, Outlanders. They will come in the spring with fire and sword. I know you suspect this already, young Fell. Still, that is not important at this moment, for we were speaking of Sigarni. Is she strong? Is she willful and obstinate? Does she have a piercing stare that strikes fear into the hearts of strong men?"

Fell laughed suddenly. "Yes, all of those." His smile

faded. "But speak plainly, old man, for I wish to hear more of this invasion you speak of. Why would they invade?"

"Why indeed? What motivates the minds of evil men? Who can truly know, save another evil man. And, testy though I have been throughout my long life, I have never been evil, and therefore cannot answer your questions with any guarantee of accuracy. I can hazard a guess, however."

"I never knew a man who could talk so long and say so little," snapped Fell.

"Youth was always impatient," Taliesen rebuked him mildly. "There are two main reasons I can think of. One concerns a prophecy being talked of in the south, about a great leader who will rise among the peoples of the Highlands. Prophecies of this nature are not usually welcomed by tyrants. Secondly, and probably more important, is the fact that the Baron Ranulph Gottasson is ambitious. He has two enemies, one is the King, and the other is the Earl of Jastey. By raising an army in the Highlands he can make himself a power again in the capital—especially with a few victories to brag of."

"How can he achieve victories when there is no army to fight him?"

Taliesen smiled and shook his head. "For that very reason, how can he not?"

"But there is no leader. God's teeth, this is insane!"

"Wrong again, boy. There is a leader. That is why I am here, sitting in this cold, inhospitable cave, with its dull company and worse porridge. *There is a leader!*"

Fell stared at him. "Me? You think it is *me*?"

"Do I look like an idiot, boy? No, Fell, you are not the leader. You are brave and intelligent, and you will be loyal." He chuckled. "But you are not gifted to command armies. You have not the talent, nor the will, nor the blood."

"Thank you for your honesty," said Fell, feeling both aggrieved and relieved. "Then who is it?"

"You will see. In three days, outside the walls of Citadel

town a sword will be raised, and the Red will be worn again. Be there, Fell. In three days, at dawn. By the light of the new sun you will see the birth of a legend."

The old man stood and his joints cracked like dry twigs.

Fell rose also. "If you are some sort of prophet, then you must know the outcome of the invasion. Will my people survive?"

"Some will, some won't. But it is not quite so simple, young man. There is only ever one past, but myriad futures, though sometimes the past can be another man's future. Now there is a riddle to spin your head like a top, eh?" The old man's features softened. "I'm not trying to baffle you, Fell. But I have knowledge gained over twenty times your lifetime. I cannot impart it to you in the brief moment we have. Let us merely say that I know what *should* happen, and I know what *could* happen. I can therefore say with certainty what *might* happen. But never can I tell you what *will* happen!"

"Even Gwalch is more sure than that," put in Fell, "and he's drunk half the time."

"Some events are set in stone, and a part of destiny," agreed Taliesen, "as you will see in three days at Citadel town. Others are more fluid." He smiled. "Don't even try to make sense of what I tell you. Just be close to Citadel town. And now I will show you something more memorable than teeth whistling. Watch carefully, Fell, for you will not see its like again."

So saying, the old man walked toward the wall—and through it. Fell gasped, blinked, then pushed himself upright and ran to the wall.

It was solid rock.

But of the old man there was no sign. For a moment Fell stood there, his broad right hand resting on the rock. Then he turned and glanced back at the fire. It had died down. Adding more wood, he waited until the flames rose and flickered high, then settled down beside the fire. It was pitch-dark and icy cold outside the cave now, but he felt the heat from the blaze and was comfortable. And as he dropped into a deep and dreamless sleep he heard again the words of the old man.

"Be there, Fell. In three days, at dawn. By the light of the new sun you will see the birth of a legend."

Will Stamper moved through the market crowds, scanning for signs of cutpurses or beggars. He had been corporal of the Watch for two years now, and the burly soldier took his job very seriously. Beside him the shorter Relph Wittersson munched on an apple.

"More people this year," said Relph, tossing away the core. A mangy mongrel sniffed at it, then moved away.

"Population's growing," Will told him, stroking a broad finger under the chin strap of his iron helmet. "All them new houses on East Street are sold now, and they're talking of building to the north. God knows why people want to come to this place."

"You did," Relph pointed out. Will nodded and was about to speak when he saw a small grey-haired man in a dirty brown tunic moving at the edge of the crowd. The man saw him at the same instant and swiftly darted down an alleyway.

"Alyn Shortblade," said Will. "I'll have the old bastard one of these days. What was I saying?"

"Can't remember, something about buildings going up and immigrants coming in," answered Relph, pausing at a meat stall and helping himself to a salt beef sausage. The stall holder said nothing and looked away. Relph bit into the sausage. "Not bad," he said, "but too much cereal. Shouldn't be allowed. Can't rightly call it a sausage if there's more bread than meat in it."

The two moved slowly through Market Street, then down Baker's Alley and into the main square, where the tents and marquees were being erected ready for Tournament Day. The sound of hammers on nails filled the square as workmen continued to build the high-banked seats for the nobles and their ladies and Will saw the slight, blond Lord Leofric directing operations. Beside him stood the captain of the Watch. Will cursed softly. Relph tapped Will's arm.

"Let's go back through Market Street," he advised. Will was about to agree when the captain saw them. With an imperious flick of his finger he summoned them over. Will took a deep breath. He had no liking for the captain, and worse, no respect. The man was a career soldier, but he cared nothing for the well-being of his men.

Redgaer Kushir-bane, Knight of the Court, son of the Earl of Cordenia, did not wait for the soldiers to reach him. Arms clasped behind his back he strode toward them, his red beard jutting. "Well?" he asked. "Caught any cutpurses?"

"Not yet, sir," said Will, giving the clenched fist salute.

"Hmmm. Nor will you if that stomach keeps spreading, man. I'll have no lard bellies under my command."

"Yes, sir." It was futile to offer any form of argument, as Will Stamper had long ago discovered to his cost. Happily for Will the captain turned his attention to Relph.

"There is no shine to your buckle, man, and your helmet plume looks like it's been used to wipe a horse's arse. That's a five-copper fine, and you will report to my adjutant for extra duty."

"Yes, sir," said Relph meekly.

"Well, get on with your rounds," commanded Redgaer, spinning on his heel, his red cloak swirling out.

"What a goat-brain," whispered Relph. *"Your plume looks like it's been used to wipe a horse's arse,"* he mimicked. "More likely it was used to brush his tongue after he'd dropped on his knees to kiss the Baron's rear." Will chuckled, and the two soldiers continued on their way through Tanner Street and back into the market.

"Whoa, look at that!" said Relph, pointing. Will saw the object of his attention and let out a low whistle. A tall woman was moving through the market, her hair shining silver despite her youth, and on her left fist sat a red hawk.

"Look at the legs on that girl, Will. All the way up to the neck. And what an arse, tight, firm. I tell you, I wouldn't crawl across her to get to you!"

"Bit thin for my taste," said the older man, "but she walks well, I'll say that. She's a Highlander."

"How do you know? Just because she's wearing buckskins? Lot of Lowlanders wear buckskins."

"Look at the way she moves," said Will. "Proud, arrogant. Nah . . . Highlander. They're all like that. I see she's not wearing a marriage bangle." As they watched they saw the hawk suddenly bait, wings flapping in panic. The woman calmed it, gently stroking its red head.

"She could stroke me like that," said Relph. "A bit lower down, though. Come on, let's talk to her."

"What for?"

"I go off duty at dusk. You never know your luck."

"I'll bet that five-copper fine that she's not interested."

"And I'll bet you I'll spear her by midnight!"

"You arrogant son of a bitch," said Will with a smile. "I'm going to enjoy watching you cut down to size." The two soldiers angled through the crowd, coming alongside the woman as she stood by the dried fruit stall.

"Good morning, miss," said Will. "That's a fine bird."

The woman offered a fleeting smile. "She hunts well" was all she said, then she turned away.

"Are you from the Highlands?" asked Relph.

The woman swung back. "I am. Why do you ask?"

"My friend here had a little bet with me. I said you were mountain-bred, he insisted you were a Lowlander. I told him you could always tell a Highland woman."

"Tell her what?" countered the woman, turning her pale gaze on the soldier.

"No . . . I mean, recognize one. It's in the . . . er . . . walk. Tell me, are you . . . er . . . staying on in Citadel tonight? There are some fine places to dine, and I'd be honored to escort you."

"No, I am not staying on. Good day to you." She walked on, but Relph hurried alongside, taking hold of her arm. This made the hawk bait once more.

"You don't know what you're missing, sweet thing. It's never wise to turn down a good opportunity."

"Oh, I never do that," said the woman. "Good-bye."

She strode off, leaving Relph red-faced. "Ah," said Will, "the sound of five fresh copper coins jingling in my palm. I can almost hear it."

Relph swore. "Who does the bitch think she is?"

"I told you, she's a Highlander. As far as she is concerned you are an occupying enemy soldier. And if she doesn't hate you—which she probably does—she despises you. Now let's move on, and you can figure out how to pay me."

"How'd she get a hawk?" said Relph. "I mean, a woman with a hawk. It's not proper. Maybe she stole it!"

"You can put that thought from your mind now, son," said Will sternly. "Just because a woman doesn't want to sleep with you, it doesn't mean you can just lock her up. I'll not have that kind of wrongdoing in my cells. Put it from your mind, and concentrate on the crowd. It'll be more than a five-copper fine if there's a purse cut while we're on duty. More like five lashes!"

"Yes," said Relph. "Plenty more sheep in the field anyway." He laughed suddenly. "Did you hear that Gryen picked up a dose of the clap from the whorehouse in North Street? His dick is covered in weeping sores. He's in a hell of a state. They put bloody leeches on it! Can you imagine that? Must be pretty small leeches, eh?"

"Serves him right," said Will. He stopped outside the apothecary shop and stepped inside.

"What are we looking for?" asked Relph.

"My youngest has the whooping cough. Betsi asked me to pick up some herb syrup."

"Always ailing, that boy, ever since the fever," said Relph. "You figure him to die?"

Will sighed. "We lost two already, Relph. One in the plague back in Angosta, and the second when I was campaigning in Kushir. Yellow fever struck him down. I don't know whether the boy will survive or not. But he's a fighter, like his dad, so he's got an even chance."

"You were lucky with Betsi," said Relph as Will waited for the apothecary to fill a small blue bottle with syrup. "She's a good woman. Cooks up a fine stew, and your place is always so clean. I'd bet you could eat off the floor and not pick up a scrap of dust. Good woman."

"The best," agreed Will. "I think when summer comes I'll try to relocate down south. Her folks is back there and she misses them. Might do that."

"There's a rumor we'll be campaigning in spring. You heard it?"

"There's always rumors, son. I don't worry about them. One of the reasons I came here was for the quiet. Betsi was always worried that I'd be killed in a battle. Ain't no battles here, so who are we going to campaign against?"

"The captain was saying that the Highland clans were getting ready for war, attacking merchants and travelers."

Will shook his head. "It's not true. There was one attack, but the Foresters caught the men and killed them. They weren't Highlanders. No, I'm looking forward to summer, son. I'll take the family south."

The apothecary handed over the bottle and Will gave him two copper coins.

Outside Relph tapped him on the arm. "How come you pay? I don't. Bastard townies can afford to look after us. After all, we look after them."

"I always pay my way," said Will. "It's an old habit."

Grame the Smith delivered the Baron's grey stallions and left the Citadel. It had been no surprise when the Baron failed to pay for the work, and Grame had been expecting nothing more. He wandered through the town, and considered buying a meal at the Blue Duck tavern. Roast pork with crackling was a speciality there. Grame tapped his ample stomach. "You're getting old and fat," he told himself. There was a time when he'd been considered one of the handsomest men in Cilfallen, and he had grown used to the eyes of women lingering on him as he passed. They didn't linger much now. His hair had long since departed his skull, and sprouted unattractively from his shoulders and back. He'd lost three front teeth and had his lips crushed at Colden Moor, the teeth smashed from his head by an iron club wielded by an Outland soldier. God, that hurt, he remembered. It was a kind of double pain. As he fell he knew his good looks were gone forever.

Now he sported the bushiest white beard, with a long, drooping mustache to cover the mouth.

He reluctantly passed the Blue Duck and continued along Market Street, catching sight of Sigarni talking to two soldiers. The first was a tall man, middle-aged, with the look of the warrior about him. The second was smaller; this one took hold of Sigarni's arm, but she spoke to him and moved away. Grame saw the man's face turn crimson. The smith chuckled, and made his way to where Sigarni was standing before a knickknack stall. She was examining a brass tail-bell.

"Good day to you," said Grame. Sigarni gave him a friendly smile, but he saw her cast her eyes back toward where the two soldiers were standing.

"I'm thinking of buying Abby a bell," she said. "All the other hawks here have them."

"For what purpose," asked the smith, "apart from the fact that all the others have them?"

Sigarni thought about it for a moment, then grinned. "I don't know, Grame," she admitted. "But they are pretty, don't you think?"

Grame took the bell from her fingers and looked at it closely. "They're well made," he said, "and they'd be silent in flight. Falconers use them to locate their birds. You can hear them when they land in a tree. Do you have trouble with Abby? Do you lose her?"

"Never."

"Then you don't need a bell. What brings you to Citadel?"

"There is a hawking tourney, with a money prize of two gold guineas. I think Abby could win it."

Grame scratched at his thick white beard. "Maybe. It will depend on how they structure the contest. If obedience is marked highly you would have a good chance. But speed? The goshawk is lighter and faster than Abby."

"You surprise me, Grame. I didn't know you understood falconry."

"Had a gos myself once. Beautiful creature . . . but willful. Lost her in the year before Colden. I take it you're trying to get Abby used to crowds before the tourney?"

"Yes," answered Sigarni, stroking Abby's sleek head. "They don't seem to bother her. She's baited a few times, but I think she'll perform well. I'll bring her again tomorrow."

"Is there an entrance fee to this tournament?"

"Yes. One silver penny. I paid it this morning." Sigarni's expression changed. "The cleric had to get permission from the captain of the tourney to allow me to enter. He wasn't sure if women were permitted to take part."

Grame chuckled. "Well, it is unusual, girl. They don't understand that Highland women are . . . shall we say different."

"From what?" she countered.

"From their own timid females," said Grame. "Their women have no rights. When they marry, all their fortunes become the property of their husbands. They can be beaten, humiliated, and cast aside, with no recourse to the law."

"That is awful. Why do the women stand for it?"

Grame shrugged. "Habit? God only knows. Their fathers choose their husbands, their husbands dominate their lives. It's a world ruled by men. So, the captain of the tourney allowed your entry? He must be an enlightened man."

"He was fascinated by Abby. I could tell. He asked me where I got her, and how many kills she had. That sort of thing. He said the Baron would be interested in her."

Grame said nothing for a moment. Then, "I'm not sure I like the sound of that, Sigarni."

"Why?"

"You don't come to the Citadel much, do you? No, of course you don't. You sell your skins to the tanner and the furrier, and you buy your supplies—what . . . three times a year?"

"Four times. What does that matter?"

"The Baron is a keen falconer. He will certainly be *interested* in Abby. He may want her for his own."

"Well, he can't have her," she said.

Grame smiled, but there was no humor in the expression. "The Baron will have anything he desires. He is the Lord here. My advice is to forget the tourney and take Abby back into the mountains."

"I paid my silver penny!"

Grame reached into his pouch and produced a coin. "I'll pay that—aye, and gladly."

"I don't want your money, Grame—though I thank you for the offer. You think he would steal her from me?" Grame nodded. "But how could he do this. By what right?"

"Conquest. You are a clanswoman. You have no rights, save those he allows."

Sigarni's face darkened. "By God, that is wrong!"

"I don't doubt that by *God* it is wrong. But it is not God who makes the laws here; it is the Baron. I have some business here, but I will be ready to leave by dusk. My wagon is by the north wall, behind the armorer's shop. I'd be pleased to have the company, if you'd like a ride back to Cilfallen."

"Yes, I would," said Sigarni. "I'll meet you there at dusk."

Grame's words both irritated and upset Sigarni. She had wanted to compete, to show Abby's skills to a wider audience, to revel in their approbation. And she wanted to show that a woman could train a hawk as well as any man. Yet Grame was no fool. If he said she was in danger of losing Abby, then she had to listen, and act accordingly. It was unfair, but then life was unfair. If not, then she would have loved Bernt, and he would still be alive.

Sigarni strolled through the crowds and on to Falcon Field, passing the rows of hutches containing the hares to be used in the falcon displays; snared over the past few days, the little beasts would be freed individually to dart and run across the field, seeking escape from the silent killers sent to dispatch them. Abby's golden eyes focused on the cowering creatures. "Not for you, pretty one," said Sigarni. "Not this time. No applause for my beautiful Abby."

The cleric was still sitting at his desk on the outer edge of the field, and several falconers were waiting to sign their names, or make their marks on the broad ledger. A cadger had been set close by, hooded falcons sitting on the many perches. All were goshawks. Abby bridled and baited as she saw them, her wings flaring out. "Hush, now," whispered Sigarni. "Best behavior from you, sweet one." Behind the cleric she saw the two soldiers who had spoken to her earlier. The big one was no problem, but the shorter man had mean eyes. Beyond them stood the captain of the tourney. She could not remember his name, save that it began with Red, which matched his beard and his complexion.

Taking her place behind the men, she waited her turn. One of the falconers looked closely at Abby. "Fine creature," he said. "Never thought to see another. Kushir bird, ain't she?"

"Yes."

"Good killers. Not as fast as my own bird, but she'll come to call a damn sight faster." Reaching out, he stroked Abby's chest with a broad forefinger. To Sigarni's annoyance Abby allowed this treatment, even seemed to enjoy it.

"Next!" called the cleric. He was ginger-haired and Sigarni remembered him riding with an escort through Cilfallen, taking the census. What was his name? Andred? No . . . Andolph.

The falconer signed his name, paid his silver, and moved away to the cadger to collect his bird. Sigarni stepped forward and Andolph glanced up. "Oh, 'tis you. You've already signed."

"And now I wish to unsign. I cannot take part after all."

"I see," said Andolph, laying down his quill. "I am afraid there are no allowances made for withdrawals. I take it you are seeking your money back?"

"Yes. Why pay for something I cannot do?"

"Why indeed? However, the rules are quite specific. If a falcon becomes ill, or the falconer fails to appear, then his entry fee is forfeit. You see it is the entry fee that creates the ultimate prize."

"I only signed an hour ago," she said, smiling sweetly. "Can you not make an exception for a poor mountain girl?"

Andolph blushed. "Well . . . as you say, it was only an hour since." Reaching into the box at his left hand, he removed a silver penny and handed it to her. Abby baited once more and the little man dropped the coin in Sigarni's palm and snatched his hand away. "I really don't like them," he confided. "I prefer the hares."

"Hares were created for sport," said Sigarni.

Four riders came galloping across the field, their horses' hooves drumming on the hard-packed clay. Abby fluffed up her feathers, but Sigarni held tightly to the flying jesses. The lead horseman, a man dressed all in black, dismounted from the grey stallion, tossing the reins to a second horseman. Sigarni stood silently, for all the men were now waiting, stiff-backed. Even the little cleric had risen from his seat. This then, she knew, must be the Baron. Inwardly Sigarni cursed herself for bothering about the entry fee, for the man was staring intently at Abby. He was a tall man, with sleek black hair drawn back tightly over his brow and tied in a short ponytail at the nape of his neck. He sported a thin, trident beard that gleamed as if oiled, and his eyes were large and wood-ash grey, hooded, and bulging from their sockets. His lips were thin, the mouth cruel, thought Sigarni.

"Where did you get the bird?" he asked, the voice so low that it was a moment before Sigarni realized he had spoken.

"A gift from a friend," she answered him. The other riders dismounted and gathered in close. Sigarni felt hemmed in, but she stood her ground.

"In return for some sexual favor, I don't doubt," said the Baron, his tone bored. "Ah well, I expect you are here to sell the creature. I'll give you ten guineas for it—assuming you haven't ruined it."

"She is not ruined, my lord, and she is not for sale," said Sigarni. "I trained her myself, and was planning to enter the tourney with her."

The Baron appeared not to notice she had spoken. Turning to the man behind him, he called out, "Ten guineas, if you please, Leofric. I'll reimburse you later. And remind me to speak to the black man next time he visits the town."

"Yes, my lord," said the blond rider, fishing in his purse for coins.

Sigarni stepped back. "She is not for sale," she said, her voice louder than she intended. This time the Baron turned and for the first time looked into her eyes.

"You are a Highlander, aren't you?" he announced.

"I am."

"There are no noble houses in the Highlands, merely a motley group of inbred savages scraping a living from the mountainsides. The law is simple, woman. A yeoman may raise a goshawk. That is the only bird of prey allowed to those not of noble blood. The bird you hold is not a goshawk; therefore you cannot own the bird. Am I speaking too fast for you? Now take the money and hand the bird to my falconer."

Sigarni knew that she should obey. It mattered not that it was unfair. Grame was right, the Baron was the law and to deny him would be futile. Yet something flickered deep within her, like the birth of a fire.

"I am of the blood of Gandarin the King," she said, "and the hawk is mine. Mine to keep, mine to free!" So saying, her arm swept up and she released the jesses. Surprised by the sudden movement, Abby spread her wings and sailed into the air. Not even a glimmer of anger showed on the Baron's face. For several heartbeats no one moved, and all watched the hawk gliding up on the thermals. Then, without speed, almost casually, the Baron's black-gloved fist cracked against the side of Sigarni's face. Half stunned, she staggered back. The Baron moved in. Sigarni lashed out with her foot, aiming for his groin, but her aim was out and she kicked him in the thigh. "Hold her!" said the Baron. She found her arms pinned and recognized the soldiers who had first spoken to her in the market square. The Baron hit her in the stomach, and she doubled forward. His voice echoed through her pain; it was not a raised voice, nor did it contain a hint of emotion. "Stupid woman," he said. "Now you have forfeited your right to the ten guineas. Any more stupidity and you will face the lash. You understand me? Call the bird!"

Sigarni looked up into the hooded eyes. Her mouth tasted of blood. "Call her yourself," she said, then spat full in his face. Blood and saliva dripped to his cheek. Taking a black handkerchief from the pocket of his tunic, he slowly wiped the offending drops from his face. "You see," he said to the gathered men, "with what we are dealing? A people who have no understanding of law, or good manners. They are barbarians, without culture, without breeding." His hand lashed out in a backward strike that cannoned his knuckles against Sigarni's right cheek. "Call the bird!" he ordered. "And if you spit at me again I will have your tongue cut out!"

Sigarni remained silent. The Baron turned to his falconer, a short, wide-shouldered Lowlander. "Can you call it in?" he asked.

"I'll do my best, my lord," he answered, moving out onto

the open ground with hawking glove aloft. He gave a long, thin whistle. High above, Abby banked and folded her wings into a stoop to dive like an arrow. Some sixty feet from the ground her wings spread again and she leveled out. "She's coming in, sir!" shouted the falconer.

The Baron turned back to Sigarni. "Ten lashes for you, I think, and a night in the cells. Perhaps you will learn from the experience, though I doubt it. You Highlanders never were given to learning from your mistakes. It is what makes you what you are." Casually he struck her again, left and right, his arm rising and falling with a sickening lack of speed. Sigarni tried to roll her head with the blows, but the soldiers were holding hard to her arms.

And then it happened. No one watching quite understood why. Some blamed confusion in the mind of the hawk, others maintained the woman was a witch, the hawk her familiar. But Abby swept down, past the falconer's outstretched glove and straight toward Sigarni, talons extended for the landing. At that moment the Baron's fist came up to strike the woman again.

"The hawk, my lord!" shouted the falconer.

The Baron turned, arm still raised. Abby's razor-sharp talons tore into his face, hooking into the left eyebrow, raking down through the socket, and tearing out his eye. He screamed as he fell back, the hawk still clinging to his face, her talons embedded in his left cheek. Abby's wings thrashed madly as she tried to free herself. The Baron's hands came up, grabbing the wings and ripping the bird clear. Blood gushed from the face wound. Staggering now, he threw the bird to the ground, and Sigarni watched in horror as one of the riders drew a sword and hacked it through Abby's neck. The wings fluttered against the clay. Men gathered around the Baron, who had fallen to his knees, pressing the palm of his black glove against the now-empty eye socket.

The three riders who had arrived with him half carried him from the field.

The captain of the tourney moved in front of Sigarni. "You'll suffer for that, bitch!" he told her. "The Baron will have your eyes put out with hot coals, your hands and feet hacked off, and then you'll be hung outside the walls in an open cage for the crows to feast on you! But first you'll answer to me!"

Sigarni said nothing as she was dragged away by the soldiers. A crowd had gathered on the edge of the field, but she did not look at them. Holding her head high she stared impassively at the keep ahead, and the double doors of the outer wall. Abby was dead. Had she given her to the Baron, she would still be alive. She saw again the fluttering wings, and the iron sword cleaving down. Tears fell to her cheeks, the salt burning the cut under her eye.

The men marched her through the Citadel entrance and then turned left, cutting across the courtyard to a narrow door and a staircase leading down into the dark. Sigarni pulled back as the men tried to force her through. The soldier whose advances she had spurned struck her over the ear with his elbow. "Git down there!" he hissed. She was propelled forward. The stairwell was dark, the stairs slippery. The soldier twisted her arm behind her back, the other man releasing his hold on her and moving ahead. For a short while they descended in total darkness, then the faint glow of a burning torch lit the bottom of the stairs and they emerged into a dungeon corridor. Two men were sitting at a table, playing dice. Both stood as the captain strode into sight.

"Open a cell!" he ordered. The men hurried to obey.

Sigarni was still in a daze as they dragged her into the cell. It was large and grey, one wall wet with damp, and it stank of rats' droppings. There was a small cot in one corner, and there were rusted chains hanging from the walls.

"How do you like this, bitch?" sneered the red-bearded captain, moving in front of her. Sigarni did not reply. His hand reached out, cupping her breast and squeezing hard. She winced, then brought up her knee, hammering it into his groin. He groaned and fell back. The soldier to her right, the short man, punched her in the side of the head, and she was hurled across the cot.

"Strip her," ordered the captain, "and we'll see how much pleasure the whore can supply."

Through her pain Sigarni heard the words, and the strength of panic surged through her. Launching herself from the cot she dived at the first soldier, but she was still groggy and he caught her by the hair. Hands grabbed at her body and she felt her leather leggings being dragged clear. Torchlight glittered from the captain's dagger.

"I'm going to put my mark on you, woman. And I'll hear you beg and scream before this night is over."

Chapter Five

Gwalchmai was sitting on the porch weeping when Asmidir rode up. As the black man climbed from the saddle and approached the old man, he could smell the fiery spirit on Gwalchmai's breath, and he saw the empty jug lying on its side. "Where is Sigarni?" he asked.

The old man looked up, blinking. "Suffering," he said. "She is the sword blade going through fire."

"What are you talking about?"

"Why do we do it?" asked Gwal. "What is it in our natures? When I was young we raided a Lowland village, stealing cattle. There was a young woman in a field. She had hidden in some bushes. But we found her. We raped her. It seemed good sport, and no harm done." He shook his head. "No *harm* done? Now that the Gift is upon me and I know the truth, I wonder if there will ever be forgiveness. Do you ever wonder that, Asmidir? Do you ever think of the Loabite woman you captured in the high mountains of Kushir? Do you lie awake at night and ask yourself why she slashed her wrists?"

Asmidir straightened as if struck, his dark eyes narrowing. "You are the Gifted One?"

"Aye. That is my curse, black man. It is only marginally worse than yours."

The sunlight was fading and Asmidir helped the old man to his feet, guiding him into the cabin where Lady was stretched out by the dying fire. Asmidir eased Gwalchmai into a chair, then sat opposite the man. Lady rose and put her head in Asmidir's lap, seeking a stroke. The black man idly patted her, rubbing his fingers behind her ears, and Lady's tail began to wag. "I need your help," Asmidir told Gwalchmai. "I need to find a man."

The old man leaned forward and gazed into the dying flames. "No, you don't," he said. "On both counts. But I will help you, Asmidir. Oh, yes, I will. First, however, tell me why are we such savages. Tell me that!"

"What do you want from me, Gifted One? The answers to questions we all know? We do what we do because we *can*. We hunt and kill because we *can*. That which is in our power belongs to us, to be used as we desire. Whether it be a round of meat, a wild-born stag, an ancient tree, or a beautiful woman. Now what is it you want to hear?"

Gwalchmai gave a long sigh, and rubbed at weary, bloodshot eyes with a gnarled hand. "As we sit and speak," he said, "in the warmth of this cabin, there is a woman in a cell, being beaten, brutalized, and raped by five men. She is bleeding, she is hurt. One of the five is a nobleman, but he is filled with a lust for inflicting pain. But the others are all *ordinary* men. Men like you and me, Asmidir. I can feel their thoughts, taste their emotions. By God, I can also sense their arousal! And I would like to kill them. But am I different? Was I different in that field? Were you different with the Loabite woman?"

"She was part of the spoils of war," said Asmidir, "and no, I do not lie awake at night and think of her. She was used. We are all used. She chose to kill herself. Her choice, Gifted One. But I have no time for these games, nor am I concerned about some whore in a prison cell. Do you know the name of the leader who is coming, or not?"

Gwalchmai swung around, his eyes bright and glittering. "Yes, I know. I have always known. From the night when the Gate was opened, when Taliesen came to me, and brought me the child to raise."

"And will you tell me?" asked Asmidir, masking his impatience.

"It is not a man."

"You make no sense, you drunken old fool. What is it then . . . a tree? A horse?"

"Are you so stupid that you cannot understand what has been said here?" asked Gwalchmai. "Where are we, for God's sake? Can you not concentrate that fine mind for a moment?"

Asmidir sat back and took a deep breath. "Humor me," he said at last. "Perhaps my mind is not as fine as you imagine." But the old man said nothing and Asmidir took a deep breath. "Very well, I will play this game. Where are we, you asked? We are in the Highlands, in the cabin of Sigarni the Huntress. And we have been talking about a woman in a cell . . ." He sat bolt upright. "Sweet Heaven, Sigarni is in the cell?"

"Sigarni is in the cell," echoed Gwalchmai, tossing a fresh log to the flames.

"Why?"

"The Baron desired her hawk. She refused to sell it. In the argument that followed the hawk tore out the Baron's left eye. Sigarni was dragged away."

"But she lives. They have not killed her?"

"No, they have not killed her. But they are giving her scars she will carry all her life, and her pain will be visited a thousand times upon their countrymen."

"What can I do? Tell me!"

"You can wait here, with me. All your questions will be answered, Asmidir. Every one."

Will Stamper sat in the Blue Duck tavern staring into the tankard. It was the fifth jug of ale he had consumed, and it could not deaden the shame he felt. Relph pushed through the crowd and sat opposite him, a bright smile on his face.

"Looks like I don't owe you that five coppers anymore, eh? Told you I'd spear her by midnight."

"Shut up, for God's sake!"

"What's wrong with you, Will? It were great, weren't it?

Nothing like it! And you had your share." He chuckled. "And the captain. Humping like a little bunny. Nice to know the nobles get boils on their arses, isn't it?"

Will lifted the tankard and half drained it. The ale was strong, and he felt his head swimming. "I've never done that before," he said. "Never will again. I'm not going to wait for the summer. I'm going south tomorrow. I'm finished here. Wish I'd never come."

"You've got blood on your hand," said Relph. "Did she bite you?"

Will jerked and rubbed the dried blood onto his leather leggings. "No. It's not my blood." He bit his lip and looked away, but Relph saw the tears spilling to his cheeks.

"What's got into you? Is it the boy? He'll get over the whoop, Will. I'm sure he will. Come on, mate, this isn't like you at all. Here, let me get you another drink." Relph stood, but Will reached out and took hold of his arm.

"It doesn't bother you, does it? She was screaming. She was cut, bitten, thrashed. It doesn't bother you?"

"It didn't bother you at the time, either. And no, why should it worry me? Worse'll happen to her tomorrow. At least she went out with a good rut, eh? Anyway, the captain told us to. So why not? God's teeth, Will, she's only a whore. Whores were made for sport."

Will released his hold and Relph moved back into the crowd. He gazed around him through bleary eyes, listening to the laughter of the revelers, and thought of Betsi; picturing her in that cell. Relph returned with two tankards. "Here, get that down you, mate. You'll feel better. There's a dice game back at the barracks at midnight. You fancy a bet?"

"No. I'll get home. Got to get Betsi to pack ready for tomorrow."

"You're not thinking this through, Will. No one will be taking on mercenaries down south. What will you do?"

"I don't care."

Relph leaned forward. "You have to care, Will. You have

a family to support, and a sick son. You can't go dragging them out into the countryside. It's not fair on them. Look, I don't know why this has got to you so bad. You stuck a few inches of gristle into a few soft warm places. Now you want to ruin your life and your family's lives. It don't make no sense. You get home and get a good night's sleep. It'll all look different in the morning."

Will shook his head. "What will be different? I'm forty-two years old. I've lived my whole life by an iron set of rules which my dad beat into me. You ever heard me lie, Relph? You ever seen me steal?"

"No, you're a regular saint, mate. They ought to put up statues to you. But what's the point you're making?"

"I just betrayed everything I've lived for. *Everything.* What we did there was wrong. Worse than that, it was evil."

"Now you're talking daft. What do you mean evil? She was a slag, and I'll bet she's been jumped before. What pigging difference does it make? She's dead anyway, come morning. You heard the captain, they're going to put out her eyes and hang her in the old cage. Bloody Hell, Will, you think what we done is any worse than that? Come on, I'll walk you home. You look all in."

Relph stood and helped Will to his feet. The big man staggered, then headed for the door.

"I should have stopped it," mumbled Will. "Not joined in. Oh, God, what will I say to Betsi?"

"Nothing, mate. Nothing at all. You just go home, and you sleep."

The relief guard was called Owen Hunter; the man he replaced told him of the sport he had missed. Owen was a Lowlander, married to a harridan named Clorrie who made his life a misery. As he sat at the dungeon table in the flickering torchlight, he tried to remember the last time he had enjoyed a woman. It was more than three years—if you didn't count the alley whore.

He had smiled when the guard told him of the afternoon's entertainment, and even managed to say, "That's life," when the man pointed out that it should have been Owen's shift, except that the Lowlander had swapped it earlier that day.

But now, as he sat alone, he allowed his bitterness to rise. Of all the women to choose he had married Clorrie: sharp-tongued, mean-spirited Clorrie. Life's a bastard and no mistake, thought Owen. Like the other soldiers, he had heard of the incident when the Baron lost his eye. Even now the surgeons were at work in the upper room of the keep, plugging the wound and feeding the Baron expensive opiates.

There was no sound in the dungeon corridor, save for the occasional hiss from the torches. Owen stood and stretched his legs, remembering the last words of the man he replaced: "What an arse on her! I tell you, Owen, she was a jump to remember."

Owen lifted a torch from its bracket and walked past the four empty cells to the locked door. Pulling open the grille he peered inside. There was no window to the cell and the torchlight did not pierce the gloom. Slipping the bolt, he opened the door. The woman was lying on the floor, her legs spread open. There was blood on her face and thighs and on one of her breasts. Owen moved closer. She was still unconscious. Despite the blood he could see that she was beautiful, her hair gleaming silver and red in the torchlight. His eyes scanned her body. Even the hair of her pubic mound was silver, he noticed. She was slim and tall, her breasts firm. Owen saw that one of her nipples was bleeding, a thin trickle of red still running down to her side. Kneeling alongside her Owen ran his hand up her thigh, his fingers stroking the silver mound, his index finger slipping inside her.

He made his decision and rose, planting the torch in a wall bracket. Swiftly he stripped off his leather leggings and knelt between the open legs, pushing his hands under her thighs to draw her onto him. Why not? he thought. Everyone else has had their pleasure. Why not me? Why shouldn't Owen Hunter have a little fun?

His last sight was of the woman suddenly rearing up. His own hands were locked beneath her thighs, but he saw her right hand stab forward, felt the terrible pain as her first two fingers struck his eyes. Then all was pain and an explosion of light that was unbearable.

Sigarni dragged her fingers from the oozing sockets and groaned. Her ribs hurt, but that was as nothing compared with the pain within. She pushed the body of the guard from her, then rolled to her knees. Nausea rose in her throat and she vomited. Her head was pounding, her body begging her to lie down, to rest, to heal. Instead she forced herself to her feet. The guard began to moan. Dropping to her knees she pulled his dagger from his belt and plunged it through the nape of his neck. His legs spasmed, one foot striking the narrow cot. Blood filled the man's throat and he began to choke. Dragging the dagger clear she held the point over the center of his back and threw her weight down upon it. The blade slid between his ribs, skewering the lungs. Now he was still. A pool of urine spread out from beneath him. Sigarni stood again, then sat on the cot looking around the cell, taking in every block and stone, every rat hole. Her leggings had been thrown into a corner. Retrieving them, she dressed. The cord of the waist had been cut. Dragging the guard's belt clear, she pierced a new buckle hole in the leather and strapped it to her waist.

Everything hurt. Her lips were swollen, her cheek cut and bruised. There was a knife cut in her right buttock and another on her left thigh. The guard moaned again. Sigarni could not believe the man could still be alive. Taking hold of the jutting knife with both hands she wrenched it clear of his back, then knelt forward to slice the razor-sharp blade across his throat. Blood gushed to the stone floor. Grabbing him by the shoulders, she rolled him to his back, slashing the sharp blade again and again across his lower body. At last, exhausted, she stopped, her hands drenched in blood.

"You've got to get out of here," she told herself. "You've got to find them." She had feigned unconsciousness at the end, even when two of them had stood and urinated over her. She had heard the small man, Relph, talking about the Blue Duck tavern. She knew it—it was close to Market Street.

Knife in hand, Sigarni walked from the cell and out into the dungeon corridor. Her legs had no strength, and she fell to her knees and vomited once more. "Don't be weak," she scolded herself. "You are Sigarni the Huntress. You are strong."

Rising unsteadily, she managed to reach the stairs and started to climb up into the darkness. Halfway up she heard footfalls. Pushing herself back against the wall she waited. Then a man called out from some distance above, "Hey, Owen, I was on my way home when I thought it would be worth a second tilt at the bitch. You fancy a double, eh?"

From out of the darkness he appeared, a looming shape with a protruding belly. Sigarni rammed the blade into that belly, ripping it up toward the heart. He grunted and fell back to the stairs. "Oh, God! Oh, God!" he screamed. Sigarni pulled the blade clear and stepped in close.

"You want to ride double with me, Outlander? You want to enjoy Sigarni?"

"Oh, please! Don't kill me!"

"You left teeth marks in my breast, you fat bastard. Now bite on this!" The knife slid between his teeth and Sigarni slammed it home to the hilt. His fat arms began to flail, but she knelt on his chest and cut his throat. Only when he was still did she mutilate him in the same way she had the first guard. Slowly she climbed the stairs, pushing open the door at the top. The courtyard was moonlit and deserted, save for a sentry sitting under the arch. He was facing out into the town. Sigarni stepped into the open air and walked across to the arch.

The sentry was not even aware of dying . . .

Blood-drenched and weak, Sigarni moved on into the silent town.

* * *

Abby was dead—killed trying to save her. And I am dead, she thought. They will kill me, for I have not the strength to find them all. Somehow the thought of dying held no fear for her. All that kept her moving on tottering feet was the need for vengeance, a need as old as the Highlands themselves. Clan laws were not subtle, precedents were rarely cited, and there were no glib-tongued lawyers to represent the factions. Wrongdoers were punished by those they had wronged, or in the case of murder were hunted down by clan warriors selected by the Hunt Lord. Justice was sudden, harsh, and final.

But Sigarni had no family, save old Gwal who had raised her after the Slaughter. There were no men to seek blood revenge.

Only me, she thought. Only Sigarni. The knife slipped from her fingers and clattered to the street. Stopping, she picked it up, then fell heavily. "Damn!" she whispered. Twisting around, she sat for a while with her back against a cool stone wall. The stars were bright, the night cool with the promise of autumn. Some distance away she could hear the sound of revelers, and knew she was close to the Blue Duck tavern. What will you do? she wondered. Walk in, covered in blood, and move from table to table until you see them? What kind of a plan is that? And if you wait past the dawn they will find you anyway, and drag you back to that cell, and who knows what torture. Are you mad, girl? Leave this place. Get back into the Highlands where you can gather your strength.

Two of them are dead, she told herself. One more, at least, is in the tavern.

One more . . .

Forcing herself to her feet, Sigarni groaned. Blood was trickling down her leg. She licked her lips with a dry tongue and tried to blank out the pain.

"Women are made for sport."

The words flashed back into her memory. The short soldier had said them at some point during her ordeal. Laughter had followed his words, then more pain. Suddenly she remembered the little Census Taker and his revulsion and fear as Abby pecked at him. What was it he had said: "I prefer the hares"? Hares are made for sport, Sigarni had told him.

Everything is made for sport, she realized, in a world ruled by Outlanders.

The rest had given her fresh strength and she walked on.

The Blue Duck tavern was an old building with frayed timbers and white walls. There were four windows on the ground floor, two either side of the old oak door. One of the windows was open and through it she could hear the sounds of the drinkers. Moving to the wall beside it, she glanced in. The place was packed and her keen eyes scanned the faces within. There were none she recognized, but then she could see only a section of the crowd. Dropping to her knees she crawled under the window, then rose and glanced in from the new angle. Two men were walking toward the door. Her heart, and her anger, lifted. Transferring the knife to her left hand, she wiped the sweat from her right, rubbing the palm down her leggings.

The door opened. "That's it, Will, one foot in front of the other. That's the way to go, son."

"Shut the bloody door!" said someone inside. Relph pulled shut the door as Will Stamper leaned against the wall.

"Be right with you, mate, but I've got to piss," said Relph, opening the front of his leggings and urinating against the wall. Sigarni moved silently alongside the drunken Will and sliced the knife back across his throat. The skin flapped open, blood bubbling clear. Then she ran forward and plunged the blade into Relph's back. He reared up and grabbing his hair, she rammed his head against the wall. Falling to his knees Relph struggled to turn. Wrenching the knife clear Sigarni, still holding to his hair, dragged his head back to expose his throat. "Women are made for sport," said

Sigarni, slashing open his jugular. Relph fell back, his arms and legs thrashing. Sigarni stepped clear and moved to where Will stood leaning against the wall, his blood gushing over the front of his tunic. Slowly he toppled to his knees and looked up at her. There was no hatred in his gaze, and no fear. He tried to speak, but could only mouth two words. Sigarni almost laughed. Then she leaned back and kicked him in the head and his body fell to the stones.

Only one more now, she thought. The captain.

But where would he be?

"Are you insane, woman!" came a voice inside her mind. *"Leave now!"*

"No!" she said aloud. "I'll find him."

"Leave and he'll find you. I promise you! Stay and you will die and he will live. I promise you that too!"

"Who are you? Where are you?" she asked, spinning around and scanning the shadows.

"I am with you, girl, and I want your trust. Leave now. Believe me, you won't like being dead. I know, I've tried it. Now go!"

Confused, Sigarni obeyed, cutting down through an alley toward the north gate.

The bastards have unhinged my mind, she thought. Now I am hearing ghost voices.

From the Citadel keep came the sound of clanging alarm bells.

I'll never get out now, she thought.

"Yes, you will," said the voice. *"Your people need you."*

Baron Ranulph Gottasson groaned. The pain had moved beyond pleasure to a burning point of agony that bordered on the exquisite. Narcotics flowed in his blood, and his waking dreams were vivid. He saw again the fall of the Kushite cities, refugees running panic-stricken from their burning homes, heard again the wailing of the soon-to-die, the piercing screams of city dwellers staring into the brutal faces of the conquering soldiers, feeling the cold bite of their blades into soft, yielding flesh.

Days of blood and glory, marching his men across inhospitable deserts, iron mountains, and lush foreign plains.

And then it was over. No one left to conquer.

At first it had not seemed so onerous: the triumphant return to the capital, the cheering crowds choking the streets, the nights of celebration at the palace, the orgies . . . The Baron groaned again. He felt someone lift his head, and a cold metal goblet was placed against his lips. He swallowed and sank back.

Then had come the day when the organization of the empire was reshaped. Plessius was made Governor General of Kushir and the east—a bumbling fool of a man with not an ounce of ambition in his fat head. A hardly surprising choice to rule a land three thousand leagues from the capital. The King had chosen wisely; there would be no rebellion from that quarter. Ranulph had let it be known he desired the north. There was nothing here of any worth, save cattle and timber. The climate was harsh in winter, perversely changeable in what passed for summer. A little coal was being mined, but there were no deposits of gold or silver, nor even iron. The people were poor and defeated.

Ranulph had waited for his appointment, sure in the knowledge that he would be offered anything *but* the north. The King possessed a mind of astonishing cunning, and would never offer any general the true object of his desires.

Ranulph's mind swam on a sea of delicious pain . . .

He had a spy in Jastey's household, and knew well that the Earl desired the west. Seventeen rich cities, scores of mines, seven ports, and a thriving commercial network. Together they created the perfect foundation for an assault on the King. Wealth to buy mercenaries, ships to ferry armies and keep them supplied.

Oh, how Ranulph had laughed when Jastey had been made High Sheriff of the Capital. Despite being a position of great influence, bringing immense wealth, it meant that Jastey was always at court and close to the King.

But Jastey's handsome face had worn a smile the following day, when Ranulph had been summoned to the palace. The memory brought a fresh spasm of agony. Ranulph had walked down the long aisle in the Chapel of the Blessed Blade, to where the King waited with his courtiers around him, Jastey at his right hand. Ranulph knelt before his sovereign, then gazed up into the dark, reptilian eyes.

"It is reported to me that you desire to govern the north, my good and dear friend," said the King. "Your services to the kingdom merit great rewards, and I can think of no greater reward than to bestow upon you that which you most desire. Rise, Baron Ranulph Gottasson, Earl of the North, Governor General of the Highlands."

To his amazement Ranulph had managed a smile. It did not match the grin on Jastey's face. The west had gone to the King's new favorite, Estelm.

The feast that followed had been bitter hard for the new Baron. The King seated him next to Jastey, and that alone made the food taste of bile and ash.

"My congratulations, Ranulph," said the Earl. "I know we do not see eye to eye on many issues, but I would like you to know that I argued most strongly for you to be given the north. I thought it would perhaps ease the animosity between us."

Ranulph looked into the man's dark eyes and saw the humor glinting there. "Animosity, cousin? Surely not. Friendly rivalry would be more apt, I believe?"

"Perhaps," agreed Jastey. "However, that should now be behind us. You have your own kingdom, as it were, while I must remain in the capital making laws, sitting in judgment, surrounded by clerics. Ah, how I envy you!"

Ranulph smiled, and pictured sliding a red-hot dagger into Jastey's belly.

Returning to his town house he had walked into his library and stood gazing at the map stretched out on the far wall.

The empire filled it, from ocean to ocean. Ranulph's mouth was dry, his hands trembling with suppressed tension. The skin of his back and buttocks was still tender, but he knew that he needed the release of the whip. Summoning a servant, he ordered him to fetch Koris.

The man's face paled. "I am sorry, my lord, but Koris packed his belongings and left this morning."

"Left? What do you mean *left*?"

The servant swallowed hard. "He has taken up a new . . . appointment . . . lord."

The shock hit him like ice upon hot skin. Koris, whom he had trusted above all men, and loved better than any woman. And he knew, without a shred of doubt, where the boy's appointment had taken him.

Jastey!

Dismissing the servant, the Baron moved to the window, opening it wide and breathing in the cold night air.

"I don't want to go north, Ranulph. It's cold there—and there are no amusements."

"We will not be going north, sweet boy."

"But isn't that what you want?"

"Be patient and all will be revealed."

"You don't trust me!"

"Of course I trust you. Now don't sulk! I hate that."

And he had explained his plans, talked of his dreams, secure in the knowledge that he was with the one person in all the empire who loved him.

Two nights later, bound, gagged, and hooded, Koris had been carried down to the secret room below the town house. Ranulph had his arms tied to posts, his legs chained to the wall. Dismissing the soldiers who had brought him, he pulled the hood clear of the boy's beautiful face.

"Oh, Ranulph, please God, don't hurt me!"

The Baron drew his dagger and pushed the blade into a brazier of hot coals. "While the blade heats," he said softly, "we will talk of love and trust."

Semiconscious now, the Baron felt the terrible stabs of fire in his eye socket, lancing their way through the opiates in his blood. Koris had been allowed no opiates throughout that long, long night.

Kollarin the Finder was comfortably asleep between the two whores when he heard the frenzied hammering at the tavern door below his room. He yawned and stretched, his right arm touching the fleshy shoulder of the plump young woman on his right. She moaned softly and turned over. The slender girl to his left awoke.

"What is happening?" she asked sleepily.

Kollarin sat up. The room was cold, the fire long dead. "I don't know, but someone is anxious to get in," he said. He heard the innkeeper tramping down the stairs, cursing as he moved.

"All right! All right, I'm coming, damn you!"

The sound of bolts being drawn back drifted up to the room and Kollarin heard his name mentioned. Now it was his turn to curse. Clambering over the slender whore he grabbed his leggings and began to climb into them. Just then the door opened and a soldier entered.

"We need you, Finder," said Captain Redgaer Kushirbane. "There has been an attack on the Citadel cells."

The fat whore woke with a start and screamed. Kollarin's head was pounding. "Be quiet, please!" he said, squeezing shut his eyes. "My head is splitting."

"Why is he here?" she asked, drawing the blanket over her large breasts. Kollarin smiled at this show of shyness. "Employment, my pretty," he said. "This gentleman has come to offer me coin, with which to pay for your expert services. Now go back to sleep." Kollarin continued to dress, pulling on a pair of brown leather boots over his green leggings. His shirt was of wool, dyed dark green, and over this he donned a sleeveless leather jerkin lined with fleece.

Moving past the captain, he descended the stairs. Two soldiers were idling there and the innkeeper was standing by, his expression cold.

"I must apologize," said Kollarin, "for the ruination of your rest, my friend. It appears there has been an emergency of some kind. I am sure the captain will reimburse you."

"Fat chance of that," snapped the innkeeper, walking to the door and holding it open.

Out in the street Redgaer started to explain, but Kollarin cut him short. "No need for words, Captain. Merely take me to the scene."

They moved swiftly through the town up the short hill to the arched gateway where a corpse lay on the cold stone. Kollarin knelt beside the body, laying his right hand just above the gaping wound in the man's neck. "This is not where it began," he said, and rose to walk across the moonlit courtyard to the dungeon stairs. Here was a second corpse. Kollarin paused, laid his hand on the man's head, then walked on.

The soldiers and the captain trooped after him and Kollarin entered the small dungeon. On the floor was the last corpse. Kollarin stood for a moment staring down at the man. He had been castrated, and then the genitalia had been pushed into his open mouth. Kneeling beside him, Kollarin touched his hand to the cold stone floor and closed his eyes. Images poured into his mind. He let them flow for a few seconds, then closed them off. Remaining where he was for a moment more, he gathered his thoughts and rose, turning to face the captain. "What do you wish to know?" he asked, keeping his tone neutral.

"How many were involved in the attack? Where are they now?"

"There was no attack, Captain," said Kollarin softly. "The raped woman lay where this man is now, pretending to be unconscious. When he too desired a piece of the vile action she stabbed out his eyes—as you can see." The captain did not look down. "She used her fingers. Then she took his dagger and killed him with it. She was in great pain herself at the time—but then you know that." Kollarin turned. "She fell to her knees and vomited there, then sat for a moment or two upon the cot." Moving past the captain, he stepped out into the dungeon corridor. "Still holding the dagger she made for the stairs. The other guard was returning. He said something, but it is unclear to me. She killed him, then made her way up the stairs." Kollarin followed in her footsteps and found a smear of blood upon the stairwell wall. Touching his fingers to it he closed his eyes once more. The captain and the soldiers were pressing in close. "Ah, yes," said Kollarin. "Here she paused for a moment. She is thinking of three men, two soldiers . . . and you, Captain. She has decided to seek them out and kill them. But she is weak, and bleeding. She castrates this guard too, but has little energy to spare. She is thinking of a tavern, trying to remember where it is. She has heard the men speak of spending the evening there."

"The Blue Duck!" said one of the soldiers.

"And that's where she is heading?" asked Redgaer. Kollarin nodded.

"*Was* heading, Captain. This was some while ago."

Redgaer Kushir-bane pushed past the Finder and ran up the stairs, the soldiers pounding after him. Kollarin followed. The four men ran through the streets, arriving at the Blue Duck tavern in time to see the crowd gathered around the bodies of the two soldiers. Kollarin pushed through and squatted down by the bodies.

"When did this happen?" he heard Redgaer demand.

"Moments ago," said a voice. "It was a woman. We saw her making off."

Kollarin touched his hand to the blood on the dead Will Stamper's throat. Then he jerked and almost fell. A voice boomed into his mind. *"Delay them!"* It was not a command, nor yet a plea. Kollarin was surprised, but not shocked. Spirits of the dead had spoken to him before. Yet none had been as powerful as this one. For one fleeting moment he saw a face, hawk-nosed, with deep-set grey eyes and a beard of bright silver. Then the face faded. Kollarin remained where he was for a few seconds more, gathering his thoughts. He was a Hunter, a Finder. His reputation was second to none, and he valued this above all else. Kollarin never failed. He had trailed killers and thieves, robbers and rapists, cattle thieves and assassins. Never before had he been asked to hunt down an innocent woman, brutalized by her captors. Never before had a long-dead spirit interceded on behalf of a victim.

Kollarin rose and stretched his back.

"Where is she heading, man?" demanded Redgaer.

"I can't say," said the Finder. "Her mind was very confused at this point."

"Can't say?" sneered Redgaer. "It's what you are paid for, man." Kollarin knew just where she was, heading out through the open north gate, with half a mile to go before the safety of the tree line. He looked at Redgaer and smiled.

"As she killed these men, Captain, she was thinking of you. She was wondering how she could reach you, and draw a sharp knife across your testicles." Redgaer winced. "After that she wandered away into that alley there. Perhaps she is still there—waiting."

"That leads to the north gate, sir," said one of the soldiers. "There is a stable there. We could get horses."

Redgaer nodded. "Follow me," he ordered, and ran off.

Kollarin remained where he was, staring down at the dead Will Stamper. The thoughts of dying men were often strange, almost mundane sometimes. But this man had tried to speak on the point of death. Two words. Kollarin shook his head.

What a time to say *"I'm sorry."*

The more Fell considered his *encounter* with the old man, the more he believed it was a dream. That being so, he asked himself, why are you sitting here in the cold waiting for dawn to rise over Citadel town? He smiled ruefully and poked the dying campfire with a long stick, trying to urge some life into the little blaze. Fell's sheepskin cloak was damp from the recent rain and the fire had not the strength to warm him. It spluttered and spat, fizzled and sank low. He glanced at the sky. Dawn was still an hour away. He was sitting with his back against the shallow depression of a deep boulder, the fire set against a second tall stone. The forester looked down at the last of the wood he had gathered. It was also damp. To his left Fell could see the twinkling lights of the *Cinder-wings*. He hoped they would come no closer. Fell had no wish to be visited by the ghosts of painful memories. The *Cinders* were clustered under an oak branch twisting and moving, their golden wings of light fluttering in the dark. When he was a child Fell had caught one of them, and rushed it home to his parents. In the light of the cabin it had proved to be nothing more than a moth, with wide, beautiful wings and a dark, hairy body. Lying dead in his hand it had seemed so ordinary, yet out in the woods, its wings glowing with bright light, it had been magical beyond imagining.

"You are lucky, boy," his father told him. "You are too young to have bad memories. Trust me, as you grow older you will avoid the *Cinders*."

How true it was. When Fell was sixteen he had been walking through the night, following the trail of a lame wolf. He saw the flickering of *Cinder-wing* lights and walked in close to see them fly. Instantly the vision of Mattick's soon-to-be-drowned face filled his mind, the child reaching out to Fell as the undertow dragged him toward the rapids. Fell couldn't swim, and could only watch helplessly as the child was swept over the rocks, the white water thrashing around him. The face hovered in Fell's mind and he dropped to his knees, tears coursing his cheeks. "It was not my fault!" he cried aloud, then scrambled back from the glowing insects. After that he gave the *Cinder-wings* a distant respect.

The rain began again, and the *Cinders* vanished from sight. Fell shook his head. "A great fool you are," he said aloud, watching the drops of rain settling on the longbow.

The bowstring was safe and dry in his belt pouch, his quiver of twelve shafts behind him and under his cloak, but Fell did not like to see his favorite hunting bow at the mercy of the weather. It was a fine bow, made by Kereth the Wingoran. Horn-tipped, it had a pull of more than ninety pounds. Fell, though not the finest of the Loda bowmen, had not missed a killing shot since purchasing the weapon. An arrow would sing from the string, streaking to its target and sinking deep through skin, flesh, and muscle. It was important for a deer to die fast. Ideally the beast would be dead before it knew it, therefore the meat remained tender and succulent; whereas if the creature was frightened, its muscles would tense and harden and the meat would stay that way. Fell's bow supplied choice meat.

"What are you doing here, Fell? Following a dream you don't believe in?" he said aloud. The words of the dream man came back to him. *"In three days outside the walls of Citadel town a sword will be raised, and the Red will be worn again. Be there, Fell. In three days, at dawn. By the light of the new sun you will see the birth of a legend."*

The rain eased once more, and as the moon showed through the break in the clouds, the *Cinders* glinted back into life. Fell hefted his bow and wiped the drops of water from its six-foot length. Amazingly the fire flared up, tongues of flame licking at the wood. Fell stretched out his hands and felt the welcome warmth.

"That is better," said Taliesen. Fell's heart hammered and he jumped like a startled squirrel. The old man had appeared from nowhere, seeming to blink into existence. "It used to be," continued the druid, his cloak of feathers shining in the moonlight, "that I enjoyed forest nights. But sometime during the last hundred years or so my blood started to run thin."

"Why can't you walk up to a fire like anyone else?" stormed Fell.

"Because I am not like everyone else. What point is there in possessing enormous talent if no one is given the opportu-

nity to appreciate it? By Heaven, boy, but you scare easily."
Taliesen rubbed a gnarled hand over his wood-smoke
whiskers. "No food this time, eh? Well, I suppose that is a
blessing."

"You didn't touch it last time, so you have no way of
knowing!" said Fell. "You are not real, old man. You are not
flesh and blood." As he spoke Fell suddenly reached out and
swept his hand across Taliesen's face. His fingers passed
through the wrinkled skin, and he felt nothing but air against
his palm.

"Good," said Taliesen. "You have intelligence. Yet you are
still wrong. I *am* flesh and blood. But I am not flesh and
blood *here*. I am sitting in my own cave in another place, and
another time. The energy needed to open the Gateways for
the flesh is immense; there is no need to waste it when an astral projection will serve the same purpose. And since my
role is merely to speak with you, my spirit image must suffice."

"You breed words like lice," snapped Fell, still rattled.
"And I don't relish having wizards at my fire. So speak your
piece and be gone."

"Tish, boy, where are your manners? Elders are to be
treated with respect, surely, even in this new and enlightened
age? Did your parents teach you nothing? Your father, I recall, was a man of good breeding."

"For pity's sake, just say what you came to say," said Fell.
"I am already sick of your lectures."

Taliesen was silent for a moment. "Very well," he said at
last, "but mark the words well. Firstly, when I leave, I want
you to string your bow. The time is drawing near when you
will have to use it. Secondly, you know the location of the
Alwen Falls?"

"Of course, where Ironhand passed over. Every Loda child
knows where it is."

"When the arrows are loosed, and blood is upon the ground,
you must take the Cloak Wearer there. You understand?"

"Understand? No, I understand nothing. Firstly, I have no intention of loosing a shaft at anyone or anything, and secondly, who is the Cloak Wearer?"

"Have a little patience, Fell. And if you do not loose a shaft a loved one of yours will die. Take me at my word, boy. And remember the pool. That is vital!"

The old man vanished. The fire died instantly.

Fell sent a whispered curse after the man. Yet even as he spoke he drew the bowstring from his pouch and strung the bow.

The first light of predawn was heralded by birdsong and Fell swung his quiver over his shoulder and walked to the top of the hill overlooking Citadel town.

There was nothing to see, save the grey walls and the rising stone of the Keep beyond the town's rooftops. Gradually the sky lightened and he saw a tiny figure emerge from the north gate and begin to run toward the hills. Fell squinted, but could not—at first—identify the runner.

Then, with a shock, he saw the dawn light glint on her silver hair. She was some three hundred yards onto open ground when the three horsemen rode from the town. The lead rider was a soldier in helm and breastplate, as was the third. But it was the second man, riding a grey stallion, who caught Fell's attention. He was brandishing a sword, and he wore a red cloak! His excitement soared.

Sigarni was running hard, but the horsemen were closing. Why do they have their swords drawn? thought Fell. And then it came to him in a sickening realization. They are chasing her. They mean to kill her!

The lead horseman was a mere fifty yards behind her when Fell drew a shaft and notched it to the bowstring. It was not an easy shot—a fast-moving horseman, downhill from him, and with the light still poor.

The enormity of what he was about to do filled Fell's mind, yet there was no hesitation. Smoothly he drew back the string until it nestled against his chin, then he took a deep

breath and slowly let it out. Between breaths and utterly motionless, he sighted carefully and loosed the shaft. The arrow
sang through the air. For a fraction of a heartbeat Fell
thought he had missed, but the shaft slammed home in the
lead rider's left eye, catapulting him from the saddle. Running forward, Fell notched a second arrow to the string; but
he shot too swiftly, and the shaft flew past the red-cloaked
officer and skimmed across the flank of the third man's
horse. The beast reared, sending the soldier tumbling over its
haunches in an ungainly somersault.

The red-cloaked officer was almost upon the fleeing
woman. Fell saw her glance back once, then turn and leap
at the grey horse, waving her arms and shouting loudly. The
grey swerved to avoid her, pitching its rider to the left. Sigarni
leaped at the man, a silver blade glinting in her right fist. Her
left hand caught hold of his cloak, dragging him from the saddle. The knife rose and fell. Blood gouted from a wound in the
man's neck and again and again the knife flashed.

Sigarni rose with the dead man's cloak in her hand. Fell
watched as she gazed back at the Citadel town. Scores of people were lining the parapets now. Sigarni swirled the crimson
cloak around her shoulders, retying the snapped neck cord.
Then she raised the dead man's sword and pointed it at the
spectators.

The sun finally rose and Sigarni was bathed in its golden
light, the iron sword shining like a torch of silver to match
her hair. For Fell it was as if time ceased to have meaning,
and he knew that this scene would shine forever in his memory. The cloak wearer was Sigarni. *She* was the legend. Fell
let out a long, slow breath.

Sigarni plunged the sword into the ground, then turned
and slowly mounted the grey stallion. The third soldier was
sitting on the ground nearby. Sigarni ignored him and urged
the horse on toward the trees and the waiting Fell.

He saw the blood upon her shirt and leggings, the bruises
and cuts on her face.

But more than this, he saw the crimson cloak around her slender shoulders.

"What now for us all, Sigarni?" he asked as she came closer. "What now?"

Her eyes seemed unfocused, and she did not appear to hear him. Her face was losing its color, the surface of the skin waxy and grey. The horse moved on, plodding into the trees. Fell ran after it, just in time to throw aside his bow and catch hold of Sigarni as she started to fall from the saddle. Pushing her foot clear of the stirrup, Fell levered himself to the stallion's back. With one arm holding the unconscious Sigarni to him, he took up the reins in his left hand and heeled the stallion forward.

The old wizard had urged him to take her to the falls, but if he did so now he would leave a clear trail behind him, the horse's hooves biting deeply into the damp earth.

The pursuit was probably already under way, and with little time to plan Fell urged the horse to greater speed and headed for the deeper forest. He rode for several miles, keeping to the deer trails, always climbing higher into the mountains. Glancing at the sky he saw thick clouds to the north, dark and angry, their tops flattened like an anvil. Fell breathed a prayer of thanks, for such clouds promised hail and thunder and powerful storms. Hauling on the reins he stepped down from the saddle, allowing Sigarni to fall into his arms and across his shoulder. The ground beneath his feet was rocky and firm, leaving no trace of his booted feet. He slapped the stallion firmly on the rump and the horse leaped forward in a run, heading on down the slope toward the valley below. Fell left the trail, forcing his way through deep undergrowth. The ground broke sharply to his right into a muddy slope; it was hard to keep his footing here, especially with the added burden of Sigarni. He moved on carefully, occasionally slithering and sliding, keeping close to the trees that grew on the hillside, using them as barriers to halt any out-of-control slide. He was halfway down the slope when he heard the sound of horsemen on the road above. Dropping to his knees behind a screen of bushes, he looked back and saw the soldiers galloping by. There were more than thirty in the group.

With a grunt Fell pushed himself to his feet and struggled on. By his own reckoning he was around four miles due east from the Alwen Falls. But that four miles would become at least six by the route he would be forced to travel, along winding trails, skirting the steeper slopes and the many acres of open grassland.

He was sweating heavily by the end of the first mile, and by the second he felt his legs trembling with the effort of carrying the unconscious woman. Sigarni had made no sound throughout and Fell paused by a stream, lowering her to the ground. Her color was not good, and her pulse was faint and erratic. Carefully he examined her, opening her torn shirt. There were bloody teeth marks on her breast, and a range of purple bruises on her rib cage and shoulders. But no deep wounds. She is in shock, he thought. It is vital to keep her warm; to find somewhere he could nurse her. Gently he stroked her bruised face. "You are safe, my love," he said softly. "Hold on for me." She did not stir as Fell wrapped the crimson cloak around her, then lifted her to his shoulders. Almost two hours had passed already since the fight above the town, and there were still four miles to go. Fell took a deep breath and struggled on, trying not to think of his aching muscles, the burning in his calves and thighs.

For three more painful hours Fell carried Sigarni through the forest. In all that time she made no sound.

At last they arrived at Alwen Falls.

There was no sign of the wizard.

In a shallow cave, a little way back from the pool, Fell built a fire. Removing his own sheepskin cloak he covered Sigarni with it and, holding her hand, talked to her as she slept. "Well," he said, squeezing her limp fingers, "this is a sorry mess and no mistake. We're wolves' heads now, my love. I wish I knew why. Why were they chasing you? Who wounded you? Ah, well, I expect you'll tell me in your own good time. Shame about the bow, though. Best I ever had. But I couldn't carry it, hold you, and guide the horse at the same time." Leaning forward, he stroked her brow. "You are the most beautiful woman, Sigarni. I never saw the like. Was that what caused your pain? Did some Outland noble desire you so badly he felt compelled to take you by force? Was it the red-bearded man whose throat you slashed to red ribbons?" Releasing her hand, he fed wood to the fire and rose, walking to the cave mouth.

What now? he wondered. Where will we go?

He had relatives among the Wingoras and the Farlain, but with a price on his head he would only endanger them by seeking their aid. No, Fell, he told himself, you are a man alone now, friendless and hunted. You have killed an Outlander and they will hunt you to your dying day. A roll of thunder boomed across the sky and lightning forked across the heavens. Fell shivered and watched as the rain hammered down on the surface of the pool, falling in sheets, thick and impenetrable. Stepping back from the cave mouth, he returned to the fire and the sleeping Sigarni.

"We will cross the sea, my love," he said, "and I'll do what I should have done. We'll marry and build a home in distant mountains."

"No, you won't," said Taliesen from the cave mouth. Fell smiled and swung to see the old man, his feather cloak dripping water, his wispy hair plastered to his skull. In his hands he carried a long staff, wrapped in sacking cloth.

"That's a more pleasing entrance," said the forester. "*Now* I believe you are flesh and blood." Taliesen removed his cloak and draped it over a rock. Squatting by the fire, he held out his ancient hands to the flames.

"You did well, boy," he said. "You have evaded the first hunters. But they will send more, canny men, skilled in tracking. And with them will be a Finder, a seeker of souls, a reader of thoughts. If you survive this, which is doubtful at best, they will send the night-stalkers, creatures from the pit."

"No, no," said Fell, "seek not to cheer me, old man, with your boundless optimism. I am a grown man, tell it to me straight."

Taliesen hawked and spat. "I have no time for your humor. We must protect her, Fell. Her importance cannot be over-stated. You must go from here to her cabin. Gather her weapons and some spare clothes; give them to the dwarf. Tell him, and the others there, what has occurred. Then you must find the hunters and lead them deep into the moun-tains."

Fell took a deep breath, fighting for calm. It didn't work. "Find the hunters? Lead them? What say you I just attack the Citadel town single-handed and raze it to the ground? Or perhaps I could borrow your feather cloak and fly south, in-vading the Outland cities and slaying the King? Are you in-sane, old man? What do you expect me to do against thirty soldiers?"

"Whatever you can." The old man looked into Fell's eyes, his expression as cold as ice on flint. "You are dispensable, Fell," said Taliesen. "Your death will matter only to you. You can be replaced. Everything can be replaced, save Sigarni. You understand? You must earn her time, time to recover, time to learn. She is the leader your people have yearned for. Only she has the power to win freedom for the clans."

"They'll never follow a woman! That much I know."

Taliesen shook his head. "They followed the Witch Queen four hundred years ago. They crossed the Gateways and died for her. They stood firm against the enemy, though they were outnumbered and faced slaughter. They will follow her, Fell."

"The Witch Queen was a sorceress. Sigarni is merely a woman."

"How blind you are," said the old man, "and rich indeed is your male conceit. This woman was dragged to a cell and raped, sodomized, and beaten senseless by four men. Like animals they fell upon her . . ."

"I don't want to hear this!" roared Fell, half rising.

"But you shall!" stormed the wizard. "They struck her with their fists, and they bit her. They cut her buttocks with their sharp knives, and forced her to unspeakable acts. Then they left her upon the floor of the cell, to lie on the cold stone floor in a pool of her own vomit and blood. Aye, well might you look shocked, for this was men at play, Fell. She lay there and after an hour or so a new guard came into the cell. He too wanted his piece of her flesh. She killed him, Fell. Then she hunted down the others. One she slew upon the dungeon stair. She killed a sentry in the courtyard and two more outside a tavern. And the last? You saw him, in his fine red cloak of wool. Him she tore the throat from. Just a woman? By all the Gods of the Nine Worlds, boy, in her tortured condition she killed six strong men!"

Fell said nothing, and transferred his gaze to the sleeping woman. "Aye, she's a Highlander," he said with pride. "But even that will not make men follow her."

"We will see," said Taliesen. "Now go to her cabin before the hunters reach it. Send the dwarf with weapons and clothes."

"You will stay with her?"

"Indeed I will."

Fell rose and swung his quiver over his shoulder, then gazed down at the unconscious Sigarni. "I will keep her warm," said Taliesen. "Oh, and I retrieved your bow." Lifting what Fell had believed to be a staff covered in sacking, Taliesen passed the weapon to the surprised forester.

"You even kept it dry. My thanks to you, wizard. I feel a whole man again."

Taliesen ignored him and turned to the sleeping Sigarni, taking her long, slim hand into his own.

Swirling his cloak around his shoulders, Fell stepped out into the rain-drenched night.

* * *

Sigarni stood silently by the grey cave wall and listened as Fell and the old man spoke. She could hear their words, see their faces, and even—though she knew not how—feel their emotions. Fell was frightened and yet trying to maintain an air of male confidence. The old man—Taliesen?—was tired, yet filled with a barely suppressed excitement. And lying by the fire, looking so sad and used, she could see herself, wrapped in the rapist's red cloak, her face bruised and swollen. *I am dying*, she thought. *My spirit has left my body and now only the Void awaits*. There was no panic in her, no fear, only a sadness built of dreams never to be realized.

Fell took his bow from the old man and walked from the cave. Sigarni tried to call out to him but he did not hear her. No one could hear her, save maybe the dead.

But she was wrong. As soon as Fell walked out into the rain the old man looked up at her, his button-bright eyes focusing on her face. "Well, now we can talk," he said. "How are you feeling?"

Sigarni was both surprised and confused. The old man was holding the hand of her body, yet looking directly into the eyes of her spirit. It was disconcerting.

"I feel . . . nothing," she said. "Is this what death is like?"

He gave a dry chuckle, like the whispering of the wind across dead leaves. "You are talking to a man who has fought back death for many centuries. I do not even wish to speculate on what death is like. Do you remember the waking of your spirit?"

"Yes, someone called me, but when I opened my eyes he was not here. How is this happening, old one?"

"I fear the answer may be too complicated for an untutored Highlander to understand. Essentially your body has been so brutalized that your mind has reeled from thoughts of it. You have entered a dream state which has freed your . . . soul, if you will. Now you feel no pain, no shame, no guilt. And while we talk your body is healing. I have, through my skill, increased the speed of the process. Even so, when you do return to the prison of flesh you will feel—shall we say—considerable discomfort."

"Do I know you?" asked Sigarni.

"Do you think that you do?" he countered.

"I can remember being held close to your chest. You have a small mole under the chin; I know this. And in looking at you I can see another man, enormously tall, broad-shouldered, wearing a buckskin shirt with a red wingspread hawk silhouette upon the breast."

Taliesen nodded. Childhood memories. Yes, you know me, child. The other man was Caswallon. One day, if God is kind, you will meet him again."

"You both saved me from the demons—out there by the pool. Gwalchmai told me. Who are you, Taliesen? Why have you helped me?"

"I am merely a man—a great man, mind! And my reasons for helping you are utterly selfish. But now is not the time to speak of things past. The days of magick and power are upon us, Sigarni, the days of blood and death are coming."

"I want no part in them," she said.

"You have little choice in the matter. And you will feel differently when you wake. In spirit form you are free of much more than merely the flesh. The human body has many weapons. Rage, which increases muscle power; fear, which can hone the mind wonderfully; love, which binds with ties of iron; and hate, which can move mountains. There are many more. But in astral form you are connected only tenuously to these emotions. It was rage and the need for revenge which saved your life, which drove you on to wear the Red. That rage is still there, Sigarni, a fire that needs no kindling, an eternal blaze that will light the road to greatness. But it rests in the flesh, awaiting your return."

"You were correct, old one. I do not understand all you say. How do I return to my flesh?"

"Not yet. First go from the cave. Walk to the pool."

She shook her head. "There is a ghost there."

"Yes," he said. "Call him."

Sigarni was on the point of refusing when Taliesen lifted his hand and pointed to the fire. The flames leaped up to form a sheer bright wall some four feet high. Then, at the center, a small spot of colorless light appeared, opening to become a pale glistening circle. It glowed snow-white, then gently became the blue of a summer sky. Sigarni watched spellbound as the blue faded and she found herself staring through the now-transparent circle into her own cabin. She was there, talking with Gwalchmai. The conversation whispered into her mind.

"Who was the ghost?" asked the image of Sigarni.

"Go and ask him, woman. Call for him." She shivered and looked away.

"I can't."

Gwalch chuckled. "There is nothing you cannot do, Sigarni. Nothing."

"Oh, come on, Gwalch, are we not friends? Why won't you help me?"

"I am helping you. I am giving you good advice. You don't remember the night of the Slaughter. You will, when the time is right. I helped take the memory from you when I found you by the pool. Madness had come upon you, girl. You were sitting in a puddle of your own urine. Your eyes were blank, and you were slack-jawed. I had a friend with me; his name was Taliesen. It was he—and another—who slew the Slaughterers. Taliesen told me we were going to lock away the memory and bring you back to the world of the living. We did exactly that. The door will open one day, when you are strong enough to turn the key. That's what he told me."

Now the circle shrank to a dot and the flames of the fire returned to normal. "Am I strong enough to turn the key?" she asked Taliesen.

"Go to the pool and find out," he advised. "Call for him!"

Sigarni stood silently for a moment, then moved past the old man and out into the night. The rain was still hammering down, but she could not feel it nor, strangely, could she hear it. Water tumbled over the falls in spectacular silence, ferocious winds tore silently at the trees and their leaf-laden branches, lightning flared in the sky, but the voice of the accompanying thunder could not be heard.

The huntress moved to the poolside. "I am here!" she called. There was no answer, no stirring upon the water. Merely silence.

"Call to him by name," came the voice of Taliesen in her mind.

And she knew, and in knowing wondered how such an obvious realization should have escaped her so long. "Ironhand!" she called. "It is I, Sigarni. Ironhand!"

The waters bubbled and rose like a fountain, the spray forming an arched Gateway lit by an eldritch light. A giant of a man appeared in the Gateway, his silver beard in twin braids, his hair tied back at the nape of his neck. He wore silver-bright armor and carried a long, leaf-bladed broadsword that glistened as if it had been carved from moonlight. He raised the sword in greeting, and then sheathed it at his side and spoke, his voice rich and resonant. "Come to me, Sigarni," he said. "Walk with me awhile."

"You spoke to me in Citadel town," she said. "You urged me to flee."

"Yes."

"And you fought for me when I was a child. You slew the last Hollow-tooth."

"That also."

"Why?"

"For love, Sigarni. For a love that will not accept death. Will you walk with me awhile?"

"I will," she said, tears brimming.

And she stepped forward to walk upon the water.

Chapter Six

Despite the excruciating pain flaring from the empty eye socket, the Baron Ranulph Gottasson enjoyed the awestruck and fearful expressions of the men before him. Idly the fingers of his left hand stroked the carved dragon claws on the arm of the ornate chair. Sharp they were as they gripped the globe of ebony. The men waited silently below the dais. He knew their thoughts and, more importantly, their growing anxiety. They had failed—the woman who had robbed him of his eye was still at large. The Baron leaned back on the high carved chair and stared balefully down at the twenty men before him, his single eye bloodshot but its gaze piercing.

"So," he said softly, his voice sibilant and chilling, "tell me that you have captured the woman and the renegade."

The officer before him, a tall man sporting a square-cut beard but no mustache, cleared his throat. His chain-mail leggings were mud-smeared, and his right arm was clumsily bandaged. "We have not caught them yet, my lord. I brought the men back for fresh supplies."

"You did not catch them," repeated the Baron, rising from his chair. "One woman and a forester, riding double on a stolen stallion. But you did not catch them." Slowly he descended the three steps from the dais and halted before the officer. The man dropped his head and mumbled something. "Speak up, Chard. Let us all hear you!"

The officer reddened, but he raised his head and his voice

boomed out. "They fooled us. They turned the stallion loose and cut out across the valleys. Then the storm came and it was impossible to read sign. But we followed as best we could, thinking the woman would return to her people. The renegade forester, Fell, shot at us from ambush, wounding two of my men. We gave chase, my lord, but heavily armed riders are useless in the thickets. We left our horses and tried to follow on foot. It was like trying to catch a ghost. I had no archers with me. Three more men were struck by his arrows. Happily their armor saved them from serious injury, though the mercenary, Lava, still has an arrowhead lodged in his shoulder." Chard fell silent.

The Baron nodded solemnly. "So, what you are saying is that thirty Outland warriors are no match for a woman and a clansman."

"No, my lord. I am saying . . ."

"Be silent, fool! Did you think, at any time during the four days you have been gone, to send back to Citadel for trackers? Did you not consider hiring the services of the Finder Kollarin? Did you set the renegade's own people to hunt him?"

"His own people . . ."

The Baron half turned away, then swung back his fist, smashing the officer's lips against his teeth. The skin split and blood sprayed out as Chard was hurled backward. He fell heavily, cracking his skull against the base of a statue. Chard gave out one grunting moan, then slid into unconsciousness. "You have all failed me," said the Baron, "but his was the greatest sin. He will suffer for it. Now you!" he said, pointing to a burly soldier with close-cropped fair hair. "You are Obrin the Southlander, yes?"

"Yes, my lord." The man bowed.

"You have fought barbarians before, I understand. In Kushir, Palol, Umbria, and Cleatia?"

"Yes, my lord. And served also in Pesht under your command. I was there when you stormed the wall, sir, though I was but a common soldier then."

"And now you are a sergeant-at-arms. Answer me well and you shall assume command of the hunt, and become a captain. Tell us all now what errors were made by the idiot lying at your feet."

Obrin drew a deep breath and was silent for a moment. The Baron smiled. He knew what was going through the man's mind. No enlisted soldier wished to be made an officer: the pay would not cover the mess bills, and from its meager supply he would have to purchase his own horse and armor and hire a manservant. Obrin's round face paled; then he spoke. "The trail was cold from the moment the storm broke, my lord. We should have headed for Cilfallen and taken hostages. Then the foresters themselves could have hunted down their comrade. I would also have posted a reward for their capture, just in case. There's not much coin in the Highlands. And there's always some bastard who'd sell his mother for a copper or two, if you take my meaning, my lord." Obrin paused and rubbed his broad chin. "You have already mentioned the Finder, Kollarin, but—I'll be honest with you, my lord—I would not have thought of him, sir, and if it please you, I don't want Captain Chard's command. I'm no nobleman. And I wouldn't fit in. I don't have the brains for it. But I am a good sergeant, sir."

The Baron ignored the soldier and climbed to the dais to return to his seat. His eye socket was throbbing and tongues of fire were lancing up into his skull. Yet he kept his expression even and showed no trace of the pain he was feeling. "Find Kollarin and take him with you when you have your supplies. Take fifty men. Split them into two sections. One will ride to Cilfallen and post a reward of one hundred guineas; this group will also take four hostages and return them to Citadel. The second group, led by you, Obrin, will include Kollarin. You will start your search at the woman's cabin. And before you leave you will take the former Captain Chard to the whipping post, where you will apply fifty lashes to his naked back. With every lash I want you to consider this: Fail, and one of your men will be lashing you."

"Yes, sir," said Obrin miserably.

The Baron waved his hand, dismissing the men. "Not you, Leofric," he said as the slender blond-haired cleric was about to leave. "Shut the door and come to me in my study." Leaving the dais the Baron strode across the hall and through a small side door, leading to a flight of steps that took him up to the parapet study. A goblet had been placed on the desk, filled with dark, noxious liquid. The Baron hated medicines of any kind, and pain-masking opiates in particular. But the injury was now interfering with his thought processes and he drained the foul brew and sat with his back to the open window.

Leofric knocked twice, then entered the study. "I am sorry, cousin, for your pain and your disappointment," he said uneasily.

"The pain is nothing, but I am not disappointed, boy," the Baron told him, motioning the younger man to a seat opposite him. "Far from it. The Highlands need to be purged, and the excuse has now fluttered in on the wings of a dead hawk. A woman rebel was arrested after attacking the King's Emissary. Highlanders raided the dungeons to release her. Then they attacked the King's soldiers. When word reaches the south the King will send another five thousand men to serve under me, and we will march from Citadel to the sea and wipe out the clans once and for all."

"I don't understand," said Leofric. "How are the clans a danger to the empire? They have no military organization, indeed no army, and there is no insurrection."

The Baron smiled. "Then we cannot lose, can we, Leofric? And at the end I will have an army as large as Jastey's. The King grows old and soft. You think Jastey has no plans to seize the crown for himself? Of course he has. And I can do nothing to stop him while I am stuck away here in this godforsaken wilderness. However, a war against the clans, well, that has great merit. In the south they still fear these northerners, and old men recall with dread how the shrieking savages erupted from the mountains bringing fire and death to the Lowlands. You will see, Leofric. As soon as news reaches the south of this latest outrage, the price of land south of the border will plummet. The weakhearted will sell up and move and panic will sweep through the immediate Lowland towns."

"That I do understand," said Leofric, "but what if the Highlanders do hunt down this . . . Fell . . . and the woman? What if they surrender them to us to save the hostages?"

The Baron shook his head. "It won't happen. I know these barbarians; they're all too proud. I'll hang the hostages as soon as they reach Citadel, and leave their bodies on the north wall for all to see. And if that doesn't force at least a show of resistance, I'll burn Cilfallen and a few of their towns."

"And what task would you have me perform, my lord?" asked Leofric.

"There will be no major invasion of the Highlands until spring. We want time for the fear to grow back home. I intend to attack with six thousand fighting men and five hundred engineers. You must put your mind to the question of how we feed and supply this army all the way to the sea. Also, I want you to study the maps and locate three sites for our fixed camps and fortifications. You know what is required: The forts should be situated close to the lands of the Pallides and the Farlain. Choose open ground, yet close enough to the woods for the men to be able to gather timber for the walls. Questions?"

"Yes, my lord, the fortifications. I am well aware of the standard design used for the construction of temporary fortifications during punitive raids into hostile territory. But these are rough constructions, not intended for more than a few nights. Will they suffice?"

The Baron considered the question. The Highland winters were notoriously savage, and the forts would need to be manned throughout the long, bitter months until the invasion. More important than this, however, was the likelihood of Highlanders attacking the outposts. There would be no way to reinforce them once the snow blocked the passes.

"You misunderstood my use of the word *standard*," said the Baron smoothly. "This is not a punitive raid, but should be considered as a full invasion. The forts therefore will have regulation defenses, earth barriers at least ten feet high, topped with timber walls to another fifteen feet. Weighted portcullis gates will also be constructed. You are familiar with the design?"

"Of course, my lord. It was devised by Driada during the Cleatian Wars in the last century, but was possibly based on an earlier . . ."

"I did not ask for a history lesson, Leofric. You will take two hundred engineers and three hundred infantrymen into the Highlands. Then you will oversee the building of these forts and within them storehouses for supplies. Make sure the storehouses are watertight. I want no rotting meat nor mildewed cereal when I arrive with the army."

Leofric stood and bowed. "I thank you for your trust in me, cousin. I will not fail you."

Sigarni opened her eyes and saw the flickering flame shadows on the cave ceiling. She watched them for a moment, then felt the onrush of pain from her wounded body. A voice spoke from her left. "She is awake. Pour some broth for her." Sigarni rolled her head toward the sound, focusing her eyes upon a wizened old man with deep-set pale eyes.

"Taliesen?" she whispered.

"Aye, lass, Taliesen. How are you feeling?"

"Hurt. What happened to me?"

"You don't remember the attack in Citadel dungeons?"

She closed her eyes. "Of course I do—but that was years

ago. I meant why am I injured *now*?" Taliesen leaned forward and helped her to sit up. Pain lanced through Sigarni's right side and she groaned.

"One of your ribs is cracked. It will heal soon," said Taliesen. Another figure moved into sight, child-small, yet bearded. Sitting at her right, Ballistar handed her a wooden bowl and spoon. The broth was thick and salty and Sigarni became acutely aware of her hunger. She ate in silence. When she had finished Ballistar took back the bowl. Sigarni felt her strength returning, but still she was confused.

"Why did you mention the . . . attack on me?" she asked Taliesen.

"Because it happened three days ago," he said slowly. "You have been spirit-wandering in a place where there is no time."

"I remember," she said. "He took me by the hand."

"Who took her?" asked Ballistar. Taliesen waved him to silence.

"Yes, you walked with him," said the wizard, taking Sigarni's hand. She wrenched it back, her eyes blazing.

"Do not touch me! No man will ever touch me again!" The violence in her voice was startling, surprising Ballistar who dropped the empty bowl. It rolled across the cave floor, coming to rest against the far wall.

Taliesen seemed unmoved by the rebuff. "I am sorry, my dear, that was remiss of me. Did you learn much in your time with him?"

"It is hazy now," she said sleepily. "But he said he would teach me . . . would always . . . be with me." Sigarni stretched out again and closed her eyes. Taliesen covered her with a blanket of wool.

"What was she talking about?" asked Ballistar. "When did she go walking? And who with?"

Taliesen rose and walked to the fire. "Time to gather more wood," he said.

"Who did she walk with?" repeated Ballistar.

"It's not for you to know, dwarf. Now go and fetch some wood. The black man will be here soon, and then you'll understand a little more of what is happening here."

"I'm not your servant!" snapped Ballistar. "I don't have to jump through hoops because you say so!"

"No," agreed Taliesen, "you don't. But I am trying to keep her warm, and I am a little too old to relish walking around a forest and stooping to collect dead wood. You, on the other hand, do not have far to stoop."

"I'll do it for her," said the dwarf. "But know this, Taliesen, I do not like you. Not one bit."

"How wise of you," Taliesen told him.

Ballistar stomped from the cave and out into the afternoon sunlight. Fallen wood was plentiful, following the storm, and he spent an idle hour gathering armfuls of fuel and carrying them back to the cave. Taliesen spent the hour sitting silently beside the sleeping Sigarni. Bored now, Ballistar returned to the poolside and stared out over the water. It was smooth and motionless here, and the reflections of the trees on the opposite shore could be seen growing upside-down in the pool. Ballistar moved to the edge and knelt, leaning out over the water. His own face looked back at him, the deep-set brown eyes gazing into his.

"What's it like in an upside-down world?" he asked his reflection. "Are you happy or sad?" The face in the pool mouthed the same words back to him. Ballistar moved back and sat with his back to the trunk of a weeping willow.

Asmidir came riding down the slope and Ballistar stood. The black man was wearing clothes of brown and russet, with a deep green cloak. He sported no burnoose and upon his head he wore a helm of burnished iron that rose to a glistening silver point at the crown. Seeing Ballistar, he drew rein and stepped from the saddle. "Where is she?" he asked.

Ballistar pointed to the cave. "There is a wizard with her. Unpleasant little man."

"How is she?"

"Beaten and abused. She will get better though. I know it."

The black man nodded. "I know it also. What news of Fell?"

"I've heard nothing," the dwarf told him. "I've been here for three nights. But I don't think they'll catch him. A canny man is Fell, and stronger than he believes."

"You see much, Ballistar. You are no man's fool. I shall be taking Sigarni to my house. You are welcome to join us. I think she will feel better with you there."

"She may not want either of us," said the dwarf. "She just told Taliesen that no man will ever touch her again—she may hate us all for the sins of a few."

Asmidir shook his head. "She is too intelligent for that, my friend. Will you come?"

"Of course I will come. She is my friend."

"Mine also," said Asmidir softly. "And I will defend her with my life. You believe me?"

Ballistar looked deeply into the man's dark eyes. "Aye, I believe you, black man. I don't like you, but I believe you."

"There is much in me to dislike, Ballistar. I have been a harsh man, and at times a cruel one. Despite this I have never betrayed a friend, and treachery is utterly alien to me. I intend to help Sigarni, to teach her all that I know."

"About what?" asked Ballistar.

"About war," Asmidir answered.

There was little conversation as the five men moved through the forest, each locked in his own thoughts. Fat Tovi the Baker kept thinking of his eldest son, and how proud he was of the boy. When the soldiers had selected him as one of the four hostages he had stood tall, straight of back, and he had shown no fear. *Like me, when I was younger,* thought Tovi. Then he shook his head. *No, he's better than me. There's a lot of his mother in him, and she comes from good stock.*

Beside him walked Grame the Smith, his thoughts dark

and brooding. Grame stood by while the soldiers selected the hostages, but he was holding the forge hammer in his hand, and using all his iron will to stop himself from running forward and braining the grinning officer. That I should live to see this, he thought, foreigners riding into our villages unopposed and stealing away our people. The smith felt the shame as if it were his alone.

Ahead of the two old men walked the three foresters, Fell at the center. Bakris Tooth-gone was to his left, Gwyn Dark-eye to the right. Gwyn's thoughts were all of Fell. He loved him better than he loved his own brothers, and was racking his brains for a fresh argument to use to stop Fell from surrendering to the Outlanders. But nothing would come. Four lives were at stake, Tovi's son, the Widow Maffrey, the cattle herder Clemet, and Nami, the fat daughter of the shepherd Maccus. Fell was a man of honor, and once he had heard about the hostages there was only one course of action left to him. It broke Gwyn's heart to make this journey.

Bakris was thinking about what would happen once the arrogant Fell had been hanged. Surely his own skills would be recognized and he would be elected Captain of Foresters?

Fell himself could think only of Sigarni, and all that might have been. Taliesen had ordered him to lead the hunters deep into the forest, and this he had done, wounding several of them. They had almost caught him twice, but his woodcraft saved him—that and his fleetness of foot. What will happen now, Sigarni? he wondered. Will you remember me kindly?

In his mind's eye he could see himself standing on the scaffold, the hemp rope at his throat. Will you die like a man, Fell, he asked himself, standing tall and proud? In that moment he knew that he would. No Outland audience would see a Highland man scream and beg for his life.

Fell glanced up at the branches above him, the sun dappling them with gold and sending shafts of brilliance to the undergrowth below. Through a break in the trees he saw

High Druin, rising majestically above the other peaks. "Be with me, Father!" he whispered to the mountain.

"What's that, Fell?" asked Gwyn.

"Talking to myself, man. Ah, but it's a fine day for a walk, to be sure."

"That it is, my friend, but I'd be happier if we were heading north."

"I cannot do that. I'll let no Highlander die for my crimes."

"Crimes? What crimes?" snorted Grame, moving alongside them. "They raped her, for God's sake, and they hunted her down like an animal. Who do they think they are, these Outlanders? First the Baron tries to steal her hawk, then they rob her of her virtue . . ."

"What virtue?" sneered Bakris. "Hell's teeth, man, that was gone long ago. She's had more pricks than an archery target."

"That's enough," hissed Fell as he swung on Grame. "Who do they think they are? They are the conquerors, and they make the laws. You, me, the whole of the Highlands, are ruled at their whim."

"There's supposed to be a leader coming," said Tovi. "I wish to God he would appear soon."

"*She* already has," said Fell. The other men looked at one another, then back at Fell. "Aye, you'll think it nonsense," he said. "But an old sorcerer came to me, and told me to be at the Citadel town at dawn on a certain day. There I would see the Red worn again, and a sword held over the town. Well, my lads, I was there. And I saw Sigarni don the Red, and watched her kill an Outlander. She's the leader prophesied. I won't live to see it, but you will."

"Have you gone mad, lad?" asked Grame. "What does she know of war and battles? She's a child. Who'd follow her?"

"I would," said Fell.

"If he would, so would I," put in Gwyn.

Bakris gave a sneering laugh. "I'd follow her into the bedroom. Anytime."

"You will all see it come true," said Fell. "Now let's be moving on. I have a wish to be in Citadel town before dusk."

Tovi put his broad hand on Fell's shoulder. "I'm not stopping you, boy," he said, his voice thick with emotion. "I'd do anything to bring my son home. Yet, even now, if you choose to take a different path I'll think none the worse of you. You understand?"

Fell nodded. "I understand, Hunt Lord. But I killed an Outlander, and they want blood. If they don't get mine they will seek it elsewhere. It is their way. I would ask you this, though—look to Sigarni, and help her all you can. Both you and Grame are battle-hardened warriors. You have lived what the rest of us only hear stories of. You know how the heart feels before a battle, and how a man's courage can turn to water. You know what it takes to stand against a foe. That knowledge will be vital in the days ahead. My death may give you breathing space to plan. But it will be no more than that."

"It may not even give us that," said Gwyn. "They want Sigarni too. They may just take you, and keep the hostages."

"I've thought of that," said Fell. "Let us hope there is a spark of honor in the Baron."

"You're doing the right thing, Fell," said Bakris. "I'd do the same in your place."

"Then let's move on," said Fell. "One more hill, lads, and we'll be home."

The five men trudged up the hill, cresting it just as the sun was turning to blood over the western mountain peaks. In the distance they could see the line of the wall around Citadel town, and the tall ramparts of the keep beyond.

By the north gate, in cages outside the wall, hung four bodies, and crows were thick around them. At this distance it was impossible to recognize faces, but all knew the worn-out black dress worn by the Widow Maffrey. "God's heart!" whispered Grame. "They've killed them already! But it has only been two days! They promised a week."

"A spark of honor, you said, Fell," muttered Gwyn. "Now we all see what Outland honor is worth."

"They'll pay for this a thousandfold," said Fell. "I swear it!"

Sigarni, her red cloak wrapped around her shoulders, sat on the mock ramparts of Asmidir's castle home and stared out over the rolling hills and woodlands to the south. Asmidir stood alongside her, leaning on the crenellated grey stone parapet. "You understand your purpose?" he asked her.

"Yes," she said, her voice cold. "I am to kill Outlanders."

Angrily he swung on her. "No! That is the first lesson you must learn. War is not just a game of killing. Any commander who thinks in this way will be destroyed, if not by the enemy then by his—or her—own troops."

"Troops? Are you insane?" she stormed. "There are no soldiers, there is no army. There is only Sigarni. And all I live for now is to kill as many as I can." Pushing herself to her feet she faced him, her own pale eyes locked to his dark orbs. "You can have no understanding of what they did to me, or what they took from me. You are a man. This whole world has been created for your pleasures, while women are here merely for sport—either that or to carry your brats for nine months, ready to feed more souls to your games of slaughter in years to come. Well, Asmidir, Sigarni will carry no brats, but she *will* play your game."

He smiled ruefully. "You cannot play until you know what you are playing for. You must have an objective, Sigarni. How else can you plan?"

"An objective?" she mocked. "I am alone, Asmidir. What would you have me do? Where is my army? You want an objective? To free the Highlands of Outland rule, to drive the enemy back into their own lands and beyond. To lead a hundred thousand men deep into their territory and sack their capital. Is that enough of an objective?"

"It is," he said. "Now examine how you will plan for this objective."

Sigarni rose and faced him. "I have no time for worthless games. There is no army."

"Then build one," he said sternly.

Spinning on her heel, Sigarni strode along the rampart, climbing down the stone stairway to the courtyard. A servant bowed as she passed him. Moving on, she entered the house where Ballistar was standing before the stuffed bear, staring up at it. "It's so lifelike," said the dwarf. "Don't you think?"

Ignoring him, she walked into the hall and seated herself in a wide leather armchair set before the log fire. Asmidir followed her, with Ballistar just behind.

"Why are they bowing to me?" demanded Sigarni. "All of them. They don't speak . . . but they bow."

"I ordered them to," said Asmidir. "You must become familiar with such treatment. From now to the end of your life you will be separated from the common man. You will become a queen, Sigarni."

"The Whore Queen, is that it? Is that how you see me, Asmidir? Or was it some other black bastard who named me a harlot?"

Asmidir pulled up a chair and sat down opposite her. "Your anger is justified," he said. "I did not know then that *you* were the leader the prophecy spoke of. I ask your forgiveness for that. But I also ask that you focus your rage, and do not allow it to swamp your reason. If the prophecy is true—and I believe it to be so—then you must be ready to act. A wise general knows that men can be replaced, weapons can be replenished. But lost time cannot be regained."

"And who will follow me, Asmidir?" she asked. "Who will follow the whore Sigarni?"

Ballistar moved between them and gave a low bow. "I will follow you, Sigarni," he said. "Will you let me be the first?" Dropping to one knee he gazed up at her.

Sigarni felt her anger drain away. "You are my friend," she said wearily. "Is that not enough?"

"No. I believe what he says. The wizard said the same. I

know I am not built to be a warrior, or to lead men into battle. I can serve you, though. I can cook, and I can think. I am not a fool, Sigarni, though nature has gifted me the appearance of one. Other men will kneel before you, and you will gather an army from among the clans. And if we are all to die, let it be while fighting a vile enemy. For from now until then, at least we will live with pride."

Sigarni stood and took his arms, helping him to his feet. "You shall be the first, Ballistar," she said. Seizing her hand he kissed it, then stepped back, blushing.

"I'll leave you now," he said. "I'll prepare breakfast. Planning should never be attempted on an empty stomach."

As the dwarf departed Asmidir leaned forward. "His words had great wisdom, Sigarni."

She said nothing, but sat silently for a while staring into the flames, seeing again the sword that crushed the life from Abby, and then the terrible ordeal in the dungeon.

"What kind of army can we raise?" she asked.

Asmidir smiled. "That is more like it! The Loda number less than two thousand people, of which no more than six hundred could fight, and only then for a short space of time, for the fields would have to be tilled and planted, crops gathered and so on. Realistically we could raise three hundred fighting men. The Pallides number more than six thousand, with approximately two thousand men between the ages of fifteen and sixty. I have no detailed information as yet about the Farlain, but judging by the areas they inhabit, there should be at least four thousand of them. The Wingoras are the smallest clan, but even they could put two hundred fighting men on the field of battle. All in all, perhaps four thousand in total."

"Such a total could not be reached," she said. "You could not assemble all the clan's fighting men in one place. If the enemy were to avoid a confrontation, or slip by, all the villages and towns would be undefended."

Asmidir clapped his hands together. "Good!" he said. "Now

you are thinking! Tell me then, what is the most important matter to be studied first?"

"The enemy leader," she said without hesitation. Then she faltered, her brow furrowing.

"What is it?" he asked. "Are you in pain again?"

"No. I am . . . remembering. How strange. It is like looking through a window and seeing myself from afar. And he is with me. Talking. Teaching. He is saying, "*Know the enemy general for he is the heart and mind of the foe. The body may be of great power, and almost invincible, but if the heart and mind are not sound he will face defeat.*"

She saw that Asmidir was surprised. "Who is saying this? And when?"

"The King who was," she told him, "and he spoke to me while I slept in the cave."

"Now you are speaking in riddles."

"Not at all, Asmidir, but let us leave it there, as a mystery for you. He also said there were five fundamentals to analyze before war was undertaken: moral influence, weather, terrain, command, and doctrine."

Asmidir's surprise turned to astonishment. His eyes narrowed and he smiled. "Did he also mention the seven elements?"

"No. He said he would leave that to you."

"Are you making mock of me, woman?" he asked, his expression softening.

She shook her head. "I am speaking the truth." Rising smoothly she stood before him. "And *woman* is no way to address a leader," she said, smiling.

Asmidir did not return the smile. Instead he moved to his knees before her and bowed his head. "I ask your forgiveness, my lady," he said, "and I further request that you allow me to be the second man to pledge his loyalty to you."

"Now you are mocking *me*, Asmidir," she admonished him.

He glanced up, his face set. "I have never been more serious, Sigarni. I offer you my sword, my experience, and—if necessary—my life. All that I have is yours . . . now and forever."

"It shall be so," she heard herself say.

At that moment a servant entered. He bowed low. "Soldiers approaching, lord. Some thirty in number. With them rides the man you spoke of, dressed all in green."

Asmidir swore softly. "Remain in your room, Sigarni. This situation may become delicate."

"Who is the man in green?" she asked.

"A Seeker, a Finder. His powers are strong, and he will sense your spirit. One of my servants will come to you. Follow where he leads, my lady, and I will come to you when I can."

Obrin removed his iron helm and pushed back his chain-mail head and shoulder guard, allowing the mountain breeze to cool his face and blow through his short-cropped hair. Resting the helm on a flat stone beside the stream, he pulled off his riding gauntlets and laid them atop the helm. "A beautiful land," observed the Finder Kollarin, moving alongside him and splashing water to his face.

"Like my homeland," replied the sergeant, scanning the mountains. Obrin said nothing more and moved away to check the horses. They had been picketed a little way upstream and a sentry was standing by them. "Give them a while to cool down, then take them to water," he told the young man.

"Yes, sir."

"Yes, Sergeant!" snapped Obrin. "I'm not a bloody officer."

"Yes, Sergeant."

Obrin's foul mood darkened further. It had started already. Word of his temporary promotion had spread fast and the men thought it humorous, but nothing could be farther from the truth. As they were leaving the Citadel barracks Obrin had seen several officers watching him. They were laughing.

One of them, Lieutenant Masrick—a potbellied second cousin of the Baron—cracked a joke, his thin voice carrying to the mounted soldiers waiting for Obrin: "Put a pig in silk and it is still a pig, eh, my friends?"

Obrin pretended not to hear. It was the best policy. His short-lived appointment would soon be forgotten, but the enmity of a man like Masrick could see him humbled—or worse. Obrin pushed thoughts of Masrick from his mind.

He had camped his men in a hollow beside a stream. From here the campfires could be seen over no great distance, and with a sentry posted on the closest hill, they could have ample warning of any hostile approach. Not that Obrin expected an attempt to rescue the prisoner. However, regulations demanded that in the absence of a fortified camp, the officer in charge observe the proper precautions. The ground was rocky, but sheltered, and two campfires had already been lit. Cooking pots were in place above them and the smell of stew was beginning to fill the air. Obrin walked to the brow of a hill overlooking the campsite and sat down on a rock. From here he could see Kollarin sitting beside the stream, and the other men moving about their chores. The prisoner was seated by a slender elm at the edge of the camp, his hands and feet tied. There was blood on his face, and his left eye was blackened and swollen.

Obrin felt uncomfortable. He had known Fell for almost four years and he liked the man. A good judge of character, Obrin knew the clansman to be strong, proud, and honest. He was no murderer, of that Obrin was sure. What difference does it make what you think? he asked himself. Who cares? You had a job to do and you did it. That's all that matters. Fell had said nothing since the capture. Kollarin had led them to a cave, in which Fell was sleeping. They had rushed him and overpowered him. But not before Fell had smashed Bakker's nose and broken the jaw of the new recruit, Klebb. Obrin grinned at the memory. There was little to like about

Bakker, a loud, greasy whoreson with shifty eyes. The flattened nose had improved his looks tenfold!

Obrin saw Kollarin rise and begin to walk up the hill. He cursed inwardly for the man unnerved him. The sergeant did not care for magickers. Obrin made the Sign of the Protective Horn as the man approached. He did not do it covertly, but allowed Kollarin to see the gesture.

The man in green smiled and nodded. "I only read minds when I am paid," he said. "Your secrets are quite safe."

"I have no secrets, Finder. I tell no lies. I deceive no one—least of all myself."

"Then why make the sign?" asked Kollarin, sitting alongside the soldier.

"A casual insult," admitted Obrin, unconcerned over any possible reaction.

"You do not like me, Sergeant. You believe Fell should have been given the chance to fight like a man, and not be taken in his sleep. You are probably right. I would go farther, though. We are all reared on stories of heroes, great warriors, or poets, or philosophers. We are told that we must aspire to be just like these heroes, for only by so doing can we ensure the survival of civilization. It is very noble. Indeed it is laudable." Kollarin chuckled. "And then we become men, and we realize that it is all nonsense."

"It is not nonsense!" said Obrin. "We need heroes."

"Of course we do," Kollarin agreed. "The nonsense is that sometimes they are the enemy. What then do we do, Obrin?"

"I'm not a philosopher. I live by my own rules. I steal from no man, and I commit no evil. God will judge me on that when my time comes."

"I am sure that He will judge all of us, my friend. Tell me, what do you think He will think of *us* when young Fell is brought before him? When his body lies broken and blinded on the Citadel rack and his spirit floats up to paradise?"

Obrin was growing more uneasy, yet he did not walk away, though he wanted to. "How should I know?"

"I think you know," said Kollarin sadly.

"What do you want me to say?" stormed Obrin. "That he has been treated unjustly? Yes, he has. That he doesn't deserve to die? No, he doesn't. None of it matters. The Baron is the law, he gave me my orders and it is my duty to obey them. What of you? You took his money, and agreed to hunt down the clansman. Why did you do it?"

Kollarin smiled. "I had my reasons, Obrin. Did you hear about what happened to the woman?"

"It is said they raped her but I find it hard to believe. Will Stamper was not that kind of man. We were friends, I knew him."

"He did it," said Kollarin. "I was in that cell. I read it in the blood. They all did it. And they cut her, and they bit her, and they beat her with fists. And all because she tried to stop the Baron stealing her hawk. Heroic, eh?"

Obrin said nothing for a moment. The light was failing and the campfires cast a gentle glow over the hollow. "I can't change the world," he said sadly. "Fell rescued the woman and I'm glad that he did. Now he has to pay for it, which saddens me. But in my life I've seen a lot of good men die, Kollarin. And a lot of evil men prosper. It is the way of things."

"You'll see worse yet," said Kollarin coldly.

"Like what?"

"The invasion in the spring, when the Baron leads an army to annihilate the Highlanders. You'll see the burning buildings, hear the screams of women and children, watch the crows feast on the bodies of farmers and shepherds."

"That's just a rumor!" snapped Obrin. "And a stupid one at that! There's no one for the army to fight here."

"I am Kollarin the Finder," said the man in green, rising. "And I do not lie either."

Obrin stood and walked down the hill. A soldier offered him a bowl of stew, which he accepted, and for a while he sat with his men, listening to them talk of whores they had known, or lands they had campaigned in. Then he ladled more stew into his bowl and walked to where Fell was tied. The clansman looked up at him, but said nothing.

Obrin squatted down. "I have some food for you," he said, lifting the bowl to Fell's lips. The clansman turned his head away and Obrin laid down the bowl. "I'm sorry, Fell," he said softly. "I like you, man, and I think you did right. I hope to God the woman gets far away from here." The clansman's eyes met his, but no words were spoken by him.

Returning to the fire, Obrin ordered the cooking pots cleaned and stowed, then set sentries for the night. Kollarin was once more sitting by the stream, his green cloak wrapped about his shoulders.

Using his saddle for a pillow, Obrin removed his chain-mail shoulder guard and his breastplate, unbuckled his sword and dagger belt, and settled down to sleep. In all his seventeen years of soldiering sleep had always come easily. In the blazing heat of the Kushir plains, in the harsh, bone-biting cold of the Cleatian mountains, at sea in a gale-tossed ship, Obrin could just close his eyes and will his body to rest. It was, he knew, a vital skill for a veteran. In sleep a man regained his strength and rested his soul. In war a soldier's life depended on his power, speed, and reflexes. There were few second chances for a tired warrior on a battlefield.

But sleep was slow to come tonight.

Obrin lay on his back, staring up at the bright stars and the lantern moon.

He was walking along a narrow trail, beneath an arched tunnel made up of the interlinked branches of colossal trees on both sides of the way. Obrin stopped and glanced back. The tunnel seemed to stretch on forever, dark and gloomy, pierced occasionally by a shaft of moonlight through a gap in the branches.

Obrin walked on. There were no night sounds, no owl calls, no rustling of wind in the leaves. All was silence, save for his soft footfalls on the soft earth. Ahead was a brilliant shaft of moonlight, a beautiful column of light that shone upon a crossroads. Obrin approached it, and saw a warrior sitting on a rock by the wayside. The man was huge, his long white hair gleaming in the moonlight. He wore his beard in two white braids that hung to his silver breastplate. A double-handed claymore was plunged into the earth before him, its hilt a glistening silver, while a huge crimson stone was set into the pommel.

"It is a fine weapon," said Obrin.

The man stood. He towered over Obrin by a good South-land foot. "It has served me well," he said, his voice rich and deep. Obrin looked up into his pale, deep-set eyes. They were the color of a winter storm cloud, grey and cold. Yet Obrin felt no fear.

"Where are we?" he asked.

The tall warrior extended his arm, sweeping it across the three paths that began in the pillar of light. "We are at the crossroads," said the warrior. Obrin's attention was caught by the man's single gauntlet of red iron. It was splendidly crafted, seemingly as supple as leather.

"Who are you?" he asked

"A man who once traveled," answered the warrior. "Many paths, many roads, many trails. I walked the mountains, Obrin, and I rode the Lowlands. Many paths, some crooked, some straight. All were hard."

"The warrior's paths," said Obrin. "Aye, I know them. No hearth, no home, no kin. Only the Way of Iron." Weariness settled upon him and he sat down.

The warrior seated himself beside the Southlander. "And which path do you walk now?" asked the stranger.

"I go where I am sent. What else can a soldier do? Seventeen years I have served the Baron. I have watched friends die, and my boots have collected the dust of many nations. Now I have an aching shoulder and a knee that does not like to march. In three years I can claim my hectare of land.

Maybe I will—if I can still remember how to farm. What of you? Where are you going?"

"Nowhere I haven't been," answered the man. *"I too wanted to farm, and to breed cattle. But I was called upon to right a wrong. It was a small matter. A nobleman and his friends were hunting, and they rode through a field and trampled a child playing there. Her legs were broken badly and the family had no coin to pay for a Wycca man to heal her. I went to the nobleman and asked for justice."*

Obrin sighed. *"I could finish that story for you, man. There's no justice for the poor. Never was, never will be. Did he laugh in your face?"*

The giant shook his head. *"He had me flogged for my impudence."*

"What happened to the girl?"

"She lived. I went back to the nobleman and this time he paid."

"What brought about his change of heart?"

"There was no change of heart. I left his head on a spike, and I burned his home to the ground. It was a grand fire, which burned bright and lit the sky for many a mile. It also lit men's hearts, and that fire burned for thirty years."

"By God, did they not hunt you?"

"Aye. And then I hunted them."

"And you were victorious?"

"Always." The warrior chuckled. *"Until the last day."*

"What happened then?"

Idly the warrior drew his sword from the earth and examined the glistening blade. The ruby shone like fresh blood, the blade gleaming like captured moonlight. *"The war was over. Victory was won. The land was at peace, and free. I thought my enemies were all dead. A dreadful mistake for a warrior. I was riding across my lands, gazing upon High Druin, watching the storm clouds gather there. They surprised me. My horse was killed, but not before the gallant beast got me to the edge of the forest. They came at me in a pack: men I had fought alongside, even promoted. Not friends, you understand, but comrades-in-arms. My heart was wounded each time I killed one of them. The wounds to my body were as nothing to my grief."*

"Why did they turn on you?"

The warrior shrugged, then thrust the sword once more into the earth. *"I was a king, Obrin. And I was arrogant and sure. I treated some of them with disdain. Others I ignored. There were always ten men queuing for every favor I could grant. And I made mistakes. Once I had freed them from the tyranny of the oppressor I became a tyrant in their eyes. Who knows, maybe they were right. I do not judge them."*

"How did you survive alone against so many?"

"I did not."

Obrin was shocked. *"You . . . you are a spirit then?"*

"We both are, Obrin. But you have a body of flesh to which you will return."

"I don't understand. Why am I here?"

"I called you."

"For what purpose?" asked Obrin. *"I am not a king, nor of any worth."*

"Do not be so harsh on yourself, man," said the warrior, laying his iron gauntlet on Obrin's shoulder. *"You have merely lost your way. And now you are at the crossroads. You may choose a new path."*

Obrin gazed around him. All the pathways looked the same, interminable tunnels beneath arched trees. *"What difference does it make?"* he asked. *"They are identical."*

The warrior nodded. *"Aye, that is true. All roads lead to death, Obrin. It is inescapable. Even so, there is a right path."*

Obrin laughed, but the sound was bitter and harsh. *"How would I know it?"*

"If you cannot recognize it, then you must find a man already upon it and follow him. You will know, Obrin. Let the heart-light shine. It will light the way."

* * *

Obrin awoke with a start. The dawn light was streaking the sky, though the stars had not yet faded. His thoughts were muddled and his mouth felt as if he'd swallowed a badger. With a groan he sat up. His right shoulder ached abominably. Rising from his blankets, he walked to a nearby tree and emptied his bladder. Everyone else was still asleep, including the prisoner. Obrin hawked and spat, then stretched his right arm over his head, seeking to ease the ache.

The hill sentry walked down and saluted. "Nothing to report from the watch, Sergeant," he said, "but there are riders to the south."

"Clansmen?" This was unlikely, for there were few horses in the mountains.

"No, sir. Soldiers from Citadel, I think. Too far away to be sure."

"Get a breakfast fire going," ordered Obrin. Moving to the stream, he stripped to the waist and washed in the cold water, splashing it over his face and hair. Kollarin joined him.

"Sleep well, Sergeant?"

"I always sleep well."

"No dreams?"

Obrin cupped some water into his hands and drank noisily. There was an edge to the man's voice, like a plea of some kind. Obrin looked at him. "Yes, I dreamed," he said. "You?"

Kollarin nodded. "Did it make sense to you?"

"Are dreams supposed to make sense?"

Kollarin moved in close, his voice dropping to a whisper. "He has come to me before—back in Citadel when I was hunting the woman. He told me to leave her be. That is why I only agreed to hunt down the man. Do you know who he is?"

"I thought you only read minds for coin," Obrin reminded him. The sergeant stood and shivered as the cold morning breeze touched his wet skin. Hastily he donned his shirt, then returned to his blankets and put on his armor. Kollarin remained by the stream.

A soldier with a swollen nose approached Obrin. "All quiet in the night," he said, his voice thick and nasal.

"How's the nose, Bakker?"

"Hurts like hell. I was tempted to cut the bastard's throat last night, but I reckon I'll just get myself dungeon duty and watch the torturer at work on him."

"We ride in one hour," said Obrin.

They breakfasted on porridge and black bread, but the prisoner steadfastly refused the food Obrin brought to him. With the meal finished, the cooking pots cleaned and stowed, Obrin's men prepared for the journey back to Citadel.

"Riders coming!" shouted one of the men. Obrin wandered to the edge of the hollow and waited as the ten-man section rode in. They were led by Lieutenant Masrick. Obrin saluted as the man dismounted.

"I see you caught him," said the officer, ignoring the salute. "About time, Sergeant. Has he told you where the girl is?"

"No, sir. I was ordered to bring him back, not interrogate him."

Masrick swung to Bakker, who was just about to douse the breakfast fire. "You there! Keep that fire going." Slipping his dagger from its sheath, he tossed it to Bakker. "Heat the point. I want it glowing red."

Masrick strode to where Fell was tied, then aimed a savage kick into the prisoner's belly, doubling him over. "That," said the officer, "is for nothing at all. What follows will, however, have value. Are you listening, clansman?"

Fell raised his head and met the officer's stare. He said nothing. Masrick knelt before him and punched him full in the face. Fell's head snapped back, cannoning against the tree trunk. "You killed a cousin of mine. He was a wretch, but he owed me money. That was bad. But it will be worth much more to me to find the woman and bring her back to the Baron. I think you'll help me. All you clansmen think you are tough. But trust me, when I have burned out your left eye you'll do anything to save the sight in the other."

The soldiers had gathered around the scene in a sweeping half circle. Obrin gazed at their faces. They were eager for the entertainment. Kollarin was standing back from them, his expression impossible to read. Bakker brought the heated knife to the officer; the hilt was wrapped in a rag, the point hissing as Masrick took it.

"Lieutenant!" Obrin's voice barked out. Masrick was startled and he almost dropped the knife.

"What? Make it quick, man, the knife is cooling!"

"Leave him be!"

Masrick ignored him and knelt before Fell, the knife moving toward the forester's eyes. Obrin's foot rose and slammed into the officer's face, spinning him to the ground. There was a gasp from the soldiers. Masrick rolled to his knees, then screamed as his hand pressed down on the red-hot blade that was smoldering in the grass. He surged to his feet, his face crimson. "By God, you'll pay for that!"

"I am an acting captain," said Obrin, "promoted by the Baron himself. You are a lieutenant who just disobeyed an order from a *superior* officer. Where does that leave you, you jumped-up toad?"

"You have lost your mind," sneered Masrick, "and I will see you hang for your impertinence. No common man may strike a nobleman, be the common man a captain or a general. That kick is going to cost you dear!"

"Ah, well," said Obrin with a broad smile, "may as well be hung for a sheep as a lamb!" So saying, he took a step forward and slammed his fist into the officer's mouth, catapulting the man from his feet. Drawing his dagger, he moved in for the kill.

Something struck him a wicked blow on the skull and he staggered, half turning. He saw Bakker raise his arm, then the cudgel struck his temple and he fell into darkness.

When he awoke he found himself tied to his saddle. Masrick was leading the column and they were approaching a small castle. Fell was walking beside Obrin's mount, his hands tied behind him and a rope around his neck. The other end of the rope was being held by the rider in front.

"You really did it this time, Sergeant," said a voice from his left. Obrin turned in the saddle to see, riding alongside him, Bakker. "Now they're going to hang you! Not before time, if you ask me. You always was a right pain in the groin. Never liked you."

Obrin ignored him.

The castle gates loomed ahead.

Chapter Seven

Asmidir had never enjoyed great talent as a magicker. Though his powers of concentration were great, and his imagination powerful, he had always lacked what his tutors termed *ability of release*. Magick, he was told, involved the user surrendering control and merging his mind with the powers hovering beyond what the five senses could experience. For all his talent Asmidir had never been able to fully *release*. Now he sat in the main hall, a huge leather-bound book open on his lap. The script was in gold, carefully set upon bleached leather; it was an ancient Kushir script and he read it with difficulty.

Closing the book, he stood and moved to the long, oval table. Upon it was a golden dish, set on a stand above three small candles. Asmidir drew his dagger and began to speak. His eyes were closed, his spirit loose within the cage of his powerful body as his breathing deepened. The dagger blade cut into his forearm and blood welled, dripping into the heated dish where it sizzled and steamed. Asmidir's voice faded away. Opening his eyes, he took a deep, shuddering breath. It was done. Not brilliantly, not even expertly. Let it at least be adequate, he thought. Returning the dagger to its sheath he pressed his thumb against the shallow wound on his arm, applying pressure for some minutes. A dark-skinned servant stepped forward with a long linen bandage. Asmidir extended his arm, and the man skillfully applied it.

"Bring the officer here to me, Ari," he told the servant.

"Also the man in green. You have prepared the refreshment I ordered for the soldiers?"

"Yes, lord. As you commanded."

The servant took the bowl and departed the room. Asmidir returned to the log fire and settled himself into an armchair. He heard the sounds of hoofbeats on stone, and felt the cold blast of air as the main doors of the castle were pulled open to admit the soldiers.

Rising from his chair, he turned toward the door just as the potbellied Lieutenant Masrick strode into sight with Kollarin the Finder behind him. Masrick's face was discolored, his lips thickened and split.

"Good day to you," said Asmidir, stepping forward with an outstretched hand. "It is good to see you again, Masrick." The officer responded with a perfunctory handshake. A servant appeared. "Fetch wine for our guests, Ari." Masrick removed his iron helm and carelessly dropped it upon the highly polished table.

"The Baron wants to see you," said Masrick. "You are to return with us to Citadel."

"I think you mean that the Baron has *requested* my presence," said Asmidir coolly.

"No, I said what I meant. He told me to bring you, and that's what I'll do." Masrick lifted a hand to his smashed lips, probing them. "I have two prisoners with me. Does this place still boast a dungeon?"

"No," Asmidir told him. He swung to Kollarin. "And you must be the Finder," he said, forcing a smile. "I take it from the fact that you have prisoners that you have been successful."

"Yes," said Kollarin. He moved to the hearth and reached out to touch the leather-bound book on the small table. Idly the man in green flipped open the cover. "Ah, a Kushir grimoire. A long time since I have seen such a work. The scripting is very fine—resin dusted with gold and then varnished. Exquisite!"

"You read Kushir?" asked Asmidir, holding his expression to one of mild interest, while his heart beat against his ribs like a drum of war.

"I read all known languages," said Kollarin. "I do not wish it to sound like a boast, since it is a Talent I have possessed all my life, and not the result of dedicated study."

The servant, Ari, returned with a flagon of wine and two goblets. Masrick accepted his without a word of thanks. Kollarin smiled at Ari and gave a short bow of the head. "Not drinking with us, Asmidir?" Masrick asked.

"No." Turning back to Kollarin, he asked, "What will you do now that your hunt has been successful?"

"Successful?" queried Kollarin.

"Two prisoners. I understood you were hunting for a man and a woman."

"We haven't caught the woman yet," said Masrick, cutting in, "but we will. We have the forester, Fell. The other prisoner is a renegade. He struck me! Loosened several teeth. By God, he'll pay for it when I get him back to Citadel."

"It does look sore," agreed Asmidir. "Ari, fetch some of the *special* camomile ointment for this gentleman." As the servant departed Asmidir seated himself before the fire, trying not to look at Kollarin as the man slowly turned the pages of the grimoire. "So," he said to Masrick, "why does the Baron request my presence so urgently?"

"That's for him to tell you," muttered Masrick. "Now where can I lodge these prisoners? Do you have no rooms with locks?"

"Sadly, no. I suggest you bring them in here. Then at least you can watch until you leave."

"Until *we* leave," corrected Masrick.

Asmidir rose and approached the officer. The black man was at least a foot taller. "At the moment, my dear Masrick, I am putting aside your bad manners on the grounds that the blow to your face, and the subsequent pain, has made you forget your breeding. Understand, however, that my patience is not limitless. Try to remember that you are an insignificant second cousin to the Baron, whereas I am a friend to the King. Now get out and fetch your prisoners. I wish to speak with the Finder."

Masrick's mouth dropped open, and his eyes narrowed. Asmidir read the fury there. The black man leaned in close. "Think carefully before you react, moron. It is considered deeply unlucky to be struck twice in the face on the same day." Masrick swallowed hard and backed away. Asmidir swung away from him and crossed the room to where Kollarin waited. For a moment only Masrick hesitated, then he marched from the hall.

"You did not need the cloak spell," said Kollarin softly. "I refused to hunt the woman."

"Very wise," Asmidir told him, keeping his voice low. "When you return to Citadel town I will see that one hundred silver pieces are delivered to you."

"Very kind." Kollarin's green eyes held Asmidir's gaze. "But I shall not be returning to Citadel."

"Neither shall I," said Asmidir with a wry smile.

Masrick returned to the hall and two soldiers led in the prisoners, ordering them to sit by the far wall. The officer marched up to Asmidir. "I fear you were right, Lord Asmidir," said Masrick. "The events of the day shortened my temper. I ask your forgiveness for my . . . abrupt manner." The anger was still present in his eyes, but Asmidir merely smiled.

"We will say no more about it, my dear Masrick. Are your men being fed?"

"Yes. Thank you. How soon will you be ready to leave?"

Asmidir did not answer, but strolled across the hall and stood before the prisoners. "I know you," he said, addressing Obrin. "You were in the fist-fighting tourney last winter. You lost in the final—stumbled and went down with an overhand right."

"You have a good memory for faces," Obrin told him.

"Now if I'd managed to hit the Cleatian with the same power that I used on goat face there, I would have won."

Masrick ran forward and aimed a savage kick that thundered against Obrin's shoulder. "Be silent, wretch!" he shouted.

"Even kicks like a goat," sneered Obrin.

Masrick drew his dagger. "I'll cut your bastard tongue out!" he threatened.

Asmidir laid his hand on the officer's arm. "Not here, my friend," he said. "The rugs were expensive, shipped all the way from Kushir."

As Obrin's laughter sounded, Masrick paled, and his hand trembled. But he slammed the dagger back in its scabbard.

The servant returned, carrying a small enameled pot. As he paused beside Masrick and bowed, the officer looked at the tall servant. "Well, what do you want?"

Ari held out the pot. "What is this?" Masrick asked Asmidir.

"A healing ointment. Apply it to the lips and you will see."

Masrick took the pot and removed the lid. The ointment was cream-colored. Dabbing a finger to it, he spread some on his injury. "That is good," he said. "Soothing! Where did you obtain it?"

"My servants are all *Al-jiin*," said Asmidir. "They are very skilled with potions."

Kollarin was only half listening to the exchange, but the words *Al-jiin* cut through him like a sword of ice. Standing beside the hearth he stiffened, his green eyes flicking to Ari. The man was tall and slender, his skin the color of age-polished oak; he had a prominent nose, not negroid like Asmidir, but curved and aquiline. In that moment Kollarin wondered how he could ever have been convinced the man was a servant. He glanced at his wine goblet. It was still almost full. How much had he drunk? One mouthful? Two?

Ari turned slowly, his deep dark stare pinning Kollarin.

The servant seemed to glide across the room. "Are you well, lord?" asked Ari. "You are looking pale."

"I am well at this moment," said Kollarin. Reaching out with his Talent, he touched the other man's mind . . . and recoiled as if he had thrust his hand into a fire.

"Perhaps you should sit down, lord," offered Ari.

"Am I to die here?" pulsed Kollarin.

"If my lord wills it so," came the response. "If you will excuse me," he said aloud, "I have duties to attend to."

"By all means," said Kollarin. Ari turned and left the hall and once more Kollarin reached out, seeking not the mind of the servant but choosing instead the soldiers who were waiting outside. He pictured the solid cavalryman, Klebb.

Nothing. One by one he sought out the others.

Still nothing. Were their thoughts being shielded? he wondered.

Sitting by the fire he closed his eyes and dropped his spirit to the second level, opening his mind to more general astral emanations. He felt the castle and its great age, and beyond it the forest and the heartbeat of eternity.

From here it was a simple matter to find the third level. Kollarin gasped. Moving through the castle he could see the restless, disembodied shapes of lost spirits, murdered men who did not yet know they had died.

His eyes snapped open.

All dead. Twenty-eight soldiers, drugged and then strangled. All that remained were the two guards in the room, and Masrick himself. Kollarin's mouth was dry and he reached out for his wine. *What are you doing, fool?* Leaving the goblet where it stood, he rose and rubbed his hand across his mouth. Am I under sentence? he wondered.

Asmidir crossed the hall. "You seem preoccupied, my boy," he said.

Kollarin looked up into the black man's face, seeing the power there, and the cruelty. "Your *Al-jiin* have completed their work," he said softly. "Where does that leave me?"

"Where would you like to be left?" Asmidir asked.

"Alive would be pleasant."

"What are you two whispering about?" asked Masrick, picking up Kollarin's goblet and draining it. He belched and then sat down.

"We were talking about life and death, Masrick," said Asmidir, "and the slender thread that separates both."

"Nothing slender about it," said the officer. "It is all a question of skill and courage."

"What about luck?" asked Asmidir. "Being in the wrong place at the wrong time?"

"A man makes his own luck," replied Masrick.

"I'm not sure that's true," said Asmidir. "But let us put it to the test. Would it be lucky or unlucky were you to find the woman, Sigarni?"

"Lucky, of course," answered Masrick. "You know where she is?"

"Indeed I do." Asmidir clapped his hands twice. A line of warriors filed silently into the room; tall men in black cloaks and helms, all carrying sabers of shining steel. They wore black mail-shirts that extended to their thighs, and black boots reinforced with strips of black steel. Across their chests each wore a thick leather baldric, complete with three throwing knives in jet-black sheaths. Kollarin moved back against the wall as the warriors fanned out. He recognized the servant Ari, though the man now looked like a prince of legend.

Masrick was also watching them. "What is the meaning of this?" he asked.

Asmidir chuckled and without turning his head he gave an order. "Kill the guards," he said, his voice even, almost regretful.

Kollarin watched as if in a dream. Two of the black-garbed warriors drew throwing knives from their sheaths and slowly turned. One of the guards, a man with a bruised and swollen nose, frantically tried to draw his sword; a knife hilt appeared in his throat and he sank back against the wall. The second guard turned to run; a black knife slashed through the air taking him in the back of the neck and he fell forward, his face striking the edge of the table; the blow dislodged his helm which rolled across the tabletop. The two dark-skinned warriors retrieved their blades and returned to stand in line with their comrades.

Masrick's face was ashen. Kollarin almost felt pity for the man. "Ari," said Asmidir softly, "is our guest ready to join us?"

"Yes, lord." Ari departed the hall and a terrible silence followed. Masrick was sweating now and Kollarin saw that the little man's hands were trembling. Despite his armor he looked nothing like a soldier.

"I . . . I . . . don't want to die, Asmidir," he whimpered, tears spilling to his cheeks. The black man ignored him. "Please don't kill me!" The hall door opened and Ari returned. Behind him came another warrior and Kollarin's breath caught in his throat. She was tall and slender, her hair silver-white like the chain-mail tunic she wore. Thigh-length and split at the sides, the links gleamed like jewels. Her long legs were encased in glistening black leggings, delicately reinforced by more silver chain links around the upper legs, and a crimson cloak hung from her shoulders. Kollarin had never seen a more beautiful woman. As she entered all the warriors, including Asmidir, bowed deeply. Kollarin followed their lead.

Masrick tried to stand, pushing his arms against the sides of the chair, but his legs would not move. He slumped back, then a convulsion jerked his body in several spasms. Asmidir leaned over him. "Your hunt was successful, Masrick. You are in the presence of Sigarni. Die happy!"

Spittle frothed at Masrick's lips and his eyes bulged. Then he was still, the open eyes staring unfocused at the man before him. The silver-armored woman approached the chair and stared down at the dead man. "Did he die of fright?" she asked Asmidir.

"No. He smeared poison upon his lips."

The woman looked at Kollarin, who bowed once more. "Why does this one live?"

"In truth I am not sure," said Asmidir. "He refused to hunt you, and I do not know why. He is the Finder, Kollarin. Do you wish him slain?"

Kollarin waited, his green eyes watching the woman's face. "Why did you refuse?" she asked him.

"That is not easy to answer, lady," he told her, surprised that his voice remained steady. "A man appeared to me and asked me to spare you."

"Describe him."

"The face was powerful, deep-set blue eyes. His hair was silver-white, like yours, and he wore his beard in two braids."

She nodded, then swung to Asmidir. "Let him live," she said.

The black man was about to speak, yet held his silence. Stepping back, he allowed Sigarni to dominate the center of the room. Her armor he had brought with him from Kushir, intended as a gift for the warrior king the seer had spoken of. Asmidir had always pictured it upon the muscular form of a young man. Yet now, as he gazed upon her martial beauty, he could scarce believe he had not purchased it with Sigarni in mind. Everything about her was regal, and he wondered how he had failed to notice it before.

His *Al-jiin* had cut the two prisoners free and both men were now standing and staring at the warrior woman. Fell bowed his head. Sigarni's eyes were fixed on the Outlander in the uniform of a soldier. Her hand closed around the hilt of her dagger, the blade whispering from its scabbard as she moved toward the man with deceptive grace. Only Fell recognized her intent. "No, Sigarni," he said, stepping in front of the soldier. "This man saved me from torture at the risk of his own life."

"No Outlander will live," she said softly, almost without anger. "Stand aside, Fell."

"I claim the *Cormaach* on this man," he said. Asmidir was puzzled, and he watched Sigarni's reaction carefully. She stood silently for a moment, then gave a cold smile.

"You would do this for an enemy?" she asked.

"I do. I sat with my arms bound and a glowing red-hot knife was before my eyes. Obrin stopped the officer, and struck him into the bargain. They were taking him back for torture and death. It would seem poor gratitude indeed if I stood by while he was casually slain. I ask for his life, Sigarni."

"Stand aside, Fell, I would speak with this man." Fell hesitated, for the dagger was still in her hand. For a moment only he failed to move, then he stepped back. Asmidir watched the soldier, Obrin. There was no sign of fear in the man.

"Are you aware," asked Sigarni, "of what has been said here? Do you understand the meaning of *Cormaach*?"

"I know nothing of your barbarian ways, madam," said Obrin. "I'm just a soldier, see. Untutored, you might say. So why don't you tell me?"

Asmidir could see Sigarni fighting for calm as she gazed upon this man in the hated uniform of those who had so brutally assaulted her. She'll kill him, he thought. She'll step in close and at his first wrong word ram the knife into his throat.

"He has offered to adopt you—to make you his son. How old are you?"

"Thirty-seven, by my own reckoning. I might be out by a year or two."

"So, your new father is some fifteen years younger than you. You wish to be adopted, Outlander?"

"Is there a choice?" he asked.

"There are always choices," she said, moving in close. "You saved Fell, therefore I am in your debt. You may leave here and make your way wherever you choose. I would like to kill you, Outlander. I would like to see the blood gush from your neck. But my word is iron. Leave now and no one will harm you."

"What's the other alternative?"

"You are not man enough for it!" she snapped. "Leave before my patience is exhausted."

"Become a clansman, is that it? A rebel against the Baron, and the King?" Obrin laughed, the sound rich and merry. "So that's what he meant, is it? This is the crossroads." He swung to Fell. "Adopted me, did you, boy? Well, by God, you could have done worse. I'll walk your road—even though we all know where it will lead. So what do I do, lady? To whom do I pledge my sword?"

Sigarni was too surprised to answer, and Asmidir stepped forward swiftly. He spoke in Kushir and the twelve *Al-jiin* all dropped to their knees around the silver-armored woman. "You are in the presence," he told Obrin, "of the Lady Sigarni, War Chief of the clans. It is to her you pledge your loyalty."

Obrin dropped to one knee before her, then lifted his hand to guide her dagger to his throat. With the point resting against his skin he spoke. "This day I become your carle, lady. I will live for you, and when the day comes I will die for you. This is the promise of Obrin, son of Engist, and sworn before God."

Sigarni was silent, then looked to Fell, who still stood. As their eyes met, the tall forester dropped to his knees, "My life is yours, Sigarni," he said, "now and forever."

Sigarni nodded, then approached Asmidir. "We need to speak," she said, and walked from the room. Asmidir followed her.

Obrin and Fell rose together. "Thank you, lad," said the soldier. "You'll not regret it."

"I believe that," Fell told him. "But will you? How will you feel when your countrymen face you sword to sword? It is no small matter."

Obrin shook his head. "Put your mind at rest, Fell. To you we are all Outlanders, yet we come from many parts of the realm. My people were mountain folk, conquered a hundred years ago. And I am the only one from my tribe at Citadel. Even that, though, misses the point. There are some things a man *must* fight for. That, I believe, is what Kollarin was trying to tell me. Is that not so?" he asked the man in green.

"Indeed it was," said Kollarin, crossing the room and stepping over the corpses of the soldiers. "I always wondered what it would be like to be a hero."

Behind them the twelve silent *Al-jiin* gathered up the bodies and left the hall.

Sigarni felt gripped by a sense of unreality as she climbed the carpeted steps to the upper balcony, and the room where Ari had shown her the armor. Beside her Asmidir said nothing as they walked. The room was small, fifteen feet by twenty, with one large window looking out over High Druin. Sigarni had donned the silver chain-mail topcoat, the armored leggings and the boots, but the sword, breastplate, and helm remained. The breastplate had been sculpted to resemble the athletic chest and belly of a young warrior, while the helm was too large for the silver-haired woman.

Sigarni walked to the window, pushing it open to allow the cool, yet gentle autumn breeze to whisper into the room. Abby was dead, and this she found almost as hurtful as the abuse she had endured. But more than this Sigarni felt a weight of sorrow for the life she would never know again, the quiet solitude of her mountain cabin, the morning hunt, and the silent nights. Grame had warned her of the Baron, and she wished now that she had heeded him. A few pennies lost and her life would have remained free. Now she was embarked on a course that could lead only to death and ruin for the people of the mountains. What are we? she thought. And the picture came to her mind of a mighty stag at bay in the Highlands, with the wolves closing in. We can run and live for a little longer, or we can fight and be dragged down.

Clouds were gathering above High Druin like a crown of grey above the white snowcapped peaks.

"Speak your thoughts, my lady," said Asmidir.

"You don't need to give me pretty titles here," she told him, still staring from the window. "There is no one to hear them."

"It has begun, Sigarni," he said softly. "It is time to make plans."

"I know. What do you suggest?"

He shook his head. "I will offer my advice in a moment," he told her. "First I would like to hear your views."

Anger almost swamped her, but she fought it back. "You are the warrior and the strategist—or so you tell me. What would you have me say, Asmidir?"

"Do not misunderstand me, Sigarni. This is not a game we are playing. You are the one the seer spoke of. Unless the gods are capricious—and perhaps they are—then you must have some special skill. If we are to form an army, if we are to defy the most brilliant military nation of the world, it will be because of *you*—you understand? At the moment you are full of bitterness and righteous rage. You must conquer that, you must reach inside yourself and find the Battle Queen. Without her we are lost even before we begin."

Sigarni turned from the window and moved to a high-backed chair. "I don't know what to say or where to begin," she said. "If there is a skill it is lost to me. I do not believe I am given to panic, Asmidir, but when I try to think of the way ahead my heart beats faster and I find myself short of breath. I look inside, but there is nothing there save regret and remembered pain."

Asmidir seated himself before her. He reached out, but she instinctively drew back her hand; his face showed his hurt.

"Let us examine then the immediate priorities," he said. "My men have been scouting the valleys and passes south of here. The Baron has ordered campaign fortifications built. These are vital for an invading army. Stores and supplies will be left at these forts so that when the invasion force moves in they will have bases from which to sally forth into the mountains. The first is being constructed no more than ten miles from here, in the Dunach Valley. It could be argued that our first task should be to halt their work, to harry them. For that we will need men. We have already discussed where to find warriors. You must seek the aid of the Pallides Hunt Lord, Fyon Sharp-axe."

Sigarni rose and returned to the window. Sunlight shone brilliantly through gaps in the distant storm clouds, and the muted sound of far-off thunder rippled across the land. She shivered. "No," she said at last. "The fortifications must wait. If I were Fyon Sharp-axe I would not turn over my men to an untried woman from another clan. Send Fell to me."

"What are you planning?" he asked.

"We will discuss it later," she told him. Asmidir smiled and rose, bowing deeply. After he had gone Sigarni drew the sword from its silver scabbard. It was a saber, thirty inches long, the blade highly polished and razor-sharp, the hilt bound with strips of dark grey speckled skin, reinforced by silver wire. It was surprisingly light in her hand, and perfectly balanced. She swung the sword to the left. It sliced through the air, creating a low hissing sound. Hearing Fell approach she moved to the chair, laying the naked blade upon the table before her. The forester entered and bowed clumsily.

"A surprising turn of events," she said. He grinned and nodded. His face was bruised and swollen, but as he smiled she saw again the handsome clansman she had loved. Motioning him to a seat she looked away, gathering her thoughts. "How many of the foresters could you gather to us?" she asked.

"Not many," he said. "Perhaps six of the fifty. You have to understand, Sigarni, that they are men of family. They know a war against the Outlanders can end only one way. Most would therefore do anything to avoid such a war. Even after the murders."

"What murders?"

Fell told her of the taking of hostages, and his decision to give himself up to the authorities. "But they did not wait the promised four days. By the following morning all four were hanging from the walls of Citadel. I believe Tovi and Grame would join us, and perhaps half of the men of Cilfallen. What are you planning?"

"I want you to go from here. Now. Find the six men, and any others you trust. We will meet at my cabin in four days. Is that enough time for you?"

"Barely. But I will be there."

"Go now," she ordered him. "And send the Outlander to me."

Gwalchmai lifted his jug from the dog cart and stared out over the hills toward Citadel town. The two hounds, Shamol and Cabris, were asleep in the sunshine. Gwalch pulled the cork from the jug and sat beside Tovi. The baker was silent, lost in thought. The sun was bright in a clear sky, the mountains shining in splendor, but Tovi was oblivious to the beauty and Gwalchmai felt for him. "Your son was a fine boy," said Gwalch, lifting the jug to his lips and taking three long swallows.

"You didn't know him," said Tovi tonelessly.

"I know you. And I can see him in your mind. You were proud of him—and rightly so."

"None of that matters now, does it? His mother weeps all the time, and his brothers and sisters walk silently around the house. What manner of men are these, Gwalch, who could hang an innocent boy? Are they monsters? Demon-driven?"

The old man shook his head. "All it takes is a monster in

charge, Tovi. Like a pinch of poison in a jug of wine. Suddenly the wine is deadly. You want a drink?"

"No, I need to keep my eyes sharp for when the devils come. You know, I can't even hate them, Gwal. I feel nothing. Is that my age, do you think? Have I lost something during these years in the bakery?"

"We've all lost something, my friend. Maybe we'll find it again." Gwalch lifted the jug to his lips—then paused. He pointed to the south. "There! What do you see? My old eyes have dimmed."

Tovi squinted. "Flashes of sunlight upon metal. The enemy are coming. It will take them at least an hour to cross the valley floor."

"How many?"

"They are too far away to count accurately. Go back to Cilfallen and tell them the Outlanders are coming."

"What about you?" asked Gwalch, pushing himself to his feet. Behind him the grey hounds rose also.

"I'll wait awhile and count them. Then I'll join you." Gwalch climbed into the cart, still nursing his jug. He flicked the reins and the two war hounds lurched into the traces. Tovi watched as the little cart trundled out of view, then he stood and stretched. His thoughts flicked to the Pallides man, Loran, and his warnings concerning the Outlanders. He had hoped the clansman was wrong, but now he knew otherwise. A few weeks ago the world had been a calm and pleasant place, filled with the smell of fresh-baked bread and the laughter and noise of his children. Now the days of blood had dawned again.

Stooping, he picked up the old claymore and stood facing the south, his hands upon the hilt, the blade resting on the earth. It was a fine weapon, and had served him well all those years ago. Yet holding it now gave him no pleasure, no surging sense of pride. All he could feel was sorrow.

The line of riders came down the long hill into the valley. Now he could count them. One hundred and fifty men and five officers. Too large a group to have come for hostages. No, he told himself, this is a killing raid. One hundred and fifty-five soldiers for a village of forty-seven men, thirty-eight women, and fifty-one children! As he thought of the little ones a spark of anger burned through his grief, flaming to life in his breast. His huge hands curled around the claymore, the blade flashing up. Once he could have taken three, maybe four enemy soldiers. Today he would find out how much he had lost.

Turning his back upon the distant enemy, Tovi laid the claymore blade on his shoulder and strode down the long road to home. He was high above Cilfallen and from here the buildings seemed tiny set against the green hills and the mighty mountains. Newer dwellings of stone alongside the older timbered houses, and ancient log cabins with roofs of turf, all clustered together in a friendly harmony of wood and stone. Aye, thought Tovi, that is the mark of Cilfallen. The village is friendly and welcoming. There were no walls, for up to now the people had lived without fear.

Cilfallen was indefensible. Tovi sighed, and paused for one last look at the village he had known all his life.

Never will you look the same to me again, he knew. For now I can see the lack of walls and parapets. I see hills from which cavalry can charge into our square. I see buildings with no strong doors, or bowmen's windows. There is no moat. Only the stream, and the white rocks upon which the women and children beat the clothes to wash them.

Tovi walked on, aware also of his own weakness, the large belly fed with too much fresh bread and country butter, and a right arm already tired from holding the claymore.

"I'll find the strength," he said aloud.

Captain Chard led his men down into the valley, riding slowly, stiff-backed in the saddle. Despite the honey salve on his back the whip wounds flared as if being constantly stung by angry wasps. The weight of his chain mail added tongues of flame to his shoulders, and his mood was foul. He knew that if Obrin had followed the Baron's orders with more relish he would not now be alive, for the three-pronged whip could kill a man within thirty lashes if delivered with venom. Obrin had been sparing with his strokes, but each of the whip-heads had a tiny piece of lead attached, adding weight to each lash, scoring the skin, opening the flesh. Chard felt sick as he remembered standing at the stake, biting into the leather belt, determined not to scream. But scream he did, until he passed out on the thirty-fourth stroke.

A mixture of honey and wine had been applied to his blood-drenched back. Three of the deeper cuts had needed stitches, twenty-two in all. Yet here he was, within a fortnight, sitting his saddle and leading his men.

He did not question the Baron's change of heart, and had accepted the commission with a burbled speech of gratitude that the Baron had cut short. "Do not fail me again, Chard," he had warned. "How many men will you need?"

"Three hundred, sir."

The Baron had laughed at him. "For a village? Why not take a thousand?"

"There are nearly two hundred of them, sir!"

The Baron had lifted a sheet of paper. "One hundred and fifty, approximately. Fifty of them are children under the age of twelve. Around forty are women. The remainder are men. Farmers, cattle herders—not a good sword among them. Take one hundred and fifty men. No prisoners, Chard. Hang all the bodies so they can be clearly seen. Burn the buildings."

"Yes, sir. When you say no prisoners . . . you mean the men?"

"Kill them *all*. I have chosen the men you will have with you. They are mercenaries, scum mostly. They'll have no problem with the task. When they're finished let them loot. They will also—most certainly—keep some of the younger women alive for a while. Let them have their enjoyment, it's good for morale." The Baron's cold eyes fixed on Chard. "You have a problem with this?"

Chard wished he had the courage to tell the man just how much a problem he had with butchery. Instead he had swallowed hard and mumbled, "No, sir."

"How is your back?"

"Healing, sir."

"You won't fail me again, will you, Chard?"

"No, sir."

The sun was high and sweat trickled down onto the whip wounds. Chard groaned. An officer rode alongside as they reached the valley floor.

"Beyond that line of hills, isn't it?" the man asked and Chard turned his head. The officer was thin-faced, with protruding eyes, his face marred by the scars of smallpox. Several white-headed pimples showed around his nostrils and a boil was beginning on the nape of his neck. "Many women there?" asked the officer as Chard ignored the first question.

"Set the men in a skirmish line," Chard ordered.

"What for? It's only a pigging village. There's no fighting men likely to ambush us."

"Give the order," said Chard.

"Whatever you say," answered the officer, with a thinly disguised sneer. Twisting in the saddle, he called out to the men, "Every second man left skirmish. All others to the right!" He swung back to Chard. "You have orders for the attack?"

"How many ways are there to attack a helpless village?"

"Depends if they know they're going to be attacked. If they don't, you just ride in and get the headman to call all the people together. When they're all in one place you slaughter 'em. If they do know, then they'll all be locked in their houses, or running for the woods. Lots of different ways, on foot, in a charge. It's up to you."

"Attacked many villages, have you?"

"Too many to count. It's good practice. I'll tell you, you

can learn a lot about your men by the way they conduct themselves in a situation like this. Not everyone can do it, you know. We had a young lad once, fearless and damn good with a sword or lance. But this sort of mission, useless. Blubbed like a baby . . . ran around witlessly. Know what happened? Some young kid ran at him and slashed his throat open with a scythe. It was a damn shame. That boy had potential, you know?"

"Send a scout up to the high ground. He'll see the village from there."

The officer wheeled his horse and rode to the left. A young mercenary kicked his horse into a run and Chard watched him climb the hill and rein in at the top. The soldier waved them on.

Chard led the men up the hill. The officer came alongside and the two men stared down at the cluster of buildings. A narrow stream cut across the south of Cilfallen, and there were two small bridges. Chard examined the line of water; the horses could cross it with ease. Beyond the stream was a low retaining wall, around two feet high and some thirty feet in length. Beyond that were the homes he had been sent to destroy. As he watched a young woman walked from one of the buildings; she was carrying a wicker basket full of clothes, and she knelt at the stream and began to wash them. Chard sighed, then he spoke. "Send fifty men around the village to the north to cut them off from the hills. The rest of us will attack from the south."

The officer gave out his orders and two troops filed off to the northeast. Then he leaned across his saddle. "Listen, Chard, I'd advise you to wait here. From what I hear your back's in a mess, so you won't be able to fight. And I guess you won't want any . . . pleasures. So leave it to me and my men. You agree?"

Chard longed to agree. Instead he shook his head. "I will ride in with the attack," he said. "When it is over I will leave you to your . . . pleasures."

"Only trying to be helpful," said the officer with a wide grin.

They waited until the fifty horsemen had reached their position to the north of the village, then Chard drew his sword. "Give the order," he told the officer.

"No prisoners!" shouted the man. "And all the looting to be left until the job is done! Forward!"

Chard wondered briefly if God would ever forgive him for this day, then touched spurs to his mount. The beast leaped forward. The soldiers around him drew their weapons and charged. The men were lighter armored than he, wearing leather breastplates and no helms, and the mercenaries soon outpaced him, forming three attacking lines.

Chard was some fifteen lengths behind the last man when the first line of mercenaries reached the stream. The woman there dropped her washing and, lifting her heavy skirts, ran back toward the buildings. The raucous cries of the mercenaries filled the air and then the horses galloped into the water, sending up glittering fountains that caught the sunlight and shone like diamonds.

The first line had reached the middle of the stream when disaster struck. Horses whinnied in fear and pain as they fell headlong, tipping their riders over their necks. For a moment only Chard was stunned.

Trip wire! Staked beneath the waterline. My God, they were ready for us!

The riders of the second line dragged on their reins, but they collided with their downed comrades in a confused mass. Chard pulled up his mount. Experienced in battle, he knew that the trip wire was only the beginning. Swiftly he scanned the buildings. There was no sign of a defensive force . . .

And then they were there!

Rising up from behind the low retaining wall, a score of bowmen sent volley after volley of shafts into the milling men. Wounded mercenaries began to scream and run, but long shafts slashed into them, slicing through their pitiful armor.

"Dismount!" shouted Chard. "Attack on foot!"

Scum though they were, the mercenaries were not afraid to fight. Leaping from their horses they rushed the bowmen, who stood their ground some thirty feet beyond the stream. More than twenty mercenaries went down, but Chard was confident that once hand-to-hand fighting began they would be swept aside by weight of numbers.

Urging his horse to the edge of the stream, he shouted encouragement to his men.

From behind the buildings came a surging mass of fighting men, armed with claymores, scythes, spears, and hammers—and women carrying knives and hatchets. They smote the mercenaries' left flank. Chard saw the baker, Fat Tovi, slash his claymore through the shoulder and chest of a mercenary, and then the white-bearded smith, Grame, grabbed the pox-marked officer by the throat, braining him with his forge hammer.

The mercenaries broke and ran. But there was no escape.

Chard wheeled his horse and galloped along the stream, crossing a small bridge, then riding for the second group. All fifty were waiting as ordered in skirmish formation some twenty yards below the tree line. With these men he could yet turn the battle.

His pain was forgotten as he urged his stallion up the hill.

As Chard came closer he watched with horror as a dozen men pitched from their saddles with arrows jutting from their backs. Horses reared, spilling their riders.

A line of mounted bowmen rode from the trees, shooting as they came: grim, dark men, clothed in black and silver. As they neared the stunned mercenaries they threw aside their bows, drawing shining silver sabers. There were no more than twenty soldiers left. A few of them tried to fight, the others fled.

Chard, his force in ruins, his fragile reputation gone forever, shouted his defiance and galloped toward the attackers. From their center, on a jet-black horse, came a red-cloaked rider in silver armor. Chard raised his sword, slamming his spurs into the weary stallion's flanks. The horse leaped forward.

The silver rider swung her horse at the last second and the two beasts collided. Chard was flung from the saddle as his stallion went down. The silver rider sprang from her mount and ran in just as he was trying to rise. Despairingly he swung his broadsword at her legs. She jumped nimbly and, as she landed, lashed her saber across his face. The blade struck his temple, biting deep and dislodging his helm.

Chard fell, rolled, and struggled to rise. The saber smashed down upon his skull, glancing from the chain-mail head guard. The blow stunned him and he sagged to his back. The saber lanced into his throat. Chard felt pain only briefly, for the sword plunged through his neck and into the cold earth beneath him.

All was quiet now, and he felt a curious sense of relief. No dead children, no raped and murdered women. Perhaps God would forgive him after all.

Perhaps . . .

Sigarni stepped back from the corpse and heard Asmidir order his men into the village to check on casualties. She was breathing heavily, yet her limbs felt light. Asmidir came alongside her. "How are you feeling?" As he spoke, his hand came down on her shoulder.

"Don't touch me!" she hissed, pulling away and turning to face him. She saw the shock and the dismay, but it was nothing to the roaring panic his contact aroused within her. "Stay away from me!" she said.

"Sigarni." His voice was soft, his eyes troubled. "You are in no danger from me. The battle is over, and I believe we have won. Calm yourself before the others see you."

The roaring receded and she began to tremble. "God, what

is happening to me?" she said, dropping her saber and sitting down on the grass.

He moved to sit opposite her. "I think we should blame it on the reaction to the battle, though we both know that is not the truth," he said sadly. "However, let us put that aside for now and enjoy the moment of victory. You risked it all, Sigarni. And I am proud of you. As I told you, I did not believe in the wisdom of this course. It was, in my view, too early for a confrontation. But you proved me wrong. Now perhaps you will explain why you were so confident."

She smiled and felt some of the tension ease from her. "It was not confidence. You told me I must have special skills. Whether or not that is true only time will tell. But I knew I could gather no support without a victory. Who would follow me? An untried woman in a world of beaten men."

"But why here in Cilfallen? How did you know they would come here? There are scores of hamlets and villages throughout the Highlands."

"Indeed there are, and we won't be able to protect them all. But Cilfallen was *my* village, and from here they took the hostages. It is also on largely open land. No major walls, no defenses. Added to this, it is the closest main settlement to Citadel."

"And why did you believe there would be an attack?"

"I questioned Obrin concerning Outland tactics. He believed they would send between one hundred and two hundred men."

Asmidir smiled. "We could have lost it all, my lady. We gambled everything on a single throw of the dice. That is not to be recommended for every occasion, I assure you."

Sigarni rose, then extended her hand to pull Asmidir to his feet. He looked up and met her eyes, and she knew he could see there her fear at the prospect of his touch. Slowly he reached out and clasped her wrist, rising smoothly and disengaging his grasp. "That took courage, did it not?" he said.

She nodded. "I am sorry, Asmidir. You are a dear friend,

and will always be so. But they took something from me and I cannot get it back."

He shook his head. "I fear they *took* nothing. They *gave* you something . . . something vile, like a poison that eats into your heart. I am your friend, Sigarni. More than that, I love you. I would die for you. But you alone must find a way to defeat the monsters tormenting you."

"What do you mean *defeat* them? I killed them!"

"You misunderstand me," he said gently. "They may be dead, but you hold them to you. They exist in every thought you have; you see their faces on all men—even your friends. I cannot advise you, for I have no . . . no *perception* of what you have been through. But you are now a fortress, barred against those who love you. Yet you have the enemy trapped within also. I think you will have to find a way to raise the portcullis and allow your friends in."

"Nonsense," she retorted. "There is no portcullis." Before he could speak again, she swung away and walked to her horse. "Let's get to the village," she said.

The two of them rode in silence.

The narrow lanes of Cilfallen were strewn with Outland corpses. Sigarni gazed on them dispassionately and guided her horse to the south of the town. The bodies of the mercenaries—stripped of all weapons—were slowly being carted across the bridge to an open field. Fell was sitting on the retaining wall surrounded by several of his foresters; they rose when they saw Sigarni. She dismounted and approached them. "You did well," she said. "Did you suffer any losses?"

"Three men wounded, none seriously. Four of the villagers were killed. Eleven others sustained wounds, most of them minor." She turned toward the waiting foresters, recognizing them all. Three of them had been casual lovers. The men stood silently, their expressions guarded.

"You have now seen how the Outlanders keep the peace. Know this: In the spring they will come with an army. Their mission will be to annihilate all clansmen, and their families, and their children. I intend to fight them—just like today. I will drench the Highlands in their blood. Today we are few, but that will change. Those who wish to serve me should make their wishes known to Fell. Those who do not should make plans to leave the mountains. There are only two sides now: Outland and Highland. Those not with me will be deemed traitors, and I will hunt them down also. That is all."

Spinning on her heel, she walked back to where Asmidir waited with the horses. "I need to see Tovi," she said. They found him at the bakery, with the ovens heating. He had discarded his sword and was kneading a batch of dough.

"One last time," he said with an embarrassed smile. "I don't know why I wanted to." He gazed around the long room with its racks of empty shelves. "This place has been my life."

"Now you have another life," she said sternly. "You were a warrior, Tovi; you understood discipline. You and Grame and Fell will train the Loda men. We will fall back into the forest and there I shall leave you. You will gather fighting men, organize stores for the winter, and put out scouts to watch for any further incursions into our territory. You understand this?"

"We can't win, Sigarni. I understand that."

"We just did!"

"Aye," he said, wiping the dough from his hands and moving to stand before her. "We defeated a band of ill-led mercenaries. We tricked them and trapped them. What happens when the Baron marches with his regular soldiers? I watched your man Obrin fight today. He was deadly. What happens when there are thousands like him against us?"

Sigarni stepped in close, her eyes cold, her voice hard as a blade. "Has all your courage gone, fat man? Has it melted into the blubber around your belly? I am Sigarni. I am of the Blood. And I wear the Crimson. I do not promise victory. I promise war and death. Now you have two choices. The first is to take your family and run, leave the Highlands. The second is to drop to your knee and pledge yourself to serve me until the day you die. Make that choice now, *Hunt Lord!*"

At the use of his title Tovi stiffened, and Sigarni saw the anger in his eyes. "You have fought one battle, Sigarni. I have fought many. I know what war is, and I know what it achieves. It is no more than a pestilence. It is a terrible thing—it consumes and destroys, birthing hatreds that last for generations. But I am the Hunt Lord, and I will not leave my people in this desperate hour."

"Then kneel," she said, her voice flat and unrelenting.

Tovi stepped forward and dropped to one knee. "My sword and my life," he said solemnly.

"Let it be so," she told him.

Sigarni left him there and walked from the bakery. Grame was sitting by his forge with a bloody bandage around his upper arm. Gwalchmai was with him. The smith grinned as he saw her. Gwalchmai belched, stood, staggered, and sat down. "He's drunk," said Grame.

"He always is," said Sigarni. "Will you serve me, Grame?"

The smith scratched his thick white beard. "You've changed, lass. You always had iron in you, but I'd guess it has been run through the fire and molded into something sharp and deadly. Aye, I'll serve you. What would you have me do?"

"Make the pledge."

"I gave that pledge once already, and the King ran away and left me and others to rot."

"I will not run, Grame. Make the pledge."

He stood and looked into her eyes. Bending his knee, he took a deep breath. "My sword and my life," he said.

"Let it be so."

"Where do I begin?" he asked, rising.

"See Tovi. He will tell you what I require in the coming weeks. For now, gather all weapons and supplies and lead our people deep into Pallides territory. We will speak again when the evacuation is complete. Any man who comes to you, Grame, and wishes to serve, make him speak the pledge. From now on we are Highlanders again. Nothing and no one will ever steal our pride. You understand?"

"Hail to thee, Battle Queen!" shouted Gwalchmai, lifting his jug in salute.

The words chilled Sigarni. "Be silent, old fool! This is no place for your drunken ramblings."

"He may be drunk," said Grame, "but he is not wrong. Only the sovereign can call for the pledge. And only to a sovereign would I make it. You are the Battle Queen, Sigarni. Nothing can change that."

Sigarni said nothing. Fell and his foresters came into sight, along with scores of villagers, forming a great semicircle around the forge. All had heard Gwalchmai's drunken salute, and Sigarni saw both confusion and apprehension on the faces of the people around her.

She walked slowly to her horse and stepped into the saddle. There was no noise now, and she felt their eyes upon her as she rode slowly toward the hills.

Chapter Eight

Like a gift from a merciful God winter came twelve days early, blizzards sweeping across the mountains, heavy snow-falls blocking narrow passes and making treacherous even the best of the roads. Sigarni sat alone on a high ridge, wrapped in a cloak of sheepskin, and stared out over the hills to the south. A mile away she could see three figures making their slow progress through the snow.

The heady days of victory at Cilfallen were weeks behind her now, and all the subsequent news had been bad. Stung by unexpected defeat the Outlanders had reacted savagely, sending three forces deep into the mountains to the east and the west. Three Farlain villages had been attacked, and more than four hundred Highlanders massacred in their homes. In the east a Pallides settlement was razed to the ground, and several Loda hamlets were struck during the same week, bringing the death total to more than five hundred.

Ten days before the slaughter Sigarni had traveled with Fell and Asmidir to the main Farlain town, seeking warriors to join their growing band. The experience had proved a hard lesson. As she sat watching the walkers in the snow, Sigarni steeled herself to recall the day.

More than five hundred people had gathered in the main square as the Hunt Lord, Torgan, waited to greet her. There were no cheers as the trio rode in. Torgan, a tall slender man, with wiry black hair cut short to expose a sharp widow's peak and a bald spot at the crown, was waiting for them. He

was sitting on a high seat in the center of the square, flanked
by six warriors carrying ritual ebony staffs, adorned with silver. Sitting at his feet was a white-bearded old man dressed
in a long robe of faded grey.

"What do you seek here, Woman of Loda?" asked Torgan,
as Sigarni dismounted. He did not rise from his seat, and his
words were spoken scornfully.

"Is this the Farlain Gifted One?" countered Sigarni, pointing at the old man.

"It is. What concern is that of yours?"

Sigarni turned away from him, scanning the faces in the
crowd. There was hostility there. "Have his dreams been
made known to the people of the Farlain?" she asked, raising
her voice so that the crowd could hear her.

Torgan rose. "Aye, they have. He told us of a troublesome
woman who would bring death and destruction upon the
clans: a Loda woman of low morals who by murder would
enrage the Outlanders. And his dreams were true!"

Despite her anger Sigarni stayed calm. "He is no Gifted
One," she said. "He is a fraud and a liar. And I will speak no
more of him. Let the Farlain know this: An Outland force
raided Cilfallen. We destroyed them. More will come, and
they will attack and butcher any in their path, whether they
be Loda, Farlain, Pallides, or Wingoras. All true Gifted Ones
know this. And you will see the truth of my words. I am
Sigarni. I am of the Blood of Kings. And I do not lie."

Torgan laughed. "Aye, we know who you are, Sigarni.
Word of your Talent has reached us even here. You will
leave the lands of the Farlain, and think yourself fortunate
that we do not bind you and deliver you to the Outlanders for
a just execution. Go back to your pitiful band and tell the id-
iots who follow you that the Farlain are not to be fooled."

"How can I tell them that," responded Sigarni, "when it is
obvious that they have been fooled already?" Spinning on
her heel she strode to her stallion and stepped into the saddle.
"There are other Gifted Ones," she told the crowd, "in other

clans. Be wise and seek their guidance. For the days of blood are here and if we do not join together we will be slaughtered separately. A leader has been prophesied—one who will unite the clans against the enemy. I am that leader."

"No whore will ever lead the Farlain," shouted the Hunt Lord. "Begone before we stone you!"

Sigarni touched heels to her stallion and rode from the town.

Now, as she sat in the icy cold beneath a darkening sky, her anger remained, hot and compelling. Sigarni had been better received among the Pallides, but even here they had promised no warriors to serve under her leadership. Arriving in the Larn Valley, she had been met outside the township by the blond warrior Loran, who had bowed as she dismounted.

"Well met, lady, and welcome," he said. "It is good to see you again." The memory of their meeting by Ironside's Falls seemed as distant as a dream of another life and she found herself gazing at the handsome Pallides as if he were a stranger. "Your armor fits you well," he said. "I am sorry that the shelters we built for the Loda people are so . . . so humble. But we did not have much time."

"They will suffice," she said. From the tree line a huge man ambled into view and waved at Loran. Sigarni watched his approach with undisguised amazement. A little over six feet tall, his shoulders seemed impossibly wide, and his neck was easily as big as her thigh. His head was large, and though beardless he had grown his sideburns long and they merged with his hairline to give him a leonine appearance.

"By God!" she whispered. "Is *it* real?"

Loran chuckled. "*It* is my cousin Mereth. And he's real enough."

"Is this her?" said Mereth, squinting at Sigarni. His voice was a low rumble like distant thunder.

"Aye, Mereth, this is Sigarni."

He moved his head close to her face. "Handsome woman," he said amiably.

"Mereth's vision is weak," explained Loran. "It is his only weakness. He's the strongest man I've ever seen."

"The strongest that ever was," said Mereth proudly. "I broke Lennox's record for the caber—and they said that couldn't be done. They said he was a giant. I broke it. Are you the Queen now?"

"This is not the time, Mereth," said Loran softly, laying his hand on the giant's shoulder.

"I heard the Loda Gifted One named her Queen. I was only asking."

"The Loda Gifted One is a drunkard. Now look after the lady's horse and I will see you at Fyon's house when you have stabled the mount."

Mereth smiled. "I can fight too," he told Sigarni. "I fear nothing."

Loran and Sigarni walked on into the town. "Poor vision is not his only weakness," she said when Mereth was out of earshot.

"Do not misjudge him, Sigarni. I admit he is not the most intelligent of men, but he is no simpleton. It just takes him a long time to work through a problem."

Fyon Sharp-axe entertained her at his home in the Larn Valley. It was a fine old house, built of stone with a roof of carefully carved slate. Fyon, Loran, and Mereth sat around the long table and listened intently as Sigarni told them of the events that had led to the battle of Cilfallen. The Hunt Lord, a squat, powerfully built warrior with a square-cut black beard, forked with silver, had waited courteously until she finished her tale. As she concluded he raised a wine cup and toasted her. "You did well, Sigarni," he said. "I applaud you for the way you saved the people of your clan. But I do not yet know if you are the leader who was prophesied. Our Gifted Ones say one is coming who will lead us, but they cannot name him. I know we have no choice now, save to battle for our lives. I will not relinquish this battle to you, for despite your victory at Cilfallen you are untried. And you are

a woman. It is not a woman's place to lead men into battle.
I do not say this slightingly, Sigarni, for I admire your
courage. It is merely common sense. Men are ultimately dispensable. If, in a war, all but ten of a clan's warriors are
killed, but the women remain, the clan would survive. But if
only ten of the clanswomen were left it would die. Men are
made for hunting and battle, women for gathering and child-
birth. This is the way of the world. I cannot see Pallides warriors fighting for a woman—even one as spirited as you."

Sigarni nodded. "I understand your fears, Fyon," she said.
"But I would like to hear the thoughts of Loran."

The blond warrior leaned back in his chair. He glanced at
Sigarni. "I have waited for a leader—as have we all. And I
was surprised when I heard that Gwalchmai had named you.
We here all know that you are of the blood of Gandarin, and
that he was directly descended from Ironhand. And a boy
child of yours would have first claim to the throne. Yet there
is no boy child, and never have the clans been led by a
woman."

"What of the Witch Queen?" countered Sigarni.

"Aye, I'll grant that," admitted Loran, "but she was from
beyond the old Gateways, drawn to our aid by sorcery. And
she did not stay to rule, but returned to her own land when
the war was won."

"As I shall," said Sigarni.

"Be that as it may," continued Loran, "I cannot as yet
make a judgment. I echo the Hunt Lord's praise for your victory at Cilfallen, and I deplore the treatment of you by the
Farlain. Even so, I do not believe we should commit ourselves to you at this time. I ask that you do not judge us too
harshly."

Sigarni rose. "I do not judge you harshly, Loran. You came
to Tovi and warned him of invasion. Because of your arguments he sent enough supplies back into Pallides lands to ensure survival for the people of Loda during the winter. You
have given us land, built us homes. For this I am grateful.

And I understand your concerns. I did not ask for this role, and would be more than happy to surrender it. But I know now that I am the one prophesied. I know it. What I need to know is what can be done to convince the Pallides. What do you require of me?"

"A good question," said Fyon, also rising. He rubbed at his silver-forked beard and moved to the fire blazing in the hearth. "And I wish I had an answer. We need a sign, Sigarni. Until then you must train your own warriors."

Ten days later Fyon had ridden his horse into the make-shift camp of the Loda, seeking out Sigarni.

"Welcome," she said as he ducked into the small log dwelling. It was dark inside, and lit by the flickering fire within a small iron brazier. Fyon seated himself opposite Sigarni and cast a nervous glance at the black man at her side. "This is Asmidir. He is my general, and a warrior of great skill." Asmidir held out his hand and Fyon shook it briefly.

"The Outlanders struck several Farlain villages," said Fyon. "Hundreds were slaughtered, women and children among them. Torgan led his men on a vengeance strike, but they were surrounded and cut to pieces. Torgan escaped, but he lost more than three hundred warriors. He has blamed you—claims you are a curse upon the people. My scouts tell me the Outlanders are marching toward us. They will be here in less than five days."

"They will not arrive," said Sigarni. "There are blizzards in the wind; they will drive them back."

"Only until the spring," said Fyon. "What then?"

"Let us hope that by then you will have had a sign," said Sigarni coldly.

High on the mountainside Sigarni wrapped her sheepskin cloak more tightly around her shoulders. Lady padded across the snow and hunkered down by her side. Sigarni pulled off her fur-lined mittens and stroked the dog's head.

"We'll soon be back in the warm, girl," she said. At the sound of her voice Lady's tail thumped against the snow.

The three walkers were at the foot of the mountain now and Sigarni could see them clearly. The first was Fell. With him were Gwyn Dark-eye and Bakris Tooth-gone. Slowly the three men climbed the flank of the mountain, reaching the ridge just before dusk. Snow was falling again, thick and fast.

Fell was the first to climb to the ridge. Snow was thick upon his hair and shoulders.

"What did you learn?" asked Sigarni.

"They have put a price of one thousand guineas upon your head, lady. And they are expecting another three thousand men by spring."

"Did you see Cilfallen?"

Fell sighed. "There is nothing there. Not one stone upon another. As if it never was."

"Come back to the settlement," she said. "You can tell me all."

"There's one piece of news I'd like to spit out now," he said, brushing the snow from his hair. "There was an arrival in Citadel—a wizard from the south. His name is Jakuta Khan. There are many stories about him, so we were told. He conjures demons."

Sigarni could see the fear in their eyes, and she hoped they could not see the same fear in hers. "I do not fear him," she heard herself say.

"He came to our fire last night," said Gwyn. "Just appeared out of nowhere, and seemed to stand within the flames. Tell her, Fell."

"He said for us to tell you he was coming for you. He said you were lucky that night by the Falls, but that this time he would not fail. You would remember him, he said, for the last time you saw him he had your father's heart in his hand. Then he vanished."

Sigarni staggered back and swung away from the men.

Her mouth was dry, her heart beating wildly. Panic welled in her breast, and she felt herself adrift on a current of fear. Her legs were weak and she reached out to grip the trunk of a tree.

The demons were coming again!

For Tovi Long-arm the onset of winter was a nightmare. The people of the Loda were spread now across two valleys, in five encampments. Food was a problem for almost three thousand refugees. Four of the Loda herds had been driven north after the attack on Cilfallen and three had been slaughtered to supply meat for the clan, leaving only breeding stock for the spring. But meat alone was not enough. There was a shortage of vegetables and dried fruit, and dysentery had spread among the old and infirm. Lung infections had begun to show among the old and the very young, and eleven greybeards had died so far in the first month of snow. Worse was to come, for soon the milk cows would go dry and then hunger would border on famine. Blizzards had closed many of the trails and communication was becoming difficult, even between camps. The structures erected by the Pallides were sound enough, but they were spartan and drafty, smoke-filled and dark.

Complaints were growing, and morale was low. Added to this there was resentment about the Outlander Obrin and his training methods. Day after day he would order the young men to engage in punishing routines, running, lifting, working in groups. It was not the Highland way, and Tovi had tried to impress this on the Outlander.

To no avail . . .

It was dawn when Tovi roused himself from his blankets. Beside him his wife groaned in her sleep. It was cold in the cabin and Tovi placed his own blanket over hers. The children were still asleep. Tovi moved to the fire, which had died down to a few smoldering ashes. With a stick he pushed the last few glowing embers together, then blew them into life, adding kindling until the flames licked up. Pulling on his boots and overshirt he tried to open the door of the cabin, but snow had piled up against the door in the night and Tovi had to squeeze through a narrow gap to emerge into the dawn light. Using his hands, he scooped the snow away from the door and then pushed it shut.

Grame was already awake when Tovi called at his small hut. The smith, wrapped in a long sheepskin coat and holding a long-handled felling axe, stepped out to join him. "The sky's clear," said Grame, "and it feels milder."

"The worst is yet to come," said Tovi.

"I know that!" snapped Grame. "God, Tovi, must you stay so gloomy?"

Tovi reddened at the rebuke and glared at the white-bearded smith. "Give me one good reason to be optimistic and I shall. I will even dance a jig for you! We have nearly three thousand people living in squalor, and what are we waiting for? To face famine or slaughter in the spring. Am I wrong?"

"I do not know if you are wrong, Tovi. That's the truth of it. But you could be. Concentrate on that. We now have five hundred fighting men, hard men, fueled by anger and the need for revenge. By spring we could have thousands. Then we will see. Why do you need to show such despair? It does no good."

"I am not skilled at hiding my feelings, Grame," admitted Tovi. "I am getting old and I have no fire in my belly. They killed my son, destroyed my village. Now I feel as if I am waiting for the rest of my family to be put to the sword. I find it hard to stomach."

Grame nodded. "You are not so old, Tovi. And as for your stomach—well, you look better than you have in years. Felling trees and building cabins has been good for you. Come the spring, that claymore will have no more weight than a goose feather. Then you'll find the fire."

Tovi forced a smile and scanned the camp. To the south

the new community hall was almost half built, the ground
leveled, the log walls already around five feet high. Eighty
feet long and thirty wide, the structure when finished would
allow many people of the encampment to gather together in
the evenings. This, Tovi knew, would encourage a greater
camaraderie and help lift morale. "How long now?" he
asked, pointing at the structure.

"Five days. We'll be felling trees on the north slope today.
If there's no fresh snow for a while we might finish in three."

All around them people were emerging from the huts.
Tovi saw the Outlander Obrin. The man was dressed now in
borrowed leggings and a leather tunic; he strolled to a tree
and urinated against the trunk. "I don't like the man," said
Tovi.

"Aye, he's iron hard," Grame agreed.

"It is not that. There is an arrogance about him that slips
under my skin like a barbed thorn. Look at the way he
walks . . . as if he is a king and all around him are serfs and
vassals."

Grame chuckled. "You are seeing too much. Fell walks
like that. Sigarni too."

"Aye, but they're Highlanders."

Grame's chuckle became a full-blooded laugh as he
clapped his hand on Tovi's shoulder. "Listen to yourself! Is
that not arrogance? Anyway, Obrin is a Highlander—Fell's
son."

"Pah! Put a wolf in a kilt and it is still a wolf!"

Grame shook his head. "You are not good company today,
Hunt Lord," he said. Tovi watched him stride away through
the snow.

He's right, thought Tovi, with a stab of guilt. I am the Hunt
Lord and I should be lifting the hearts of my people. He
sighed and trudged off toward Obrin. The warrior had removed his shirt and was kneeling and rubbing snow over his
upper body. As Tovi came closer he saw the web of scars on

Obrin's chest and upper arms. The man looked up at him, his eyes cold.

"Good morning, Hunt Lord."

"And to you, Obrin. How is the training progressing?"

Obrin rose and pulled on his shirt and tunic. "Six of the groups are proving adequate. No more than that. The others . . ." He shrugged. "If they don't want to learn, then I cannot force them."

"You don't need to teach a Highlander to fight," said Tovi. Obrin gave a rare smile but it did not soften his face. If anything, Tovi realized, it made him look more deadly.

"That is true, Hunt Lord. They know how to fight, and they know how to die. What they don't comprehend is that war is not about fighting and dying. It is about winning. And no army can win without discipline. A general must know that when he—or in our case *she*—gives an order it will be obeyed without question. We don't have that here. What we have is five hundred arrogant warriors who, upon seeing the enemy, will brandish their claymores and rush down to die. Just like the Farlain."

Tovi's first response was one of anger, but he swallowed it down. What would this Outlander understand of Highland pride, of the warrior's code? Fighting involved honor and courage. These Outlanders treated it as a trade. Even so, he knew that the man was speaking honestly. Worse, he was not wrong. "Try to understand, Obrin," he said softly. "Here each man is an individual. Wars between clans always come down to man against man. There was never any question of tactics. Even when we fought . . . your people . . . we did not learn. We charged. We died. You are dealing with a people who have fought this way for generations. I don't even know whether the older warriors can absorb these new ideas. So be patient. Try to find some way to appeal to the younger men. Convince them."

"I have already told them what is real," said Obrin stubbornly. "And if that wasn't enough they have the example of the Farlain."

"We are a proud people, Obrin. We can be led to the borders of Hell itself, but we cannot be driven. Can you understand that?"

"I'll think on it," said the Outlander. "But I never was an officer, and I'm no leader. All I know is what I've learned through seventeen years of bloody war. But I'll think on it."

A young woman approached them, a heavy woolen shawl wrapped around her slender shoulders. "By your leave, Hunt Lord," she said with a curtsy. "My grandfather is sick and cannot rise from his bed. Can you come?"

"Aye, lass," said Tovi wearily.

Obrin watched the Hunt Lord trudge off through the snow, saw the weariness in the man. He wears defeat like a cloak, thought the warrior. The former Outlander wandered away from the camp, climbing high onto the mountainside to the meeting cave. Three men were already present, and they had lit a fire. Their conversation faded away as Obrin entered. He walked slowly to the far side of the fire and sat, glancing down at the two bundles he had left there earlier; they were untouched. Obrin waited in silence until others arrived, some singly, some in pairs, others in small groups until twenty-five were assembled. Obrin rose and looked at their faces. Many of them were scarce more than children. They waited, sullen and wary.

"No work today," said Obrin, breaking the silence. "Today we talk. Now I am not a great talker—and even less of a teacher. But at this moment I am all that you have. So open your ears and listen."

"Why should we listen?" asked a young man in the front row. He was no more, Obrin guessed, than around fourteen years of age. "You tell us to carry rocks, we carry rocks. You tell us to run and we run. I do not need to hear the words of an Outland traitor. Just give us your orders and we shall obey them."

"Then I order you to listen," said Obrin, without trace of anger. His eyes raked the group. "Your friendship means nothing to me," he told them. "It is worth less than a sparrow's droppings. We are not here for friendship. What I am trying to do is give you a chance—a tiny chance—to defend your loved ones against a powerful enemy. Oh, I know you are prepared to die. The Farlain have shown us all how well a Highlander can give up his life. But you don't *win* by dying. You win by causing your enemy to die. Is that so hard to understand? The Hunt Lord says a Highlander cannot be driven. Is he incapable also of learning? If not, how did he acquire the skills to build homes, weave cloth, make bows and swords? What is so different about war? It is a game of skill and daring, of move and countermove. The Outlanders—as you call them—are masters of war."

"Masters of slaughter more like!" came a voice from the middle rows.

"Aye, and slaughter," agreed Obrin. "But in a battle they hold together. It is called discipline. It is nothing to do with honor, or glory. Yet all victories are based upon it." Obrin walked to the first of the bundles and flipped back the blanket covering it. Stooping, he lifted a dozen sticks, each no thicker than his thumb and no longer than his forearm. Tossing them one by one to the nearest clansmen, he said, "Break them!"

The first man chuckled and glanced down at the thin length of wood. "Why?" he asked.

"Just do it."

The sound of snapping wood echoed in the cave, followed by laughter as someone said, "The great warrior has certainly taught us to master stick splitting."

"Easy, was it not?" said Obrin amiably. "No trouble. A child could do it. And that, my fine clansmen, is how the Outlanders will deal with you. It is not a question of bravery, or honor. You fight as individuals, single sticks. Now, this is how the Outlanders fight." Taking up the second bundle, which was also composed of a dozen sticks, but tightly bound with twine, he tossed it to the jester. "Come then," said Obrin, "show me how you have mastered stick splitting. Break them!"

The man stood and held the bundle at both ends. Suddenly he bent his knee and brought the sticks down hard across his thigh. Several sticks gave, but the bundle remained intact. Angrily he hurled the sticks on the fire. "What does it prove?" he snarled. "But give me a claymore and I'll show you what I can do!"

"Sit down, lad," said Obrin. "I do not doubt your courage. The lesson is a simple one to absorb. What you saw was two bundles. Each bundle had twelve sticks. One could be broken, the other could not. It is the same with armies. When the clans fought at Colden Moor they fought in the only way they knew, shoulder to shoulder, claymores swinging. They were brought down by archers and slingers, lancers and pikemen, heavy cavalry and armored swordsmen. They were beaten decisively, but not routed. They stood their ground and died like men. By God, what a waste of courage! Did any here see the Farlain dead?"

Several men spoke up. Obrin nodded and waved them to silence. "What you saw was easy to read. The Outlanders were in the valley. The Farlain attacked from the high ground, sweeping down on them, their claymores bright in the morning sun. The Outlanders formed a tight shield wall, their spears extending. The Farlain ran upon the spears, trying to beat a path through. Then the cavalry came from the right, from their hiding places in a wood. Archers appeared on the left sending volley after volley into the Highland ranks. How long did the battle last? Not an hour. Not even half that. According to Fell it was probably over in a few short minutes. The Outlanders carried their dead away in a single wagon—ten . . . fifteen . . . twenty bodies at the most.

The Farlain lost hundreds. Are the clans too stupid to learn from their errors?" They were listening now, intently, their eyes locked to Obrin's face. "We all know the animals of the forest, and their ways. When faced with wolves, a stag will run. The wolves lope after him, slowly robbing him of strength. At last he turns at bay, and they come at him from all sides. If he is strong his horns will kill some, then he dies. You are like the stag. The Outlanders are the wolves; only they are worse than wolves. They have the horns of the stag, the stamina and cunning of the wolf pack, the claws of the bear, and the fangs of the lion. To defeat them, we must emulate them."

"How do we do this?" asked the boy who made the earlier jest.

"Your question is a good beginning," Obrin told him. "Understanding is the first key. All war is based on deception. When you are weak, you make the enemy think you are strong; when you are strong, make him think you are weak. When you are far away, make him believe you are near, and when you are near, lead him to think you are far away. The Outlanders did this to the Farlain. Their scouts must have told them the clansmen were near, so they hid their cavalry and archers. The Farlain saw the infantry occupying a weak position and attacked. In doing so, they walked into the iron jaws of the monster. We will not follow their example. We will fight on our own terms, choosing our own ground. If necessary, we will fight and run. We will make them the stag, and we shall be the wolves.

"To fight like this takes great discipline and enormous strength of heart, but it is the only way to win. Go now and talk among yourselves. Choose a unit leader from among you; he will be your officer. Pass the word to the other twenty-five groups. Tell them to appoint one man to represent them. Then I want all officers to report to me here at dawn tomorrow."

As the men stood to leave Obrin lifted his hand. "One

more point, my lads. I am from a Highland people far to the south. We are called the Arekki. I am the only man of my clan within three hundred miles. I am Obrin, and I do not lie, cheat, or steal. Not once in my life have I betrayed a friend or comrade, nor have I ever fled from an enemy. The next man to call me a traitor to my face will die on my sword. Go now!"

Sleeting hail beat against the windows as Asmidir sat at his desk with quill pen in hand, poring over maps of the Highlands. Two lanterns were glowing close by, casting gentle light on the sheets of paper littering the desktop. Asmidir stared hard at the lines on the ancient parchment, trying to picture the pass of Duane. Sheer to the east, mildly sloping to the west, it opened out into two box canyons and a long, narrow plain. Dipping his pen into the ink jar he sketched the pass, adding notations concerning distance and height.

Ari entered, still dressed in his armor of silver and black. He bowed. "Shall I bring your food here, lord?" he asked.

"I'm not hungry. Sit you down." The tall warrior pulled up a chair and sat. Leaning forward, Ari's dark eyes scanned the lines of the new map Asmidir was creating.

"Duane Pass," he said. "A good battle site—if the defenders number more than two thousand. Five hundred could not hold the ridges and would be flanked to the west. Cavalry would encircle them, then no escape would be possible."

"Aye, it is a problem. We need more men. I'd give half of all I own to see Kalia here with her regiment."

Ari gave a rare smile. "Kalia and Sigarni? Panther and hawk. It would be . . . interesting."

"She is three thousand miles away—if she still lives. But you are right, it would be fascinating to see them together. Now, you know these maps as well as I. Where will the first attack come?"

Ari sifted through the sheets. "They will bring an army to the first invasion fort. From there I would think they would swing northeast toward the deeper lands of the Farlain. They may even split their force and push northwest into Pallides territory. I think you are right to choose Duane; it is three miles south of their first fort."

Asmidir leaned back and rubbed his tired eyes. "Duane is a natural battle site. The enemy trapped below with only one means of escape, the defenders with their backs to the mountains, able to slip away at the first sign of impending defeat. As you say, however, we need at least two thousand. Where else?"

Ari shuffled through the maps. "With five hundred? Nowhere."

"Precisely my thoughts. And the Baron is no fool, he will know our approximate number. Son of a whore!" Lifting a detailed sketch of an Outland fort, he passed it to Ari. "What if we took it before they arrived? They'd have no supplies. How long could we hold them?"

"Four or five days. But they have three supply forts, not one. They will merely send a force around us. And then there would be no escape for the defenders. No prospect of victory either."

Asmidir pushed himself to his feet and wandered to the window. The snow was falling thick and fast, piling against the base of the leaded panes. "My head is spinning," he said. "Tell me something good. Anything."

Ari chuckled. "Our enemy is the Baron. He is hotheaded and reckless. Better yet, he is impatient and will not give us respect in the first battle. That is an advantage."

"That is true," agreed Asmidir. "But it is not enough to give him a bloody nose. The first battle must be decisive."

"And that means Duane Pass," said Ari.

"Which the Baron will also be aware of." Asmidir shook his head and laughed. "Are we being fools, Ari? Have we waited this long merely to stand and die on a foreign mountain?"

"Perhaps," agreed the warrior. "Yet a man has to die some-where."

"I'm not ready to die yet. I swore an oath to make the Out-landers pay for the rape of Kushir. I must honor it—or my spirit will walk forever through the Valley of Desolation and Despair."

"I also swore that oath, lord," said Ari. "We all did. Now our hopes rest with the silver woman."

Asmidir returned to the table and stared into the dark eyes of the man opposite. "What do you think of her, Ari? Could she truly be the One?"

The warrior shrugged. "I do not know the answer to the second question. As to the first—I admire her. That is all I can say."

"It does not bother you that this Chosen One is a woman?"

"Kalia is a woman—and she has fought in many wars. And Sigarni's battle plan at Cilfallen was inspired. Fraught with peril—but inspired."

Asmidir gathered up the maps and sketches. "I must be heading back to the mountains tomorrow. I need to see her."

"It will take around four days now," said Ari. "The snows have blocked many passes. Perhaps you should wait for more clement weather."

"These mountains do not know the meaning of clement weather," said Asmidir with a wry smile. "Even in summer the wind can chill a man to the bone."

"It is a hard land," agreed Ari, "and it breeds hard men. That is another advantage."

Another warrior entered and bowed. "There is a man to see you, lord," he said. "He came out of the snow."

"Do we know him?" Asmidir asked.

"I have not seen him before, lord. He is very old, and wears a cloak of feathers."

"Bring him in."

The warrior stepped aside and Taliesen entered. He did not pause or bow but strode straight to the table. Snow had gathered on his feathered cloak and his eyebrows and eyelids were tinged with ice.

"She is gone," he said. "The demons are coming—and she has gone!"

The blizzard came suddenly, fierce winds slashing across the mountains, sending up flurries of ground snow to mix with biting sleet. Sigarni was on open ground with the temperature dropping fast. Shielding her eyes with a gloved hand, she looked for shelter. Nothing could be seen. To be caught outside was to die, she knew, for already the sleet was penetrating her leggings and soaking into the sheepskin coat she wore; her fur-lined hood was white with ice and her face was burning with pain.

There was no panic in her, and in the distance she saw a huge fir tree, part buried in the snow. Striking out for it she waded through a thick drift, half climbing and half crawling until she reached the lee side of the tree. The branches of such a fir would spread in a radius of at least ten feet from the trunk, she knew, and that meant there was likely to be a natural cave below the buried branches. Lying on her belly, Sigarni began to dig with her hands and arms pushing aside the freezing snow, burrowing down beneath the boughs. Her pack snagged against a branch, and snow cascaded down on her. Digging deeper, she squeezed herself under the bough. Suddenly the snow beneath her gave way and she slid head-first into the natural pocket below. The snow cave was around seven feet deep and eight feet across, the fir branches above forming the roof. Out of the biting wind, Sigarni shivered with pleasure. From the side pocket of her pack she took a small tinderbox and the stub of a thick candle. Striking the flint, she ignited the dried bark scrapings, gently blowing them to life, before holding the candle wick over the tiny flames. With the candle lit, she set it on the ground beside her and leaned back against the trunk of the fir.

She was cold, and she stared lovingly at the flickering candle flame. The heat from it would gather in the snow cave—not enough to melt the snow overhead but more than ample to prevent death from cold. Above her she could hear the ferocity of the blizzard raking across the mountains, talons of icy sleet ripping at the land.

Here I am safe, she thought. She closed her eyes. Safe? Only from the blizzard.

She had seen the fear in Fell's eyes as he promised to stand beside her against the wizard and his demons, but more than this she had remembered the awful events of her childhood . . .

They had been enjoying a supper by the fire—when all the lanterns went out, as if struck by a fierce wind. Only there was no wind—only a terrible cold that swept across the room, drowning the heat of the fire under an invisible wave. Mother had not screamed, or shown any sign of panic, though the fear was there on her careworn features. She had leaped to the far wall, dragging down a saber and tossing it to Father who stood silently in the center of the room staring at the door. He looked so strong then, with his full red beard glistening in the cold firelight.

"Get under the table, girl," he told the six-year-old Sigarni. But she had scrambled to be beside her mother, who had drawn two hunting knives from their sheaths. Sigarni tugged her mother's skirt.

"I want a knife," she said. Her mother forced a smile and looked at her father. Little Sigarni didn't understand the look then, but now viewing it from the distance between adulthood and infancy, she knew they were proud of her.

The door exploded inward and a tall man stood there, dressed in crimson. Sigarni remembered his face; it was long and lantern-jawed, the eyes deep-set and small, the mouth full-lipped. He was carrying no weapon.

"Ah," he said, "everyone ready to die, I see. Let it be so!" In that moment a huge tear appeared in her mother's side, blood gushing from the wound. Father leaped forward, but staggered and shouted in pain as blood welled from talon marks on his neck. Something brushed Sigarni's dress and she saw the tear across her shoulder.

Father swung his claymore. It struck something invisible, black blood appearing in the air. Screaming his battle cry, he swung on his heel and sent the sword out in a second whistling arc. It thudded into another unseen assailant—and stuck there. Blood gushed from Father's mouth and Sigarni saw his chest rip open, his heart explode from the cavity and fly across the room into the outstretched hands of the man in red. Sigarni's mother hurled one of her knives at the man, but it flew by him. Turning, she leaped for the window, pushing it open, then swung back into the room and sprang toward Sigarni, grabbing her by her dress and lifting her from her feet. Spinning, she hurled the terrified child through the window.

Sigarni hit hard and rolled, then came upright and looked back at the cabin. Her mother shouted: "Run!"

Then her head toppled slowly from her shoulders . . .

And Sigarni had run, slipping and sliding down muddy slopes, panic-stricken and lost, until at last she came to the pool by the Falls . . .

Jerking her mind back to the present, she peeled off her gloves and extended her hands to the candle flame. Fell would be angry that she had left him behind, but he could not fight the demons. The forester would fare no better than her parents. No. If she had to die it would be alone.

No, she decided, not alone. I will find a way to kill some of them at least.

She sat for more than an hour, listening to the storm. Finally it swept by and the silence of the night fell on the mountains. Lifting the candle she blew it out, returning it to her pocket. Then slowly she climbed from the ice cave, and continued on her way to the pool by the Falls.

The journey was not an easy one. Many natural landmarks were hidden under drifts, the very shape of the land subtly altered by wind-sculpted snow. Above her the clouds cleared, the stars shining bright. The temperature plummeted. Sigarni pushed on, careful to move with the minimum of effort, anxious not to waste energy or to become too hot within her winter clothing. Sweat could be deadly, for it formed a sheet of freezing ice on the skin.

It was close to midnight when Sigarni struggled over the last rise. Below her the Falls were silent, frozen in midfall, and the pool was a field of snow over thick ice. Sigarni clambered down to the cave where Taliesen had nursed her. There was still some firewood stacked against the far wall. Releasing her pack, she built a blaze. The skin of her face prickled painfully as the heat touched her, and her fingers were thick and clumsy as she added fuel to the fire.

Removing her topcoat, she opened the pack and lifted clear the contents, setting them out in neat rows.

When to begin? Tomorrow? Tonight? Fear made her consider tackling the tasks now—immediately—but she was a Highlander and well understood the perils of fatigue in blizzard conditions.

No. Tonight she would rest, gathering her strength. Tomorrow the work could begin.

Ballistar awoke when he heard one of the warriors walk along the corridor outside and knock quietly at Kollarin's door. The dwarf sat up. He could hear voices, but the words were muffled by the wall. Curious, he scrambled from the bed and ambled to the door. Outside, the former servant, Ari, was talking to Kollarin. The Outlander was bare-chested, his dark hair hanging loose. "The lord needs you—now," said Ari.

"In the middle of the night?" queried Kollarin. "Can it not wait?"

"Now," repeated Ari. "It is a matter of great urgency."

"Does he want me also?" asked Ballistar.

Ari glanced down at the dwarf. "He did not say so—but I

think your counsel would be most welcome. He will meet you in the Long Hall."

Minutes later, as Ballistar and Kollarin entered the hall, they saw Taliesen and the black man sitting by the fire. Ballistar cursed under his breath. He tugged the hem of Kollarin's green tunic. "Sorcerer," he whispered. As the two men approached the fire, Asmidir beckoned them to sit.

"Sigarni has left the encampment," he said. "It is imperative that we find her swiftly."

"Why would she go?" asked Ballistar. Asmidir switched his gaze to Taliesen and the old man took a deep breath.

"How much do you know of her childhood?" he asked.

"Everything."

"Then you will recall how her . . . parents were killed."

Ballistar felt his heartbeat quicken, and his mouth was suddenly dry. "They were killed by . . . by demons."

"By demons, yes. Summoned by an enchanter who calls himself Jakuta Khan. There is much that I cannot tell you, but you should know this: Jakuta has returned. Twice already he has tried to capture Sigarni. Once as a babe. I thwarted him then, with the help of Caswallon. Then he found where we had hidden her and came again, killing her guardians. I thought he was finished then, but somehow he survived. We must find her."

"Why does he want to kill her? Is he hired by the Baron?" asked Kollarin.

"No. This goes back a very long way. As I said, I cannot tell you everything. But the heart of the matter is Sigarni's blood, or more accurately her bloodline. She is of the Blood of Kings. Those who understand the mystic arts will know why that is important to Jakuta."

Kollarin nodded. Ballistar looked from one to the other. "Well, I don't know," he said. "Why?"

"Power," Kollarin told him. "It is believed that the soul of a king carries great power. To sacrifice such a man would bestow enormous power on the one who carried out the deed.

It is said that the Demon Lord, Salaimun, conquered the world after killing three kings. I don't know whether there be truth in such tales."

"Some truth," said Taliesen. "Salaimun made pacts with the Lords of the Pits. He fed them blood and souls in return for power. Jakuta made a similar pact. But he has failed—twice."

"As far as I understand it," said Asmidir, "if you fail then your own soul is consumed. Is that not one of the dangers of necromancy?"

"It should be," agreed Taliesen. "I can only surmise that Jakuta used a familiar through which to cast his spells of summoning."

"A familiar?" echoed Ballistar.

"A conduit," Kollarin told him. "The sorcerer uses an apprentice, who is placed in a trance. The spell is then spoken through the apprentice. If it fails, the demons take the soul of the conduit . . . the familiar."

"Enough of this!" stormed Taliesen. "We are not here to educate the dwarf! Can you find her, Kollarin?"

Kollarin shook his head. "Not from here. I must go to where she last slept, then I will pick up her spirit trail."

"It will take three days in the snow," said Asmidir. The black man swung to the sorcerer. "However, it did not take you three days, Taliesen. Do you know another path?"

"Aye, but none of you could walk it," he said despondently.

"Why do you need to be in the hut, Kollarin?" asked Ballistar. "Could you not merely track her by using a piece of her clothing?"

"I am not a bloodhound, you idiot! I don't follow the trail with my snout to the snow!"

"Then how do you hone your Talent?" asked Asmidir.

"It is hard to explain. But for me a person leaves an essence of themselves in any building. It fades over a period of weeks, but once I hook to it I can follow it anywhere."

"And where is such an . . . essence . . . most strongly felt?"

"In a bed, or a favorite chair. Sometimes attached to a family member, or a close friend."

"By going to the hut, could you gain a sense of her ultimate destination?"

"No," admitted Kollarin. "I would follow the trail."

"Damn!" said Asmidir. "It brings us no closer. What of you, Taliesen? You are a sorcerer. You claim to be able to see the future. How then do you not know her whereabouts?"

"Pah!" said the old man. "You think in straight lines. You talk of *a* future. There are thousands upon thousands. New futures begin with every heartbeat. Aye, in all of them Sigarni is the Chosen One. In some of them she even succeeds for a while. In most of them she dies, young and unfulfilled. I am seeking the one future among so many. I do not know where she is; I don't know why she has run away. Perhaps in this future she lacks courage."

"Nonsense," said Ballistar, reddening. "She would not flee. If she knew the demons were coming she would try to think of a way of fighting them. I know her—better than any of you. She has gone to choose her ground."

"Where would that be?" asked Asmidir. "That is the question. And why did she not come to us to aid her?"

"Her father was a great fighter," said Ballistar, "but he was torn to pieces. She would not take her friends into such peril. Who among us could fight demons?"

"I could, but I wasn't here," said Taliesen. "My people are fighting a war in another time. They needed me."

"There was no one she could turn to," said the dwarf. "Therefore she will fight alone."

"Wait!" said Taliesen, his eyes brightening. "There is one she would turn to. I know where she is!"

"Where?" Asmidir asked.

"The cave by the pool. She has an ally there. I must go!" Taliesen rose.

Ballistar lifted his hand. "A moment, please," said the dwarf. "Do you know what Sigarni took with her when she left?"

"Knives, balls of twine, some food, a bow, arrows. What does it matter?" asked the sorcerer.

"It matters more than you think," said Ballistar. "You had better let me come with you."

Chapter Nine

Sigarni put out her hand to the fire. The warmth was both welcoming and reassuring. When the demons had killed her parents all heat had vanished from the blaze in the hearth. This, she reasoned, would be her only warning that death was close. She stared at her hands. There were blisters on her palms and on the inside joints of her fingers; one had bled profusely and they were painful.

It was the eve of her second day by the frozen Falls and she had worked hard through the hours of daylight. Fear was a constant companion, but somehow that fear was eased merely by being alone. Sigarni the Huntress had no other concerns now save to stay alive. To do that she must somehow defeat a wizard and his demons.

They can be killed, she thought. Father struck one of them and black blood flowed from it. And that which bleeds can die. Banking up the fire, she drew her saber and honed the edge with a whetstone. Outside the light was failing fast. Sigarni hooked her quiver of arrows over her shoulder and kept the bow close at hand.

Will it be like last time? she wondered. Will the man in red come first? And if he does, how many creatures of the dark will be with him? How many had been back at the cabin on that awful day? One? Two? More? How could she tell? Father had been struck first. Perhaps it was the same creature that slew her mother.

Sigarni had made plans for three.

The wind was building outside, and flurries of snow were blowing into the cave mouth. A distant wolf howled. The fire crackled and spat and Sigarni knocked a burning cinder from her leggings. Feeling drowsy, she took up her bow and walked to the mouth of the cave, drawing a deep, cold breath. *How long since you slept?* Too long, she realized. If they did not come tonight, she would catch a few hours after dawn.

Perhaps they won't find me here, she thought suddenly. Perhaps I am safe.

The moon shone in a cloudless sky, but the wind continued to blow flurries of snow across the frozen pool, rising like a white mist and sparkling in the moonlight. The air was cold against her face, but she could just feel the warmth of the fire behind her.

Alone in the wilderness of white Sigarni found herself thinking of her life, and the great joys she had known. It saddened her that she had not appreciated those joys when she had them; those glorious golden days with Abby and Lady, walking the high country without a care. Recalling them was a strange experience, as if she was looking through a window onto the life of a twin. And she wondered about the white-haired girl she could remember. How could she have lived in such a carefree manner?

Her thoughts roved on, and Bernt's sweet face appeared from nowhere. Sigarni felt a swelling in her throat and her eyes misted. He had loved her. Truly loved her. How callous she had been. *Is this all a punishment for my treatment of you, Bernt? Is God angry with me?* There was no way of knowing. *If it is, I will bear it.*

A white owl swooped over the trees—silent killer, silent flight. Sigarni remembered the first time she had seen such a creature. After the murder of her parents she had lived with old Gwalchmai. He had walked her through the woods on many a night, educating her to the habits of the nocturnal creatures of the forest. The old drunkard had proved a fine foster father, restricting his drinking to when Sigarni was asleep.

Sigarni sighed. Only a few short months ago she had been a willful and selfish woman, reveling in her freedom. Now she was the leader of a fledgling army with little hope of survival.

Survival? She shivered. *Will you survive the night?*

Weariness sat upon her like a boulder, but the bow felt good in her hands. I am not a child now, she thought, running from peril. I am Sigarni the Huntress, and those who come for me do so at the risk of their lives.

Moving back into the cave, she added two large chunks of deadwood to the fire, then returned to the entrance.

Doubts blossomed constantly. *Your father was a great fighter, but he lasted only a few heartbeats.*

"He did not know they were coming," she said aloud. "He was not prepared."

How can you prepare against demons of the dark?

"They have flesh, even if they cannot be seen. Flesh can be cut."

Fear rose like a fire in her belly, and she allowed the flames to flicker. Fear is life, fear is caution, she told herself.

You are a woman alone!

"I am a Highlander and a hunter. I am of the blood of heroes, and they will not bring me to despair and panic. They will *not*!"

A silver fox moved out into the open and padded across to the poolside. "Hola!" shouted Sigarni. The noise startled the beast and it leaped out onto the ice and ran across the pool. As it reached the center it swerved to the left, then raced to the other side. Sigarni's eyes narrowed. Why had it swerved? What did it see? Whatever it was remained invisible within the snow mist. Sigarni ran back to the fire; it was still warm. Notching an arrow to her short hunting bow, she returned to the cave mouth and waited.

Long minutes passed. Then he appeared, walking with

care upon the ice. He was not as tall as she remembered, but then she had only looked upon him with the eyes of a child. Shorter than Fell, he was a stocky man, his belly straining at the red leather coat he wore. His hair was black, close-cropped, silver at the temples, his face fleshy and round. His leggings and boots were red, as was the ankle-length cloak he wore.

Sigarni drew back the bowstring, took careful aim, and waited as he approached. The man saw her, and continued to move closer. Forty feet, thirty. He looked up and smiled. Sigarni let fly and the arrow flashed through the air. He raised his hand and the shaft burst into flame. She notched another.

"Don't waste your energy, child," he said, his voice surprisingly light and pleasant. "This is the day you die—and move on to worlds undreamed of. Great adventures await you. Accept your destiny with joy!"

The temperature in the cave plummeted. Something moved behind her . . . instantly Sigarni leaped out and ran to the right, toward a gentle, tree-covered slope. She did not look back, keeping her eyes to the trail. Halfway up the slope she suddenly twisted to the right once more, cutting behind a snow-covered screen of low bushes. The moonlight was bright and she stared at the snow, and the footprints she had left behind.

Alongside them now she saw other footprints, huge and appearing as if by magic. They were moving inexorably toward her at great speed. Drawing back the bowstring, she aimed high and released the shaft. It traveled no more than twenty feet before stopping suddenly, half of its length disappearing. A terrible screech sounded, and she saw dark blood pumping out around the arrow. She loosed a second. This too thudded home into her invisible assailant. "Come on, you whoreson!" shouted Sigarni. The creature roared and charged, much faster now, smashing aside the screen of bushes. An invisible leg punched against a hidden length of twine, dislodging the slip ring and springing the toggle. Released from tension, a spear-thick sapling whiplashed back into a vertical position. The three sharpened stakes bound to it, each more than a foot long, plunged into the creature's chest. It thrashed and screamed. The sapling was snapped, but the stakes remained embedded in the invisible flesh. Then it fell and the roaring faded to a low moan. This too died away.

Sigarni did not wait for the death throes, and was already running as the trap was sprung. Angling across the fresh-fallen snow she ran up the slope, cutting to the left until she was just below the crest of the hill. There were no trees or bushes close by. Dropping to her knees, she notched an arrow and waited.

No more than a few heartbeats passed before she saw first one, then two sets of footprints being stamped into the snow. Anger flared in her, fueling her determination. The closet of the creatures struck the first trip wire. As the trigger bar was dislodged the rough-made longbow hidden beneath a snow-covered lattice of thin branches released its deadly missile. Four feet long, the sharpened stick had been barbed all along its length. It slammed into the first creature at what to Sigarni appeared to be lower belly height. She had no time to revel in the strike, for the second creature was almost upon her.

The second hidden bow loosed its deadly shaft—and missed!

With no time to shoot, Sigarni dropped the bow and took a running dive down the hill, landing on her shoulder and rolling headlong toward the lake. Halfway down she felt her saber snap, then belt and scabbard tore free. Sigarni staggered to her feet. There was one more trap, but it was some way to the left of the cave.

Too far.

Spinning around, she saw the terrifying footprints closing in on her right. A low sound came from the left. Sigarni ducked down—just as talons ripped into her shoulder. The silver chain mail she wore stopped her flesh from being ripped from her bone, but even so she was picked up and hurled ten feet through the air, landing hard on the snow-covered ice pool.

Both creatures now made their way after her.

Sigarni pushed herself upright and began to run. She had one hope now—perhaps the ice at the pool's center would not support the weight of the beasts pursuing her.

The creatures were closing on her and Sigarni could hear the pounding of their taloned feet upon the ice. The saber was gone, but she still had her knife.

Damned if I'll die running, she thought. Skidding to a stop, she drew the hunting knife and spun to face them. The swirling snow highlighted their bulk, plastering against the skin of their chests and bellies. In the moonlight they appeared as hairless bears. Flipping the knife and taking the blade in her hand, "Bite on this, you ugly bastard!" she yelled, hurling the weapon with all her might. The point lanced home in the belly of the first; she saw its head go back and a terrible cry of pain and rage echoed in the mountains.

The creature took two steps forward, then fell to the ice. The last of them closed in on Sigarni . . . and stopped.

An eerie glow was enveloping it now, faint and golden. It was indeed a hairless bear, though the head was round, the ears and nose humanoid. The beast's eyes were large, and slitted like a great cat. Malevolence shone in the creature's golden gaze as it stood blinking in the strange light.

"Kill her!" shouted the man in red, beginning to run across the ice. "Kill her!"

The noise caused the creature to jerk its head. It blinked, then focused again on Sigarni. Thin lips drew back to expose a set of sharp teeth. Long arms came up, talons gleaming in the moonlight.

"Step aside, girl," came a calm voice. Sigarni scrambled back.

The glowing figure of Ironhand was standing before the creature now, a two-handed sword held ready. He was translucent and shimmering, and Sigarni could not believe such an insubstantial figure could hold back the power of the beast. As the creature growled and leaped, the golden-lit sword flashed out, cleaving through the huge chest. There was no blood, and no visible wound. But the demon tottered back and then sank into the ice.

The red-garbed wizard looked horror-struck as the last of the beasts fell. Ironhand swung to him. "It's been a long time, Jakuta," he said.

"You can't hurt me. You might be able to slay a demon's soul—but you cannot harm the living!"

"Indeed I cannot. Nor will I have to. Is this not the third time you have tried to steal Sigarni's soul? And where is your familiar?"

The wizard blanched. Slowly he drew a wickedly curved dagger. "There is still time," he said. "She cannot stand against me."

"There is no time, Jakuta," Ironhand told him. "I can see them now!"

The wizard spun. Heavy footprints were thumping down in the snow. Scores of them . . .

Dropping his knife, the wizard began to run. Sigarni saw him make fewer than twenty paces before his body was lifted into the air. His arms and legs were torn from him and his screams were awful to hear. They were cut off abruptly as his head rolled to the ice.

"You should have called upon me," Ironhand told the stunned woman.

"I needed to fight them alone," she said.

"I would expect no less from Ironhand's daughter," he told her.

Just as the dawn light crept over the mountains a tiny pocket of darkness opened like a black teardrop on the hillside overlooking the frozen falls. Taliesen stepped from it, leading a blindfolded Ballistar. As his feet touched the snow-covered earth Ballistar collapsed to the ground, trembling. Tearing loose the blindfold, he blinked in the light. Taliesen gave a dry chuckle. "I told you the way would not be to your liking," he said.

"Sweet Heaven," whispered the dwarf. "What kind of beasts made the noises I heard?"

"You do not wish to know," said Taliesen. "Now let us find Sigarni, for I am already growing cold."

"Wait!" ordered the dwarf, pushing himself to his feet and brushing snow from his leggings.

"What now?"

"There are traps set," Ballistar told him. "She did not come here to hide—she came to fight. Now give me a moment to gather my wits, and I will lead you to her."

"There may be no need," said Taliesen softly, pointing to the ice-covered pool. Ballistar saw the patches of blood smeared across the ice. He and Taliesen moved carefully down the slope. Then the dwarf spotted what appeared to be two boulders close to the center of the pool. "Atrolls," said Taliesen. "Creatures of the First Pit."

A severed human leg was half buried in snow. Taliesen tugged it clear. The boot was still in place. "Not hers," said the wizard. "That is promising." Ballistar backed away from the grisly find—and stepped on a human hand.

"Dear God, what happened here?" he said.

"Aha!" hissed Taliesen, finding the head of Jakuta Khan. Lifting it by the ears, he brought it up until he could look into the grey corpse face. "Well, well," he said. "Come to me, Jakuta!"

The corpse eyes flipped open, and blinked twice. The mouth began to move, but there were no sounds. "No good trying to speak, my boy," said Taliesen with a cruel smile. "You have no throat. I take it I called you back from your torment. It must be so very terrible. Are they still hunting you? Of course they are." Ballistar saw tears form in the sunken eyes. "Well, I can help you there, Jakuta. Would you prefer your spirit to live for a while in this hapless skull, free from terror? You would?" Gently he laid the head upon the ice, then spoke in a harsh tongue unknown to Ballistar. The ice around the severed head began to melt away. Taliesen knelt by it. "As long as there is still flesh upon the skull you will be safe here, Jakuta. But when the fishes have stripped it away, you will return to the pit." The ice gave, the head falling into the cold water beneath as Taliesen stood.

"How was it still alive?" asked Ballistar.

"I called him back. I fear his stay will be brief."

"It was terribly cruel."

Taliesen laughed. "Cruel? You have no idea of what he suffered where he was. He called upon the Creatures of the Pit for help—and failed them. Now he dwells with them in perpetual torment. I have given him a short respite from that."

"At the bottom of an ice lake. How kind you are!" sneered Ballistar.

"I never claimed to be kind. I am certainly not disposed toward mercy for such as he. Jakuta Khan caused the death of Ironhand and destroyed a dynasty that might have changed the course of our history. He did it for profit, for greed. Now he pays. You want me to grieve for him, dwarf?"

Ballistar nodded. "Yes, that would be good. For in what way are you different from him, Taliesen? You delight in his suffering and you add to his torment. Is that not evil?"

Taliesen's eyes narrowed. "Who are you, dwarf, to lecture me? I have fought evil for ten times your lifetime. Even now in my own land the ancestors of these Outlanders are waging a war that will see hundreds, perhaps thousands, of my people die. What pity I have is for them. And there is nothing that I would not do to save them. Now, find me the woman!"

Ballistar swung away from him and walked back across the ice. With care he climbed the slope before the cave, feeling his way forward. "For the sake of Heaven!" hissed Taliesen. "Why the delay? I am freezing to death out here!" Ballistar ignored him. Some way to the left he halted, his hands burrowing into the snow. "What now?" asked Taliesen, exasperated.

There was a sharp hiss, then a sapling reared upright, whiplashing back and forth. Three sharpened stakes were bound to it. "It is a pig spear-trap," said Ballistar, "but angled to strike high. The twine is connected to a ring at the end of the trip wire . . ."

"Yes, yes, I need no instruction. Are there more?"

"We will see," said Ballistar. The cave was no more than forty feet away, yet it took the two men almost half an hour to reach it. Taliesen was the first inside, where Sigarni was sleeping by a dying fire. The wizard sat down beside her.

Satisfied that she was alive, Ballistar walked away. "Where are you going?"

"There may be more traps. I don't want some unsuspecting traveler to spring one."

Outside the dwarf took several deep breaths. His relief was almost palpable: Sigarni was alive! Ballistar stood for a moment scanning the area. To the right he could see a huge grey corpse, two arrows in its chest and three stakes in its back. One trap. On the hillside there was another body.

Ballistar trudged out toward it.

For two hours he searched the land around the pool. There were no more traps. Returning to the cave he found Sigarni still asleep, with the wizard dozing beside her. Taliesen awoke as he entered. "Four creatures were killed," said the dwarf, squatting by the fire and extending his hands to the heat. "One had a dagger in its heart, one was slain by a pig spear-trap, the third by a lance arrow. There was no mark on the fourth."

"She did well," agreed the sorcerer.

"How did she pierce their skin?" asked Ballistar. "I could

not pull her dagger free. It was as if it was embedded in stone."

"It was," said Taliesen. "You have seen the corpses of men stiffen in death?" Ballistar nodded. "With the Atrolls it is many times as powerful. The corpses turn grey, like rocks, then within a few days they putrefy and disappear. Even the bones rot."

"Will more come?"

"It is unlikely, though not impossible. Jakuta pursued Sigarni through the Gateways of Time. He had to, for his soul was pledged against her death. I know of no other sorcerer hunting her."

"Why did he seek her?"

"Perhaps she will tell you that when she wakes," said Taliesen. "And now I am tired. I shall sleep. Be so kind as to fetch wood and keep the fire blazing."

Sigarni stood on the battlements, staring out over the flanks of the mountains and the distant peak of High Druin. Ironhand stood beside her, his huge hand on her shoulder. Moonlight glistened on his braided silver beard, and shone from his silver chain mail and breastplate. She felt power radiating from him, encompassing her, bathing her in its warmth. "Where are we?" she asked.

"You mean you don't recognize it?" he said, mystified. "I'm sure that I have created it perfectly. Perhaps you need to see it from the outside?"

"I know this area," she told him. "There is nothing here save a few wooded hills."

"That cannot be!" he said, his hand of red iron sweeping out to encompass the hills. "This is my stronghold of Al-Druin. It was here that I fought the Four Armies, and slew their champion, Grayle." Sigarni saw the sadness in his eyes.

"I'm sorry, Ironhand. I have traveled these hills all my life. There are some broken stones that show there was once a large dwelling place here. But it is long gone. And not even the eldest of the Loda know what stood here."

"Ah, well," he said, turning from the parapet, "it is . . . was . . . merely stone. And at least you can see it now. Come inside and we will talk. I have a fire prepared; it will offer no heat, but is pretty to look upon." The scene shimmered and Sigarni found herself in a rectangular room, velvet curtains covering the high windows. A log fire blazed in the hearth, but as Ironhand predicted, it burned without heat.

"How is it done?" she asked, running her hand through the flames.

"Here all is illusion. We are spirits, you and I." The giant warrior, clad now in a simple tunic of green, with soft leather trews, sat himself down in a deep chair. Sigarni seated herself on the bearskin rug before the fire. "It took a long time to learn how to do all this," he said, waving his hand to encompass the room. "I do not know how long, for there is no sense of the passage of time. To me it was an eternity. Now it is the only home I know—save for the pool by the Falls where my body lies." Sigarni sat silently, aware that his sorrow was great. "Ironhand's Falls. It is a beautiful place," he continued, forcing a smile. "A man could choose far worse for his death. During the centuries I have watched the trees grow and die in that wondrous cycle of birth, growth, and death. People too—hunters, wanderers, tinkers, clansmen, foreign soldiers. And I saw you, Sigarni, diving from the edge of the Falls, straight as an arrow. I was there when you found my bones. But I could not speak, for you were not ready to listen. You can have no idea how good it is to speak to another soul."

"Are there no others here?" she asked.

"No, not now. This is my world, the silent kingdom of Ironhand. Others have come, demons and evil spirits. I slew them, and now the others avoid my . . . lands."

"You must be lonely."

He nodded. "I hope you will never know how much. I

would give anything—accept the darkness and solitude of the true grave for just one hour in your mother's company. It is not yet to be. I can accept that."

"My mother?" asked Sigarni. "You knew her?"

"Did you not listen to me back at the pool? You are my daughter, Sigarni. Your mother was my wife, Elarine. I see her in you, the same strength of purpose, the same pride."

"But you lived hundreds and hundreds of years ago. I can't be your daughter! It is not possible! I knew my mother and father—lived with them until they were slain."

"For all my faults, Sigarni, I was never a liar. Not in life, and certainly not in death. You were born in the last year of my life, when enemies I thought were friends were meeting in secret with plans to destroy me. When I did learn of their plans I urged Elarine to run, to cross the water. She would not." He smiled at the memory. " 'We will fight them,' she said. 'We will conquer once more.' I tried. My wizards were slain, all mystic protection lost to me. That was the work of Jakuta Khan. I tried to reach Elarine, but the assassins trapped me at the Falls. I died there. Elarine died at Kashar. I learned this from Taliesen, when he summoned my spirit to the Falls. You were a babe then. He and Caswallon carried you through a Gateway and left you with your *new* parents: a fine couple, unable to have children of their own. Taliesen disguised you, changing the color of your hair." Reaching out, he stroked her head. "All our family are born with silver hair. We took it as a sign of greatness. Perhaps that was arrogance. Perhaps not. We did become kings, after all. And not one foreign enemy ever brought us low."

"How did my mother die?" asked Sigarni. "Did Taliesen tell you this?"

"Aye, he told me. She had a saber in her hand, the blood of the enemy staining it. And as she died she cursed them." He rose and turned away from her, a tall man of immense power and even stronger grief. His head was bowed and Sigarni went to him, taking his hand in hers.

"Why are you here?" asked Sigarni tenderly. "Why not in paradise, or wherever it is that heroes go?"

He smiled. "I had to wait, Sigarni. I made a promise, a sacred oath, that I would come again when my people needed me. I have felt the desire to quit this place many times, seen the far light shining. But I will not travel the swans' path until the time is right."

"Perhaps she waits for you there, Elarine."

"Aye, I have thought of that often. But I never made a promise I did not fight to keep. Now that promise is upon me. For you are the heir to Ironhand, you are the hope of the Highlands."

"But how can you help me?" she asked. "You are a spirit, a ghost. What can you do within the world of men?"

"Nothing," he admitted. "But you can. And I shall continue to teach you what it means to be a king. I will re-create battles for you, and you shall see how they are fought and won. I will show you my life, the traitors and the friends, the good and the deceitful, the brave and the unmanly. All of this and more you will experience here."

"How long will this take?"

"As before, you could be with me for what seems like years, yet when you awake only a single night will have passed. Trust me, my daughter. When you return you will be closer to the warrior queen they have longed for."

"I forgot much of what passed between us before. In the true world all this will seem a hazy dream."

"The knowledge will be there," he said. "As it was at Cilfallen."

"That was your doing?"

Ironhand shook his head and led her back to the fire. "Not at all. It was you! What I did was to open your mind to the ways of war. I never lost a battle, Sigarni, for when forced to fight I was always prepared with lines of retreat and secondary plans. And I understood the importance of *speed*—of thought, of action. You have a fast mind, and great courage. You will teach your enemies to fear you."

"We have a very small army," said Sigarni. "The enemy is large, well disciplined, and used to the ways of war."

"Aye, it was the same with me, at the very beginning. There is, however, an advantage in such a situation. An army is like a man. It needs a head, and a heart, two good arms, two sound legs. It requires a strong belly and a solid backbone. Now, while it is yet small, is the time to lay the foundations of your force."

"Which is the leader," asked Sigarni, "the head or the heart?"

He chuckled. "Neither. He—or in this case *she*—must be the soul. Take heed, my daughter. Choose your men with great care, for some will be exceptional when commanding small forces, less capable with larger groups. Others will seem too cautious, yet when the swords are drawn will fight like devils."

"And how do I know which to choose?"

"Honor your instincts, and never cease to be vigilant. You can read a general by the attitudes of his men. They may fear him or love him—that is generally of no consequence. Look at their discipline. See how fast or how badly they react. The men are merely an extension of the captain commanding them."

"How then does the *soul* operate?"

"The head suggests the plans, the heart gives men spirit, the backbone gives them strength, the belly gives them confidence. The soul gives them the *cause* to fight for. Men will fight well for loot and plunder, for pride and honor. But when the *cause* is perceived as noble they will fight like demigods."

Sigarni sighed. "All this I can understand. But when the war starts I cannot keep traveling to the Falls to speak with you, to ask your advice. I will be alone then, and my lack of experience could condemn us all."

"I cannot be with you always, Sigarni, for this is your world and your time. When the spring comes, dive once more into the pool and swim to where my bones rest. Take one small fragment and keep it with you. Then you may call upon me and I will be with you. Let no one know of this, and never speak to me unless you are alone. Now let us begin with your lessons."

Fell was tired, his spirits low as he stood in the new long hut, watching Sigarni discussing tactics and strategies with Asmidir, Obrin, Tovi, and Grame. The Pallides man, Loran, was present, sitting quietly, offering nothing but listening intently. Beside him was the colossal Mereth. Gwyn Dark-eye, Bakris Tooth-gone, and other group leaders were also seated on the floor before Sigarni, who occupied the only chair. In all there were close to forty people present. It seemed to Fell that the meeting was drifting aimlessly, yet Sigarni seemed unperturbed. Some were for storming the three Outland forts, others for sending raiding parties into the Lowlands. Voice after voice was raised in the debate, often resulting in petty arguments.

Fell soon became oblivious to it all, allowing the sound to wash over him. Tired, he sat with his back to the wall, resting his head against the wood. The late summer seemed so far away now, when he had traveled to Sigarni's cabin to have his wound stitched. Her beauty had dazzled him, and left a heaviness in his heart that would not ease. She was so different now, tense as a bowstring, her eyes cold and distant. She no longer laughed, and gone was the lightness of heart and the carefree joy she once exhibited. Now she kept a distance from her followers, allowing no man to come close. A week before Fell had been explaining some of the logistical problems to her and had touched her arm. Sigarni had drawn back as if stung. She had said nothing, but had moved farther away from him. Though hurt by it, Fell saw that he was not the only man to affect Sigarni in the same way. No one could approach within touching distance of her, save the dwarf. He would sit at her feet, as he was doing now.

Fell rubbed his bloodshot eyes. Food was running low. There had not been enough salt to preserve all the meat, and much of it was now bad. The only cattle left were breeding stock, and to kill these would cause great grief among the clan, and ensure future famine. It had been bad enough slaughtering all the others. Grown men had wept at the loss. All cattlemen understood the need of the winter cull, for there was not enough fodder gathered to feed all the animals through this hardest of seasons. But to lose all the hay meant the destruction of whole herds, the loss of prize bulls that were the result of generations of breeding.

The period of late midwinter was always a time of hardship, when the milk cows dried and the meat was all but gone. This year would be ten times worse, and it would be followed by a terrible war.

Fell drifted into a troubled sleep, only to be awoken by the sounds of men pushing themselves to their feet. Cold air touched him as the doors were pushed open and the forester struggled to his feet, dizzy and disoriented. Loran, Asmidir, Obrin, Tovi, and Grame all remained behind, as did Ballistar. Fell decided to leave them to it and moved to the door, but Sigarni called him back. "I need some sleep," he said.

"You can sleep later," she told him, then turned to the others. Fell walked to where they all sat and joined them. Sigarni stood. "Obrin has now appointed twenty-five group leaders," she said. "It is therefore time for our warriors to know the structure of our leadership. There will be two wings in the army. Grame will lead one, and Fell the other. Obrin will retain responsibility for training, and will also captain a third and smaller force; the role of this third force I will discuss with you later. Tovi, you will relinquish the role of Hunt Lord, passing it to me. From that moment you will remain in charge of all supplies, the gathering of food and its distribution; you will liaise with Loran. Later you will have a second role, and that we will discuss tomorrow."

Fell glanced at the former baker, and saw that his face had grown pale. Tovi had worked as hard as any during and after the exodus from Loda lands. To lose his role as Hunt Lord was bitterly hard, and would be seen as a humiliation. No one spoke. All waited for Tovi's reaction.

The man pushed himself to his feet and walked slowly from the building. As the door closed Fell spoke. "That was not right," he said. "It was cold cruelty and the man deserved more than that."

"Deserve?" countered Sigarni. "Did his son deserve to die? Do the Loda deserve to be living in the mountains as beggars, their homes destroyed? Did I deserve . . . ?" Abruptly Sigarni returned to her seat, and Fell could see her struggling to control her anger. "The decision is made," she said at last. "The left and right wings of the army will be led by you and Grame. Obrin will select your groups tomorrow; discuss the dispositions with him. Once your wings are organized you will work with them, testing your officers, and if necessary promoting others."

"Does Asmidir have no role?" asked Fell. "I understood he was once a general."

"He will advise me. Now the hour is late, and as you said, Fell, you are in need of sleep. We will meet here tomorrow night, and then I will tell you of Obrin's force and what they must do."

The men rose to their feet and walked from the room, leaving only Obrin with Sigarni.

Fell stepped into the moonlight, Grame beside him. The white-bearded smith clapped him on the shoulder. "Do not be so downhearted, general," he said. "If Tovi is honest he will admit to his relief. His heart is not in war."

"It would have been more kind had she spoken to him alone."

The smith nodded. "She's been through the fire, boy, and

it does tend to burn away softness. And she'll need to be harder yet, if the Loda are to survive."

"Those words should be chiseled in stone," said Asmidir softly, from behind them. The two clansmen said nothing. Neither was comfortable in the presence of the black man. He smiled and shook his head, then politely bade them good night and headed for his own small hut.

"I don't like that man," said Grame.

"He can be trusted," said Ballistar, from where he was standing unnoticed by the door. "I'd stake my life on it."

"I didn't say he couldn't be *trusted*, little man. I just don't like him; there's no heart in him."

Snow began to fall once more and the bitter wind came down from the north. Fell pulled his cloak around his shoulders. "I'm for sleep," he said. "I feel like I haven't closed my eyes since autumn."

"I'll stay up for a while yet," said Grame. "She gave us much to think about." He grinned at Ballistar. "I still have a jug of Gwalchmai's throat burner. You're welcome to a dram."

Ballistar chuckled. "Just the one, mind."

Fell left them and wandered away.

Obrin's anger was hard to contain as he stood before Sigarni. "If you want me to die, why not just ask one of your soldiers to do it? Or you could cut my throat now!"

"I am not looking for you to die, Outlander." The coldness of her tone only served to inflame him further.

Obrin forced a laugh. "Come now, lady, there's no one else here. I see the way you look at me: loathing and hatred. You think I've never seen it before? What I don't understand is why you'd want to send a hundred of your own men to die with me."

"Are you finished?" stormed Sigarni, rising from her chair. "Or have you still some whining to do?" She stood directly before him, her eyes blazing. "You are entirely correct in your assessment of my feelings toward you. Perhaps toward all men, including clansmen. There is no room in my heart for love. No room. In less than twelve weeks an army will descend on these mountains, and I *must* have a force to oppose them. Not only that, but they must be denied supplies. They have three forts built deep into our territory—tell me what they contain?"

"You know the answer."

"Tell me. *Exactly!*"

"Food and supplies, weapons—bows, arrows, lances, swords, helms. But more importantly they each contain one hundred fighting men, and are impregnable against all but a huge encircling force. The palisade walls are twenty-five feet high, the entrance guarded by drop-gates. Any force approaching would be open to bowshot for one hundred paces all around the fort. Once they arrived they would have to scale the walls. I've done that, lady, and I can tell you that a man with a good sword can kill twenty men scaling. You can't defend yourself when you're scrambling up a rope."

"I am not asking you to scramble up ropes, Obrin. I did not ask you to *assault* the fort on Farlain land. I said you were to *take* it. Now will you listen to my plan?"

"I'm listening," he said, "but I spent half my life building those damned forts. I know what goes into their construction."

"I want you to ride up to the drop-gate, with your hundred men, and I want you to relieve the defenders of their command."

Obrin's jaw dropped. "Relieve? What are you talking about?"

"When we were both at Asmidir's home I asked you about the forts. You said the men who manned them would expect to serve no more than two months, then a relief force would arrive."

"But the snow? There's no way through those southern passes."

"They won't know that, will they? You are a former officer . . ."

"Sergeant," he corrected.

"Whatever!" she snapped. "Some of them may know you and that is good. They have been trapped in those forts and will have no knowledge of your . . . change of loyalty. We still have the weapons, and what passed for uniforms, of the mercenaries who attacked Cilfallen. We also have the horses. I want you to choose a hundred men and take over the Farlain fort."

He said nothing for a moment, his mind racing. They *would* be hoping for a relief force. Most of the men would be thinking about the Midwinter celebrations in Citadel, the parties, the dancing, the women. "It's a fine idea," he said, "but I should be carrying sealed orders from the Baron. Without them no officer will turn over his command."

Sigarni returned to her seat, and he could see her pondering his words. "Discipline," she said softly. "Orders and rules." She nodded. "Tell me this, Obrin, what would happen if a *verbal* order reached a commander, and when refusing to obey it, the Baron's plans were thrown into chaos? Would the Baron merely congratulate the commander on holding to the rules?"

"It is not quite that easy," replied Obrin. "In that situation the Baron would have the man flogged or hanged for not acting on his own initiative. But if the commander did obey the verbal order, and then failed, he would still be blamed for not holding fast to the regulations."

"I see," said Sigarni. "Then you will ride to the Farlain fort with only . . . say . . . eighty-five men. Get some bandages soaked in cattle blood and disguise some of your men as wounded. You will ride to the fort and tell the commander that your officer was slain, and that you are the relief force. You will say that the Pallides fort is under attack and that the Baron has ordered the commander to reinforce it."

"But there are no sealed orders!"

"You will tell him that when you were surrounded your officer, thinking all was lost, destroyed the orders so that the enemy would not see them. Then a blizzard broke and you were able to lead your men to safety."

"He won't relinquish the fort," said Obrin stubbornly. "You have to understand the officer mentality."

"Oh, I think I understand it, Obrin. Hear me out. The commander will be caught on twin horns. If he disobeys an order you tell him was issued by the Baron and the Pallides fort falls, he will be hanged or flogged. If he obeys and everything goes wrong, he will be asked why he did not follow the rules and remain where he was."

"Exactly," said Obrin.

"Then, as a good sergeant, you will help him. You will offer to lead the rescue of the Pallides fort. That way he has not disobeyed an order, and he has not left his post."

"Aye," said Obrin slowly. "He might go for such a plan. But where does that leave us? I'll be riding out again with my men."

"No, *his* men. You will explain that your forces are exhausted, whereas his are fresh."

"So I ride out with a hundred enemy soldiers behind me? What then?"

"You lead them into an ambush. Grame will tell you where."

Obrin stared hard at the tall young woman. Her face, though beautiful, was emotionless, the eyes cold now and cruel. "You are a canny woman, Sigarni," he said. "It has a good chance of success."

"Make it succeed," she urged him. "I need those supplies and weapons. More importantly, I need to deny them to the Baron."

"I can understand that, lady, but why that fort? The Pallides is closer. Even if we do take the Farlain fort we have a great distance to cover carrying the supplies back here, much of it over rough country."

"You will take all three forts," she assured him. "The Farlain will be first. And you will not carry the supplies far—only to Torgan's town. Then you will move on to the others. Now get some rest and be here tomorrow at dawn with Grame and Tovi."

Obrin bowed and walked out into the night. He could hear the sounds of laughter from Grame's hut, but elsewhere all was quiet.

She was canny all right. Not only would the plan—if it succeeded—ease the food shortage, and rob the Baron of spring supplies, but it would also impress the Farlain, who had lost scores of men in useless assaults on the fortification. And the chances of success, he knew, were high indeed. Sigarni was using the enemy's great strength against them. Discipline. Blind obedience.

Who would have thought that an untutored clanswoman could have such a devious mind?

"All women have devious minds," he said aloud. "It's why I never wed."

Sigarni rapped on the door of the small hut. "Who's there?" called Tovi. Stepping inside, she saw the Hunt Lord sitting by an open fire. He glanced up as she entered. "How did you find me?" he asked.

"Kollarin has a talent for these matters. Why are you not with your family?"

"I need time to think."

Sigarni sat down opposite the man. "You are angry."

"What do you expect? I know I was a better baker than a Hunt Lord, but I have done my best since the attack. I could do no more."

"I do not ask for more," said Sigarni. "I need your skills in other areas."

"What skills?" he asked bitterly. "You want me to bake bread for you? I can do that. Just build me an oven."

"Yes, I want bread," she said softly. "I want the people fed.

Battles alone will not win us this war, Tovi. Once we have defeated the first Outland army we will need to move from defense to attack and that means invading the Lowlands. The army will need to be supplied with food. We will need mercenaries, and that means we must have gold; a treasury. Our forces will be spread, and that requires lines of communication. You understand? The role I need you for will stretch your talents to the limit. You will have no time for other burdens."

"Why could you not say this in front of the others? Why did I need to suffer humiliation, Sigarni?"

She looked at the older man, saw the hurt in his eyes. "They did not need to know my plans. There are hard days coming, Tovi. Some of the men in that room will die in our cause: they may even be captured and tortured. Worse, one or more of them will seek to betray us. What I say to you here is not to be repeated."

"I may be captured and tortured," he pointed out.

"It is unlikely, for you will not be fighting."

"You deny me even that? A chance for revenge, to restore the honor of my family?"

"Listen to me! What is more important, that you drive your claymore into one enemy heart, or your skills bring down a thousand? You are vital to me, Tovi. You have a feel for organization, and a mind that can cope with a score of problems simultaneously. I have seen those talents here, in the four encampments. Few could have achieved what you have. When the war comes I will need your skills."

He laughed and scratched his beard. "Here we sit with a tiny force made up of many old men and young lads, and you speak of invading the Lowlands! Better still, I believe you when you speak of it. What has happened to you, Sigarni? From where do these ideas spring?"

"From my blood, Tovi."

"All these years I have watched you, and never seen you. When you were a child you used to hide behind my bakery and wait until I stepped out at the front for a breath of air. Fast as a hawk, you would sprint inside to steal a cake—just the one from the middle of the tray, then you would push the others together, disguising the gap."

"You knew?"

"I knew. You hid behind the water barrel."

"How did you know?"

"Lemon mint. Gwalchmai always loved that scent and you used to rub the leaves over your body when you bathed. Every time I stepped back inside I could smell lemon mint."

"You never caught me," she said softly.

He shrugged. "I never wanted to. You were a child of sorrow, Sigarni. Everyone loved you. And I could spare a morsel on Cake Day."

Sigarni fed some wood to the fire and they sat in companionable silence for a while. "I am not that child any longer," she said.

"I know. Yet she is still there, deep down inside. She will always be there." He sighed, then smiled. "I will serve you, Sigarni, in any way that you want me."

"Thank you, Tovi," she said, her voice tender. "For this—and for the cakes." Rising smoothly, she moved to the door. "Be at the log hall at dawn."

"Why?"

"Because I need you there," she said.

Chapter Ten

Torgan's mood was not enhanced by the news from his scouts that the Loda woman was riding toward the town. At first the people of the Farlain had talked of little else—how strong she was, how noble she looked, how brave. Torgan had fast become heartily sick of it. That was why he had led his rash raid on the Outlanders, to prove that *he* was the natural leader of the clans. It might have worked too, save for the craven tactics of the enemy, drawing back and then loosing cavalry upon him. Had they stood and fought like men he was sure the Farlain warriors would have cut them to pieces. After that he had led two spectacularly unsuccessful attacks on their fort. Another forty men had been struck by arrows; seven had died.

Now the Farlain were talking about Sigarni once more, how she had supposedly killed demons sent against her, and how successful *she* had been against the Outlanders at Cilfallen. God, could they not see what she was? Just a Loda whore in pretty armor! There was little doubt in Torgan's mind that the battle at Cilfallen had been masterminded by the black-skinned bastard who rode with her. Rode with her? Rode her, more like!

Now she was coming here again.

This time I'll make her humiliation complete, he thought.

His wife, Layelia, entered the room, bearing a cup of sweet tisane. He took it without a word and sipped it. Layelia did not depart, but stood staring at him. He looked up into her large, soft brown eyes. "What?" he asked gruffly.

"She is coming," said his wife.

"I know that. I'll deal with her."

"Are you sure you are in the right?"

"What is that supposed to mean?" he snapped. She flinched, which pleased him. A woman should know her place.

"I've heard talk that she *is* the Chosen One. Carela told me . . ."

"I'm not interested in women's gossip, Layelia. And I've heard enough!"

For a moment he thought she would stand her ground, but she bowed her head and left him alone once more. Torgan ran his hand over his close-cropped back hair. The bald spot was growing on the crown and his widow's peak was becoming more pronounced by the day. He swore softly. Why should he alone of his family lose his hair? His father had a shock of white hair, like a lion's mane, until the day he died at eighty.

Torgan threw his cloak around his shoulders and stepped out into the winter sunlight. It was bright, the day clear and cold. He could see the Loda woman in the distance. The black man was not with her, but there were a dozen or so riders following her as she made her way down the long slope. More people were on the streets than was normal for this time of day. They were making their way to the square, ready to hear the whore's words.

Torgan strode out, looking to neither left nor right. His chair had been set at the center of the square, his lieutenants were already standing beside it. This time there was no Neren, or Calias, or Pimali. All had fallen in the battle.

I never would have acted so fast had the woman not inflamed my anger, he thought. It's her fault they are dead.

By the time Sigarni and her followers rode into the square, there were more than two hundred Farlain gathered to witness the exchange. She did not dismount, but sat her horse staring at Torgan.

"Well, woman?" he called out. "What now? Why are you here?"

"Perhaps I just wanted to look at a fool," she said, her words colder than the wind. "Perhaps I wondered whether the Outlanders had made you a general in return for the number of clansmen you killed for them."

Torgan was outraged. "How dare you?" he shouted, surging to his feet. "I did not come here to listen to your insults."

"Where do you normally go?" she said. "By God, I'd think you'd have to travel far from the Highlands *not* to hear insults. Three hundred men! You led them into a trap that a child could have seen. Or did no one mention cavalry to you? Did your scouts not see their hiding places? Come to that, Torgan, did you even send out scouts?"

"I don't answer to you."

"That is where you are wrong," Sigarni told him as, dismounting, she walked toward him. "You answer to me, Torgan, because you have wasted three hundred Highlanders. Thrown their lives away in a moment of crass stupidity. Aye, you'll answer to me!"

Stepping in close, she slammed a right-hand punch to his chin. The blow shocked him and he stepped back, trying to ready himself. She turned away from him, then spun back and leaped, her boot cannoning against his jaw. Torgan hit the seat and fell heavily, striking his temple against the cold flagstones. Dazed, he heard her carrying on speaking as if nothing had happened. Only she wasn't talking to him, she was addressing the Farlain. "In eleven weeks," she said, "an army will come to these Highlands of ours—a murderous force intent on butchery. If we are to destroy them we need to act together, under a single leader. The fool lying there will lead you to destruction. I think you already know that. Pick him up!"

Torgan felt strong arms lifting him to his feet, then sitting him in his chair. "The position of Hunt Lord *can* be passed from father to son," he heard her say, "but that has not always been the Highland way. We are in a war, and it is up to you to choose a Hunt Lord who can best serve the needs of the people. *All* the people—Farlain, Loda, Pallides, and Wingoras. I do not care who you choose. But whoever it is will serve under my leadership."

"By what right?" asked a tall, broad-shouldered warrior with a silver mustache. Torgan blinked as Harcanan stepped up to stand before the woman. His uncle would put her in her place. He was a man of iron principles, not one to be fooled by this whore in scarlet.

"By what right?" echoed Sigarni. "By right of blood and right of battle. By virtue of my sword and my skills."

He shook his head. "I do not know of your blood, Sigarni, but your battle was one skirmish fought at Cilfallen. As to your sword and your skills, I have seen no evidence that you can carry a fight with either. I say this with no disrespect, for I applaud your defense of Cilfallen and your determination to fight against the Outlanders. But I need more proof that you are the war leader we should follow."

"Well said," she told him. "And how would you like this proof delivered?"

"I cannot say—but one battle does not convince me. Even now the Outlanders are camped on our land, their position impregnable. A war leader should be able to free us of their presence."

"What is your name?"

"I am Harcanan."

"I have heard of you," she said. "You fought at Colden Moor. It is said you killed twenty Outlanders, and led the King to safety."

He smiled grimly. "An exaggeration, Sigarni. But I was there the last time the clans gathered against the Outlanders and I will be there the next time, God willing."

"So then, Harcanan, will you follow me?"

"I have already said that I need more proof."

Sigarni stood silently for a moment. "I will make a bargain with you, Harcanan," she said at last. "Pledge yourself to me, and *then* I will show you proof."

"Why not the other way around?" he countered.

"Because I require your faith, as well as your sword."

He smiled. "I hear you require men to bend the knee to you, as if to a monarch. Is that what you are asking?"

"Aye, Harcanan. Exactly that. As in the old days. But you will not need to lead me to safety; you will live to see the Outlanders crushed and broken, begging for mercy. Now give me your pledge."

Torgan sat quietly, waiting for the old warrior to laugh in her face. He did not. Instead he walked slowly forward and dropped to one knee before her. "My sword and my life," he said.

Sigarni swung to the crowd. Throwing up her arm, she pointed to the line of horse-drawn wagons making their slow way over the crest of the hill. "Those wagons you see are loaded with the spoils of war, taken from the fort on Farlain land. My forces took that fort two days ago. Even as we speak, the Pallides fort is falling to us."

Harcanan rose. "How many men did you lose?" he asked.

"None," she told him. "Assemble the council, for I would address them."

Harcanan bowed, and Sigarni turned to Torgan. "I could—and probably should—kill you," she said. "But you are a Highlander, and not without courage. Be at the council meeting."

Torgan rose and stumbled away, his mind reeling.

Gwalchmai was sober. It was not an uplifting experience. As he sat in the log hall, surrounded by the younger children of the encampment, he found himself yearning for the sanctuary of the jug. There were several older women present, dishing out the last of the milk to the eager young, and about a dozen younger mothers sitting in a group, holding their babies and talking animatedly. Gwalchmai could not hear their conversation, for most of the smaller children had gathered around him and were asking questions he found it hard to answer. For some weeks now his powers had been waning, and he found himself unable to summon visions. It was ironic, that now of all times his Talent should desert him. He had often prayed to be released from the gift—the curse—and now that it had happened he felt terribly alone, and very frightened.

The clan needed him—and he had nothing more to give.

"Why do they want to kill us all, Gwalchmai?" asked a bright-eyed young boy of around twelve. "Have we done something wrong?"

"No, nothing wrong," he grunted, feeling himself hemmed in by the youngsters.

"Then why are we being punished?"

"It's no good asking me to make sense of it, lad. It's a war. There's no sense in war."

"Then why are we doing it?" questioned another boy.

"We don't have a choice," said Gwalchmai. There was still a little left in the jug, he remembered. But where had he put it?

"Are we all going to be killed?" asked a girl with long red hair. Gwalchmai cleared his throat. A man's voice cut in and Gwalchmai looked up to see Kollarin, moving through the youngsters. The younger man grinned at Gwalch, patted his shoulder, and then sat down beside him. "When a thief enters your house," he told the children, "to take what is yours, then you either allow him to roam unchecked or you stop him. When a wolf pack attacks your cattle, you slay the wolves. That is the way of the hunter. The Outlanders have decided to take all that is yours. Your fathers have decided to stop them."

"My father is a great hunter," declared the girl. "Last year he killed a rogue bear."

"Not on his own," said the boy. "My father was with him. He shot it too."

"He did not!" A squabble broke out between the two. Kollarin's laughter boomed out.

"Come, come, clansmen, this is no way to behave. I did not have a father—well, not that I recall. I had a mother who could shoot a bow, or wield a sword. Once, when a lioness got in among our sheep she strode out to the pasture, carrying only a long staff, and frightened it away. She was a fine woman."

"You are an Outlander," said the first boy, his earnest gaze fixed to Kollarin's face. "Why do you want to kill us?"

"I never wanted to kill anyone," Kollarin told him. "There are many . . . Outlanders, as you call them, from many nations. They have built an empire; I am from one part of that empire. They conquered my country a hundred and ten years ago. The Outlanders are not, by nature, evil; they do not eat babies, or make blood sacrifices to vile gods. Their problem is that they believe in their own destiny as masters of the world. They respect strength and courage above all else. Therefore the strongest, the most ruthless, tend to achieve high rank. The Baron is such a man; he is evil, and because he leads in the north his evil spreads through the men under his command."

"What happened to your father?" asked the red-haired girl.

"He ran away when I was a babe."

"Why?"

Kollarin shrugged. "I cannot answer for him. My mother told me he found life on the farm too dull."

"Did people torment you?" asked a small boy with thick curly hair.

Kollarin nodded. "Aye, they did. A boy without a father becomes, for some reason, an object of scorn."

"Me too," said the boy. "My father ran away before I was born."

"He didn't run away," put in another child scornfully. "Not even your mother could have said who he was."

The curly-haired boy reddened and started to rise. Kollarin spoke swiftly. "Let us have no violence here. You are all of the clan, and the clan is in danger; it is no time to argue with another. But there is something else you could think about. How does evil grow? What makes it appear in a human heart, growing like a weed among the blooms? I tell you. It is born from anger and injustice, from resentment and jealousy. You have all witnessed the tiniest seed of it here in this hall. A boy with no father has been insulted for what may—or may not—have been the sin of his mother. That insult, and others like it, will simmer inside him as he grows. And by what right is he treated so unjustly?" Kollarin fixed his eyes on the older boy. "Has his birth damaged you in some way?"

"Everyone knows his mother is a—"

"Do not say it!" said Kollarin icily. "For when you speak thus, you give birth to evil."

"It's the truth!"

"No, it is a *perception* of the truth. There is a difference. To the Outlanders *you* are an untutored barbarian, worth less than a pig. You are not even human: Your mother is a whore and your father is a stinking piece of filth who needs to be eradicated. That is their *perception* of the truth. They are wrong—and so are you. I do not say this to you in anger, boy. In fact, it saddens me."

"I will tell my father what you said about him, Outlander!" shouted the boy. "He will kill you for it!"

"If that is true," said Kollarin softly, "there will be one less person to fight the Baron's men. No, I do not think that he will. I think it more likely he will be saddened, as I am, that you should insult a brother at a time like this."

"He's not my brother! He's the son of a whore!"

"That's enough!" roared Gwalchmai, surging to his feet. "I am the Clan Dreamer, and I know the truth. Kollarin has spoken it, though perhaps he should not. What festers inside you, young man, is that everyone can see the resemblance between you and Kellin. You *are* brothers, and no amount of harsh words will change that. You have a great deal of growing up to do. Start now."

The older boy ran from the hall, leaving the door swinging on its canvas hinges. Snow blew in and another child moved to the door, pushing it shut and dropping the latch. The children gathered again around the two men, their faces fearful. "Sometimes," said Kollarin, "life can be needlessly cruel. You have witnessed such a time. Evil does not grow from the head of a devil with horns—if it did we would all run from it. It springs from an angry word, and settles in the ears of the hearers. It can grow almost unnoticed until it flowers in rage and envy, jealousy and greed. The next time you have an angry thought about a clan brother or sister, remember this."

"He will kill you, you know," said the curly-haired Kellin. "Jaren's father has a terrible temper. You should get a sword."

"I will, should the need arise," said Kollarin sadly. "But now I think we should play a game, and change the mood. How many here know Catch the Bear?"

Gwalchmai quietly left the hall with the game still in progress, and the squeals and laughter of the children ringing in his ears. It was bright and cold outside, but the old man could smell the approach of distant spring upon the wind. He shivered.

Kollarin was right. Evil was not an external force waiting to seize upon a wandering heart. It dwelled within the heart, a cocooned maggot waiting for the moment to break out and feed, gorging itself on the darker forces of the human soul. This was well understood by the founders of the clan, who instilled the stories and myths for youngsters to emulate. Heroes *never* oppressed or tormented the weak, *never* lied or stole or used their powers for selfish purposes. Heroes were always subject to such dark desires, but resisted them manfully. All such stories had but one purpose—to encourage the young to battle the demons inside.

Even with his Talent fading, Gwalchmai knew what demons drove young Jaren. Other children whispered that Kellin was his brother . . . this meant that his father had been unfaithful to his mother, and had then betrayed another woman leaving her to bring up a son in shame. Jaren would not have his father slandered in such a way, and had turned his anger toward little Kellin, blaming him for the lies. His anger and his hatred were born of love for his father.

Gwalchmai stood in the cold sunlight, waiting.

It was not long before he saw the boy heading back with a stocky clansman beside him. For a moment he could not remember the man's name, then it came to him—Kars. When Gwalchmai called out to him, the man let go of his son's hand and strode toward the Dreamer. His square, beardless face was pale with anger.

"You lied about me, Dreamer," he said, his tone icy. "If you were a younger man I would slay you where you stand. The Outlander is different; he will die for the honor of my family."

"And will the blood wash away the shame?" asked Gwalchmai, holding to the man's gaze.

Kars stepped in close. "The woman was any man's for a copper farthing. That was her work and her pleasure. Aye, I rutted with her. Find me a man who did not."

"That is inconsequential," said Gwalchmai. "Good God, man, have you not looked at the boy? Every line of his face mirrors yours. Yet even that is beside the point. Why should the child carry the sins of his mother? What has he done, save to serve as a reminder of a night of casual coupling? And as for the Outlander, he spoke only the truth."

"He called me a piece of filth!" snarled Kars. "Is that the truth, old man?"

"He did not call you anything, Kars. He was explaining to

the children about how the Outlanders perceive us. Jaren became angry and took it all personally."

"Enough talk!" snapped the man, drawing his claymore and turning away.

"What now, Kars?" asked Gwalchmai softly. "Will you walk into a children's gathering and slaughter the man who leads them in games? Can you not hear the laughter? The joy? How long since the clan children knew such moments?"

At that instant the doors opened and the children moved out into the light. Kars stood stock-still, his sword in his hand. The laughter of the young faded away, and they stood by silently as Kollarin stepped out and swung his green cloak around his slender shoulders. A small boy moved out to stand beside him. Kars looked at the child, then at his own son, Jaren. No one moved. Kars plunged his sword into the snow and stepped forward to drop on one knee before Kellin. The little boy did not flinch, but stared back at the warrior.

Gwalchmai felt his heart beating erratically, his breathing shallow. For Kars to accept the boy as his own would mean a loss of honor to the proud clansman, causing grief to himself and shame to his family. To reject the evidence of his eyes would bring a different kind of shame, but one that was at least private.

The warrior reached out and placed his hands on Kellin's shoulders. "You are a fine lad," he said, his voice choked with emotion. "A fine lad. Should you wish it, you would be welcome at my fire, and at my home."

Gwalchmai could scarce believe he had heard the words. Switching his gaze to Jaren, who was standing near to his father, he saw that the boy looked close to tears. Kars glanced up and called to his son and Jaren ran to him. Kars stood, then offered his hand to Kellin. "Let us walk for a while," he said. Kellin took his left hand, Jaren his right.

Together they walked away toward the trees.

Kollarin strolled across to where Gwalchmai stood. "A curious encounter," observed the younger man.

"There is still nobility within the clan," said Gwalchmai proudly. "And I will die happy."

Kollarin's face showed his sorrow. "You are going back to your cabin, to meet the soldiers who will kill you. Why? You know that if you stay here you will thwart them."

"Aye," agreed Gwalchmai. "There are magical moments when a man can change the future. But not this time. I still have one small task to perform, one last gift for Sigarni."

"You will plant a seed," said Kollarin sadly, "and you will die for it."

"Take care of my dogs, young man. I have grown to love them. And now I must go." Suddenly Gwalchmai chuckled. "There are two jugs of honey mead liquor hidden in my loft back home. I can hear them calling to me!"

Kollarin put out his hand. "You are a good man, Gwalchmai, and a brave one. I know you are concerned about Sigarni, and how she will fare without your guidance. I will be her Gifted One . . . and I will never betray her."

"There is one who will," said the old man. "I do not know who."

"I will watch for him," promised Kollarin.

Leofric's servant banked up the fire and brought in fresh candles which he lit and placed atop the dying stubs. The blond-haired young man did not acknowledge his presence, but remained poring over maps and calculations. Leofric was not a happy man. Much as he enjoyed the logistics of a campaign, he could not divorce himself from the feeling that it was all so unnecessary. The clans had been peaceful for years, and now the Baron was set to bring fire and death into their lands. And for what? A little glory and the chance to rise again in the King's eyes. That and the speculation on land prices south of the border.

It was all so meaningless.

The servant placed a goblet of steaming tisane before him. Leofric lifted it and sipped the brew, which was sweet and spiced with liquor. "Thank you. Most thoughtful," he said, looking up at the servant. The man disappeared from his mind instantly.

The army would march in ten weeks. Each of the six thousand men would carry four days' food supply with them. Leofric lifted a quill pen. One pound of oats, eight ounces of dried beef, half an ounce of salt. Seven pennies for each pack, multiplied by six thousand. He shook his head. The Baron would not be pleased at such an outlay.

Sipping his tisane, he leaned back in his chair.

By his reckoning this war would cost twelve thousand four hundred gold pieces in wages, food, and materials. But the Baron had budgeted for ten thousand.

Where to make cuts? Salt was expensive, but soldiers would not march without it, and it was common knowledge that an absence of beef in the diet led to cowardly behavior. But halving the oats ration would mean less bulk food, and besides would save only . . . he scribbled down a calculation, then multiplied it. Three hundred and forty-two gold pieces.

Then he brightened. You have not considered the dead, he thought. The Highlanders will fight, and that means a percentage of the army would not be requiring food or payment. But how many? On a normal campaign with the Baron the losses could be as high as thirty percent, but that would not be the situation here. Half that? A quarter? Say five percent: three hundred men. Once more he bent over his calculations.

Almost there, he decided.

The servant returned. "Begging your pardon, my lord, but there is a man to see you."

"What time is it?"

"A little before midnight, sir."

"An odd time to be calling. Who is it?"

"I do not know him, sir. He is a stranger. He asked for you and said he had information you would find invaluable."

Leofric sighed; he was tired. "Very well, show him in. Give us no more than ten minutes, then interrupt me on a matter of importance—you understand?"

"Of course, sir." The man bowed and departed.

Leofric rubbed his eyes and yawned. Midnight. Dear God, I have been working on these papers for seven hours! Hastily he gathered them together, pushing them into a drawer. The servant returned, ushering in a middle-aged man with a round fleshy face and glittering eyes.

"I trust you will forgive this intrusion," said the newcomer. "But the news I have could not wait for the morning."

"And why is that, pray?" countered Leofric, gesturing the man to a seat.

"You were working on the invasion plans," said the other with a smile. "My information will force substantial changes."

"How do you know what I was working on?"

"Let us come back to that, Leofric," said the man with a wide smile. "For now, let me tell you that two of your three forts have fallen to the clansmen, and all the supplies they contain are now being consumed by your enemies."

Leofric's weariness vanished immediately. "That's not possible! I supervised the structures myself. They were impregnable!"

"Not from deceit, it appears."

Leofric sat down. "Deceit?"

"The woman Sigarni sent the traitor, Obrin, and a hundred men posing as a relief force. Both forts surrendered without a fight."

"How . . . ? Who are you?"

"I think you can fairly assume that I am a friend, Lord Leofric. I also have information concerning Sigarni and her plans. She is gathering an army, you know."

"Under whose leadership?"

"Her own, of course. She is of the blood royal, and she

masterminded the defeat of your forces at Cilfallen. Fine credentials, don't you think?"

"How many men does she command now?"

"Close to two thousand. The Farlain are with her, and the Pallides will soon follow. Unless she is stopped, that is."

"We cannot get through until the thaw. All the northern passes are blocked."

"*You* cannot get through but I can. I have already, in a manner of speaking."

The servant entered. "My lord, I think you should . . ."

"Yes, yes, no need for that now. Bring me another tisane, and one for our guest."

The man nodded and bowed as Leofric returned his attention to his guest. "I think it is time you declared your interest in this matter," he said.

"Of course. I am hunting the witch, Sigarni. My reasons are of no concern to you, but it is important to me that I find her. Surrounded as she is now by loyal clansmen, it might be . . . difficult for me to reach her. You can help me in my quest—as I can help you in yours."

"You're a magicker?"

The man laughed. "Nothing so dainty, my lord. I am a sorcerer. Some time ago I was paid to . . . remove the problem Sigarni posed. I failed. Three times. I say this without shame, for my opponents were mighty indeed. Happily, they now believe me to be dead, which leaves me free to enjoy the success I have waited for."

"Why would they think you dead?"

"A man was torn to pieces by demons. I made sure he resembled me in every way. You wish to hear more?"

Leofric shook his head. "Absolutely not. What is it you require of me, in return for your information?"

"I find that I am short of funds in Citadel town. I am far from my own bankers, and would be grateful for a gratuity that would enable me to rent a house in Citadel. There is much I must do to prepare for my next attempt. Men and materials, that sort of thing."

"Of course. Where are you staying at present?"

"A hostelry nearby, the Blue Duck tavern."

"I will have one of my servants bring you money tomorrow morning. I would also appreciate any further information you can supply concerning the plans of the rebels."

The man rubbed his fleshy chin. "I will consider that," he said. "It is a delicate business. You see, I don't want you to capture or kill Sigarni. That delight is for me. I'll think on it, and let you know my decision."

"The Baron will almost certainly want to see you."

"I don't believe so, Lord Leofric. Tell him you have a spy who brought you this information. That, after all, is the truth. Do not mention me to him. It would displease me."

"Who shall my servant ask for tomorrow?" Leofric inquired.

"Oh, I am sorry, I did not introduce myself. My name is Jakuta Khan."

Ballistar's hatred for winter was deep and perfect, for it was the one season designed to highlight his deformity. His short, stumpy legs could not cope with deep snow and he felt a prisoner in Asmidir's house. Ballistar longed to be with Sigarni again, planning for the spring and the coming war.

"You would be useless now," he said aloud as he perched on the battlements staring out over the winter landscape. "Useless."

Scrambling to his feet, he stood. Yet today there was no enjoyment in being so high. It served only to emphasize how tiny he was. Snow began to fall as Ballistar dropped to his belly and lowered himself to the parapet.

Back inside his upper room, he stoked the fire and sat down on the rug staring into the flames. The chairs were all too tall, and Ari had brought a wooden box to the room so that Ballistar could climb into bed. Why was I born like this?

he wondered. What sin could a child be guilty of that a vengeful God would condemn him to a life such as this.

No one understood his torment. How could they? Even Sigarni had once said, "Perhaps one day you will meet a beautiful dwarf woman and be happy."

I don't want a dwarf woman, he thought. Just because I am deformed, it does not mean I will find deformity attractive in others.

I want you, Sigarni. I want you to love me, to see me as a *man*.

It won't happen. He remembered the taunts that marked his childhood and adolescence. Bakris Tooth-gone had once caused great merriment with a joke about Ballistar and his inability to find love. "How could he make love to a woman?" Bakris had said. "If they were nose to nose, he'd have his toes in it, toes to toes he'd have his nose in it, and if he ever got there he'd have no one to talk to."

Oh, yes, great roars of laughter had greeted the jest. Even Ballistar had chuckled. What other choice was there?

Ballistar left his room and wandered downstairs and out into the stable yard. The little white pony was in her stall and the dwarf climbed to the rail by her head and stroked her neck. The pony swung her head and nuzzled him. "Do you worry about being a dwarf horse?" he said. "Do you look at the tall mares with envy?" The pony returned to munching the straw in her feed box. It was cold in the stable and Ballistar saw that the pony's blanket had slipped from her back. Climbing to the floor he retrieved it, and tried to flip it back into place. It was a large blanket, and as he tried to throw it high, it fell back over Ballistar's head. Three times he tried. On the last it was almost in place, but the pony moved to its right and the blanket fell to the left.

It was the final humiliation for Ballistar. Tears welled in his dark eyes, and he thought again of the high parapet. On the north side, at the base of the wall, there were sharp rocks.

If I were to throw myself from the battlements I would die, he thought. No more pain, no more humiliation . . .

Ballistar returned to the house and began to climb the stairs.

The servant-warrior, Ari, moved out of the library and saw him. "Good morning, Ballistar."

"Good morning," mumbled the dwarf, continuing his climb.

"I was wondering if you could assist me."

Ballistar hesitated, and glanced down through the stair rails at the tall black man.

"Not today," he said.

"It is important," said Ari softly. "I am studying the maps of the Duane Pass, for that is where we believe the first battle will be fought. Do you know it?"

"I know it."

"Good, then you will be of great assistance." Ari turned away and reentered the library. Ballistar stood for a moment, then slowly climbed down the stairs and followed the man. Ari was sitting on the floor with maps all around him. A coal fire was burning in the hearth.

Ballistar slumped down beside the man. "What do you need?" he asked.

"These woods here," said Ari, pointing to a green section, "are they thick and dense, or light and open?"

"Reasonably light. Firs, mostly. You thought to hide men there?"

"It was a possibility."

Ballistar shook his head. "Not possible. But there is a gully just beyond the woods where a force could be concealed. There!" he said, stabbing his index finger on the map. "Now I will leave you."

"Ah, but we have just begun," said Ari with a smile. "Look at this." He passed Ballistar a sketch and the dwarf took it. Upon it was an outline of Duane Pass and a series of rectangles, some blacked in, others in various colors.

"What are these?"

"The classic Outland battle formation—infantry at the center, the heavy black blocks. Two divisions. The blue represents the cavalry, the yellow archers and slingers. The cavalry also may be in two divisions, lightly armored and heavily armored. But this we do not yet know. Where would you place our forces?"

"I'm not a soldier!" snapped Ballistar.

"Indeed not, but you are a bright, intelligent man. Skills can be learned. Let me give you an example: Where would cavalry be of limited use?"

"In a forest," answered Ballistar, "where the trees and undergrowth would restrict a mounted man."

"And what slows down infantry?"

"Hills, mountains, rivers. Forests again."

"There, you see?" Ari told him. "Having established that, then we look for ways to ensure that battles are fought where *we* desire them—in forests, on hills. So, where in Duane would you position our forces?"

Ballistar gazed at the map. "There is only one good defensive point. There is a flat-topped hill at the northern end of the pass—but it would be surrounded swiftly."

"Yes," said Ari, "it would. How many people could gather there?"

"I don't know. A thousand?"

"I would think two thousand," said Ari. "Which is our entire force."

"What would be the point of such an action?" asked Ballistar. "Once surrounded there would be no way to retreat, and even the advantage of occupying a hill would be overcome by an Outland army numbering more than five thousand men."

"Yet it remains the only true defensive position," insisted Ari. "Once the Outlanders are through Duane Pass, they can spread out and attack isolated hamlets and villages. Nothing could stop them."

"I don't know the answer," Ballistar admitted.

"Nor I, but we will speak of it again. Tonight at dinner." He looked directly into Ballistar's eyes. "Or did you have other plans?"

Ballistar took a deep breath. "No, no other plans."

"That is good. I will see you later."

"You really believe I can be of help in this?" asked Ballistar, struggling to his feet.

"Of course. Take the sketches with you, and think about them."

Ballistar smiled. "I will, Ari. Thank you."

The black man shrugged and returned to his studies.

Chapter Eleven

"By God, she's some woman," said Obrin, peeling off his jerkin and sitting by the fire. "They fell just like she said they would. Like skittles! I could scarce believe it, Fell. When I rode up to that Farlain fort my heart was in my mouth. The officer just ordered the gates opened, listened to my report, then turned over command to me and rode out. What a moment! I even told him the best route through the snow, and he rode his men into Grame's trap."

"Grame lost no men in that first encounter, yet more than twenty when the Pallides detachment was ambushed," said Fell.

"That's nothing compared with the two hundred we slew in those engagements," pointed out Obrin. "But it's a damn shame the men from the Loda fort escaped. I still don't know what went wrong there."

"They simply got lost," said Fell, "and missed the trap. No one's fault."

Obrin reached for a pottery jug and pulled the cork. "The Baron's wine," he said with a dry chuckle. "There were six jugs in each fort. It's a good vintage—try some."

Fell shook his head. "I think I'll take a walk," he said.

"What's wrong, Fell?"

"Nothing. I just need to walk."

Obrin replaced the cork and looked hard at the handsome forester. "I'm not the most intuitive of men, Fell. But I've been a sergeant for twelve years and I know when something is eating at a man. What is it? Fear? Apprehension?"

Fell smiled wearily. "Is it so obvious then?"

"It is to me, but your men must not see it. That is one of the secrets of leadership, Fell. Your confidence becomes their confidence. They feed off you, like wolf cubs suckling at the mother's teats. If you despair, they despair."

Fell chuckled. "I've never been compared with a mother wolf before. Pass the jug!" He took several long swallows. "You're right," he said, wiping his lips with the back of his hand. "The wine is good. But I don't fear the Outlanders, Obrin. I am not afraid to die for my people. What gnaws at me is more personal. I shall make sure that my feelings do not show as strongly in the future."

"Sigarni," said Obrin, lifting the jug.

"How would you know that?" asked Fell, surprised.

Obrin grinned. "I listen, Fell. That's another secret of leadership. You were lovers, but now you are not. Don't let it concern you. You're a good-looking lad and there are plenty of women who'd love to warm your bed."

Fell shook his head. "That's not the *whole* reason for my sadness. You didn't know her when she was just the huntress. God, man, she was a wonder! Strong and fearless, but more than that she had a love for life and a laugh that was magical. She could make a cold day of drizzle and grey sky suddenly seem beautiful. She was a *woman*. What is she now? Have you ever seen her laugh? Or even smile at a jest? Sweet Heaven, she's become a creature of ice, a winter queen." Fell drank again, long and deeply.

"There's not been a great deal to laugh about," observed Obrin, "but I hear what you say. I once owned a crystal sphere. There was a rose set inside, as if trapped in ice. I've always loved roses, and this was one of the most beautiful blooms, rich and velvet red. It would live forever. Yet it had no scent, and would not seed."

"That is it," said Fell. "Exactly that! Like the Crown of Alwen—all men can see it, none can touch it."

Obrin smiled. "I've often heard Highlanders talk of the lost Crown. Is it a myth?"

Fell shook his head. "I saw it when I was ten. It appears once every twenty-five years, at the center of the pool at Ironhand's Falls. It's beautiful, man. It is more a helmet than a crown, and the silver shines like captured moonlight. There are silver wings, flat against the helm like those of a hawk when it dives, and a golden band around the brow inscribed with ancient runes. It has a nasal guard—like an Outland helm—and this is also silver, as are the cheek guards. I was there with my father. It was the winter before he went down with the plague, my last winter with him. He took me to the Falls and we stood there with the gathered clans. I could not see at first, and he lifted me to his shoulders. A man cursed behind us, but then the Crown appeared. It shimmered for maybe ten, twelve heartbeats. Then it was gone. Man, what a night!"

"Sounds like a conjuring trick to me," said Obrin. "I've seen magickers make birds of gold that fly high into the air and explode in showers of colored sparks."

"It was no trick," said Fell without a hint of anger. "Alwen was Ironhand's uncle. He had no children, and he hated Ironhand. When he was dying he ordered one of his wizards to hide the Crown where Ironhand would never find it, thus condemning his nephew to a reign fraught with civil war and insurrection. Without it, Ironhand was a king with no credentials. You understand?"

"It makes no sense to me," said Obrin. "He had right of blood. Why did he need a piece of metal?"

"The Crown had magical properties. Only a true king could wear it. It was not made by Alwen's order, it was far older. Once, when a usurper killed the King and placed the Crown on his head, his skin turned black and fire erupted from his eyes. He melted away like snow in the sunshine."

"Hmmm," muttered Obrin, unconvinced. " 'Tis a pretty tale. My tribe has many such, the Spear of Goldark, the Sword of Kal-thyn. Maybe one day I'll see this Crown. But you were talking of Sigarni. If you loved her, and she you, why did it end?"

"I was a fool. I wanted sons, Obrin. It's important in the Highlands. I had a need to watch my boys grow, to teach them of forestry and hunting, to instill in them a love of the land. Sigarni is barren—like your rose in crystal. I walked away from her. But not an hour has passed since then that her face does not shine in my memories. Even when I lay with my wife, Gwen, all I could see was Sigarni. It was the worst mistake of my life." Fell drained the last of the wine and lay back on the floor of the hut. "I'd just like to see her laugh once more . . . to be the way she was." He closed his eyes.

Obrin sat quietly as Fell's breathing deepened.

You're wrong, Fell, he thought. I know what war is, and I know the pain and terror that is coming. Given a choice I'd keep Sigarni the way she is, the Ice Queen, the coldhearted warrior woman whose strategies have already seen three enemy forts overcome, and several tons of supplies brought into the encampments.

Obrin pulled on his jerkin and stepped out into the night.

Sigarni was tired. The morning had been a long one, discussing supplies with Tovi, organizing patrols with Grame and Fell, then poring over the battle plans drawn up by Asmidir and Ari, listening to Obrin's tales of woe concerning training.

"We've not the time to train them properly," said the stocky Outlander. "I've got them responding to the hunting horn for attack and retreat and re-form. But that is it! Your army will be like a spear, Sigarni. One throw is all you get."

She felt as if her mind could take not one more ounce of pressure, and had walked with Lady to a hilltop to look upon the ageless beauty of High Druin, hoping to steal a fragment of its eternal peace.

Two of Asmidir's *Al-jiin* walked twenty paces behind her, never speaking but always present. At first their ceaseless vigilance had been a source of irritation, but now she found their silent presence reassuring. A stand of trees grew across the hilltop, and these gave some shelter from the wind as Sigarni stared out over the winter landscape at the brooding magnificence of High Druin, its sharp peaks spearing the clouds. Down on the slopes leading to the valley she could see Loda children tobogganing, and hear the squeals of their laughter. The sounds were shrill, and echoed in the mountains.

Will they still be laughing in a few weeks? she wondered.

Taliesen had disappeared again, gone to whatever secret place wizards inhabit, and his last words to her echoed constantly in her memory: *"The Pallides will ask for a sign."*

"They already have," she had told him.

"No, no, listen to me! They will ask for something specific. When they do, agree to it. Don't hesitate. I will be back when I have prepared the way. Will you trust me?"

"You have given me no reason to distrust you. But what if they ask me to supply the moon on a silver salver?"

"Say that you will," he said with a dry laugh. He threw his tattered cloak of feathers around his scrawny frame, and his smile faded. "They will not ask that, but it will seem as difficult. Remember my words, Sigarni. I will be back before the first snowdrops of spring. We will meet by Ironhand's Falls in twelve days."

Lady brushed against her leg and whined. Sigarni knelt and stroked her long ears. "I have neglected you, my lovely," she said. "I am sorry." Lady's long nose pushed against Sigarni's cheek and she felt the hound's warm tongue on her face. "You are so forgiving." She patted Lady's dark flank.

"She wishes solitude," she heard one of her guards say.

Sigarni turned to see a tall, dark-haired woman standing with the two men.

"Let her through," she called. The woman gave the black men a wide berth and walked up the hillside. She was thin of face, with a prominent nose, but her large brown eyes gave her face a semblance of beauty. "You wish to speak with me?" said Sigarni.

"I do. I am Layelia, the wife of Torgan."

"There is no place for him among my officers," said Sigarni sternly. "He is a fool."

"That is a trait shared by most men I have met," said Layelia. "But then war is a foolish game."

"Have you come to plead for him?"

"No. He will regain his honor—or he will not. That is for him. I came to speak with you. I have questions."

Sigarni removed her cloak and spread it over the snow. "Come, sit with me. Why not more questions? That is my life now. Endless questions, each with a hundred answers."

"You look tired," said Layelia. "You should rest more."

"I will when there is time. Now ask your questions."

The dark-haired woman was silent for a moment, staring deeply into Sigarni's pale blue eyes. "What if we win?" she asked, at last.

Sigarni laughed. "If we lose we die. That is all I know. My God, I certainly have no time to think of the aftermath of a victory that is by no means certain."

"I think you should," said Layelia softly. "If you don't, then you are just like a man, never seeing beyond the end of your nose."

Sigarni sighed. "You are correct, I am tired. So let us assume the hare is bagged, and move on to the cooking. What do you want?"

Layelia chuckled. "I have heard a lot about you, Sigarni. You have lived a life many women—myself included—would envy. But I don't envy you now, trying to adjust to a world of men. I ask about victory for a simple, selfish reason. I have children, and I want those children to grow in the Highland way, with their father beside them, learning about cattle and crops, family, clan and honor. The Outlanders threaten our way of life—not just by their invasion, but by our resistance. Tell me this, if you beat the Baron, what then? Is it over?"

"No," admitted Sigarni. "They will send another army."

"And how will you combat them?"

"In whatever way I can," said Sigarni guardedly.

"You will be forced to attack the Lowland cities, sack their treasuries, and hire mercenaries."

Sigarni smiled grimly. "Perhaps."

"And if you defeat the next army, will that end the war?"

"I don't know," snapped Sigarni, "but I doubt it. Where is this leading?"

"It seems to me," said Layelia sadly, "that win or lose our way of life is finished. The war will go on and on. The more you win, the farther away you will take our men—perhaps all the way to the Outland capital. What then, when the outlying armies of their empire gather? Will you be fighting in Kushir in ten years?"

"If I am, it will not be from choice," Sigarni told her. "I hear you, Layelia, and I understand what you are saying. If there is a way I can avoid what you fear, then I will. You have my word on that."

The dark-haired woman smiled, and laid her hand on Sigarni's arm. "I believe you. You know, I have always thought the world would be a better place with women as leaders. We wouldn't fight stupid wars over worthless pieces of land; we would talk to one another, and reach compromises that would suit both factions. I know that you have to be a war leader, Sigarni, but I ask that you be a *woman* leader, and not just a pretend man in armor."

"You are very forthright, Layelia. A shame you were not so forthright with Torgan."

"I did my best," said the other with a wry smile, "but he

was not gifted with a good brain. He is, however, a fine partner in bed, so I will not complain too much."

Sigarni's laughter rang out. "I'm glad he is good at something."

"He is also a good father," said Layelia. "The children adore him, and he plays with them constantly."

"I am sorry," said Sigarni. "I have obviously not seen the best of him. Have you been married long?"

"Fourteen years come summer." She smiled. "He hasn't changed much in those years, save to lose some of his hair. It's beautiful here, isn't it, the sun gleaming on High Druin?"

"Yes," Sigarni agreed.

Layelia rose. "I have taken too much of your time. I will leave you to your thoughts."

Sigarni stood. "Thank you, Layelia. I feel refreshed, though I don't know why."

"You've spent too long in the company of men," said Layelia. "Perhaps we should talk again?"

"I would enjoy that."

Layelia stepped forward and embraced the silver-haired warrior woman, kissing her on both cheeks. Sigarni felt hot tears spill to her face. Abruptly she pulled clear and turned back toward High Druin.

"You shouldn't have brought me," grumbled Ballistar. "I'm slowing you down."

"That's true," grunted Sigarni as they faced yet another deep snowdrift. "But you're such good company!"

Ballistar shifted on her shoulders. "Put me down and we'll see if we can crawl along the top of it. There should be solid ground about thirty feet ahead. Then it is just one more hill to the Falls."

Sigarni swiveled and tipped the little man from her shoulders. He fell headfirst into the drift, and came up spluttering and spitting snow. "You are heavy for a small man," she said, laughing.

"And you have the boniest shoulders I ever sat upon," he told her, brushing snow from his beard. Turning to his stomach, Ballistar began to squirm across the snow. Sigarni followed him, using her arms to force a path. After an hour of effort they reached solid ground and sat for a while, gathering their strength. "I'm freezing to death," muttered Ballistar. "I hope you left enough firewood in the cave. I'm in no mood to go gathering."

"Enough for a couple of hours," she reassured him.

The Falls were still frozen at the center, but at the sides water had begun to trickle through the ice. "The thaw is coming," said the dwarf.

"I know," said Sigarni softly.

Inside the cave Sigarni started a fire and they shrugged out of their soaked outer clothing. "So why did you bring me?" asked Ballistar.

"I thought you'd enjoy my company," she told him.

"That's not very convincing."

She looked at him, and remembered how out of place he had seemed back at the encampment, how lonely and sad. "I wanted company," she said, "and I could think of no one else I would rather have with me."

He blushed and looked away. "I'll accept that," he said brightly. "Do you remember when we used to play here as children? You, me, Fell, and Bernt built a tree house. It fell apart in the big storm. Fell was climbing and the floor gave way. You remember?"

Sigarni nodded. "Bernt stole the nails from Grame. More nails in that structure than wood."

"It was fun, wasn't it?"

"Fun? You were always arguing with the others, getting into scrapes and fights."

"I know," he said. "I was young then, and not growing like the rest of you. But I look back on those times as the happiest of my life. Do you think the others would?"

"Bernt no longer looks back," she said, her voice almost a whisper.

"Oh, I'm sorry, Sigarni. I wasn't thinking." Reaching out, he took her slender hand in his own, his stubby fingers caressing her wrist. "It wasn't your fault, not really. I think if you had gone he would still have killed himself had you turned him down. It was his life; he chose to take it."

Sigarni shook her head. "I don't think that is the whole truth. Had I known the outcome beforehand I would have acted differently. But now I think about how I was lying in bed with Asmidir, enjoying myself utterly." She sighed. "And while I was being pleasured, Bernt was tying a rope around his neck."

Ballistar looked away and fiddled with the fire, poking small sticks into the flames. "Now I have embarrassed you," she said.

"Yes, you have," he told her, reddening. "But we are friends, Sigarni. We always will be. I don't want you to feel there are words you cannot say in my presence. When is the wizard due?" he asked, changing the subject.

"Tomorrow."

"I wish he'd chosen a more hospitable meeting place."

"It had to be here," she said. "He knew what the Pallides would ask of me."

"Madness!" snapped Ballistar. "Who do they think they are? Here we sit on the verge of war and they play games. Do they believe they can win without us?"

"No, my friend, they don't think that. Their Dreamers have told them that the leader will wear the Crown of Alwen. If that is true, then I must find it. Taliesen will have a plan."

"I don't like wizards," said the dwarf.

"I remember you saying that about Asmidir. A black sorcerer, you called him."

"I still don't like him. Are you still lovers?"

"No!" Her voice was sharper than she intended and Ballistar gazed at her quizzically.

"Did he wrong you?"

She shook her head. "I don't want to talk about it. I want your help before dusk. I want you to come with me to the far side of the pool and break the ice."

"Why?" he asked, mystified.

"I need to swim."

"That's ridiculous! The cold will kill you."

"You can wait for me with a blanket," she said.

"There's something you are not telling me. What are you looking for?"

Sigarni stretched out her hand to the fire. The cave was glowing now in the firelight, and the sounds of winter outside only served to make it seem more cozy within. "I am going to find a small bone," she said. "A talisman if you like, a good-luck charm."

"Whose bones?" he asked, wide-eyed.

"Ironhand."

Ballistar's jaw dropped. "You found his bones? He didn't pass over the Gateway?"

"No. He died here fighting his enemies."

"How will a bone help you?"

"Enough questions, Balli. Come on, we're warm enough now."

Together they left the cave and trudged across the snow-covered ice of the pool. Sigarni found the boulder under which the bones lay, and she and Ballistar began to chip away at the surrounding ice with their knives. It was slow work and Ballistar lost his patience. Climbing to the top of the jutting boulder he jumped to the ice, landing hard. Four times more he did so, then on the fifth a large crack appeared. "Almost there," he said. Suddenly the ice gave and he fell through into the dark water beneath. Sigarni dived across the ice, her hand snaking out to grab his collar just as he was about to sink. With a great effort she hauled him back.

"You'd better get back to the cave," she said.

"No, no, I'm all right," he said, shivering. "Can you reach the bones from here?"

"I don't know. I'll have to be fast." Slipping out of her clothes, she slithered into the water.

"Be careful, there's an undertow," warned Ballistar.

The cold chilled her to the bone, and all was darkness. Holding to the boulder, she released some air and dived deeper. Her hand touched the bottom and she scrabbled around, but could feel nothing but stones. Something sharp cut the palm of her hand. The sudden shock caused her to breathe out and, her lungs aching, she rose toward the surface. Her head thumped against ice.

She had missed the opening.

Holding down panic she rolled to her back, pushing her face toward the ice. There was always a tiny gap between ice and water, and she breathed in deeply. The cold was bitter now and she could not feel her fingers.

You stupid woman! she thought. To come so far and die so stupidly.

A faint glow surrounded her. "Why do you never call for me, child?" asked Ironhand. "Dive to the bottom and collect what you came for, then follow me to the surface."

Filling her lungs with air she rolled and dived, kicking out against the ice to propel herself down. In the glow she saw Ironhand sitting on the pool floor; beside him was a human head but she did not recognize the face. On the other side of the ghostly giant lay his bones. Swiftly she grabbed a finger bone and rose toward the surface.

As she broke clear Ballistar took hold of her arm and dragged her onto the ice.

"I was worried near to death," complained the dwarf. Sigarni could not speak; she had begun to shake uncontrollably. "And look, you've cut your hand," he said, pointing to the trickle of blood on her palm.

Ballistar took up her clothes and led her back to the cave,

where she sat wrapped in a blanket, her face and hands blue. "I hope that bone was worth it," he said.

"It . . . was," she told him. "He . . . is . . . here."

"Who is?"

"Ironhand."

"Ironhand?" he repeated. "In the cave? With us?" Ballistar gazed around fearfully. "I don't see him."

Sigarni shrugged off the blanket and moved a little way from the fire. "Come and rub my skin," she said. Ballistar put his hands on her shoulders and began to massage the flesh.

"So now we are dealing with wizards *and* ghosts," he said.

"Lower. On my back," she ordered.

Ballistar knelt behind her and rubbed gently at the cold skin. "You should sit closer to the fire."

"No. It would do more harm than good. When I am a little warmer . . . That is nice. Now my arms."

He sat beside her, kneading her flesh, encouraging the blood to flow. He tried not to stare at her breasts, but failed. Sigarni did not seem to notice. Of course she doesn't, he thought. I am not a man to her.

"I am going to sleep now, Balli. Watch over me, and keep the fire going."

Holding fast to the bone, she lay down by the fire. Ballistar covered her with two blankets. As she closed her eyes, he leaned down and kissed her cheek.

"What was that for?" she asked sleepily.

"I love you," he said.

"I love you too," she whispered. And slept.

The fire burned low and Ballistar added the last of the wood. Sigarni's flesh was still cool and the dwarf wandered out into the cold of the night to gather deadwood. The carcasses of the demons still lay where Sigarni had slain them, but they were not rotting; it was too cold for that. They'll smell bad come spring, thought Ballistar as he wandered beneath the trees, kicking at the snow and seeking fuel.

"Over there," said a voice. "Beneath the oaks."

Ballister leaped, turned, and fell over. Standing beside him was a glowing figure in ancient armor, his white beard braided into forks. He wore a long, double-handed broadsword in a scabbard of embossed silver—and the hand resting on it was made of red iron. "By Heaven, you are skittish," said the ghost. "Are you going to fetch the wood or not?"

"Yes, lord," answered Ballistar.

"I'm not your lord, dwarf. I am merely a spirit. Now fetch the wood before she freezes to death."

Ballistar nodded, and dug around in the snow beneath the oaks, gathering deadwood, then returning to the cave. The glowing figure stayed by him, watching his efforts. "It cannot be easy to live in such a body," he said.

"A choice would be pleasant," muttered Ballistar.

"You've a handsome face, lad. Be thankful for small gifts."

"All my gifts are small—bar one. And I'll never get to use that," answered Ballistar, kneeling by the fire and placing two long sticks upon it.

The ghost assumed a sitting position by the fire. "You can never be sure," he said. "I had two dwarfs at my court and they were always in demand. Once I had to adjudicate in a very delicate matter, where a knight cited one of my dwarfs as his wife's secret lover. He wanted the dwarf hanged and his wife burned at the stake."

"What did you do? Did you kill them?"

"Do I look like a barbarian? I told the knight that he would be laughed out of the kingdom if he sought a public trial. The wife was sent back to her family in disgrace. I had the dwarf castrated. However, that is not the point. Never lose faith, little man."

"Well, thank you for your advice," snapped Ballistar.

"However, I have not yet met a woman who would wish to have me clamber all over her." He told the spirit of Bakris's jest and Ironhand laughed.

"Nose to nose . . . yes, that's very good. How did you respond?"

"I laughed with them—though it broke my heart."

"Aye, it's the best way." He leaned forward, peering at Sigarni. "Is she warming up?" he asked.

Ballistar moved alongside the sleeping woman and touched the flesh of her arm. "A little. She was seeking your bones. Damn near died for it."

"I know, I was there. Willful child." The ghost smiled. "She can't help it, it is in her blood. I was willful myself. How is the war progressing?"

"I would have thought you'd know more about that than a mere dwarf," said Ballistar. "Can spirits not fly around the world?"

"I don't know any spirits," said Ironhand. "But *I* cannot. I'm trapped here, where I died. Well, until now. Wherever Sigarni goes, I shall go too."

"That's a comforting thought. I think you'll cause a certain amount of panic back at the encampment."

Ironhand shook his head. "No one will see me, boy—not even you. I only showed myself to you since Sigarni was foolish enough to tell you about me. So, what is happening?"

Ballistar told the King of the Pallides' request that Sigarni should find the lost Crown. "We are waiting for Taliesen," he concluded. "He'll show us where it is."

"Oh, I know where it is," said Ironhand. "That won't be the problem. Getting there and out again alive is the issue."

"Where is it?"

"In a dying world of sorcery, a dark malevolent place. Even the air is poisonous with magick. No true man can live there for more than a few months. He would sicken and die. One of my wizards tracked it down and passed through a Gateway to retrieve it; we never saw him again. A second followed him; he came back broken and diseased, not all our medicines and charms could heal him. But while he lived he told us of the world, its beasts, and its wars. I decided then to send no more of my people in search of the Crown."

"But Sigarni *must* go there," said Ballistar. "Without the Crown the Pallides will not accept her leadership. They might believe you, though. You could appear to Fyon Sharp-axe and tell him Sigarni is the chosen one."

The ghost shook his head. "It might work, but then Sigarni would rule only through a long-dead king. No, Ballistar, she must win the right for herself. When my wizard returned he told me the Crown was in a temple, at the center of a city at war. He saw it, was even allowed to touch it. I think he believed that to do so would heal him of his afflictions in that world. It didn't."

"You say *allowed* to touch it. There are people there?"

"Aye, there are people. They cling to life in a world of death."

"What is killing them?"

"There is no sun to bring life to the land. The city was built inside a forest of dead trees. There is no grass, and no crops grow. The land is in perpetual twilight. The mountains there spew fire and ash, and occasionally rip themselves apart with sounds like a thousand thunders. You can see why I forbade any further ventures into that land."

"But without cattle and crops, how do they survive?" asked Ballistar.

"On war," the King told him.

"That makes no sense," said the dwarf.

"It does, lad, if you have a mind dark enough to examine it."

Ballistar awoke with a start and sat up blinking and afraid. He had failed Sigarni and slept. Swiftly he rushed to her side. She was warm to the touch and sleeping deeply. Relieved, the dwarf knelt by the fire and blew the coals to glowing life, adding shreds of bark to feed the tiny flames. Once it had flared he placed two small logs atop the coals.

From Sigarni's pack he took a flat-bottomed pot and a sack of dried oats. Filling the pot with snow, he stood it upon the fire. Despite being full of snow it melted to only a tiny amount of water and Ballistar spent some time moving back and forth bringing handfuls of snow from outside the cave. When the pot was half full of water he added oats and a pinch of salt.

The sun was up, the cave mouth lit with golden light. Birdsong could be heard from the trees outside and the air was fresh with the promise of the coming spring.

Sigarni awoke and stretched. The blanket slid from her naked body. "Ah, breakfast," she said. "What a fine companion you are, Ballistar."

"I live to serve, my Queen," he said, making an elaborate bow.

"No sign of Taliesen?"

"Not yet, but the dawn has only just arrived." Using two long sticks, Ballistar lifted the pot from the fire and stirred the contents, which had thickened considerably. "You brought no honey," he chided her. "Porridge is bland and tasteless without it."

"I had to carry enough food for two. Come to think of it, I had to carry you as well for a while. There was no room for honey. Have you slept?"

"A little," he admitted.

She smiled. "The next time I suggest a swim under the ice, be so kind as to remind me of my previous stupidity."

"I will. How are you feeling?"

"Rested, and at peace for the first time in weeks. No plans to study, no quarrels to adjudicate, no ruffled feathers to smooth. Just breakfast at dawn in a peaceful cave, enjoying good company."

"I trust you include me in that description?" said Taliesen, stepping into the cave and brushing snow from his tattered cloak of feathers. Sigarni nodded, but her smile had faded.

"Welcome, Taliesen."

The old man made his way to the fire and sat. "You have a beautiful body, Sigarni. Fifty years ago it would have inspired me to carnal thoughts. Now, however, I can appreciate its beauty on an entirely different level. I take it the Pallides asked for the Crown?" Sigarni nodded and rose from bed, dressing swiftly. "It will not be easy—and yet you must not dally," continued Taliesen. "I will send you through the Gateway as soon as you are dressed."

"The world beyond is poisonous," said Ballistar coldly. "She could die there."

Taliesen swung to him. "It is very rare that I am surprised, dwarf. Yet you have accomplished it. How is it that you know of Yur-vale?"

"I am a creature of legend," said Ballistar with a wide grin. "I know many things."

"Then perhaps you would like to continue my story?"

"Gladly," said Ballistar, who then told Sigarni all that Ironhand had confided to him the night before. The dwarf took great pleasure in the look of amazement that Taliesen sought to disguise. When he had finished Ballistar moved to Sigarni's pack, pulling out two shallow bowls. Ladling porridge into each, he passed one to Sigarni. "You are welcome to eat from the pot," he told Taliesen.

"I am not hungry!" snapped the wizard. "Is there anything else you wish to add about Yur-vale?"

"No," said Ballistar happily. "Do continue."

The wizard cast him a baleful glance. "Yur-vale was once a paradise. There was no physical ugliness there, and no natural disease—at least no disease that affects the inhabitants. It was a land of beauty and light. Now it is the opposite. It is an ocean world, with a very small land mass at the equator. The land mass has two great cities, and these are in a perpetual state of war. The war is necessary, for reasons we do not need to trouble ourselves with. The Crown is in a temple at the center of the city of Zir-vak. It is a city under siege and you will need to enter it by means of a black river which flows through it. Do not drink the water; it has been polluted by volcanic ash. The city's inhabitants have a way of purifying the water, involving filters. Once inside the city, the water you find will be good to drink. Take food with you, and eat nothing offered to you during your stay—no matter how appetizing it looks."

"How do I get there?" asked Sigarni.

"There is a Gateway close to the Falls. I will send you through and you will arrive at a point some seven miles south of the city. Since you will not see the sun, you must head for a set of twin peaks you will see to the north. When you return to the Gateway you will make a cut upon your arm and allow blood to drop on each of the six standing stones that make up the circle. I will then bring you back."

"Bring *us* back," put in Ballistar.

"I go alone," said Sigarni. Ballistar was about to argue when Taliesen cut in.

"I agree with him," said Taliesen with a rare smile. "Take the dwarf. He will be of use."

Ballistar was surprised. "Why do you support me, wizard? I know you have no love for me."

"Perhaps that is why I support you," said Taliesen. "Have you brought weapons?"

"Yes," said Sigarni. "Bows, knives, and my saber."

"Good. Now, if you are both ready, we should depart."

Sigarni took a small pouch from her pack and dropped the finger bone of Ironhand into it. Looping a thong through the pouch, she tied it around her neck.

"What is that?" asked Taliesen.

"A talisman," she told him.

Ballistar thought he was about to speak, but Taliesen said nothing. The wizard rose. "When you have cleaned and stowed your pots, I will be waiting for you on the other side of the pool," he said, and padded out of the cave.

"Are you sure you want to come with me, Balli?" asked Sigarni.

"Always," he said.

They found Taliesen waiting by a cliff face some two hundred yards from Ironhand's burial place. Sigarni had played there as a child, and she and her friends had often debated the meaning of the strange symbols carved on the rocks. The area was flat, as if smoothed by man, and deep grooves had been chiseled from the rock in the shape of a tall rectangular door. There was also evidence of an inscription, though wind and rain, snow and hail, had long since eroded the greater part of it.

"This is one of the Lesser Gateways," said Taliesen. "It does not allow movement through *our* time, but does serve to open time doorways to other realities. Now remember what I said. Do not drink of the water of the black river, nor eat any meat offered to you. This is vital. I knew a sorcerer once who went there and ate a little pork; it swelled inside him and ripped him apart. Yur-vale is a world of great magic, and you are strangers to it. Because of your very *strangeness* its power will be many times greater around you. Bear this in mind. Now, you know where you are heading?"

"Seven miles toward the twin peaks," said Sigarni.

"Good. Now my bones are freezing here, so let us begin. Are you ready?" Sigarni nodded and Taliesen turned to Ballistar. "And you, dwarf? There is still time to change your mind. What awaits you is not pleasant. Your worst nightmare is beyond this Gate."

Ballistar thought he detected a note of concern in the wizard's voice, and felt his fears rise. "I will travel with Sigarni," he said stoutly. Reaching up, he took hold of her hand.

"Then let it begin," said Taliesen. The old wizard closed

his eyes and spoke softly in a language unknown to either of the Highlanders. It was soft and fluent, almost musical. Pale light flooded from the rectangular grooves in the rock face, which became translucent, and then transparent, and Sigarni found herself staring through it at a cold, grey landscape. "Step through quickly," said Taliesen. "It will hold for a few seconds only."

The silver-haired woman and the dwarf stepped through the portal. Sigarni shivered as she passed through, for it was like walking through a waterfall, cold and yet not as refreshing. On the other side they found themselves standing within a circle of six tall granite stones. Sigarni swung around in time to see Taliesen fade away to nothing.

"Well, we are here," she said, turning back to Ballistar. The dwarf was lying on the ground, his body twitching. "Balli! Are you ill?"

His body began to writhe.

And stretch . . .

Dropping her bow and loosing her pack, Sigarni knelt beside him. His limbs were thrashing around, his legs jutting now from his tiny trousers. The small doeskin boots split as his feet grew. His black leather belt snapped. Sigarni moved back from him and waited. Finally the spasmodic twitching eased and she found herself gazing down at a healthy young man in torn clothes and shredded boots. Part of one boot was still around the ankle like an adornment. Ballistar groaned and sat up. "What happened to me?" he asked. Then he saw his arms, full length and strong, with long, slender fingers, and his legs. He scrambled to his feet and found himself staring into Sigarni's eyes. "Oh, God, dear God," he said. "I'm a man!"

Throwing his arms around the stunned Sigarni, he kissed her cheek. "I'm a man," he said again. "Look at me, Sigarni!"

"You look very fine," she said with a smile. "Truly this is a magical place."

"He said my worst nightmare awaited me. How wrong can a man be? This is everything I dreamed of. Now I will be able to stand with the others and fight the Outlanders. No more jibes and cruel jokes. Oh, Sigarni . . ." Abruptly he sat down and began to weep.

"I brought a spare tunic and leggings," said Sigarni. "I think they might fit you. Even if they don't, they'll look better than the rags you are wearing."

He nodded and moved to her pack. "I could even get married," he said, "and sire sons. Tall sons!"

"You always were handsome, Balli, and you'll make a fine father. Now stop talking and get dressed, we must be moving on."

Sigarni gazed at the bleak landscape; the sky was slate-grey and the air smelled acrid. Far to the east she could see fires on the horizon as two distant volcanoes spewed hot ash and lava out over the land. "Not a hospitable place," she said.

"I think it's wonderful," said Ballistar.

She turned to see him struggling out of his ruined leggings. "By Heaven, Balli, has *that* grown also?"

He giggled. "No, it was always this big. Do you like it?"

She laughed. "Just cover it, you fool!"

Ballistar dressed and tied the thongs of his new green leggings. "They are a little tight," he said. "Am I as tall as Fell?"

"No. But you are taller than Bakris and Gwyn. That will have to do."

Sigarni reached for her bow—and froze. The weapon had rooted itself in the ground and small, slender branches were growing from it. "Would you look at that!" she said. Roots were spreading out from the bow, delving into the grey, ash-covered ground.

"What about your arrows?" asked Ballistar. Sigarni swung her quiver clear and pulled a shaft from it; it was unmarked. At that moment a single ray of sunshine seared through the ash-grey sky, a pillar of light bathing what had once been a bow and was now a swiftly growing tree. The sudden warmth was welcome and Sigarni glanced up at the sky, enjoying the feeling of sunlight on her skin. Then it was gone.

Something moved against her chest and, startled, Sigarni glanced down. The small leather pouch was bulging now, and writhing, as if a large rat were inside. Swiftly she ripped it from her neck and hurled it to the ground. The leather split and a white bone protruded, others joining to it. As with Ballistar the bones stretched and grew, cartilage and ligaments slithering over them, pulling joints into sockets. At last a huge skeleton lay on the volcanic ash.

For a moment nothing more happened. Then suddenly, in a vivid burst of color, red muscle and sinew, flesh and veins, danced along its frame, covering lungs and liver, heart and kidneys. Skin flowed over the whole, and silver hair sprouted from head and chin.

For a while Ironhand lay naked on the ground, then took a long shuddering breath. His eyes opened, and he saw Sigarni. "I can feel," he said. "The ground beneath me, the air in my lungs. How is this possible?"

"I have no idea," said Sigarni, removing her green cloak. She cut a hole in the center and passed it to the naked man.

Ironhand stood and looped it over his head. "Where are we?"

"In the land of Yur-vale," Sigarni told him. "Taliesen sent us through a magical Gateway."

"It is puzzling, but by Grievak, it is good to feel again— and to have two good hands of flesh and blood," he added, clenching his fists. "Who is this?" he asked, turning to the young man at her side.

"It is me, Ballistar the Dwarf. The magick made me grow. Though not as tall as you," he added with a frown.

Ironhand chuckled. "You are tall enough, boy. What now, daughter?"

She pointed to the twin peaks. "We make for the city and find the Crown."

Yos-shiel had been a Black River trader for more than two hundred and seventy years, and remembered with great regret the ending of all that was beautiful in Yur-vale. He had been celebrating his twenty-fourth birthday when the first mountain had erupted, spewing molten lava down the hillside, destroying the vineyards and the cornfields.

It had been a bitter summer. First the war, and then the natural upheavals that hid the sun from the sky. Year by year it had grown steadily worse. Yos-shiel pushed his thin fingers through his thick white hair, and stared out of the window at the quay, where men were loading supplies onto one of the three barges he would send down to Zir-vak after dusk. Smoked fish and timber: the only two items of any worth in Yur-vale. Yos-shiel sold them for gold and water, in the vain hope that one day gold would be a viable currency once more.

The old man rose and stretched. From his window he saw a single ray of sunshine to the south and his heart swelled. How long since there had been a break in the clouds? A year? Two? Several of the loaders saw it also, and all ceased their work.

A young man, seeing Yos-shiel at the window, called out, "Is it a sign, master? Is the sun returning?"

The pillar of light vanished. "I do not look for signs anymore," he said softly.

Stepping out into the dull light, he counted the barrels of fish. "There should be fifty," he said.

A huge man wearing a red shirt embroidered with gold moved into sight. "Two were spoiled," he said, his voice low, rumbling like distant thunder. Yos-shiel looked into the man's small, round eyes. He knew Cris-yen was lying, but the man was a thug and, he suspected, a killer. The two guards Yos-shiel had appointed to supervise the loads had mysteriously disappeared. He feared them dead.

"Very well, Cris-yen, carry on." With a contemptuous smile the big man swung away.

I never should have employed him, thought Yos-shiel. He and his brothers will strip me of all I have. I will be lucky to escape with my life. Glancing up at the iron sky, he suddenly smiled. What is life worth now? he wondered. Would I miss it?

Soldiers manned the ramparts of the stockade and Yos-shiel considered asking them for help in dealing with Cris-yen. The supplies he sent were vital to the city, and his plea deserved to be heard. But then *deserve* has nothing to do with it, he realized. Cris-yen had made friends with the officers, giving them presents. If I go to them and they turn against me my death will come all the sooner, he thought.

Strolling to the edge of the quay, he stared down into the inky depths of the river. No fish swam there now. The fleets were forced to put out far to sea in order to make their catches.

The barge from the city came into sight, its cargo of barrels lashed to the deck. Fresh drinking water, cleaned in the charcoal filters of Zir-vak, and fresh meat for the soldiers.

Yos-shiel wandered back to his small office and continued working on his ledgers.

Just before noon he heard a commotion from outside, and saw his workers moving toward the stockade gates. Yos-shiel closed the books, cleaned the quill pen, and followed them. The gates were open and three people had entered the stockade, two men and a woman. The woman was silver-haired and strikingly beautiful. Beside her was a giant in an ill-fitting green tunic, tied at the waist with what looked like an old bowstring; he too was silver-haired. The last of the trio was a young man, dressed in green trews and a shirt too small for him.

"Where are you from?" asked Cris-yen, pushing to the

front of the crowd and standing before the woman, his hands on his hips.

"South," she said. "We're looking for passage into the city."

"And how will you pay me?"

The woman produced a small gold coin and Cris-yen laughed. "That's no good here, my pretty; it doesn't put food in mouths any longer. I'll tell you what I'll do, you and me will go to the warehouse and we'll arrange something."

"We'll find passage elsewhere," she said, turning away. One of Cris-yen's brothers stepped forward, grabbing her arm.

"There's nowhere else, you'd better listen to him," he said.

"Take your hand off my arm," said the woman icily.

The man laughed. "Or what?"

The woman ducked her head, hammering her brow into his nose. The man released her and staggered back but she leaped, her foot cracking against his chin and catapulting him back into the crowd. Yos-shiel saw the soldiers watching from the ramparts but they made no move to interfere.

"That was an assault!" yelled Cris-yen. "Take her!" Several men rushed forward. The woman downed the first with a straight left. The smaller of her companions rushed in and threw himself at the others; he and several men tumbled to the ground.

"That's enough!" bellowed the silver-bearded giant. The sound boomed around the stockade and all activity ceased as he stepped in close to Cris-yen. "Well," he said, "you seem to be the lead bull of the pox-ridden herd. Perhaps you and I should decide the issue."

Cris-yen said nothing, but his huge fist hammered into the man's chin. The giant took the blow and did not move. He merely grinned. "By God, son, if that is the best you have to offer you are in serious trouble," he said. Cris-yen tried to throw a left, whereupon the giant blocked it with his right and slapped Cris-yen openhanded across the cheek. The sound was like snapping timber. Cris-yen staggered to his right—then, head down, rushed the giant. The charge was met by a right cross that smashed Cris-yen's jaw and spun him from his feet. He hit the ground facedown, twitched once, and was still.

"A chin like crystal," muttered the giant. "Any more for the fray?" No one moved. The man walked to the unconscious Cris-yen and calmly removed the embroidered red shirt. Pulling off his own tunic, he donned the garment. "A little tight," he said, "but it will do." Without hurry he stripped Cris-yen naked and clothed himself in the man's leather leggings and black boots. "That feels better," he said. "Now, who is in charge here?"

Yos-shiel stepped from the crowd. "I am, sir."

"Then it is with you we should discuss passage?"

"It is. And you are welcome to travel free of any charges."

"Good. That is most hospitable. I am Ironhand, this is my daughter Sigarni and her friend Ballistar."

"I can see why you earned your name," said Yos-shiel.

Yos-shiel offered his guests wine and food, and if he was offended by their refusal to eat, he did not show it. Ballistar liked the little old man, and listened with relish as he told of his troubles with Cris-yen.

"I don't believe he will cause you more trouble for a while yet," said Ironhand, "but if you'll take my advice you'll promote a man to take his place immediately, and then dismiss all of his henchmen."

"I shall," said Yos-shiel, "although I would be grateful if you could stay beside me while I do the deed."

"Gladly," promised Ironhand.

"I was amazed that Cris-yen fell so swiftly to you. I have seen him break men's arms, and cudgel them down with hammer blows from his fists."

"They breed them tough where we come from," said Ballistar.

"And where is that?" asked Yos-shiel.

"South," answered Ballistar vaguely, wishing he had kept his mouth shut.

"We are from another world, Yos-shiel," said Sigarni, moving to sit on the desk opposite the old man. "We passed through a magical Gateway."

The trader smiled, waiting for the end of the joke. When it didn't come his smile vanished. "You . . . are wizards?"

"No," said Sigarni, "but a wizard sent us. We have come to reclaim something that was lost in this world, and return it to our own."

"The sunlight," said the old man. "That was you, in the south. What did you do?"

"I don't know what you mean," said Sigarni. "You mean the break in the clouds?"

"Yes. It's been years since we've seen the sun. Can you make it come at will?"

"I did nothing, Yos-shiel. It was merely my bow. The wood began to sprout leaves and root itself in the soil. Then the sun shone."

"We had wizards once—a whole temple of them. They supervised the building of the Great Library in Zir-vak. They were blamed when the sun went away and sacrificed on the high altar. The King promised that with their deaths the mountains would stop spewing fire, but it didn't happen. In the last two hundred years there have been other prophets who claimed that blood sacrifice would appease the gods, and they would relent of their punishment. But they have not. We are a dying people, Sigarni; there is no hope for us."

"And yet amid all this turmoil you fight a war," she said. "Why?"

"It was originally over a woman. The King's grandfather fell in love with a noblewoman from the east, but she was betrothed to the King of Kal-vak. Despite her pleas her father made her honor her promise, and she was sent to Kal-vak. Our King was furious—and swore he would free her. We went to war. Our troops attacked Kal-vak and were repulsed. Then the first of the mountains exploded. Each side blamed the other for the catastrophe, claiming that treachery had alienated the gods against us. At first it wasn't too terrible; the summers got shorter, and less warm, but crops still grew. But gradually the sky turned darker, and fine ash was deposited over the farmlands. Food grew scarce, save for the fish. But even these are swimming far from shore now."

"Yet the war goes on," said Ironhand. "How is it that neither side has won? You said the battle was begun by the King's grandfather. How long ago was that?"

"A little more than two hundred and forty years. Most of the principal players are now dead though the war goes on for other reasons. People need to eat."

"They eat the corpses!" whispered Ballistar.

"It is a little like pork, I am told," said Yos-shiel. "I have not eaten it myself, but when the time comes I don't doubt that I shall. Life is always sweet—even in the Hell of Yurvale." The old man sighed. "But tell me, my friend, what is the object you seek? I may be of some assistance."

"The Crown of Alwen," said Sigarni.

"I know of no such object."

"It is a winged helm, bright silver, embossed with gold."

"The Paradise Helm," said Yos-shiel, his eyes widening. "You cannot take that! It is all that gives the people hope. Every twenty-five years it shows us a vision of paradise, waterfalls and green trees, and a multitude standing around it, happy and smiling. That is our most prized artifact."

Sigarni laid her hand on the old man's shoulders. "What you see is my people standing by the Alwen Falls. Every quarter of a century the Crown reappears there, shimmering over the water. We all gather to see it, and you in turn, it seems, gather to see us. Tell me, Yos-shiel, of the last time the sun shone."

"It was on the day of the old King's burial. I was there as they laid him on the funeral ship and sent it blazing on the river. The clouds broke and the sun shone for a full day.

It was magnificent, there was singing and dancing in the streets."

"And before that?"

"I don't remember exactly. Wait . . . yes, I do. Twelve years ago, at the Feast of Athling. We saw the dawn on the following day, the sun huge and red. That lasted only minutes."

"What happened on the next feast day?"

"You don't understand, the Feast of Athling corresponds with the public display of the Paradise Helm. It happens only four times a century."

For some time Sigarni questioned the old man and soon Ballistar became bored with the dialogue. He wandered to the window, leaned on the sill, and watched the barges being loaded.

At last the conversation died away and Ironhand broke in. "Best bring your men in for dismissal, old fellow," he said, "for we have a hankering to be on one of those barges when it pulls away."

"Yes, I will," said Yos-shiel. "Thank you."

An hour later the three sat at the stern of a forty-foot barge as the crew poled it steadily upriver. The vessel was fortified by hinged wooden flaps along both rails, which could be raised to offer protection from an assault. Huge rocks had been left at intervals along both sides of the deck, ready to be hurled down on any boat that sought to impede the barge's progress. Armed men sat at the prow, and all of the barge workers carried long knives.

"So we find the temple and steal the Crown?" said Ballistar. "It would be best to enter it at night."

Sigarni rose, stretched, and walked away down the port side of the vessel. A soldier smiled at her. "Stay with your friends," he said. "Soon it will be so dark you will not be able to see your hand before your face."

She thanked him and returned to the others, seating herself on a coil of rope. The light faded fast, and soon the barge was engulfed in a darkness so complete that Sigarni felt an edge of panic.

"It's like being dead," whispered Ballistar. Sigarni felt his hand brush against her arm; she took hold of it and squeezed his fingers.

"No, it isn't," said Ironhand. "Death is not dark; it is bright and vile."

"How can they see to steer?" Ballistar asked.

"Quiet back there," came a voice. "We'll see the city within an hour."

There was little sensation of movement within the all-encompassing blackness and Sigarni found herself thinking back to her days with Fell, when they had hunted together and made love before the fire. He had been able to read her moods so well. There were times when she had wanted nothing more than to curl up beside him, stroking his skin. On such occasions he would hug her and kiss her fondly. On other nights, when the fey mood was upon her she would desire to make love with passion and fire. Always he responded. I was good for you too, Fell, she thought. I knew you, your thoughts and your dreams.

The first kiss had been shared on the slopes of High Druin, on a bright summer's day. They had raced over the four miles from Goring's Rock to the White Stream. Fell was faster and stronger, but his staying power could not match Sigarni's; she had doggedly clung to his trail, always keeping him in sight until the last long rise. Then, as he faltered, she drew on her reserves and passed him.

At the White Stream he had sunk back to his haunches and fought for breath. Sigarni brought him water in a hastily made cup of bark.

"You are a wonder, Sigarni," he said at last, taking her hand and kissing it.

She sat beside him, looping her arm around his neck. "My poor Fell! Is your pride damaged beyond repair?"

He looked at her quizzically. "Why would my pride be hurt? I did my best."

"I liked it when you kissed my hand," she said, changing the subject.

"Then I shall do it again."

"I would like it more if you kissed my mouth."

He smiled then. "You are very forward for a Highland girl—I shall put it down to Gwalchmai's poor teaching. I don't mind losing a race to a woman like you, but it is not meet for you to do the seducing."

"Why?"

"Because I sat up through most of the night trying to think of a way to get you to kiss me. It makes a mockery of all my planning."

Sigarni lay back on the soft grass. "Not at all. Go ahead. Show me your strategy."

He chuckled. "Too late. I think the fox is already in the henhouse."

"Even so, I would like to hear it."

Rolling to his elbow he lay beside her, looking down. "I wanted to tell you that I have never known anyone like you, and that when I am with you I am happier than at any other time. You are the delight in my life, Sigarni. Now and always."

"You've won me over with your fine words," she said. "Now the kiss, if you please."

Ballistar's voice cut through her thoughts. "Your hand is very warm," he whispered.

"I was thinking good thoughts," she told him, keeping her voice low.

The journey continued, until at last they could see the faint lights of the city ahead. The barge moved on, approaching an arched portcullis gate. The helmsman flashed a signal with his lantern that was answered from above the arch. Then, with a great creaking and groaning, the portcullis rose and the barge passed beneath it.

Lanterns hung from poles all along the quayside and Sigarni heard Ballistar breathe a sigh of relief. "It was awful," he said, "like being blind."

"It was not awful," said Sigarni wistfully.

The barge clanked against the stone quay. Ironhand was the first ashore, followed by Sigarni and Ballistar.

"What now?" asked the warrior.

"We'll find some sheltered place to sleep," Sigarni told him. "Tomorrow we'll see the King."

"For what purpose?" Ballistar asked.

"I shall ask for the Crown to be returned."

"And he will just give it to you?"

"Of course not, Balli. I shall offer him something in return."

"It will need to be a very large gift," Ironhand pointed out.

"It will be," she promised.

Chapter Twelve

The city was unlike anything Sigarni had ever seen. Crammed together, the houses reared like cliff faces, dotted with lighted windows. Narrow alleyways filtered off like veins in the flesh of a stone giant. Arched tunnels led deeper into the city, and these boasted oil lamps, hung at regular intervals to guide the traveler. There were signs on every alley, giving names to the streets and the wider avenues that led off from them. Sigarni felt hemmed in and dwarfed by the colossal nature of Zir-vak.

Ironhand was less impressed. "They have structures in Kushir of far greater beauty," he said, "and there is evidence at least of planning there. These . . . huge hovels give a man no space to breathe."

"It is oppressive," agreed Ballistar. They wandered on aimlessly for a while until they saw the lights of a tavern. Ironhand headed for it. "Wait!" called Ballistar. "How will we pay?"

"I'll think of something," said Ironhand.

The tavern was more than half empty, and few diners sat at the rough-built tables. There was a long, timbered drinking area at which several men stood, downing ale. Ironhand moved to the bar and a serving maid approached him. She was extraordinarily fat, her mouth turned down at the corners, her eyes small and seemingly set in several acres of unnecessary flesh; her enormous breasts sagged over the bar.

"What is there on offer?" asked Ironhand as Sigarni and Ballistar moved alongside.

"To eat or to drink, or both?" she countered, idly wiping at the counter with a stained rag.

"Just to drink," said the silver-bearded giant.

"We have ale or water, or if you'd rather something hot we have a dry root tisane."

"And with what do we pay?"

"What?"

"What currency do we need? We are strangers here and have been told that gold is of no use."

"You don't pay," she said, as if talking to someone retarded. "Everything's free . . . has been for years. So what will it be?"

"Ale," said Ironhand.

"I'll have water," said Sigarni. "Where can we find lodgings for the night?"

"Wherever you choose. There's a room upstairs that you're welcome to. There's no fire, mind—no wood, you see. But the oil lamps keep the room warm enough. There's only one bed, but it's big enough for the two of you," she said, gesturing toward Ballistar and Sigarni. "As for him . . . well."

"I could always share your bed, my pretty," said Ironhand. "I expect it's a large one."

"The cheek of the man!" said the woman, blushing.

"Those that don't ask never get," said Ironhand with a wink. "And you've no idea how long it has been since I've enjoyed the company of a handsome woman."

"Handsome, indeed! I *was* a fine-looking young woman, I'll have you know. Men traveled far to court me—and I don't take kindly to being mocked."

"I would never mock you, my lovely. I've always preferred my women with a little meat on their bones. You think on it, while you fetch us our drinks. I'm a man of considerable patience."

Ironhand turned away and strode to a nearby table, where

Ballistar sat alongside him. "Good God, man, how could you make love to that . . . that . . . sow?"

"She looks mighty good to me, lad. Now there's your sort of woman," he added, pointing to another serving maid carrying a tray to the far table. She was slim and dark-haired, no more than seventeen. Ballistar stared at her with undisguised longing. "I'll call her over," whispered Ironhand.

"No!" squealed Ballistar.

It was too late, for Ironhand waved at the girl. She finished delivering the dishes to a table by the window, then walked over. "My friend, here . . ." began Ironhand.

"For pity's sake!" snapped Ballistar. He smiled sheepishly at the maid. "I'm . . . er . . . sorry."

"What he's trying to say, my lovely," continued Ironhand, "is that he is smitten by your beauty. If I were a younger man I'd fight him to the death for you. Now, we are strangers in this city, and have no understanding of the normal practices. It will have to suffice that he finds you astonishingly attractive and would like to spend a little time with you when you are finished with your work. What do you say?"

The girl smiled and stared hard at Ballistar, who felt he had reddened to his toes.

"He is a handsome boy," she said, "and you are an old devil. However, since you've already seduced my mother—and that puts me out for the night—I think I will spend a little time with the young man. The rooms upstairs are all numbered. I shall be in room eleven in an hour or so." Reaching out, she cupped Ballistar's chin. "Your beard is soft," she said. "I like that."

Her mother appeared, bearing a wooden tray on which was set a pitcher of ale, a jug of water, and three tankards. She set it down carefully and turned to Ironhand. "Don't you be drinking too much of that," she said. "It has a habit of turning hard men to softness, if you take my meaning."

Ironhand's laughter bellowed out. Grasping the woman around her ample waist, he drew her into his lap. Then taking the pitcher, he raised it to his lips and began to drink. Ballistar and Sigarni watched in amazement as he downed more than half of it. "By God, that's better," he said. Then he rose, lifted the astonished woman into the air, and began to spin and dance.

"She must weigh a ton," whispered Ballistar to Sigarni. "How does he do that?"

Ironhand returned to the table, still carrying the woman. "It's no good," he said. "I can wait not a moment longer. I'll see you both in the morning." So saying, he carried his conquest from the room.

For a little while Ballistar and Sigarni sat in silence. At last he spoke. "The woman I'm going to see . . . I don't . . . what should I . . . ?"

Sigarni laughed softly. "Do whatever comes naturally. Sit with her and talk for a while. My advice would be to tell her that she is your first, and that you are unskilled."

"I couldn't do that!"

"She will know anyway. Enjoy yourself, Ballistar. And make sure that she too has fond memories of the meeting. Too many men get carried away by their lust, and forget that their partners need loving too."

"How do I . . . ?"

"This is not a lesson, Balli. Kiss, touch, and explore. Make it last. This is the one experience you will never forget."

He grinned. "I can't believe this. When we get back I'm going to pick up the little wizard and kiss both his wizened cheeks!"

"He'll turn you into a spider and tread on you."

"Will you be all right alone?"

Leaning forward, she covered his hand with her own. "I stood in a cave and waited for demons, Balli. I think I'll probably survive a night in a strange inn, don't you?"

They sat and talked for a while, then the young maid came for Ballistar and Sigarni smiled at the look of sudden panic that flashed across his handsome face. "Go," she said, "enjoy yourself."

Alone now, she sipped the water and concentrated on the magical events that had overtaken them in Yur-vale. Three separate bursts of magick: the growth of Ballistar, the sprouting of the bow, and the rebirth of Ironhand. The dwarf had become a man, strong and straight. Why? And why the bow, and not the arrows? She had tried to discuss it with Ballistar, but he had merely shrugged and said, "It was magick. Who cares why?"

But there must be laws governing magick, she thought. Ironhand had been reborn through a piece of dried bone. But what of the bone tips on her arrows? Why had they not grown into deer? And the leather of her belt or boots—why had these items remained intact?

Taliesen had warned that this was a world of strong magick, and that it would affect them far more than the inhabitants of Yur-vale. What had he said about his fellow sorcerer? He had eaten pork and it had swelled inside him? Sigarni shuddered. Like the bone of Ironhand, the flesh had reconstituted itself in his belly and he had been ripped to pieces from within by a live and panic-stricken boar.

Reaching for the water goblet, she winced as the cold metal edge pushed at the still-healing cut on her palm.

And instantly she had the answer. On the night before the journey she had held Ironhand's bone. On the journey itself through the Gateway she had gripped Ballistar's hand.

My blood touched them. The bow also—but not the arrows!

Sigarni rose from her seat and walked upstairs to her room. The bed was deep and soft, but she did not sleep for several hours. When she awoke Ironhand was sitting beside the bed.

"I hope your dreams were good ones," he said.

"I had none that I can recall," she told him. "You?"

"I didn't sleep a wink," he said with a grin. "But I could eat a horse."

"That would not be advisable. The horse would eat you."

He looked at her quizzically and she explained about Taliesen's warning. "Well, then, we had better find the Crown and head back to the Highlands. I want to taste a good steak again, and smell the pines."

"First we must find the palace, or wherever it is that the King resides."

"You think he will just give you a national treasure?"

"We'll see."

The King stared from the window of his eighth-floor study and watched as the enemy siege engines slowly approached the city's north wall. There were seven of them, each around eighty feet high, clad in sheets of hammered iron and impervious to flame arrows. When they reached the walls, which they would within the hour, the fighting would be hard. Close to the wall the towers would lower their drawbridges, and fighting men would pour out onto the ramparts.

His guards would meet them, blade to blade, hacking and slaying, buying time for the engineers to hurl firebombs through the apertures. The iron cladding outside would offer no protection to the scores of men waiting on the siege tower stairs.

You are coming to your doom, he told himself. He glanced to his left, where his ceremonial armor was laid out on a bench of oak. You are getting too old to fight, he thought. And what will happen to Zir-vak when you fall in battle? Neither of his sons had yet reached one hundred—and even if they had, he thought with regret, they could not shoulder the responsibilities of command. Perhaps I have been too easy on them.

Stepping back from the window he moved to his desk, lifting a bronze-rimmed oval mirror. The face that peered back at him was grey with fatigue, the eyes dull. Dropping the mirror, he picked up the letter that had arrived the previous evening from the merchant Yos-shiel. Three strangers had come to the city, intent on stealing the Paradise Helm. They would find a fine surprise waiting for them!

A servant entered the room and bowed deeply. "Majesty, there is a woman who wishes to see you."

"Tell her I have no time today. Let her make her entreaty to Pasan-Yol!"

"With respect, Majesty, I feel you may wish to speak with the woman. She says she wishes to see you in connection with the Paradise Helm—and she matches the description you gave to the soldiers."

The King turned. "Is she alone?"

"No, her companions are with her, Majesty—a white-haired giant and a young man."

"Are they armed?"

"They gave their weapons to the Royal Sentries."

Intrigued, the King moved to his desk. "Show them in—and fetch Pasan-Yol."

Bowing once more, the servant departed.

As Yos-shiel had reported, the woman was very beautiful, and moved with a grace that stirred the King's blood. "I understand you claim to be from another land," he said. "Where might that be?"

"I could not say where in relation to Yur-vale," she told him, her voice deep, almost husky. "We were sent through a magical Gateway."

The King picked up the letter. "So Yos-shiel tells me. I must say I find it hard to believe. Could it be that you are spies, sent by the enemy?"

A squad of guards moved in behind the newcomers. "You wish them arrested, Majesty?" asked Pasan-Yol.

"Not yet," the King told the young guardsman. "They interest me. So tell me, woman, why you are here."

"To bring back the sun," she said. The silence in the room grew as the listeners took in her words.

"You are a witch?" asked the King.

"I am."

"Sorcery has long been considered a crime here, punishable by death."

The woman smiled. "Whereas stupidity has obviously not. Do you wish to see the sun shine over Yur-vale?"

The King leaned back in his chair. "Let us suppose—merely for the sake of argument—that you could achieve this . . . this miracle. What do you desire in return?"

"I think the letter from Yos-shiel will answer that," she told him.

"You know of that—and yet you come here? Was that wise, witch?"

She shrugged. "The wisdom of any course can only be judged by the outcome. I offer you the sun for a piece of metal. You make whatever choice seems fitting."

"What do you think, Pasan?" asked the King.

The young guardsman gave a derisory laugh. "I think they are spies, Father. Let me interrogate them."

"Yet another numbskull," said Ironhand to Sigarni, in the same tone of voice. "You think they are all victims of inbreeding?" The guardsman's sword snaked from its scabbard. "Put it away, boy," said Ironhand, "before I take it away from you and swat your backside." The guardsman took a deep breath and dropped into a fighting position with sword extended.

"That's enough!" said the King. "Put up your blade, Pasan!"

"You heard what he said, Father!"

"Aye, I did," answered the King wearily. "So let us not be too swift to prove his point."

"I think a little proof would not go amiss," put in Sigarni to the King. "Do you have a garden here?"

"Nothing grows in Zir-vak," he said. "But, yes, there was a garden. I do not go there now, for the sight of it saddens me."

"Take me there," she said, "and I will show you something to lift your heart."

The King stood and moved to the window, where the siege towers were inching ever closer. He swung back to the woman. "Very well, I will humor you. But know this, if there is no miracle I shall not be best pleased—and the charge of sorcery will be laid against you."

"If there is no miracle," said the woman, "then the charge will be hard to prove."

For the first time the King smiled. "Let us go to the garden," he said.

The garden was more than two hundred feet long, and had been designed around a series of winding white-paved pathways. There were three fountains, none of them in use, and the flowerbeds were covered with thick grey ash. Scores of dead trees lined the marble walls at the outer edges of the garden, and the area was devoid of any life.

Sigarni felt a moment of fear as she surveyed the landscape. What if her reasoning was flawed?

"I'm looking forward to this," said Ironhand with a wink.

"Well," said the King, "we are here, and you promised a miracle." He was standing with his arms folded, his son beside him with hand on sword. The six guards stood nervously by.

Sigarni approached the King. "May I borrow your dagger, my lord?" she asked.

"What nonsense is this?" stormed the young man at his side.

Sigarni frowned, then raised her arm before him. "Make a shallow cut, here," she said, pointing to her forearm.

Pasan-Yol drew his dagger, and drew the blade slowly across her skin. Blood welled, and Sigarni walked to a line of dead bushes, kneeling down before the first and holding her arm above the dry branches. Slowly drops of blood dripped to the wood.

Nothing happened. Sigarni stayed where she was, and glanced at Ironhand, who was watching her intently. She had explained her theory to him, and he had listened thoughtfully.

"Well, where is this miracle?" asked the King, his tone hardening.

Ironhand stepped forward and knelt beside Sigarni. "Touch the bush," he whispered.

Lowering her arm, her fingers brushed against the wood and she felt her hand grow hot. The blood upon the branches disappeared into the grey wood, which began to swell and grow. Buds appeared, pushing out into new red growth, stretching up toward the iron sky, then darkened to green and finally to brown. Three blooms appeared, opening to roses the color of Sigarni's blood.

She stood and turned toward the King, ready to present her arguments.

Just then a beam of sunlight pierced the clouds, illuminating the garden. In its bright light the King looked older, more weary, his face lined, dark rings beneath his eyes. "How have you done this?" he whispered, moving to the rose and kneeling before it to smell the blooms.

"The war must end," she said. "That is all that keeps the sun at bay."

"What are you saying?"

"This is a magical land, Majesty, where the war and the devastation feed the dark side of the magic. Every act of hate, of malice, of bloodlust, only serves to fuel the fires beneath the mountains. You are destroying this world with your fighting. Think back to the days before, when the sun shone. The Feast of Athling. There was a three-day truce between the armies; when the fighting stopped the sun shone. It was the same when your father was buried: a day of truce. And before the war Yur-vale was a paradise. Can you not see it? In some way the feelings of the people are magnified by the land itself. All this hatred and violence is reflected by the land which, like the people here, is turning on itself."

"I told you she was a spy!" roared Pasan-Yol. "This is all a trick to lull us."

From some distance away came a series of dull, booming sounds, and the faint clash of steel upon steel. The sunlight faded away.

"The siege towers have reached the walls," said the King. "I must go now. But I will give your words serious consideration and we will meet again this afternoon. In the meantime I will ask one of my servants to show you the palace museum. There are many wonders there—including the Helm you seek."

Sigarni and Ballistar bowed. Ironhand merely inclined his head.

"Your tall friend does not care for the formalities. Does he not know it is wise always to pay respects to a king?"

"He does, my lord," said Sigarni. "But he is a king himself, and is unused to bowing before others."

The King chuckled. "A monarch should have better dress sense," he said, pointing to Ironhand's ill-fitting red shirt. "And you, young lady, should have that wound dressed— unless of course you plan to revive my entire garden." He swung to the young man. "You cut too deeply, Pasan. See that the surgeon is sent for, and that our guests are looked after."

"But, Father . . ."

"Just do it, Pasan. I have no time for further debate." The King strolled away, followed by four of the guards.

Pasan glared at Sigarni. "You may have fooled him with your witchery, but not me. You are an enemy—and enemies are to be destroyed. And look at your rose," he said triumphantly. "It is already dying."

"Aye," she agreed sadly. "With every death upon the walls. With every mouthful of corpse meat. With every word of hate."

Summoning Ballistar and Ironhand, Sigarni walked back toward the palace.

Her arm bandaged, the blood still seeping through, Sigarni sat with Ironhand and Ballistar in the main hall of the Palace Museum. There were statues lining the walls, paintings hung in alcoves, but pride of place went to the Crown of Alwen, which sat upon a slim column of gold within a crystal case. The Helm shimmered in the lamplight and Ironhand gazed upon it with undisguised admiration. "Had I retained the Crown," he said softly, "there would have been no civil war. Elarine and I could have enjoyed a peaceful reign and you, Sigarni, would have known great joy."

"I have known great joy," she said. "Gwalchmai was a fine foster father, and I have lived a free life in the Highlands."

"Even so, I wish it had been different."

"It is never wise to long for days past," she told him. "They cannot come again. What will you do when we get back? Will you announce yourself and lead the army? You are much more suited to the task than I."

"I think not," said the giant. "You are the new Battle Queen. Let it be so. I will advise—and take an hour or two to smite the enemy," he added with a grin.

"*If* we get back," pointed out Ballistar. "There is no certainty. What if you are wrong about this war, Sigarni? What if the sun does not shine again?"

"I am not wrong," she said. "I sensed it from the moment the bow sprouted leaves. This is a land in torment. Everything here is unnatural. When the war ends, so will the upheavals of nature—I am convinced of it."

"I think you are correct," said Ironhand, "but the fact remains that for the war to end, both sides must agree on terms. After fighting for this long, such a decision will be hard. There is something else too, daughter. If there is no peace, and the King refuses to give you the Crown, what then?"

"We will leave without it—and fight the Outlanders without the aid of the Pallides."

"I'm hungry," said Ballistar. "Do you think they would allow us a cooking pot? We still have some oats."

"You could ask," said Sigarni, gesturing toward the silent guards at the door. But the request was refused, and the trio moved around the museum, studying the various artifacts.

Toward dusk several servants entered, filling the oil lamps and lighting more. Huge velvet curtains were drawn across the high, arched windows.

At last the King returned. He was wearing armor now, and looked even more weary than he had in the morning. "Their siege engines were destroyed," he said, "but the death toll was very high. I have asked for a truce, and will meet with their King outside the walls in an hour. I want you with me when I speak with him."

"Gladly, sire," said Sigarni.

More than fifty lanterns had been set on poles outside the main gates, and a score of chairs were set out in two lines of ten, facing one another. The night was pitch-black, the lanterns barely giving out sufficient light to see more than a few paces. "Fetch more," ordered the King, and two officers moved away into the blackness. The King, now dressed in a simple tunic of blue, sat down, with Sigarni on his left and Pasan-Yol on his right.

Twenty more lanterns were set out.

They waited for some time, and then saw a slow-moving column of men walking from the enemy camp, their King in the lead, wearing silver armor embossed with gold. He had no helm and Sigarni saw that his lean face showed the same edge of weariness as that of the man beside her.

He did not look at the waiting party, but strode directly to a chair opposite the King of Zir-vak and sat down.

"Well, Nashan," he said at last, as his twenty-man escort fanned out behind him, "for what purpose do you call this meeting?"

The King told him of Sigarni's arrival, and of the miracle in the rose garden. The enemy leader was less than impressed.

"Today you destroyed a few siege towers, but they proved their worth, did they not? You were hard-pressed to stop them. I have now ordered fifty to be built, then Zir-vak will fall. You think me a fool, cousin? You seek to stave off defeat with this nonsense?"

"It is all nonsense, Reva. We fight a war our grandfathers began. And for what? For the honor of our Houses. Where is the honor in what we do?"

"I will find honor," stormed Reva, "when I have your head impaled on a lance over the gates of Zir-vak."

"Then you may have it," said the King. "You may take it now. If that will end the war and bring the sun back to our lands, I will die gladly. Is that all you desire?"

"The surrender of all your forces, and the opening of the gates," demanded Reva.

"The gates are already open," pointed out the King. "And we will fight no more."

"No!" screamed Pasan-Yol. "You cannot betray us all."

"It is not betrayal, Pasan, it is a new beginning."

The young man lurched to his feet, a dagger in his hand. Before anyone could stop him he had rammed the blade into his father's breast. The King groaned and fell against Sigarni. Ironhand, standing behind the King, reached over and grabbed Pasan-Yol by the throat, dragging him away. Ballistar threw himself at the young man, wrenching the knife from his grasp.

Sigarni lowered the dying King to the ground. "Reva!" he called.

The enemy King knelt by his side. "I spoke the truth, cousin. This war is killing the land and it must end. Not just for you and I, and our Houses, but for the land itself. You now have my head, and my city. Let the hatred pass away with my death."

For a moment Reva said nothing, then he sighed. "It will be as you say, Nashan. I too have a need to see the sun." Pulling off his gauntlet, Reva took Nashan's hand.

A man cried out and pointed upward. A full moon had appeared in the night sky, and the glimmering of distant stars could be clearly seen. "It begins," whispered Nashan.

And he died.

Sigarni closed the King's eyes and stood. "A sad end to a fine man," she said, turning and walking away. Ironhand released Pasan-Yol, who stood staring at the moon and stars. Then he ran to his father's body, hurling himself across it and sobbing.

Sigarni, Ballistar, and Ironhand returned to the museum. Ironhand thundered his fist against the crystal case, which exploded into fragments. Reaching inside, he drew out the Crown and passed it to Sigarni.

"It is time to go," she said, opening her pack and stowing the Crown inside.

Vast numbers of people thronged the streets, staring up at the sky as the trio made their slow way down to the river. There were several boats moored there and Sigarni chose a small craft, with two oars. Loosing it from its moorings, they climbed aboard, and set out on the journey downstream.

Sigarni sat staring back at the receding city. Ballistar put his arm around her shoulder. "Why so sad, Sigarni? You saved them."

"I liked him," she said. "He was a good man."

"But there is something else, I think?" he probed.

She nodded. "We stopped one war, and now we have the means to pursue another. Is our land any different from this one? How does High Druin feel about the slaughter that is coming?"

"Our fight is not about honor, or a stolen wife," said Ballistar. "We fight for survival against a pitiless enemy. There is a difference."

"Is there? My hatred is all used up, Balli. When they raped

me, I wanted to see every Outlander slain. That is not what I desire anymore."

Later the following day, in bright sunlight, the three stood at the circle of stones. Sigarni unwound the bandage on her forearm and used it to press her blood against each of the six stones. Then the three of them stood at the center, holding hands and waiting.

"I'm anticipating that steak with great pleasure," said Ironhand.

"And I can't wait to see their faces when they see what I have become," said Ballistar happily.

Light grew around them and Sigarni felt dizziness swamp her. Then Taliesen appeared before her, and a cold winter breeze touched her face.

"Did you get it?" the wizard asked.

Sigarni did not answer. In her right hand lay the tiny bone fragment of Ironhand, while clinging to her left was Ballistar the Dwarf, tears flowing from his eyes as he stood, dressed in her outsize leggings.

Like all Highlanders, Gwalchmai loved the spring. Life in the mountains was always harsh, and people lived with the constant knowledge that death waited like a monster beyond the firelight. Winter fell upon the mountains like a mythical beast, robbing the land of crops, of food, sucking the heat from the soil and from the bones of Man.

But spring, with her promise of sunshine and plenty, was a season to be loved. The burst of color that appeared on the hillsides as the first flowers pushed their way through the cold earth, the singing of birds in the trees, the fragrant blossom on bush and branch—all these things spoke of *life*.

The ache in Gwalchmai's back had faded away in the morning sunlight, as he sat in the old chair on the porch of his cabin. I almost feel young again, he thought happily. A faint touch of regret whispered across his mind, and he opened the parchment he had held folded in his hand. It had been so long since he had written anything that the words seemed spidery and overlarge, like a child's. Still, it was legible.

Time for the last of the mead, he thought. Leaning to his right, he lifted the jug and removed the stopper. Tipping it, he filled his mouth with the sweet liquor and rolled it over his tongue. He had hidden the mead the year Sigarni was brought to him, which had been a vintage year. Gwalchmai smiled at the memory. Taliesen had walked into the clearing, leading the child by the hand. In that moment Gwalchmai had seen the vision of his death. That night, as the child slept, he had taken two jugs and hidden them in the loft, ready for this day.

This day . . .

The old man pushed himself to his feet and stretched his back. The joints creaked and cracked like tinder twigs. Drawing in a deep breath, he swirled the last of the liquor in the jug. Less than half a cup left, he realized. Shall I save it until they come? He thought about it for a moment—then drained the jug. Letting out a satisfied sigh, he sank back to the chair.

The sound of horses' hooves on the hard-packed ground made him start and panic flickered within his breast. He had waited so long for this moment—and now he was afraid, fearful of the long journey into the dark. His mouth was dry, and he regretted the last swallow of mead.

"Calm yourself, old fool," he said aloud. Rising, he strolled out into the wide yard and waited for the horsemen.

There were six scouts, clad in iron helms and baked leather breastplates. They saw him and drew their weapons, fanning out around him in a semicircle. "Good morning, my brave boys!" said Gwalchmai.

The riders edged their horses closer, while scanning the surrounding trees. "I am alone, boys. I have been waiting for you. I have a message here that you may read," he added, waving the scrap of parchment.

"Who are you, old man?" asked a rider, heeling his horse forward.

Gwalchmai chuckled. "I am the reader of souls, the speaker of truths, the voice of the slain to come. They found the body, you know, back in your village. Upon your return they intend to hang you. But do not let it concern you—you will not return."

The man blanched, his jaw hanging slack.

"What's he talking about?" demanded another rider. "What body?"

Gwalchmai swung to the speaker. "Ah, Bello, what a delight to see you again! And you, Jeraime," he added, smiling up at a third rider. "Neither of you like each other, and yet, together you will stand back-to-back at the last, and you will die together, and take the long walk into Hell side by side. Is that a comforting thought? I hope not!"

"Give me the message, old man!" demanded the first rider, holding out his hand.

"Not yet, Gaele. There is much to say. You are all riding to your deaths. Sigarni will see you slain."

"How is it you know my name?" demanded Gaele.

"I know all your names, and your sordid pasts," sneered Gwalchmai. "That is my Gift—though when I gaze upon your lives it becomes a curse. You buried her deep, Gaele, by the riverbank—but you never thought that the old willow would one day fall . . . and in so doing expose the grave. Worse yet, you left the ring upon her finger, the topaz ring you brought back from Kushir. All the village knows you killed her. Even now a message is on its way asking that you be returned for trial! Fear not, brave boy, for your belly will be opened at the Duane Pass. No hanging for you!"

"Shut up!" screamed Gaele, spurring his horse forward. His sword lashed down, striking the old man on the crown of his head and smashing him from his feet. Blood gushed from the wound but Gwalchmai struggled to his knees.

"You will all die!" he shouted. "The whole army. And the

crows will feast on your eyes!" The sword slashed down again and Gwalchmai fell to his face in the dirt. All tension eased from his frame, and he did not feel the blades lance into his body.

All these years, he thought, and at the last I lied. I do not know whether Sigarni will win or lose, but these cowards will carry the tale of my prophecy back to the army, and it will rage like a forest fire through their ranks.

As if from a great distance, Gwalchmai heard his name being called.

"I am coming," he said.

Gaele dragged his sword clear of the old man's back, wiping the blade clean on the dead man's tunic. Stooping, he plucked the parchment from the dead fingers and opened it.

"What does it say?" asked Bello as the others gathered around the corpse.

"You know I can't read," snapped Gaele.

Jeraime stepped forward. "Give it to me," he said. Gaele passed it over and Jeraime scanned the spidery text.

"Well?" demanded Gaele.

Jeraime was silent for a moment, and when he spoke his voice was trembling. "It says, *'There will be six. One of them a wife-killer. Gaele will strike me down. Jeraime will read my message.'* "

Jeraime let the parchment fall and backed away to his horse.

"He was a sorcerer," whispered Bello. "He said we were all going to die. The whole army! Dear God, why did we come here?"

The army made camp near the ruins of Cilfallen: seven thousand men, incorporating four thousand heavily armored foot soldiers, fifteen hundred archers and slingers, five hundred assorted engineers, cooks, foragers, and scouts, and a thousand cavalry. The Baron's long black tent was erected near the Cilfallen stream, while the cavalry camped to the north, the foot soldiers to the east and west, and other personnel to the south. Leofric set sentry rotas and dispatched scouts to the north; then he returned, weary, to his own tent.

Jakuta Khan was sitting on a canvas-backed chair, sipping fine wine. He smiled as Leofric entered the tent. "Such a long face," said the sorcerer, "and here you are on the verge of a glorious expedition."

"I dislike lying to the Baron," said Leofric, opening a travel chair and seating himself opposite the red-clad man.

"I told you, it was not a lie. I *am* a merchant—of sorts. Where do you think the first battle will be fought?"

"The Baron believes they will fortify the Duane Pass. We have several contingency plans for such an eventuality. Can you not tell me what they are planning? The fall of the forts has left me out of favor with the Baron. He blames me!"

Jakuta Khan shook his head and adopted a suitably apologetic expression. "My dear Leofric, I would dearly love to help you. But to use my powers while Taliesen is nearby would be costly to me—perhaps fatal. The old man is not without Talent. When he departs I will reach out and, shall we say, observe them. Relax, my boy. Enjoy the wine. It really is very good."

Leofric sighed. He knew the wine was good; it had cost a small fortune. Accepting a goblet, he sipped the liquid appreciatively. "You said you had tried to capture the woman before, and had failed. Is she charmed? Is this Taliesen as powerful as you?"

"Interesting questions," said Jakuta Khan, his jovial round face now looking serious and thoughtful. "I have pondered them often. The first attempt was thwarted by Taliesen and a Highlander named Caswallon. They took her as a babe, and hid her . . . here. At that time I did not know of Taliesen's existence, and therefore had no plan to cope with him. By the time I found her hiding place she was a small child; her foster mother threw her from the cabin window, and she ran to a nearby waterfall. There Caswallon and Taliesen once more intervened, though how they came to be there at that precise time, I do not know. They could not have stopped me, for I was well prepared. Sadly, a third force intervened; I believe it was a spirit. He aided her again—and that cost the life of the dearest of my acolytes. But there it is. That is life and we cannot grumble. But last week I used one of the four great spells. Infallible. Either the victim dies, or the sender. I risked everything. And nothing happened. Curiously, the demon I summoned disappeared as soon as my spell was complete. I can tell you, Leofric, I have spent many a long night since thinking over that problem. I know it is hard for you to imagine, but think of aiming a bow at an enemy and loosing the shaft. As it flies through the air, it disappears. It was like that. The question is, where did the demon go?"

"Did you find an answer?" asked Leofric, intrigued.

"I believe so. I cast the spell just outside Citadel town, inside a circle of ancient stones. They are believed to be Gateways to other worlds. In some way I believe I activated the Gateway. Even so, the creature was completely attuned to Sigarni. Therefore wherever it went, she would have been there also. Mystifying."

Leofric refilled his goblet. "Does that mean the creature is still looking for her?"

"It is possible. In fact, it is more than likely. The Gateways operate through time as well as space, and even now he is winging his way toward her. What a cheering prospect—I'll drink to that!"

"Why do you hate her so? Has she done you some harm?"

"Good Heavens, Leofric, I do not hate her. I don't hate anyone. Such a harmful emotion! I rather admire her, don't you? But I need what she has. The blood royal! All the great spells require blood royal. And anything can be achieved with it, lead to gold, immortality—of a kind—physical strength. As limitless as the imagination."

"She's just a Highland woman, for God's sake. What royal blood does she carry?"

"What blood? How arrogant of you, Leofric. Your own King does not carry the blood royal, though his grandsons might. Sigarni is the daughter of the great King, Ironhand, who was done to death by assassins centuries ago. He had a fortress near here, colossal and impregnable. Only the foundation stones are left."

"Then how could she be his daughter?"

"She was carried through a Gateway in time. Do you not listen, my boy?"

"I think the wine must be going to my head," Leofric admitted. "It all sounds like gibberish."

"Of course it does," said Jakuta Khan soothingly, leaning forward and patting the young man's knee. "But that is the simple answer to your question. Her blood carries power, and I need that power. If there was a way to utilize it without killing her, I would. For I am not fond of death."

Leofric refilled his glass for the second time. "You are a strange man, Jakuta. Perhaps you are insane. Have you thought of that?"

"You are full of interesting ideas, Leofric. It makes you a joy to be with. Let us examine the premise. Insanity: not being sane. Yet how do we establish sanity? Would we, for example, look to the majority of people and claim them as normal and sane?"

"That seems reasonable," agreed Leofric.

"But the King is not normal like them, is he? He is an extraordinary man, as is the Baron. Does that make them insane?"

"Ah, I see what you are saying," said Leofric, leaning forward and spilling his wine. "But then normality is not just a question of who farms or who rules. It is surely an ability to discern right from wrong, or good from evil, perhaps."

"Now the waters become even muddier, my boy. If a farmer sees a neighbor with a bigger section of land, and more wealth, and sets out to murder him, is he evil?"

"Of course."

"But if a king sets out to destroy his enemy's kingdom in order to swell his own treasury, then he, by that example, is evil also."

"Not so!" insisted Leofric, aware he was on dangerous ground. "There may be many reasons why a nation goes to war. Security, for example, protecting one's borders."

"Of course, of course," agreed Jakuta. "And this war? Against an enemy with no army to speak of, a pretend war for the purpose of self-glorification, is this evil?"

"For God's sake keep your voice down!"

"Sanity is not easy to establish, is it, Leofric? All I know is that one man's good is another man's evil. That is the way life works: It favors the rich and the powerful, it always has and I suspect it always will. I am not rich, but I am powerful. I intend to become more powerful."

"As powerful as this Taliesen?"

"Less and more. He is a curious fellow. He has vast resources, and chooses not to use them. You would like him, I think, Leofric. He knows more about the Gateways than any man alive. Yet he lives like a peasant, and dresses worse. He has a cloak of feathers that has seen better days, and he has allowed his body to become old and wizened. We have not conversed, but I would make a wager that he believes his powers to be a gift from some supreme source, to be used wisely and carefully."

"Perhaps he is right."

"Perhaps. I cannot disprove his theories, but I tend toward disbelief. I have conversed with demons who serve a greater demon, and I have known holy men who claim to have spoken with God. Whereas I, more powerful than most, have never felt the need to serve either God or the Devil, and neither of them has seen fit to approach me."

"How will you know when Taliesen has left the Highlands?"

"Oh, I will know."

*   *   *

In the morning Leofric felt that he had a caged horse inside his skull, trying to kick its way to freedom. His head pounded and the bright sunlight induced a feeling of nausea. Jakuta Khan, who seemed untouched by the excesses of the night before, sat quietly, watching the dawn. Leofric stumbled from the tent and made his way to the stream, where he stripped off his tunic and bathed in the clear, cold water.

Wet and shivering, he dressed and walked to the Baron's tent. As he had expected the Baron was already awake, and was sitting at his travel desk examining maps. Leofric entered and bowed. "Good morning, my lord. I trust you slept well?"

The Baron rubbed at the black leather eye patch he wore. "I have not slept well since that damned bird tore out my eye. What news?"

"The scouts are not in yet, sir. Shall I fetch you breakfast?"

"Not yet. How do you think they will defend the pass?" The Baron spread out a series of maps on the rug at his feet. Leofric crouched down and studied them.

"They have few choices, sir. My spies tell me the Pallides had pledged themselves to Sigarni. That brings the total of her force to just over three thousand—not quite enough, I would imagine, to defend the eastern slope. They would be too thinly stretched and we could outflank them. The western slope is shorter, but that would mean leaving a gap in their eastern defenses, through which a force of cavalry could ride, creating havoc in their villages. Of course, they may try to defend both slopes, or they may, if desperate, choose to occupy the flat-topped hill at the north end of the pass. The slopes are steep and a shield-ring would be hard to penetrate."

"In what way do you see this as a desperate move?" inquired the Baron.

"We would surround them, and there would be no means of escape. They would be gambling all on being able to hold us, wear us down, then counterattack."

"I agree," said the Baron. "So which do you believe they will choose?"

"I am not a warrior, my lord, and I do not fully understand their mentality. I would, however, think it likely they will try to occupy the western slope. It is wooded, and covered with boulders. We would be forced to attack many times to discover the areas in which they are weak."

"Aye, they'll try to be canny," said the Baron. "That black traitor Asmidir will see to that. Their line will be of varying strength, at its most powerful where an attack is likely." He stabbed his forefinger at a point on the first map. "Here, where the slope is not so steep, and here, where the tree line thins. We will attack both simultaneously with the infantry. But the cavalry will strike here!"

"The highest ground? Is that wise, my lord?"

"Asmidir knows the way we fight, Leofric. Therefore we change. If I am wrong we will lose a few score cavalry, but the outcome will remain the same. What of supplies?"

Leofric rubbed at his eyes, praying that his head would stop pounding. "I commandeered as many wagons as were available, my lord, and they should start arriving by late this afternoon. The men will be on short rations until we take the Pallides villages and the cattle there."

"We have your negligence to thank for that," snapped the Baron. "I shall not swiftly forget the fall of your *impregnable* forts. If you were not my cousin, I would have had you flayed alive."

"I am very grateful to you, sir," said Leofric dutifully. The sound of horsemen approaching allowed him to avoid further embarrassment and he rose swiftly and moved outside. The first of the scout troops were returning. Lightly armed on fast horses, they could move swiftly across the countryside. All were veterans of many campaigns, and had traveled with the Census Taker in the autumn in order to accustom themselves to the land.

The lead rider dismounted, the other four riding off toward the cook-fires. The man saluted.

"Your report?" demanded Leofric.

"No sign of the enemy, sir. We killed one old man who ran at us with an ancient broadsword, and we spotted some foresters heading south, but as ordered, we avoided contact. The Loda fort has been plundered and the walls part dismantled. We rode to the Pallides fort, and this has seen similar treatment."

"Any activity at Duane?"

"None that I could see, sir, and I thought it best not to push too far. We'll head out again after the men have eaten and acquired fresh mounts."

"Good. We will be moving on to the Loda fort within the hour. When you return, make your report to me there."

"Yes, sir."

The Baron appeared and called out to the man as he was about to mount his horse.

"You, how many foresters were heading south?"

"Around a score, sir. Maybe a few more hidden by the trees."

"Not an attacking force, then?"

"I don't believe so, sir. I think they may have been hunting. I expect food is scarce about now."

"That's all," said the Baron, moving alongside Leofric as the man saluted and turned away. "How many men do you have guarding the supply wagons?"

"Two troops, my lord, and a section of infantrymen."

"Send back another fifty cavalrymen. I don't think they are hunting deer, they are seeking to cut our supply line."

"Yes, sir. I'll do that immediately."

"And give the orders to take some of them alive for questioning."

"Yes, sir."

"Now you can order me that breakfast," said the Baron, returning to his tent.

* * *

Asmidir fought to keep himself calm. "Sigarni, listen to me; you cannot continue to risk everything on a single throw of the dice. We have enough men now to hold the western slope. We can wear them down, harry their flanks, disrupt their supply lines. There is simply no need for us to take unnecessary chances."

"I hear what you say, Asmidir, and I will consider it," she said. "Leave me now."

She watched him depart, knowing his turmoil. He was a soldier, a strategist, and his hatred of the Outlanders had seeped into his bones. He had traveled far to find an enemy capable of inflicting savage defeats on his enemies, and now he felt it was all at risk. As indeed it was . . .

Fell had stood by silently during the exchange, and she turned to him. "You are slow to offer your opinions, general?"

He laughed. "I'm no general. I am a forester and proud of it. What he says makes sense to me, but who am I to argue with the great Battle Queen of the Highlands?"

"Stop it, Fell," she said, irritated. "Just tell me what you think."

"The man understands war—and he knows the ways of the Outlanders. The western slope must be defended, for it leads into our heartland. He knows it. You know it. The Outlanders know it."

"Exactly my point," said Sigarni. "We all know where the dangers lie—therefore it is time to think of something different. And, by God, I shall!" She sat in silence for a few moments. "Any sign of Gwalchmai yet?" she asked.

"No. I think he headed home."

"To die," she said softly.

"Aye. His time had come, he said. He told me he was due to die in the spring—even knew the face of the soldier who would do the deed."

"He did not say good-bye," she said. "He took me in when

the beasts slew my . . . parents, and he cherished me through-out my childhood. Why would he leave without saying good-bye?"

"He knew the day and the hour, Sigarni. He left soon after you set off for the Crown. He spoke to Taliesen just before he departed; maybe the wizard can tell you more."

"And what of Ballistar?"

Fell shook his head. "Nothing yet, but Kollarin is seeking him."

"It broke his heart, Fell. He wanted you to see him as he was in that other world, strong and straight. He even bedded a woman there. It is often said that what is never had cannot be missed. I think that is true. All his life he has yearned to be like us. Then it happened, and he experienced a joy he could not have dreamed of. The return was a living night-mare for him."

"You look tired, Sigarni. Perhaps you should rest for a while."

"No," she told him, "I need to see Taliesen before he leaves. Will you fetch him?"

"And then you will rest?"

She nodded. As Fell left the cabin Sigarni felt the truth of his words. Her bones ached with weariness, and her mind seemed to float from problem to problem, never settling. How long since you slept? she asked herself. Three days? Four?

Taliesen entered. "The enemy is six thousand strong," he said, "and they will be here in two days. I wish you good for-tune, Sigarni. It all rests now on your skill, and the courage of your men."

"I wish you could stay, Taliesen. Your powers would be more than useful."

"I shall return when the battle is over."

"You are assuming that we will conquer?"

"No," he said sadly. "I am making no assumptions. I have

seen many futures, Sigarni. In some you win, in others you die."

"They cannot all be true," she pointed out.

"Oh, they can," he said softly. "I long ago learned that there are many worlds identical to our own. When we travel between them, all things are possible. If you are dead when I return I will travel more Gateways, seeking a Sigarni who survived."

"Why not seek her now—and then tell me how she did it?"

He smiled. "I like you, Battle Queen. Truly. And now I must go. Have you spoken to Ironhand since he lost his second life?"

"Yes. His hurt is considerable, but he is still with me," she said, touching the pouch hanging at her throat.

"I am sorry for the dwarf. I did not know that he would be so affected beyond the Gate."

"Kollarin will find him. Ballistar is strong; he will recover. Go in peace, Taliesen."

The old man bowed once more and walked to the door. Sigarni stretched herself out on the narrow pallet bed.

And drifted into the bliss of a dreamless sleep.

When she awoke Ironhand was sitting beside her. The old King was clad once more in his silver armor, with a great winged helm upon his head, his beard braided. "How long have I been asleep?" she asked.

"Three hours. Fell is outside the cabin and is allowing no one in."

"Now is the time for decisions," she said, sitting up and rubbing the sand of sleep from her eyes. "And it frightens me."

"As it should. A little fear is like yeast to the spirit, encouraging it to grow strong."

"What if I make a mistake now?"

"Then all die," he told her bluntly.

She took a deep, calming breath. "What advice can you offer me?"

"You are the Queen of the Highlands, my daughter, and I am proud of you. But now you must learn the one terrible lesson of monarchy. That you are alone. The decision is yours. Win or lose, *you* carry the weight. For what it is worth, however, I will offer one thought—seek out the wife of Torgan."

"You know her?"

"I was with you when you spoke last to her. She made you smile, and she made you cry. Both were good for you."

"Then you cannot say which defensive plan would be the best for us? I was relying on you, Ironhand. You have fought so many battles. You won them all."

"No, I didn't. Wish I had. I was always too headstrong. I just won the important ones. Seek out the woman, then make a decision. Stick to it, and be firm in your leadership. If you have doubts, hide them. You are the Battle Queen. They will all look to you, now and always."

"You will be with me on the battlefield?"

"Aye, then I will seek Elarine and the fields of glory."

The image shimmered and vanished. Sigarni rose and called out to Fell, who entered the room and knelt beside her. "You were talking in your sleep," he said. "I could not make out the words."

"I am going for a walk. Will you join me?"

"I am at your command," he told her.

"I am asking you as a *friend*, Fell," she told him, holding out her hand. For a moment only he stared at it, then their fingers touched. She looked into his deep brown eyes, and watched his smile grow.

"I love you, Sigarni," he said, his voice thickening. "Always did, always will. Welcome home."

Together they walked from the cabin and down the hillside. The snow was melting fast, and spring flowers were everywhere. "Is Torgan still here?" she asked.

"As far as I know. He and his wife have taken lodging with Fyon Sharp-axe. Are you going to give him a command?"

"Yes," she said, "under you."

"Why? The man insulted you—and all of us."

"But he's a Highlander, Fell, and a brave man. He deserves a second chance—for his wife and family if for nothing else."

"Why the change, Sigarni? What has happened to you?"

"Perhaps it is High Druin," she said with a smile. "Perhaps he spoke to me. When I went through the Gateway to that strange land I could almost feel its emotions. Yet the people there could not. I think it is the same here. The land cannot abide hatred, Fell. And I have no place left in my heart for it. Tomorrow we fight the Outlanders—because we must. We will destroy them if we can—but only because we must. Torgan was wrong, but he believed himself right and acted with the best interests of his clan at heart. Now he suffers shame. I shall end that."

As they approached the end of the tree line Sigarni turned toward Fell and curled her arms around his neck. "I hated you when you left me, and when I heard about the death of your wife I was glad. It shames me to admit, and I feel sorrow now."

Dipping his head he kissed her tenderly. "This is all I ever wanted, Sigarni. I know that now."

"Leave me here, Fell. I will see you later—at the meeting hall. There I will announce our battle plan."

"And after that?"

"We will go home. Together."

Sigarni walked down the winding lane to the home of Fyon Sharp-axe. Loran, Torgan, and the huge warrior Mereth were sitting in the sunshine with the Hunt Lord. All rose as Sigarni approached.

"You are welcome, lady," said Fyon with a short bow.

Loran fetched a chair for her, and they sat. Torgan remained standing, then turned toward the house. "Wait," said Sigarni, "I would value your counsel."

"Do you wish to shame me again?" he asked, standing tall, his eyes angry.

"No. I want you to be at the meeting tonight. Tomorrow you will command the Farlain wing, under Fell's leadership."

Torgan stood stock-still, and she could see the anger replaced by wariness. "Why are you doing this?" he asked.

"I need strong men in positions of authority. You may decline if you choose."

"No! I accept."

"Good. The meeting begins at dusk. Is Layelia in the house?"

"Yes," said Torgan, still stunned. "Shall I fetch her?"

"No. I will find her." Sigarni rose and left the men to their conversation. As she passed Torgan he called out to her.

"Wait!" Dropping to one knee, he bowed his head. "My sword and my life," he said.

It was an hour before dusk as Sigarni set out from the Pallides village. The afternoon was clear and bright, the sun dappling the new leaves on the trees. She felt better than she had in days, her mind cleansed of doubt. Whatever the outcome now, she felt that her plan was the best chance for Highland success.

Breaking into a run, she raced up the track, her body reveling in the exertion. As she ran she noticed a mist spreading out from the undergrowth. At first she ignored it, but it thickened suddenly, swirling around her. Sigarni slowed. The trees were indistinct now, mere faint shadows in the grey. Glancing up she saw that the mist was also above her, blocking the sun.

Unafraid, yet with growing concern, she walked on, heading upward. The trail was no longer beneath her feet, but if she continued climbing she would arrive at the encampment.

A line of bushes appeared directly before her and she tried to skirt them, moving to the left. The undergrowth was thicker here, the ground flat.

Her irritation grew, but she pushed on.

After a while she came to a gap in the mist, a small hollow inside a ring of oak trees. The mist clung to the outer ring, and rose up over the dip to form a grey dome. There was a man sitting on the grass at the center of the hollow, portly and friendly of face. Looking up, he smiled broadly.

"Welcome, Sigarni. At last we meet in perfect circumstances."

"I saw you die at the Falls, ripped to pieces," she said, her hand closing around the hilt of her dagger.

"Happily that was an acolyte of mine. I say happily, though I miss him dreadfully. Happily for me, I should have said."

"You will not find today so happy," she told him, drawing the blade and advancing toward him. Her legs felt suddenly heavy, as if she were wading through knee-deep mud. The knife was a terrible weight in her hand . . . it dropped slowly toward her side, then tumbled from her trembling fingers.

"You are quite correct," he said, "I do not find this a happy experience. You have done well among your barbarian friends, and were you to live, I believe you could cause the Outlanders considerable embarrassment. Sadly you must die—would that it were different." Pushing himself to his feet, he drew a slender curved blade and advanced toward her. Sigarni fought to move, but could not. The knife came up and he took the neck of her tunic between the pudgy fingers of his left hand and cut away the cloth, exposing her breasts. "I apologize for this apparently unseemly behavior," he said amiably. "I have no intention of soiling your virtue. It is just that I need to make the correct incision for the removal of your heart."

"Why are you doing this?" she asked him. "What have I ever done to you?"

"As I recall, my dear, you used to hunt hares for sport. What had they ever done to you? We are not dealing here in petty squabbles or feuds. I am a sorcerer and a student of the universe. It is well known among my peers that certain sacrifices are considerably more powerful than others. A man, for example, will provide more power than . . . a hare. But the blood royal! Ah now, that is a priceless commodity." Taking a small chunk of charcoal from his pocket, he drew a line between her breasts and along the rib line on her left side.

"Ironhand!" she cried.

"Ah," he said, stepping back, "so he was the mysterious force. Fascinating! Sadly, however, my dear, I have established a mystic wall around this hollow. No spirit can enter here, so save your breath. Your friend will not hear you either, for the mist dampens all sound. Now what I am about to do is remove your heart. There will be no pain. I am not a savage, and your death will be swift."

"Give me until tomorrow," she begged him. "Let me save my people first!"

He chuckled. "And you, of course, will give me your word to return?"

"Yes, I will. I swear it."

"Ah, but you know what you hunters say—a hare in the bag is worth ten in the burrow. Let us merely hope that your officers will perform ably without you. Now, do you have a God you wish to make a final prayer to?"

"Yes," she said, silently praying for the return of Taliesen.

"Then make it brief, my dear, for I wish to return to Leofric's tent. He has a fine stock of wine which I am looking forward to savoring. This country air does not suit me. I was born to exist within well-stocked cities. Let me know when you are finished, Sigarni. And do not waste your time seeking to contact Taliesen. He has gone back to his own time and is too far away to be of assistance—even could he hear your thoughts, which he cannot. I am afraid, dear lady, you are all alone. There are no creatures of myth or legend to help you now."

"Don't be too sure," she said with a smile.

"Oh, I am sure," he said. The knife rose and Jakuta Khan leaned forward, then arched back with a cry. He staggered several paces, his hand scrabbling at his back, where a bone-handled knife jutted from his kidneys. Sigarni felt the spell holding her dissipate and fall away. She lunged for her dagger and sprang at the sorcerer, ramming her blade into his fat belly and ripping it up toward his lungs. His scream was high-pitched and pain-filled as he sank to the ground. "Oh, you have wounded me!" he cried.

Ballistar ran forward to stand beside Sigarni and Jakuta Khan looked up at him, his eyes already misting in death. "A dwarf," he whispered, surprised. "I have been killed by a dwarf!"

He turned his dying eyes upon Sigarni. "It is . . . not over. I sent a . . . demon. He is lost somewhere in time. But one day . . . when you look into his eyes . . . remember me!" And he slumped facedown on the grass.

"Your arrival was most timely," she said, kneeling beside the dwarf and kissing his bearded cheek.

"Gwalchmai appeared to me. Told me to be here. I was ready to kill myself, but he said I would be needed, that I could help the clans."

"Oh, Balli, if you had died my heart would have been broken. Come, let us go to the meeting!"

"I suggest you dress yourself first," he said.

Chapter Thirteen

Fell lay awake, Sigarni's sleeping body pressed closely against him and her head upon his shoulder. Lady lay at Sigarni's left, her black flanks gleaming in the firelight. The coals in the iron brazier were burning low now, and the cabin was bathed in a gentle red glow.

Fell had stood at the back of the meeting hall and watched the faces of her officers as she outlined her battle plans. At first they had been shocked, but they had listened to her arguments, delivered quietly but forcefully, and had offered no objections. Each of the officers had been given a task—save for Fell.

He had returned to the cabin with Sigarni, and their lovemaking had been tender and joyous. No words spoken throughout, but both experiencing an intensity that led to tears. Fell had never known anything like it; he felt both complete and fulfilled. In all his adult life he had dreamed of moments like this, to be at one with the object of his love.

The night was quiet, and the entire world consisted of nothing more than the four walls he could see and the glowing fire that warmed the cabin. Tomorrow the great battle would begin and, God willing, after that he and Sigarni could begin a new life together. Once the Baron was defeated, they could send emissaries to the Outland King and end a war neither side had truly wanted. Then he and Sigarni could build a home near the Falls.

She moaned in her sleep and he stroked her silver hair. She awoke and smiled sleepily. "You should be asleep," she said.

"I am too happy for sleep," he told her. Her hand stroked down his warm belly and arousal flared instantly.

"Then I shall tire you," she said, sliding her body over his. Her mouth tasted sweet and he smelled the perfume of her hair, felt the warmth of her body.

At last the passion subsided and he sighed. "Are you ready for sleep now?" she whispered into his ear.

"You held them, Sigarni," he said proudly. "All those warriors and greybeards! They stood and listened and they believed. I believe! It is so hard to think of you now as the huntress who lived alone and sold her furs. It is as if you were always waiting to be a queen. Even Bakris Tooth-gone speaks of you with awe. Where did you send him, by the way?"

"South," she said.

"Why?"

"To cut their supply lines. God, Fell, I wish this was over. I don't want to be a Battle Queen."

"We can end it tomorrow," he said. "Then we'll build a house. You know the flat land to the west of the Falls? I've often thought that it would make a splendid home. A little back from the pool, so that the noise of the Falls would be filtered by the willows. There's good grazing land close by, and I know Grame will loan me some breed cattle."

"It sounds . . . wonderful," she told him.

"There's good hunting too."

At the sound of their voices Lady awoke and pushed herself between them. Sigarni stroked the hound's ears. "It is a fine dream," said Sigarni. "Now let's get some rest."

"What do you mean, a dream?" Fell asked.

"The war will not be over with one battle," she said sadly. "If we win, the Outlanders will see it as a blow to their pride. They will have no alternative but to send another army north."

"But it makes no sense!"

"War makes no sense, Fell. Let's talk about it all to-morrow."

"Aye, we'll do that," he said. "I will be proud to stand beside you."

"You won't be beside me, Fell. I need you and your men to take up a position away from the battle, on the right. They will break through on the western slope, and head for the encampments. They must be stopped. Destroyed. Hold the right, Fell. Do it for me!"

"Oh, God!" he whispered, his stomach knotting.

"What is it?" she asked, concern in her voice.

"Nothing," he assured her. "It is all right, just a little cramp in my leg. You are right, Sigarni. We should sleep now. Come, put your head on my shoulder."

Sigarni sat up and pushed Lady away. "Back to your blanket, you hussy!" she said. "He is mine alone!"

Settling down beside him with her arm across his chest, she fell asleep almost immediately. But for Fell there would be no rest that night. He remembered the night at Gwalchmai's cabin, and the drunken words of the Dreamer.

"But I know what I know, Fell. I know you'll live for her. And I know you'll die for her. 'Hold the right, Fell. Do it for me!' she'll say. And they'll fall on you with their swords of fire, and their lances of pain, and their arrows of farewell. Will you hold, Fell, when she asks you?" Gwalch looked up, his eyes bleary. *"I wish I was young again, Fell. I'd stand alongside you. By God, I'd even take that arrow for you."*

No house by the Falls. No golden future in the sunshine on the mountains. This one night is all there is, he realized. He felt the panic in the pit of his belly, and in the palpitations of his heart. Fell so wanted to wake Sigarni again, to tell her of Gwalchmai's prophecy. Yet he did not.

Instead he held her to him and listened to her soft breathing.

"Will you hold, Fell?"

Aye, he thought, I will hold.

The loss of a group of his scouts was not entirely unexpected, and the Baron had dispatched four more men to scout the Duane Pass. Only one returned—and he had an arrow wound high on the right shoulder.

"Well?" asked the Baron.

The man's face was grey, and he was in great pain. "As you predicted, lord, they have taken up a position on the flat hill. A wall of shields. I estimate there are almost three thousand warriors there."

"Their full force?" The Baron laughed and turned to his officers. "See what happens when a woman leads? What fools they are!" Swinging again to the wounded scout, he asked, "What of the western slope?"

"Around a hundred men hidden in the trees. I got pretty close before they saw me."

"To the east?"

"I saw no one, sir."

"Good. Go and get that wound seen to."

"Yes, sir. Thank you, sir."

The Baron gathered his officers around him. "You have all studied the maps, and you will realize that their position is a strong one. We must first encircle the hill; that will stretch us thin in places, but it is too high for them to make a swift sally down upon us." He fixed his attention on a tall, lean cavalryman. "Chaldis, you will take half the cavalry and a thousand foot. Kill the defenders on the western slope and attack their encampment and the surrounding Pallides villages."

"Yes, my lord," Chaldis responded.

"Where is Cheops?" asked the Baron.

"Here, my lord," answered a short, stocky figure in a uniform of brown leather, pushing forward from the back.

"You will take your archers to the eastern slope and pepper them. I will initiate attacks from the western side. Be wary, Cheops. I would sooner your arrows fell a little short than sailed over the defenders and struck our own men. Nothing so demoralizes a fighting man as to fear death from the shafts of his own archers."

"You can rely on us, my lord."

"Leofric, you will command the cavalry wing. Skirt the hill and continue sporadic raids from the north side. Use only the heaviest armored lancers. The enemy will have good bowmen on that hilltop. Do not push too far. Hit hard, then break away. It will be the infantry who apply the hammer blow."

"Understood, my lord."

"Gentlemen," said the Baron with a rare smile. "A magnificent opportunity lies ahead of us. In the south there is a great panic concerning these rebel Highlanders, and when we have defeated them the King will make sure you are rewarded for your efforts. But remember this, though they are barbarians and scum they still know how to fight. I want the woman alive; I will send her in chains to the capital. As to the rest, slaughter them to a man. God is with us, gentlemen. Now let us be about our duties."

The Baron strode to his tent and ducked below the flap. Once inside he turned his attention to the Highlander, sitting flanked by two guards. The man was of medium height, with greasy dark hair and a wide mouth. He did not look the Baron in the eye.

"Your information was correct," said the Baron. "The bitch has fortified the hilltop."

"As I told you, my lord," said Bakris Tooth-gone, starting to rise from his chair. But a soldier pressed his hand on Bakris's shoulder, easing him back into the seat.

"Treachery always fascinates me," said the Baron, flicking his fingers and pointing to a jug of wine. A servant filled a goblet and passed it to his lord; the Baron sipped it. "Why would one of Sigarni's captains betray her?"

"It's a lost cause, my lord," said Bakris bitterly. "They're all going to die. And I want to live. What's wrong with that? In this life a man must look out for himself. I've never had nothing. Now by your leave, I'll have some gold and some land."

"Gold and land," echoed the Baron. "I have sworn to see every Highlander slain and you are a Highlander. Why should I not kill you?"

Bakris grinned, showing stained and broken teeth. "You won't get them all in this one battle, lord. I know all the hiding places. I was a forester; I can lead your soldiers to where they run to. And I'll serve you well, lord."

"I think you will," the Baron agreed.

Three servants set about dressing the Baron in his black armor, buckling his breastplate, hooking the gorget into place, attaching his greaves and hinged knee protectors. Accoutred for war, he strode to his black stallion and was helped into the saddle.

Touching heels to the stallion's flanks, he rode to the front of the battle line and lifted his arm.

The army moved on toward the mouth of the Duane Pass.

To the Baron's surprise there were no flights of arrows from the rearing cliff faces on either side, nor any sign of defenders on the gentle slopes to left and right. Ahead the sun glimmered on the shield wall of the defenders, as they ringed the flat-topped hill half a mile distant.

A long time ago the Outlanders themselves had employed the shield-ring defense. It was strong against cavalry, but weak against a concerted attack from infantry, with support from archers. Bowmen could send volley after volley of arrows over the shields, cutting away at the heart of the defenders.

The Baron rode on. Now he could see the tightly packed clansmen, and just make out the silver-armored figure standing in the front line.

I should be grateful to you, he thought, for you have made my glory all the greater. Swinging in the saddle, he glanced back at his fighting men. If the losses were too light the victory would appear shallow, too high and he would be deemed an incompetent. Around three hundred dead would be perfect, he thought.

Leofric rode past him on the right, leading the cavalry in columns of three. On the left, Chaldis led his fifteen hundred men up the western slope to the enemy's right. "That's good, Chaldis," shouted the Baron admiringly. "Let them see where you are heading; it will give them time to think about the fate of their wives and sons. Fire some buildings as soon as you can. I want them to see the smoke!"

"Aye, my lord," the captain replied.

The Baron rode on, leading his infantry to the foot of the hill but remaining out of bowshot. Custom demanded that he give the enemy the opportunity to surrender, but today was not a time to consider custom. Good God, they might accept!

Glancing to his right, he saw Cheops and his fifteen hundred lightly armored archers toiling up the slope. Each man carried thirty shafts. Four thousand five hundred sharp missiles to rain down upon the unprotected defenders!

The Baron ordered the encirclement of the hill and the three thousand remaining infantrymen, holding tightly to their formations, spread out to obey.

There was no movement from the defenders, and no sound. No harsh, boastful challenges, no jeering. It was unusual. The Baron could see the woman, Sigarni, moving among the men. The helm she wore was truly magnificent and would make a fine trophy.

Dark storm clouds obscured the sun, and a rumble of distant thunder could be heard from the north. "The Gods of War are preparing for the feast!" he shouted. "Let us not disappoint them."

Fell waited behind the cover of the trees, Torgan beside him. They could not yet see the lancers, but they could hear the thundering of their hooves on the hard-packed earth of the hill. Fell glanced to his right, and saw the Highlanders notching arrows to their bows. To his left the swordsmen waited, their two-handed claymores held ready. Five hundred fighting men, ready to defend their homes, their families, and their clans.

The first of the lancers breasted the hill: tall men on high horses, their breastplates shining like silver in the sunlight, their long lances glittering. Each man carried a figure-of-eight shield on his left arm. They were still traveling in a column of fours, but as they reached open ground they spread out. The officer drew rein, shading his eyes to study the tree line.

Fifty Highlanders moved out onto open ground and loosed their longbows. Some of the shafts struck home, and several men and half a dozen horses fell, but most were blocked by the shields of the lancers. Leveling their lances, the riders charged.

"Now?" whispered Torgan.

"No," Fell told him. "Wait until they are closer."

The fifty exposed Highland bowmen continued to loose shaft after shaft at the oncoming riders. Horses tumbled under the deadly volleys, but the lancers rode on. The distance closed between them, until no more than thirty paces separated the two groups.

"Now!" said Fell. Torgan lifted his hunting horn to his lips and blew two short blasts. Another hundred bowmen ran from the trees to stand beside their comrades. Hundreds of shafts tore into the lancers; the charging line faltered as the missiles slashed home into unprotected horseflesh. Horses reared and fell, bringing down following riders. Amid the sudden confusion the Highland swordsmen charged from cover, screaming their battle cries. The lancers panicked, though many tried to swing to meet this unexpected attack. Horses reared, throwing their riders, then the Highlanders were among the lancers, dragging riders from their saddles and hacking them to death upon the ground.

Among the first to die was the enemy officer, hit by four shafts, one taking him through his right eye. The horsemen at the rear pulled back, galloping toward the safety of open ground. Torgan blew three blasts on his horn, and a chasing group of Highlanders reluctantly halted and jogged back to the tree line.

Over the hilltop marched a thousand Outland infantry, flanked by a score of archers. They drew up and surveyed the scene of carnage, then locked shields and advanced in broad battle formation, one hundred shields wide, ten deep.

"More than we thought would come," said Torgan.

"They can't hold that formation within the woods," said Fell. "Fall back fifty paces."

Torgan's hunting horn sounded once more, in one long baleful note.

Highland archers continued to shoot into the advancing mass of men, but to little effect. Some fell, but the infantry held their long rectangular shields high and most of the shafts bounced from them.

The lancers had re-formed now, and galloped forward to try an encircling sweep of the woods. Obrin and two hundred riders countercharged them from the left, cleaving into their flank, hacking and cutting. The lances of the Outland riders were useless in such close quarters and they frantically threw aside their long weapons, drawing their sabers. But this second attack demoralized them, and they were pushed steadily back.

The Outland infantry slowed its advance, their leader unsure whether to push into the trees or swing and defend the beleaguered cavalry.

"Come on, you bastard!" whispered Fell. "Come to us!"

The line began to move once more, the formation breaking into a skirmish line as each of the soldiers increased the distance between himself and his fellows by around three feet. Fell was forced to admire the smoothness of the switch from tight ranks to open formation.

These were enemies to respect.

Less able to protect one another in this new formation, however, the Outlanders began to take heavy losses from the retreating archers.

"This is it," Fell told Torgan. "By God, we'd better get it right!" Torgan gave a wide grin, and sprinted off to the left where his hundred men waited. With a harsh battle cry Torgan led his warriors in a frenzied assault on the enemy's right flank, just as they crossed the tree line. Fell saw the Farlain leader push himself deep into the fray, his claymore rising and falling with deadly skill.

Drawing his own sword, Fell signaled his own hundred and they crept through the undergrowth toward the enemy's left flank. Outnumbered ten to one, Torgan's men were being driven back as the wings of the Outland force pushed out to encircle the defenders.

With all attention on the right Fell charged the left, his claymore smashing through a soldier's helm and scattering his brains over his comrades. The Outlanders fell back but re-formed smoothly, trying to close ranks. The thick undergrowth and the trunks of tall trees prevented them re-forming into a tight single unit and the Highlanders, unencumbered by heavy armor, tore at them like wolves around a stag at bay.

A sword flashed for Fell's face. Swaying aside, he swept up a vicious two-handed cut that glanced from the tip of the soldier's shield and smashed into his cheekbone. The soldier was punched from his feet by the blow.

On the right Torgan had pulled back his men. Some Outlanders had given chase, but Torgan swung back his group and cut them down.

Out on open ground the lancers broke into a full retreat. Obrin made no attempt to give chase, but gathered his men and galloped for the woods. Leaping from their horses, the Highlanders ran to the aid of their comrades. Torgan saw them coming and blew on his horn. Highland archers dropped their bows, drew their swords, and joined him.

Again he charged the enemy right, and such was the ferocity of the charge that the Outlanders buckled and broke, losing formation. Beside him the giant Mereth, wielding a club
of oak reinforced with iron studs, hammered his way forward with Loran beside him.

"Pallides! Pallides!" roared Mereth.

Torgan hurdled a fallen tree and shoulder-charged an Outland soldier. The man staggered back, falling into his comrades. Torgan's claymore sang through the air as three men
hurled themselves at him. He blocked the lunge of the first,
all but decapitating him with a reverse cut. The second
man's sword cut into Torgan's side, the third aimed a blow at
his face. It was blocked by an upraised sword, and Torgan
saw Obrin smash the man from his feet.

Ignoring his own wound, Torgan leaped once more into
the action. To his right Mereth was surrounded by swordsmen, but was holding them at bay with great sweeps of his
murderous club. "Farlain!" shouted Torgan, rushing to his
aid. Several men followed him, including Loran. An arrow
sliced by Torgan's cheek, taking Loran in the side of the
neck; the handsome Pallides staggered to his right and fell.
Ignoring the bowmen Torgan raced into the fray, ducking beneath a wild sweep and slashing his sword through the knee
of the wielder; the leg broke with a sickening snap and the
swordsman fell, screaming. Mereth bellowed a war cry and
ran at a second group of men. One of them rammed a spear
through the giant's belly and Mereth staggered to a stop.
Then his club swept up and across to smash the skull of the
spear-wielder. A sword clove into Mereth's bull neck. Blood
spurted from the severed jugular as Torgan stabbed his own
sword into the killer's belly.

On the left Fell was battling furiously. Here the Outlanders
retained at least a semblance of order, and were pulling back
toward open ground. Again and again Fell led his men in in-
creasingly desperate charges.

But there were fewer of them now. Obrin and twenty

Highlanders ran to his aid. Fell had been cut on the right cheek, and blood was flowing from a deep wound in his thigh. His claymore, though, felt light in his hand as he charged again, Obrin beside him.

"Don't let them re-form!" he bellowed.

The archer captain Cheops reached the crest of the eastern slope and glanced across at the enemy defensive wall. Beyond that he could see the cavalry charging the woods. It was all going well; the range from his position to the enemy was less than two hundred yards, well within killing distance. It was hot, and today would be thirsty work. Glancing behind him he saw a heavy stand of gorse, and beyond it a grove of trees.

"You!" he shouted to a young recruit. "Go back into the trees and see if there's a stream or a pond. If there is, you can refill our canteens."

"Yes, sir!" the boy called out, setting off at a run.

Cheops strung his longbow. He had made it himself five years ago, a splendid weapon tipped with horn. Pulling his shafts from his quiver, he pushed them point first into the earth. For some reason that Cheops had never been able to fathom, arrowheads with a little clay stuck to them pierced armor all the better.

Selecting his first shaft, he notched it to the bow. There was little point in trying to select a target, since he would have to arc the arrow over the shield wall. Still, the Highlanders were densely packed on the hilltop, and any hit would be an advantage. Cheops drew back on the string and sent the shaft in a long, looping flight.

This was going to be a good day. No sign of rain to warp the arrows. Not much wind.

His archers gathered on both sides of him, selecting their arrows and removing their cloaks.

It was all so easy . . .

Idly he wondered why the Highland bitch had decided to make a stand here.

Cheops did not have long to wait for an answer. From behind there came a scream and he swung around to see the boy he had sent looking for water running for all he was worth. The lad had discarded his longbow, which amazed Cheops, for the loss of a weapon meant a thirty-lash flogging. What had he seen? A bear?

The boy glanced back as he ran and tripped, rolling headlong. Gripped by panic, he scrambled to his feet. From the gorse and the undergrowth came thousands of Highland warriors.

Cheops stood transfixed. It was not possible. They had an army of three thousand—and there were at least that many on the hilltop opposite.

Impossible or not, they were here!

"Back! Back!" yelled Cheops. His men hardly needed the order. Lightly armed with bow and knife, they were no match for sword-wielding warriors and began to stream back down the hill, leaving their arrows stuck in the soft earth. The Highlanders poured after them.

Cheops hurled aside his longbow and pumped his arms for extra speed. Ahead he could see the Baron, directing an attack on the western side of the hilltop.

The Baron swung around, and stood openmouthed as his archers hurtled down into the pass. The thin circle of soldiers around the hill also glanced up. Cheops knew that his dignity was fleeing ahead of him, but he didn't care. Dignity could be regained. Life was another matter entirely. He reached the foot of the pass just ahead of the fastest of his men, and slipped through the infantry to what appeared the relative safety behind the infantry lines.

There he stopped and looked back.

The Highlanders were pouring down the hillside, screaming some incomprehensible battle cry. They struck the infantry like a hammer.

Then they were through.

With nowhere left to run, Cheops drew his dagger. As a burly white-bearded warrior carrying a battle-axe charged him, Cheops ducked under the swinging blade and thrust his knife at the man. The blade was turned by a breastplate and Cheops stumbled and fell. The axe clove him between the shoulder blades.

On the hillside the Baron shouted orders to the infantry to form a defensive square and retreat down the pass. With fine discipline they gathered, the Baron at the center.

The Highlanders beat ineffectually against the shield wall, and the withdrawal began.

Leofric had never wanted to be a soldier, or any kind of fighting man. His loves were numbers, logistics, and organization. As he sat his gelding on the north side of the hill he found himself contemplating his future. Never having seen a battle, he was unprepared for the ferocity, the screams, and the cries. It was all so . . . barbaric, he realized.

Once it is over I will return to the capital, he decided. The University had offered him a teaching post in languages. I will accept it, he thought.

"Do we attack, sir?" asked the lieutenant at his side. The man had drawn his sword, and seemed eager to lead the five hundred cavalrymen up the steep slope. Leofric glanced up at the shield wall above.

"I suppose so," he said. "The Baron ordered us to make probing assaults."

"I understand," said the officer. "Wasp formation, sting and run. How many should I take, sir?"

Leofric swung in the saddle and gazed at his five centuries. "Take three," he said. "Harry them!"

"Yes, sir."

The remnants of Chaldis's cavalry came galloping down the western slope—no more than thirty men, some of them wounded. An officer rode up to Leofric. "We were ambushed, sir. More than a thousand Highlanders were waiting for us in the woods. They are cutting the infantry to pieces."

At that moment the archers led by the sprinting Cheops came racing down the slope—pursued by, Leofric gauged, some two thousand Highlanders.

"Son of a whore!" hissed the officer. "Where in Hell did they come from?"

Leofric was momentarily stunned. He had an eye for numbers, and had already estimated there to be around three thousand on the hilltop. Now from nowhere the number of the enemy had risen to six thousand, which was not even within the bounds of possibility.

"God's blood!" said the lieutenant. "What now, sir?"

Leofric needed a moment to think. Looking up at the shield wall above him, the answer came like a blinding revelation. "There are no men on the hilltop," he said. "We are besieging the Highland women!"

All around them the infantry was falling back around the Baron. Raising his arm, Leofric led his cavalry in a charge against the enemy's left. Cutting through to where the Baron stood, Leofric leaped from his mount and ran to him. Swiftly he told him of the Highland deception.

The Baron swore. "How many do we have left?" he asked.

Leofric cast his eyes at the sea of fighting men. "Two thousand. Perhaps less."

"Advance on the hill!" shouted the Baron. "Formation One!"

"What is the point!" screamed Leofric. "It is over!"

"It will be over when I've killed the bitch!"

With a discipline gained during decades of warfare, the Outland troops re-formed into a fighting square one hundred shields wide and ten deep. "Double time!" shouted the Baron, and the men began to run. Leofric, caught in the center, had no choice but to run alongside the Baron. On the outer edges of the battle his cavalry was being cut to pieces trying to protect the exposed right flank of the square. Even so, inexorably the phalanx moved up the hill toward the waiting women.

"I'm coming for you, you whore!" bellowed the Baron, his voice rising above the clashing swords and the screams of the wounded and dying.

A black cloud of arrows slashed into the advancing line and Leofric could see scores of women loosing their shafts. He felt sickened by it all. The finest soldiers in the empire were now charging a force of wives and mothers.

Behind them the Highlanders were assaulting the troops at the rear of the phalanx, slashing their swords at unprotected backs. Many men turned to face the enemy, and this thinned the square. The Baron seemed unconcerned.

The enemy archers fell back behind the shield wall and a volley of iron-tipped spears sliced down into the advancing men. The Highlanders were all around them now, a pack of wolves ripping at their flesh. The square began to break up but the Baron ignored the threat, urging his front line on and up.

The shield wall opened and Leofric saw Asmidir charge out, with a group of men in black and silver armor. They came in a tight wedge that clove through the advancing line. Behind them, bearing spears and swords, the Highland women rushed at the attackers.

The sight of thousands of fighters streaming from the hilltop finally unnerved the advancing men. They broke and ran.

Asmidir leaped at the Baron, his two-handed sword slashing toward the Baron's neck. The Baron blocked it with his shield and gave a return blow that crashed against Asmidir's shoulder plate, dislodging it. The black man dropped to one knee and sent a wild cut that thundered against the Baron's calf, smashing his greave to shards and knocking him to the ground. Rolling to his left, the Baron clambered to his feet and threw aside his shield. Holding his own blade two-handed, he rushed the black man. "You treacherous bastard!" he screamed.

Their swords clashed again and again. A blow from Asmidir smashed the links on the Baron's neck protector and slashed up to open his cheek. Blood streamed from the cut.

Suddenly weary, Leofric sat down and watched the duel. All around him men were dying, but no one attacked the slightly built spectator who sat quietly with his hands hugging his knees.

Both men were strong and the fight continued at a savage pace. Asmidir was bleeding from wounds in both arms and a cut on his temple. The Baron blocked an overhead cut and, as Asmidir pressed in close, head-butted the black man, sending him staggering back. Dropping his sword, the Baron hurled himself at his half-stunned opponent and both men fell to the ground. The Baron drew his dagger and raised it high.

An arrow punched through his leather eye patch, slicing deep into his brain. Leofric glanced to his right and saw the warrior queen, Sigarni, in armor of bright silver, a winged helm upon her head, a short hunting bow in her hand. The Baron gave a choking cry, and toppled from Asmidir.

Leofric stood and walked over to the black man, kneeling beside him. "Are you all right?" he inquired.

"How is it that you live?" asked Asmidir, surprised.

Leofric shrugged. "Forgot to draw my sword." He helped Asmidir to his feet and the two men approached Sigarni.

Handing the bow to a dark-haired woman on her right, she surveyed the battlefield. There were still isolated pockets of fighting, but the battle was over.

She swung to Leofric and Asmidir introduced them. "You have a charmed life, Leofric," she said. "Thousands of men died today, and you have not even been scratched."

"I'm not much of a soldier," he said. "I've been offered a teaching post at the capital's University. With your leave, I think I'll accept it."

She nodded. "There has been enough bloodletting today. Go from here, Leofric, ride south to your King. Tell him the truth about all that happened here. I fear it will make little difference."

"It won't, lady. He'll come with an army ten times the size of the one you defeated here. It will never end."

Stepping forward, she placed her hands upon his shoulders and brought her face close to his. "Look into my eyes, Leofric, and hear me well. It *will* end, for I will end it. Tell him these words from Sigarni, the Queen of the North: Advance against me and I will destroy you. I will bring fire and death into your kingdom, and I will snatch you from your throne and throw your body to the dogs."

Sigarni turned away from him and walked down the hillside. Asmidir took the young man's arm and led him down into the pass. They found a horse and Leofric climbed into the saddle. "Your strategy was masterful," he said. "I congratulate you."

Asmidir smiled. "Not my strategy, boy. Hers. All war is based on deception and she learned that lesson well. Go in peace, Leofric, and be sure never to cross my path again."

"I wish you well, Asmidir," said the young man, "but I fear there will be no happy ending here."

"The man who ripped the heart from my country is dead. That is a good enough ending for today. Now ride!"

Leofric touched spurs to the stallion and cantered from the battlefield.

High in the skies above, the crows were already gathering for the feast.

Bakris was dragged before Sigarni. "They captured me," he said, "but I told them nothing."

Sigarni sighed. "You told them everything that you were supposed to," she said. "Kollarin warned me that you were a treacherous cur, who would sell your people for a handful of gold. But know this, Bakris, your treachery helped us. Without it the Baron might have sent out more scouts, and found our hidden forces. As the rope settles around your neck, think on that. Now get him from my sight—and hang him from the nearest tree!"

Fell sat quietly with his back against the tree trunk, Obrin and Torgan beside him. "It was a good day," he said. "We broke them. By God, we broke them!"

"Aye," said Obrin softly, his eyes drawn to the black-feathered arrow jutting from Fell's chest. The clansman's face was pale, there were dark rings beneath his eyes, and his lips had a bluish tinge that Obrin had seen all too often before.

"Fetch Sigarni," Obrin told Torgan. The Farlain leader nodded, and loped away. "Maybe if I removed the arrow you would have a chance," said Obrin, but Fell shook his head.

"I can feel the life draining from me. Nothing will stop it now. We won, though, didn't we?"

"Aye, we won."

Fell looked up at the sky and watched the crows swooping and diving. It was a beautiful day. High Druin wore a crown of clouds and the sun was bright behind them.

"It is a Highland custom," said Fell, "that a man's son sends him on the swans' path. I have no children of my blood, Obrin." He smiled. "But I used the *Cormaach* to save you, and that means you are my son. I want my best bow beside me, and two knives. Some bread and some wine should be wrapped in leaves. Lastly, two coins should be placed . . . upon my eyes. The coins are for the gatekeeper, who will usher me through. Will you do this for me?"

"I will, man."

"I want to be buried on the flanks of High Druin. Sigarni will know where. I want to sleep forever beneath the spot where we became lovers. And if I must walk as a spirit, and be chained to any part of the land, it should be there."

"God's eyes, Fell, I thought we had made it through together. One cursed archer hiding in the undergrowth."

"It's done now. It cannot be undone. I have often said that

a man should never dwell on regrets, but I find that hard to maintain now, Obrin. You will need a sword-bearer at my funeral. Choose a good one."

"I shall."

Fell closed his eyes. "She's a wonder, isn't she? A hilltop defended by women. Who would have considered it?"

"Aye, she's a wonder, Fell. She'll be here soon. Hang on, man."

"I don't think I can. I can hear the cry of gulls. Can you?"

"No, just the crows."

Fell opened his eyes and looked past Obrin. He smiled, as if in greeting, but when Obrin glanced back there was no one there. "Come to walk with me, you old drunkard?" said Fell. "Ah, but it is good to see you, man. Give me your hand, for my strength is all but gone."

Fell reached out, then his hand fell limply into his lap and his head sagged back against the tree. Obrin leaned in and closed Fell's eyes. "You were a fine man," he said, "and a true friend. I hope you find what you deserve."

Obrin rose and turned toward the battlefield as Sigarni came running, with Torgan alongside her. She sped past Obrin and knelt by Fell's body. Torgan paused beside Obrin and the two men moved away to a respectful distance.

Sigarni had knelt down at Fell's side. She was holding his hand, and speaking to him. Obrin saw the tears on her face and, taking Torgan's arm, drew the Farlain warrior away from the scene. "You ought to get that wound stitched," said Obrin, pointing to the congealed blood on Torgan's side.

"It'll mend," said the Highlander. "A shame he had no sons to speak his name on High Druin."

"I'll do that," said Obrin.

"Ah yes, the *Cormaach*. I had forgotten. Do you know the ritual?"

"I can learn it."

"I would be proud to teach you," said Torgan. "And if you

choose, I will stand beside you on High Druin as Fell's sword-bearer."

The two men reached the crest of the western slope and looked down over the battlefield. The Outlanders lay dead in their thousands, but many also of the Highland were slain. Women were moving around the pass, tending to the wounded. Later they would strip the Outland dead of their weapons. To the south Obrin could see Grame's warriors marching to capture the enemy's supply wagons. "What now, do you think?" asked Torgan. "Will the Outlanders listen to reason?"

Obrin shook his head. "No, they'll send Jastey and twenty thousand men. They'll be here by summer's end."

"Well," said Torgan grimly, "we'll be here to meet them!"

It was dusk when Asmidir and Kollarin found Sigarni. She was sitting alone on a distant hilltop, her red cloak wrapped tight around her.

"Thank you, my friend," said Asmidir. "I would be grateful if you would leave us alone now." Kollarin nodded and trudged away back to the encampment as Asmidir moved alongside Sigarni and sat down with his arm across her shoulder, drawing her in to him.

"Dear God, I am so sorry," he said.

"He was gone when I arrived," she told him. "Not even a farewell."

Asmidir said nothing, but held her tightly. "One arrow," she continued. "A piece of wood and a chunk of iron. And Fell is no more. Why him? Why not me, or you, or a thousand others?"

"In my land we believe in fate, Sigarni. It was his time . . . it was not yours, or mine."

"I can't believe that he's gone. I try to concentrate on it, but I see his face smiling at me. I find myself thinking that if I walk back to the encampment he will be waiting for me. It is so unreal."

"I never really spoke to Fell," said Asmidir. "I think he saw me as a rival, and he was jealous of our . . . friendship. But he was a man I was proud to fight alongside. I do not know whether there is a paradise, or a hall of heroes, or a field of glory. But I hope there is, for his sake."

"There is," she told him. "Fell will be there now, with Gwalchmai, and Fyon Sharp-axe, and Loran and Mereth, and hundreds of others who died today. But that is of little comfort to the widows they left behind, and the children who now sit crying. I never saw a battle before. It is the most evil sight. Why do men lust after it so?"

"Few soldiers do," he told her. "They know the reality of it. But your warriors will grow old, and they will remember this day above all others. The sun shining, the enemy defeated. They will remember it as a golden day, and they will tell their children of it, and their children will long to know a day like it. That is the way of things, Sigarni. I wish Fell had lived, for I can feel your sorrow and it pains me. But he did not, and you must put off your tears for another day. Your men are waiting for you. They wish to cheer you, and to celebrate their victory."

She pulled away from him. "It is not over, Asmidir; you know that. What is there to celebrate? We have won a reprieve until the summer. Before that we will have to take Citadel town, and establish strongholds in the Lowlands."

"But not tonight. Come, this is your moment, Sigarni. You are their queen, their promised one, their savior. You must walk among them like a queen."

Sigarni glanced up and saw the shimmering figure of Ironhand standing before her. Asmidir was oblivious to his presence.

"The black man is right," said Ironhand.

Sigarni leaned in to Asmidir and kissed his cheek. "Go back and tell them I am coming," she said.

"I will walk with you."

"No, I will come alone. Soon."

Asmidir rose and as he walked away, Ironhand's spirit settled down beside her. "Fell died," she said.

"I know. I saw him walk the path toward the Light. The old man, Gwalchmai, was beside him. I tried to follow but the way was closed to me. I stayed too long, Sigarni. Now I am trapped."

"That is so unfair," she told him.

He smiled. "In all my dealings in life—and subsequently in death—fairness has never seemed apparent. It is not important. My spirit lived to see your day, and to know that my blood, and Elaine's, ran true in our daughter. The future is fraught with peril, but you will lead your people well. I know this, and my pride soars higher than High Druin. Now it is time for you to meet with your generals. To thank them, and praise them, and promote others to take the place of those who lie dead."

"I cannot think of that now!"

"You can and you *must*! You restored Torgan's pride, and he fought like a lion for you. He should take Fell's place."

"He is too headstrong. Harcanan would be better."

Ironhand chuckled. "You see, you *can* think of it! Go now, my daughter. And think of me once in a while."

"You're not leaving me?"

"It is time. The Path of Light is closed to me, but perhaps there are other paths. Who knows?"

"I've lost Fell, and now I am losing you."

"You will find others, Sigarni. You will never be short of friends and advisors. I wish that I could hug you, but such pleasures are not for the dead. Go back now, my daughter."

Without a word more of farewell, he faded away.

Sigarni stood for a moment, then turned and strode back toward the victory fires at the encampment.

Epilogue

The summer had just begun when Sigarni the Queen rode with her retainers to Ironhand's Falls. Taliesen was waiting at the cave, as he had promised. The Queen dismounted and walked through to where he sat, a small fire taking the chill from the damp air within the cave.

"Well met, Taliesen."

"And you, Battle Queen. Are you ready for the next battle?"

"Time will tell, Taliesen. What of you? Are you ready to tell me why you gave me your aid?"

"Not yet," he said with a smile. "But my land is also at war, and I cannot dally here long. I have a queen to meet; she is old, but iron-hard, and she has faced her enemies all her life, and now waits to meet the last of them—a demon sent through time to hunt her."

"Sent by Jakuta Khan," she said. "I know; he told me just before he died."

"I have no doubt you will kill it, my lady," he said solemnly.

"I have much to do, Taliesen. You asked me to meet you here, and now I ask you to tell me why."

"I thought you might wish to say good-bye to a friend."

"Are we friends, sorcerer?"

"I hope so, but I was not speaking of myself. The dwarf Ballistar came to me, and asked a favor. I said I would grant it and by your leave I shall."

Sigarni sighed. "He wants to go back to Yur-vale?"

"That is what he requested."

"But he will die there."

"I think so. But, in his own words, he will die as a whole man. He will stand tall again before the end. It could even be that, with the new order there, the air will not be as poisonous or the food so deadly. I do not know. What I do know is that without your blessing, and a drop of your blood, he will be a dwarf on the other side also."

"You are asking me to send a friend to his death."

"No, my lady, I am asking you to give him a chance at a life he desperately desires."

Sigarni sat down by the fire. "I love that man," she said, "and I would do anything in my power to make him happy. If that is what he wants, then of course I shall grant it."

"It is what he wants. Are you ready?"

"I am."

Together the Queen and the sorcerer left the cave and began the long walk around the pool to the engravings on the cliff face. Ballistar was waiting there, a large pack beside him. He stood as she approached.

"Will you forgive me for leaving you?" he asked, reaching up to take hold of her hand.

"There is nothing to forgive, Balli. You are my dearest friend."

"There may be some magick beyond the Gate that will allow me to come back—and still be tall," he said.

"Yes," she said. Drawing her dagger, she made a small cut in the palm of her hand, then gripped his pudgy fingers. Reaching into the pouch that hung from her neck, she drew out a small bone, pressing this against the trickling wound. Passing it to Ballistar, she smiled. "You may need a friend on the road," she told him, "and I think Ironhand would welcome a second tilt at the fat tavern woman."

Holding tightly to the bone he looked up at her, tears spilling to his cheeks.

"I will always love you," he said.

"And I you. Go now, Balli. And know joy."

The Gateway shimmered and the dwarf hoisted his pack and stepped through.

Sigarni's adventures continue!

Read on for a sneak preview of

THE HAWK ETERNAL

Available in September 2005 from Del Rey Books

Caswallon watched the murderous assault on Ateris, a strange sense of unreality gripping him. The clansman sat down on a boulder and gazed from the mountainside at the gleaming city below, white and glorious, like a child's castle set on a carpet of green.

The enemy had surprised the city dwellers some three hours before, and black smoke billowed now from the turrets and homes. The distant sound of screaming floated to his ears, disembodied, like the echo of a nightmare upon awakening.

The clansman's sea-green eyes narrowed as he watched the enemy hacking and slaying. He shook his head, sadness and anger competing within him. He had no love for these doomed Lowlanders and their duplicitous ways. But, equally, this wanton slaughter filled him with sorrow.

The enemy warriors were new to Caswallon. Never had he seen the horned helms of the Aenir, the double-headed axes, nor the oval shields painted with hideous faces of crimson and black. He had heard of them, of course, butchering and killing far to the south, but of their war against the Lowlanders he knew little until now.

But then, why should he? He was a clansman of the Farlain, and they had little time for Lowland politics. His was a mountain race, tough and hardy and more than solitary. The mountains were forbidden ground for any Lowlander and the clans mixed not at all with other races.

Save for trade. Clan beef and woven cloth for Lowland sugar, fruits, and iron.

In the distance Caswallon saw a young girl speared and lifted into the air, thrashing and screaming. This is war no longer, he thought, this is merely blood sport.

Tearing his gaze from the murderous scene he glanced back at the mountains rearing like spearpoints toward the sky, snowcapped and proud, jagged and powerful. At their center the cloud-wreathed magnificence of High Druin towered above the land. Caswallon shivered, drawing his brown leather cloak about his shoulders. It was said that the clans were vicious and hostile to outsiders, and so they were. Any Lowlander found hunting clan lands was sent home minus the fingers of his right hand. But such punishments were intended to deter poachers. The scenes of carnage on the plain below had nothing to do with such practices; this was lust of the most vile kind.

The clansman looked back at the city. Old men in white robes were being nailed to the black gates. Even at this distance Caswallon recognized Bacheron, the chief elder, a man of little honesty. Even so, he did not deserve such a death.

By all the gods, no one deserved such a death!

On the plain three horsemen rode into sight, the leader pulling a young boy who was tied to a rope behind his mount. Caswallon recognized the boy as Gaelen, a thief and an orphan who lived on scraps and stolen fruit. The clansman's fingers curled around the hilt of his hunting dagger as he watched the boy straining at the rope.

The lead rider, a man in shining breastplate and raven-winged helm, cut the rope and the boy began to run toward the mountains. The riders set off after him, lances leveled.

Caswallon took a deep breath, releasing it slowly. The flame-haired boy ducked and weaved, stopping to pick up a stone and hurl it at the nearest horse. The beast shied, pitching its rider.

"Good for you, Gaelen," whispered Caswallon.

A rider in a white cloak wheeled his mount, cutting across the boy's path. The youngster turned to sprint away and the lance took him deep in the back, lifting him from his feet and hurling him to the ground. He struggled to rise and a second rider ended his torment, slashing a sword blade to his face. The riders cantered back to the city.

Caswallon found his hands shaking uncontrollably, and his heart pounded, reflecting his anger and shame.

How could men do such a thing to a youth?

Caswallon recalled his last visit to Ateris three weeks before, when he had driven in twenty long-horned Highland cattle to the market stalls in the west of the city. He had stolen the beasts from the pastures of the Pallides two days before. At the market he had seen a crowd chasing the red-haired youngster as he sprinted through the streets, his skinny legs pounding the marble walkway, his arms pumping furiously.

Gaelen had shinnied up a trellis by the side of the inn and leaped across the rooftops, stopping only to make an obscene gesture to his pursuers. Spotting Caswallon watching, he drew back his shoulders and swaggered across the rooftops. Caswallon had grinned then. He liked the boy; he had style.

The fat butcher Leon had chuckled beside him. "He's a character, is Gaelen. Every city needs one."

"Parents?" asked Caswallon.

"Dead. He's been alone five years—since he was nine or ten."

"How does he survive?"

"He steals. I let him get away with a chicken now and then. He sneaks up on me and I chase him for a while, shouting curses."

"You like him, Leon?"

"Yes. As I like you, Caswallon, you rascal. But then he reminds me of you. You are both thieves and you are both good at what you do—and there is no evil in either of you."

"Nice of you to say so," said Caswallon, grinning. "Now, how much for the Pallides cattle?"

"Why do you do it?"

"What?" asked Caswallon innocently.

"Steal cattle. By all accounts you are one of the richest clansmen in the Farlain. It doesn't make any sense."

"Tradition," answered Caswallon. "I'm a great believer in it."

Leon shook his head. "One of these days you'll be caught and hanged—or worse, knowing the Pallides. You baffle me."

"No, I don't. I make you rich. Yours is the cheapest beef in Ateris."

"True. How is the lovely Maeg?"

"She's well."

"And Donal?"

"Lungs like bellows."

"Keeping you awake at night, is he?"

"When I'm not out hunting," said Caswallon with a wink.

Leon chuckled. "I'm going to be sorry when they catch you, clansman. Truly."

For an hour they haggled over the prices until Leon parted with a small pouch of gold, which Caswallon handed to his man Arcis, a taciturn clan crofter who accompanied him on his raids.

Now Caswallon stood on the mountainside soaking in the horror of Aenir warfare. Arcis moved alongside him. Both men had heard tales of war in the south and the awful atrocities committed by the Aenir. Foremost among these was the blood-eagle: Aenir victims were nailed to trees, their ribs splayed like tiny wings, their innards held in place with wooden strips.

Caswallon had only half believed these tales. Now the evidence hung on the blood-drenched gates of Ateris.

"Go back to the valley, my friend," Caswallon told Arcis.

"What about the cattle?"

"Drive them back into the mountains. There are no buyers today."

"Gods, Caswallon! Why do they go on killing? There's no one fighting them."

"I don't know. Tell Cambil what we have seen today."

"What about you?"

"I'll stay for a while."

Arcis nodded and set off across the slopes, running smoothly.

After a while the Aenir warriors drifted into the city. The plain before the gates was littered with corpses. Caswallon moved closer, stopping when he neared the tree line. Now he could see the full scale of the horror and his anger settled, cold and malignant. The cattle dealer, Leon, lay in a pool of blood, his throat torn open. Near him was the boy thief Gaelen.

Caswallon swung away and moved back toward the trees.

I am dying. There was no doubt in Gaelen's mind. The pain from his lower back was close to unbearable, his head ached, the blood was seeping from his left eye. For a long while he lay still, not knowing if the enemy was close by; whether indeed an Aenir warrior was at this moment poised above him with a spear or a sharp-edged sword.

Fear cut through his pain but he quelled it savagely. He could feel the soft, dusty clay against his face and smell the smoke from the burning city. He tried to open his eyes, but blood had congealed on the lashes. *I have been unconscious for some time,* he thought.

An hour? Less? Carefully, he moved his right arm, bringing his hand to his face, rubbing his right eye with his knuckle to free the lashes. The pain from his left eye intensified and he left it alone, sealed shut. He was facing the shuttered gates and the ghastly ornaments they now carried.

Around him the crows were already settling, their sharp beaks ripping at moist flesh. Two of them had landed on the chest of Leon. Gaelen looked away. There were no Aenir in sight. Gingerly he probed the wound above his left hip, remembering the lance that had cut through him as he ran. The wound still bled on both sides, and the flesh was angry and raw to the touch.

Turning his head toward the mountains, and the tall pine trees on the nearest slope, he tried to estimate the time it would take him to reach the safety of the woods. He made an effort to stand, but a roaring began in his ears, like an angry sea. Dizziness swamped him and he lost consciousness.

When he awoke it was close to dusk. His side was still bleeding, though it had slowed to a trickle and once again he had to clear his eye of blood. When he had done so he saw that he had crawled twenty paces. He couldn't remember doing it, but the trail of blood and scored dust could not lie.

Behind him the city burned. It would not be long before the Aenir returned to the plain. If he was found he would be hauled back and blood-eagled like the elders.

The boy began to crawl, not daring to look up lest the distance demoralize him, forcing him to give in.

Twice he passed out for short periods. After the last he cursed himself for a fool and rolled to his back, ripping two strips of cloth from his ragged tunic. These he pressed into the wounds on his hip, grunting as the pain tore into him. They should slow the bleeding, he thought. He crawled on. The journey, begun in pain and weakness, became a torment. Delirious, Gaelen lived again the horror of the attack. He had stolen a chicken from Leon and was racing through the market when the sound of screaming women and pounding hooves made him forget the burly butcher. Hundreds of horsemen came in sight, slashing at the crowd with long swords and plunging lances.

All was chaos and the boy had been petrified. He had hidden in a barn for several hours, but then had been discovered by three Aenir soldiers. Gaelen had run through the alleys, outpacing them, but had emerged into the city square where a rider looped a rope over his shoulders, dragging him out through the broken gates. All around him were fierce-eyed warriors with horned helms, screaming and chanting, their faces bestial.

The rider with the rope hailed two others at the city gates.

"Sport, Father!" yelled the man, his voice muffled by his helm.

"From that wretch?" answered the other contemptuously, leaning across the neck of his horse. The helm he wore carried curved horns, and a face mask in bronze fashioned into a leering demon. Through the upper slits Gaelen could see a glint of ice-blue eyes, and fear turned to terror within him.

The rider who had roped Gaelen laughed. "I saw this boy on my last scouting visit. He was running from a crowd. He's fast. I'll wager I land him before you."

"You couldn't land a fish from a bowl," said the third rider, a tall wide-shouldered warrior with an open helm. His face was broad and flat, the eyes small and glittering like blue beads. His beard was yellow and grimy, his teeth crooked and broken. "But I'll get him, by Vatan!"

"Always the first to boast and the last to do, Tostig," sneered the first rider.

"Be silent, Ongist," ordered the older man in the horned helm. "All right, I'll wager ten gold pieces I gut him."

"Done!" The rider leaned over toward the boy, slicing the dagger through the rope. "Go on, boy, run."

Gaelen heard the horse start after him, and throwing himself to the ground, he grabbed a rock and hurled it. The yellow-bearded warrior—Tostig?—pitched from his rearing mount.

Then the lance struck him. He tried to rise, only to see a sword blade flash down.

"Well ridden, Father!" were the last words he heard before the darkness engulfed him.

Now as he crawled all sense of time and place deserted him. He was a turtle on a beach of hot coals, slowly burning; a spider within an enamel bowl of pain, circling; a lobster within a pan as the heat rose.

But still he crawled.

Behind him walked the yellow-bearded warrior he had pitched to the ground. In his hand was a sword and upon his lips a smile.

Tostig was growing bored now. At first he had been intrigued by the wounded boy, wondering how far he could crawl, and imagining the horror and despair when he discovered the effort was for nothing. But now the boy was obviously delirious, and there was little point in wasting time. He raised the sword, pointing downward above the boy's back.

"Kill him, my bonny, and you will follow him."

Tostig leaped back a pace, his sword flashing up to point toward the shadow-haunted trees as a figure stepped out into the fading light. He was tall, wearing a leather cloak and carrying an iron-tipped quarterstaff. Two daggers hung from a black leather baldric across his chest, and a long hunting knife dangled by his hip. He was green-eyed, and a dark trident beard gave him a sardonic appearance.

Tostig looked beyond the man, straining to pierce the gathering darkness of the undergrowth. The warrior seemed to be alone.

The clansman stepped forward and stopped just out of reach of the Aenir's sword. Then he leaned on his staff and smiled. "You're on Farlain land," he said.

"The Aenir walk where they will," Tostig replied.

"Not here, my bonny. Not ever. Now, what's it to be? Do you leave or die?"

Tostig pondered a moment. His father Asbidag had warned the army not to alienate the clans. Not yet. One mouthful at a time, that was Asbidag's way.

And yet this clansman had robbed Tostig of his prey.

"Who are you?" Tostig countered.

"Your heart has about five beats of life left in it, barbarian," said Caswallon.

Tostig stared deeply into the sea-green eyes. Had he been sure the man was alone, he would have risked battle. But he was not sure. The man was too confident, too relaxed. No clansman alive would face an armed Aenir in such a way. Unless he had an edge. Tostig glanced once more at the trees. Archers no doubt had him in range at this moment.

"We will meet again," he said, backing away down the slope.

Caswallon ignored him, and knelt by the bleeding youngster.

Gently he turned him to his back, checking his wounds. Satisfied they were plugged, he lifted the boy to his shoulder, gathered up his staff, entered the shadows, and was gone from the sight of the Aenir.

Gaelen turned in his bed and groaned as the stitches front and back pulled at tender, bruised flesh. He opened his eyes and found himself staring at a grey cave wall. The smell of burning beechwood was in his nostrils. Carefully he moved onto his good side. He was lying on a broad bed, crafted from pine and expertly joined; over his body were two woolen blankets and a bearskin cloak. The cave was large, maybe twenty paces wide and thirty deep, and at the far end it curved into a corridor. Looking back, the boy saw that the entrance was covered with a hide curtain. Gingerly he sat up. Somebody had bandaged his side and his injured eye. Gently he probed both areas. The pain was still there, but more of a throbbing reminder of the acute agony he remembered from his long crawl.

Across from the bed, beyond a table and some chairs rough-cut from logs, was a man-made hearth skillfully chipped away at the base of a natural chimney in the cave wall. A fire was burning brightly. Beside it were chunks of beechwood, a long iron rod, and a copper shovel.

Bright sunlight shafted past the edges of the curtain and the boy's gaze was drawn to the cave entrance. Groaning as he rose, he limped across the cave, lifting the flap and looking out over the mountains beyond. He found himself gazing down into a green and gold valley dotted with stone buildings and wooden barns, sectioned fields and ribbon streams. Away to his left was a herd of shaggy long-horned cattle, and elsewhere he could see sheep and goats, and even a few horses in a paddock by a small wood. His legs began to tremble and he dropped the curtain.

Slowly he made his way to the table and sat down. Upon it was an oatmeal loaf and a jug of spring water. His stomach tightened, hunger surging within him as he tore a chunk from the loaf and poured a little water into a clay goblet.

Gaelen was confused. He had never been this far into the Highlands. No Lowlander had. This was forbidden territory. The clansmen were not a friendly people, and though they occasionally came into Ateris to trade, it was well known to be folly for any city dweller to attempt a return visit.

He tried to remember how he had come here. He seemed to recall voices as he struggled to reach the trees, but the memory was elusive and there had been so many dreams.

At the back of the cave the man called Oracle watched the boy eating and smiled. The lad was strong and wolf-tough. For the five days he had been here he had battled grimly against his wounds, never crying—even when, in his delirium, he had relived fear-filled moments of his young life. He had regained consciousness only twice in that time, accepting silently the warm broth that Oracle held to his lips.

"I see you are feeling better," said the old man, stepping from the shadows.

The boy jumped and winced as the stitches pulled. Looking around, he saw a tall, frail, white-bearded man dressed in grey robes, belted at the waist with a goat-hair rope.

"Yes. Thank you."

"What is your name?"

"Gaelen. And you?"

"I no longer use my name, but it pleases the Farlain to call me Oracle. If you are hungry I shall warm some broth; it is made from the liver of pigs and will give you strength."

Oracle moved to the fire, stooping to lift a covered pot to the flames. "It will be ready soon. How are your wounds?"

"Better."

The old man nodded. "The eye caused me the most trouble. But I think it will serve you. You will not be blind, I think. The wound in your side is not serious, the lance piercing just above the flesh of the hip. No vital organ was cut."

"Did you bring me here?"

"No." Using the iron rod, Oracle lifted the lid from the pot. Taking a long-handled wooden spoon from a shelf, he stirred the contents. Gaelen watched him in silence. In his youth he must have been a mighty man, thought the boy. Oracle's arms were bony now, but the wrists were thick and his frame broad. The old man's eyes were light blue under thick brows, and they glittered like water on ice. Seeing the boy staring at him, he chuckled. "I was the Farlain Hunt Lord," he said, grinning. "And I was strong. I carried the Whorl boulder for forty-two paces. No man has bettered that in thirty years."

"Were my thoughts so obvious?" Gaelen asked.

"Yes," answered the Oracle. "The broth is ready."

They ate in silence, spooning the thick soup from wooden bowls and dipping chunks of oatmeal loaf into the steaming liquid.

Gaelen could not finish the broth. He apologized, but the old man shrugged.

"You've hardly eaten at all in five days, and though you are ravenous your stomach has shrunk. Give it a few moments, then try a little more."

"Thank you."

"You ask few questions, young Gaelen. Is it that you lack curiosity?"

The boy smiled for the first time. "No, I just don't want any answers yet."

Oracle nodded. "You are safe here. No one will send you back to the Aenir. You are welcome, free to do as you wish. You are not a prisoner. Now, do you have any questions?"

"How did I get here?"

"Caswallon brought you. He is a clansman, a Hunt Master."

"Why did he save me?"

"Why does Caswallon do the things he does? I don't know. Caswallon doesn't know. He is a man of impulse. A good friend, a terrible enemy, and a fine clansman—but still a man of impulse. When he was a youth he went tracking deer. He was following a doe when he came upon it caught in a Pallides snare. Now the Farlain have no love for the Pallides, so Caswallon cut the deer loose—only to find it had an injured leg. He brought the little beast home upon his back and nursed it to health; then he released it. There's no accounting for Caswallon. Had the beast been fit he would have slain it for meat and hide."

"And I am like that injured doe," said Gaelen. "Had I run into the trees unharmed, Caswallon might have killed me."

"Yes, you are sharp, Gaelen. I like quick wits in a boy. How old are you?"

The boy shrugged. "I don't know. Fourteen, fifteen . . ."

"I'd say nearer fourteen, but it doesn't matter. A man is judged here by how he lives and not by the weight of his years."

"Will I be allowed to stay, then? I thought only clansmen could live in the Druin mountains?"

"Indeed you can, for indeed you are," said Oracle.

"I don't understand."

"You are a clansman, Gaelen. Of the Farlain. You see, Caswallon invoked the *Cormaach*. He has made you his son."

"Why?"

"Because he had no choice. As you said yourself, only a clansman can live here and Caswallon—like all other clansmen—cannot bring strangers into the Farlain. Therefore in the very act of rescuing you he became your guardian, responsible in law for everything you do."

"I don't want a father," said Gaelen. "I get by on my own."

"Then you will leave," agreed Oracle, amiably. "And Caswallon will give you a cloak, a dagger, and two gold coins for the road."

"And if I stay?"

"Then you will move into Caswallon's house."

Needing time to think, Gaelen broke off a piece of bread and dipped it into the now-lukewarm broth.

Become a clansman? A wild warrior of the mountains? And what would it be like to have a father? Caswallon, whoever he was, wouldn't care for him. Why should he? He was just a wounded doe brought home on a whim. "When must I decide?"

"When your wounds are fully healed."

"How long will that be?"

"When you say they are," said the old man.

"I don't know if I want to be a clansman."

"Reserve your judgment, Gaelen, until you know what it entails."

That night Gaelen awoke in a cold sweat, screaming.

The old man ran from the back of the cave, where he slept on a narrow pallet bed, and sat down beside the boy. "What is it?" he asked, stroking Gaelen's brow, pushing back the sweat-drenched hair from the boy's eyes.

"The Aenir! I dreamed they had come for me and I couldn't get away."

"Do not fear, Gaelen. They have conquered the Lowlands, but they will not come here. Not yet. Believe me. You are safe."

"They took the city," said Gaelen, "and the militia were overrun. They didn't even hold for a day."

"You have much to learn, boy. About war. About warriors. Aye, the city fell, and before it other cities. But we don't have cities here, and we need no walls. The mountains are like a fortress, with walls that pierce the clouds. And the clansmen don't wear bright breastplates and parade at festivals, they don't march in unison. Stand a clansman against a Lowlander and you will see two men, but you will not be seeing clearly. The one is like a dog, well trained and well fed. It looks good and it barks loud. The other is like a wolf, lean and deadly. It barks not at all. It kills. The Aenir will not come here yet. Trust me."